I0563642

CIRQUE
DU
PHANTASTIQUE

By

Claire Marie Clements

Cirque du Phantastique
by Claire Marie Clements

Published 2018 by The Light Network
Copyright © Claire Marie Clements

All rights reserved. No part of this publication may be reproduced, stored in or introduced into a retrieval system, or transmitted in any form, or by any means (electronic, mechanical, photocopying, recording, or otherwise) without the prior written consent of the publisher.

This book is sold subject to the condition that it shall not, by way of trade or otherwise, be resold, hired out, or otherwise circulated without the publisher's prior consent in any form of binding or cover other than that in which it is published and without a similar condition including this condition being imposed on the subsequent purchaser.

Printed in the United States

Interior layout by Christi Koehl

Edited by Keidi Keating

Map design by Funky Book Designs

ISBN: 978-0-9975727-3-5

ACKNOWLEDGEMENTS

I want to thank Alain du Maurier and his troupe for choosing me to tell their story and for keeping me company during a very difficult time in my life. I hope they bring comfort and joy to you as well, dear Reader.

Music, being the magical healer that it is, also helped me through this time and kept me going when things were challenging, particularly the music of Tori Amos, and so I wish to thank her – Asseniah will always have a voice through your music. Also, the music of Sarah McLachlan, Coldplay, Taylor Swift, the Country Music Channel, and many other artists. I may not know you personally, but the art you make helps bring down dragons and for that I thank you.

Likewise, the always entertaining and inspiring Tweets of one Earthling Wordmaster provided tiny sparks of light during the storms and for this I am grateful.

As this is my first novel, I wish to thank all the teachers, friends, and family members who have encouraged my literary pursuits along the way:

Claire Marie Clements

Paul Hollis, Anne Kay, Greg Simon, Nicole Moxham, Angela Fleming, Carmen Stacey, Shaun Beilby. Oliver de Rohan & Louise Myers for being my very first publishers. Jennifer Chapman-Winter, Tina Panagaris, Cara Lacota. Kimberly Clements & Simon Malessa & Nicole Langes for being my readers and providing feedback. All my incredibly supportive and inspiring friends, you are amazing. The Horatians and Jamie Beck for first using the term 'Auditory Chocolate'. Malcolm Harslett, Melanie Connole, Geri Neiswander, Kylie Braddock. Anthony O'Donohue. Carolyn Bond. Mum and Dad for supplying copious amounts of ink and paper and computer time. My family. Mina. And last but by no means least, Dr Nick Prescott for whom not even Alain du Maurier would be able to find the words to thank.

Thanks also to Victoria Gutierrez for her advice on the manuscript, all those years ago.

And to Keidi Keating for bringing this novel to life.

Thanks must also go to the Muses, who inspire me daily:
The Crush, The King, The Angel, The Wolf, The Lord of Lost Souls, The Goddess, The Summer Fairy, The Quarter of Colour, The Goddess with the Glorious Soul, The Lion, The English Gentleman, The Warrior Woman, and for this novel particularly, The Light, The Rose, and The Porcelain Doll.

My heartfelt thanks to each and every name on this page.

THE HIGHWAY BE

NOIR ETERNALE

DA' LAARWICK

FERDE
IN

ARELIA

KARANTALE'S
INN

TERRENVA

LANDAU

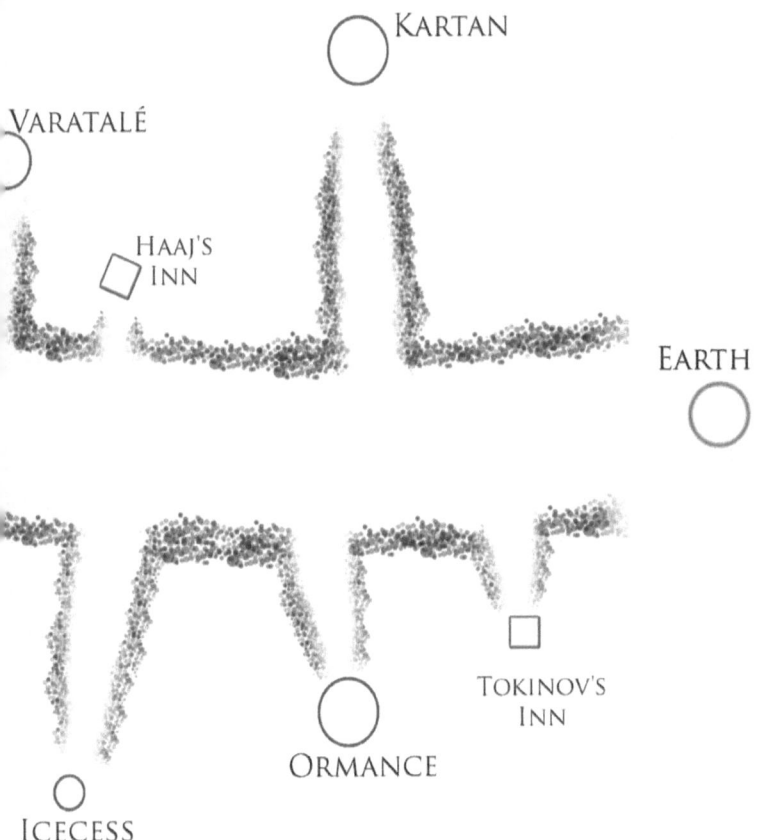

...EEN THE WORLDS

KARTAN

VARATALÉ

HAAJ'S
INN

EARTH

TOKINOV'S
INN

ORMANCE

ICECESS

PROLOGUE

Present Day – Varatalé

Alain du Maurier couldn't resist. Carefully, he reached out and pulled back the edge of the red velvet curtain, just enough to allow him a glimpse of the audience. The tiered, curved wooden benches were almost completely full; only a few empty spaces remained in the top back rows. Nobody noticed him; all eyes were on Alain's assistant, Mariette, who was providing the pre-show entertainment on the front of the stage, dancing gracefully in a whirlwind of pink feathers and sequins, the music provided by three dwarves who sat to the left in a small bandstand.

Alain watched Mariette for a moment, then once the last seat had been filled and the tent flaps drawn, he repositioned the curtain and left to check his troupe for the final time.

The cosy backstage area was warmly lit with lamps and mirrors and divided into four preparation areas by walls of flowing red material.

'All set, Melody?' Alain asked his trapeze artist, who was stretching on the floor of one of the areas.

The teenager smiled. 'Yes, Alain.' She was shivering, but she always shivered before a show.

One of the walls shifted slightly and Chester entered, dressed in his colourful jester's outfit, his face painted in a fantastic design.

'Ready, Alain,' he said.

Melody leapt up and snuggled into Chester's arms, her shivers easing and then ceasing altogether as his warmth calmed her nerves. Smiling, Alain continued on to the next room where Melody's brother was sitting in front of a mirror lit by bulbs of stardust, making sure every hair was in its rightful place and every eyelash properly separated.

'Three minutes, Izan.'

'No worries,' the magician replied, without looking up.

'And please get to the stage *before* your act starts this time.'

Izan snorted. 'Where's the suspense in that, my good man?'

Alain shook his head but could not suppress a smile. He turned away as Dell, another of the dwarf clan, and Oleg, the circus' strong man, appeared beside him.

'The ticket booth is packed up and everyone's seated,' Dell informed him.

'Excellent. Thank you, both.'

Dell hurried away to take up his violin in the bandstand while Oleg went to smother his body in Quartz Juice so his muscles would shine under the stage lights.

On the other side of the stage, Sora was checking her knives for the fourth time that night, commanding them to fly around her once before settling back into the velvet-lined case they lived in. Next to her, Fenton, the oldest of the dwarves, was readying himself by the controls.

Alain nodded to them both and walked onto the closed stage, positioning himself in the centre. He rolled his head from side to side then shook himself from the shoulders down, feeling a familiar rush of nerves tingle through him. Looking up, he saw Asseniah blinking down at him from her nest of red aerial silks, content to watch the show from above until her turn to perform arrived. Alain winked at her before turning his gaze back to the curtains.

'Have a good show, Alain,' said a voice in his head. The voice belonged to his wife, Arrahbella, who was back at the troupe's manor preparing supper for them all. She would come to the tent once the show had finished to offer psychic readings to anyone who was interested.

'Thank you, Bella,' Alain replied.

The Ringmaster had been through this exact routine many times before, seeing his troupe nervously waiting around him, bursting to get onto the stage, hungry for an audience, hearts beating fast, blood rushing through their quivering, rubber-like bodies, and, yet, every time, his heart swelled with pride and happiness at his little band of travellers, all bonded by the same insatiable, overwhelming, seductive desire; the desire to entertain.

Applause brought Alain out of his thoughts as Mariette finished her dance and joined him behind the curtain, standing so close her feathers tickled his arm. Alain nodded to Fenton and he opened the velvet dividers that separated two very different worlds. Blinded by the dazzling lights, surrounded by applause, Alain du Maurier stepped forward and began the show in his rich, seductive tones.

'Ladies and Gentlemen, welcome to Cirque du Phantastique.'

CHAPTER 1

฿EGINNINGS

Thirty-Six Years Ago – Noir Eternale

As the snow drifted slowly down, settling on the loose cobblestones and crooked cottages of Reine, Evette le'Chuse hurried along the winding streets, holding her daughter's hand tightly and keeping to the shadows.

'Where are we going, Mama?' the four-year-old asked, cheerfully. She was the image of her mother with blonde hair, blue eyes, and thin lips that curved upwards at the corners.

'Shush, Mariette, we must keep quiet,' Evette whispered, glancing nervously at a pair of watching vampires who were loitering under one of the many, ever-glowing, rust-covered lamp posts that lined the street. Despite the fact that all of the clocks in Reine currently agreed it was nine o'clock in the morning, there was no sign of any daylight; this mountainous, medium-sized planet had existed in a constant state of night ever since its creation.

Mariette kicked at a cobblestone and it rolled away, creating a barrage of noise in the otherwise silent streets.

'Mariette, what did I…' Evette stopped suddenly as they reached their destination.

The splintered door in front of her was decorated with broken brass letters, which stated that it was the house of a DOCTOR FREDERICK COTARD. Apart from that, there was nothing to distinguish it from the row of identical, dark cottages it was wedged among.

Evette looked down at Mariette, took a deep breath, and knocked tentatively. They heard shuffling and a lock being turned, then the door opened to reveal a tall man with a grizzled appearance, a bottle of brandy hanging limply in his left hand. His brown, blood-shot eyes took a moment to focus before recognising her.

'Evette.' His gaze travelled down her neck to the bare V of chest that her black coat was not quite covering.

'Doctor Cotard, I need you to 'ave a look at Mariette,' Evette said, quietly and urgently.

The doctor's eyes slid to Mariette who blinked up at him adorably. 'Of course, bring her in.' His voice was, like most Noir Eternalans, damaged from too much alcohol and nicotine consumption, and, because he was male, accented differently to hers.

Inside was an exact replica of every other cottage in Reine; two main rooms on the ground floor and two bedrooms above. Evette pulled her daughter into the cramped, brightly lit sitting room and sat her on the uneven table amongst the clutter and lamps. Strong odours of liquor and damp, rotting wood clung to the furniture and fittings.

'What seems to be the problem?' Cotard asked, already examining the young girl who was glancing around with unreserved curiosity at the various medical tools and equipment.

Evette hesitated, her hand discreetly slipping into her coat pocket and resting on the hilt of a small dagger. 'She is not displaying any signs of magic.'

Cotard stared at her for a moment then burst out laughing.

'Oh, Evette, I thought there was a serious problem. You looked so worried.'

'Zis *is* serious.' She lowered her voice. 'I am really starting to believe zat she does not 'ave any magic at all.'

Cotard laughed harder. 'No magic?! No magic?! Well, that's just absurd. There's never been a Noir Eternalan without magic. The whole world would fear for their lives if such a thing occurred. What a monstrous idea.'

Evette gulped. 'But, she is four. Surely she should be showing some sort of magic by now.'

'Not necessarily,' Cotard replied, wiping tears from his eyes. 'I once heard of a case in Caine where the child was seven before he started pouring forth poetry. Mind you, he was a ratbag up until then because of all the pressure building in his system. It's not unusual, Evette. If she's inherited your sexual powers, they won't show until she's old enough to use them. You must know that.'

'Yes, I do know, but somezing just does not feel right.'

'Tell you what, how about I measure how much magic she has stored away in there and that will put your mind at ease?'

Evette nodded. 'Yes, zank you.'

Cotard took a step closer to her and leered greedily. 'And then you can pay me for my services.'

'Of course.'

His eyes trailed to her ample cleavage once more before turning back to Mariette who was now playing with a stethoscope. Humming cheerfully, Cotard picked up a long, brass, wave-shaped wand and attached a rainbow-tinted glass ball to it. In the presence of magic, the ball would fill with a smoky substance, the volume determining how much a person had in them.

Evette sat in the mould-stained armchair and watched anxiously. Cotard continued to hum, occasionally saying something to Mariette or chuckling again at Evette's outrageous fear. He placed the tip of the wand over Mariette's heart and waited. The clock on the wall ticked ominously until Evette wanted nothing more than to throw it out onto the street. When the glass ball remained empty, Cotard's humming grew quieter and then ceased altogether. He frowned, shook the instrument, and tried again. Evette's breath caught in her throat. Slowly, she pulled the dagger out of her pocket and held it ready. Cotard stood up slowly, looking warily at the young girl. Hesitantly, he placed the wand tip over his own heart and the ball started to fill up quickly. His eyes widened in horror and he gasped loudly before pointing a shaking finger at Mariette.

'You're right! This child has no magic!' he declared in a voice so loud that Evette was sure the whole town would have heard. 'She must be killed immediately!'

As Mariette started crying, Cotard lunged for a large

rust-covered knife that was sitting on the table. Without hesitation, Evette leapt from her chair and plunged her dagger into the doctor's back. He spun around, the terror on his face increasing when he saw the primitive maternal instinct in her eyes. Quickly, he raised the rusted knife, but Evette was faster, plunging her dagger into his heart. Cotard dropped his weapon and stumbled forward with a grunt, his hands grabbing her by the shoulders and pulling her down with him as he fell to his knees. She drew the blade out of his chest and stabbed him in the neck. A horrible wet choking sound filled the room, mixing with Mariette's screams.

Certain he was now beyond help, Evette pushed the bloody knife into her pocket, grabbed her daughter, and fled the cottage, hiding her face in Mariette's hair to avoid being recognised by those who were peering out of their windows. She ran back up through the streets, heading toward the town's main centre, not stopping until she had reached her own cottage and locked the door.

Cotard's body was found that same day and no time was lost spreading rumours about who his killer might be. But, it wasn't the murder that had everyone suddenly fearing for their lives, for that sort of thing happened all the time in Noir Eternale; it was the legend that was now being whispered into every ear.

'A child born without magic!' one of Evette's male clients said to her at the beginning of their session, as he took off his shoes. 'Have you ever heard of anything so repulsive?'

Evette bit her bottom lip and looked at her daughter who was sitting on the floor, playing with an empty whiskey bottle.

'You're not going to let her watch, are you?' the man asked, looking at the young child with obvious disdain.

'Of course not,' Evette replied, tersely.

She scooped Mariette up, placed her in the neighbouring room, and shut the door. From then on, that was where Mariette would hide whenever a client or visitor called on her mother, until everyone had forgotten she had ever existed. A small hole in the wall allowed her to observe her mother at work and this, combined with the more formal lessons Evette gave her, soon made her an expert in the art of moving her body.

On the morning of her thirteenth birthday, Mariette came out of her room to find her mother dead. The cause was, most likely, the same as that of the thousands more who had died from the excessive Noir Eternalan lifestyle. The young girl cried until her tears stopped flowing, hauled her mother's body out onto the street so it would be found, and then she journeyed into the city she had grown up in but had never known.

Ten years after Evette's death, a handsome young man named Jean-Luc Montague stopped at the edge of Reine's main street and took a moment to observe all that stretched out before him: poets and players lined the sidewalks, reciting lines at the top of their beautiful voices; artists painted away, attempting to turn their seedy reality into a glorious fantasy; musicians sat on the side of the road, their haunting melodies mixing with the screams of pleasure that floated out of the brothels; families, couples, and tourists ate, chatted, and laughed at the numerous eateries; werewolves howled at the moon and smoked cigars in the shadows; and vampires chased each other into dark corners where they fed from an endless supply of blood.

Inhaling deeply, Jean-Luc detected the familiar scents of chocolate, wine, coffee, blood, and cigarettes, as well as the unfamiliar crispness of the mountains. Smiling, he set off into the commotion, his black coat billowing out behind him, small piles of snow crunching under his boots.

He stopped when he reached the Silhouette Brothel; a tall, narrow building that sat about halfway down the main street. A voluptuous naked woman was leaning over one of the black, iron-lace balconies, smoking while watching the activities below.

'Hey, whore,' a man from one of the café tables called up to her in a husky voice. 'Why don't you come down here and you and I can entertain these people?'

Laughter erupted from the onlookers, along with a few shouts of agreement.

''ow about you come up 'ere and give me some entertainment instead, 'andsome?' the woman replied.

The man whooped and ran into the brothel, appearing moments later on the balcony where he gave the watching crowd a victory wave, pulled the woman inside, and closed the doors.

Jean-Luc smiled and entered more slowly.

The rooms of the brothel were hazy with cigarette smoke and bursting with people. He fought his way through to the bar, reaching it just as one man fell off of his barstool in an intoxicated stupor. Jean-Luc quickly claimed the empty seat, lit up a cigar, and waited to be served.

'You're not from these parts,' the man sitting next to him observed.

'Nope. Cheyenne, down on the coast.'

'Ah. And how are you finding our town?'

'Well, apart from the setting, there's really not much difference.'

The man gave a short laugh and shook his head, creating a shower of dandruff, the tiny white specks floating down on to the shoulders of his crumpled tuxedo and settling on top of the layer already there. 'That's Noir Eternale for you,' he said.

'Not that it matters, I didn't come for the scenery. I've heard that Reine has the best gamblers in the region.'

'That we do, sir. But, most folks get scared off by The Legend. Tend to go to Caine or Evira instead.'

'You mean The Legend of the Freak of Reine? The child born without any magical ability at all?'

The man shuddered.

Jean-Luc shook his head. 'Doesn't scare me. That monster's probably long dead by now, or fled. I don't see why it should stop me from having some fun.'

The man smiled, revealing a set of yellowed teeth. 'I like you.' He reached out his hand. 'Maurice Chabert.'

Jean-Luc shook with him. 'Jean-Luc Montague.'

'Well, why don't you get yourself a drink, Jean-Luc Montague, and I'll introduce you to some of the best poker players in the world.'

Jean-Luc took the glass of whiskey the barman poured him and (after stepping over the intoxicated man who was still lying on the floor, snoring loudly) followed Maurice through to the gambling room. Long, and dotted with about ten round tables, all of them in use, the room also had a stage at one end where two workers were performing a tantalising striptease. Maurice found a table with three vacant places, introduced Jean-Luc to the others, and sat down.

As there was no money in Noir Eternale, the gamblers played with objects and powers. An hour into the game, when Jean-Luc had won two cottages, a four-course meal, a watch, and a poem dedicated to his name, his attention was drawn away from the table by a woman taking to the stage. She had blue eyes and long blonde hair that was tied back in a high ponytail, and her tall, curvy form was enhanced by a pink sequined corset, black, slightly torn stockings, and black lace briefs. A trio of similarly dressed women sitting beside the stage started playing their stringed instruments and the woman began to dance, fluidly and effortlessly. Jean-Luc's new friends, seeing his attention diverted, gave him up as a lost cause and played on without him.

An hour later, the dancer took a bow amid some light applause and moved through to the bar.

'Who is that woman?' Jean-Luc asked Maurice, his trance finally broken.

'Why, that is Mariette le'Chuse, the most famous whore in Reine. She can do things no other woman can, or will, do.'

Excusing himself from the table, Jean-Luc approached

the bar and introduced himself to Mariette. She responded politely and let him talk for a while, as her job required. He was a charming man and she was soon caught up in his spell, admiring his dark looks, greying beard, and refreshing attentiveness.

'Mariette, a client is waiting for you,' an older woman with harsh features interrupted some time later.

'Of course, Madam Amerie.' Mariette stood up as the woman gave Jean-Luc a piercing stare through her bedazzled spectacles and moved away. 'I am sorry but I 'ave to go.'

'Wait, when do you finish?'

Mariette laughed a beautiful bubbly laugh. 'I am afraid I am always working. Everyone always wants me. You will 'ave to make an appointment if you wish to see me for longer.'

Jean-Luc did make an appointment, but he had to wait until the following fortnight before it came around. Over the next few months, they saw each other often, and Mariette fell deeply in love.

Three months after their first encounter, Mariette went to visit her Madam, finding her in the elaborately decorated office she worked in at the top of the brothel.

'Madam Amerie?'

'Yes, Mariette?' she replied, not looking up from her accounts.

'Madam, I am pregnant.'

'You 'ave been pregnant before, Mariette. Many times, I assume.'

'Yes, but zis one I wish to keep.'

Madam Amerie looked up and took off her spectacles. Her eyes were so blood-shot it was hard to tell their original colour.

'And I wish to leave ze brozel.'

'Zis is about zat man, isn't it?'

'Yes, Madam. I love 'im.'

Amerie gave a frustrated sigh. 'Men are trouble, Mariette. It will not last. 'e will get tired of you soon enough and move on to someone else.'

'Jean-Luc is not like zat, zough, Madam Amerie. 'e looks me in ze eye when 'e talks to me, not at my body, and 'is 'ands do not touch wizout my permission. We did not even make love until our fourz session togezer and it was like nozing I 'ave ever experienced before. 'e does love me, Madam.'

The Madam sighed. 'Fine. Go. I see I cannot change your mind. Your room will be waiting for you when you come crawling back.' She looked at Mariette's stomach. 'And if zat baby turns out to 'ave your powers I will expect you to bring 'er 'ere for work.'

Mariette bit her bottom lip. She knew that by keeping the child she was risking the birth of another "monster," but, if that happened, she was confident that she could teach it all the necessary skills, just as her mother had done.

'Of course,' she replied.

The Madam returned to her accounts and Mariette knew she had been dismissed. She collected her things and moved into one of the cottages that Jean-Luc had won in the poker game.

It was a typical dark morning when Mariette's secret was finally revealed. The pair had just woken up and was lying in bed, talking as they stroked the growing baby bump.

'Mariette, how come you've never asked me what my power is?' Jean-Luc asked her, quietly.

Mariette felt a tingle of nerves run down her spine. 'I know what your power is. You never lose at cards, not unless you intend to anyway, and you stare at Monique's scars even when she 'as clozing on.' Monique, a fellow prostitute, had been burned by a jealous lover, leaving the lower half of her body covered in scars, which some men found repulsive and others found arousing. 'You can see zrough zings, my dear.' Mariette traced her finger over Jean-Luc's lips as he smiled.

'Very good, my love. I had, in fact, seen you naked five minutes after I first laid eyes on you.'

Mariette giggled.

'And it's well known throughout the town that you have physical abilities, but is that the extent of your powers? There's something different about you that I can't quite work out. You have a secret, don't you, my love?'

Mariette bit her lower lip, feeling a rush of anxiety and excitement. 'You are right. I do.'

Jean-Luc took her hand in his and kissed her fingertips. 'Whatever it is, you can tell me.'

Mariette felt a quiver in her womb. She took a deep breath. 'I 'ave no magic. I am ze Legend Child of Reine. My mozer 'id me and when she died, I came to ze brozel where I was so skilled zat Madam just assumed my powers lay in entertaining. Now everyone believes it. I never lied.' An

21

immense wave of relief washed over her, leaving her feeling slightly giddy.

Jean-Luc stared at her with blank eyes for some moments.

'You're playing games with me, my love,' he finally said.

'No, it is ze truz, and I am so glad I can finally share it wiz someone.'

Horror distorted Jean-Luc's face. He leapt from the bed and pointed a shaking finger at her. Mariette was stunned and suddenly afraid. The doctor had looked at her in exactly the same way, just before Evette had stabbed him. Her body turned ice cold.

'You monster!' he shouted. 'You harpy. You've tricked me, you... you devil.'

'No, please, Jean-Luc, I am not a monster. I am just like everyone else.'

He was pulling his clothes on clumsily while simultaneously trying to keep an eye on her. 'You're nothing like us.' He pulled too hard on his trousers and they ripped. 'You're a freak of nature. Repulsive. And you seduced me so that I would do your evil biddings.'

'No, Jean-Luc, please, please! I love you.' She was in tears, kneeling up on the bed, reaching out to him.

But Jean-Luc was dressed now, haphazardly. He ran out of the house and into the street, calling her names, and brushing himself off as though he were suddenly unclean.

Mariette knew she had no time to linger in sadness. They would come and kill her in a matter of seconds if she stayed, and she might have let them if it weren't for her unborn child. She climbed out of the bed and hurried out of the small house, into the street. Still naked, she ran, tears clouding her vision, not knowing or caring where she was going, just trying to get out of the city. She passed a number of people, all of whom didn't look twice at such a common sight. She headed downhill, tripping a number of times but managing not to fall completely. Above her, she heard faint shouts and commands of the people as the news spread. Mariette picked up her pace until her breath came in painful gasps and her chest hurt. Turning to look over her shoulder, she saw flames and smoke lighting up the dark sky; they were coming with torches.

Turning to face the street once more, she saw a white blur only moments before colliding with it. Both she and the white figure tumbled to the ground but the white figure was up again almost instantly, helping her up and wrapping their cloak around her, muttering apologies. As Mariette's senses returned she tried to push the figure away but they – he – was holding her tightly and speaking in such a deep, soothing voice that she found herself wanting to collapse in a heap and cry into his arms.

'Are you alright?' he asked.

'Please, I 'ave to go…'

'Is someone after you?'

Mariette looked into the stranger's clear blue eyes. 'My boyfriend, 'e is in a rage and I am scared for our baby.'

'Come with me, I'll take you to my house and you can hide there.'

'I cannot go wiz you, sir. Ze whole town is after me. I am

ze Legend Child. I 'ave no powers. I am a monster. Go on, turn me over to zem. I am done for anyway.' She started crying.

The stranger's eyes widened in surprise then narrowed in concern.

'Please, come with me,' he said, gently. 'I promise I'll hide you.'

There was a moon beam shining down on them, tickling Mariette's skin, and she couldn't help but notice a similarity between that and the way his voice tickled her heart. But, despite his soothing tones, she didn't believe him. She didn't think she could ever trust anyone again, especially nobody kind.

'No, you will just turn me over to zem. You are all ze same.' She tried to break free of his grasp again.

Suddenly, the stranger's voice became stern and urgent. 'Lady, the mob is getting nearer. We only have a matter of seconds before they're in this street. You have to come with me now if you wish to protect your child. Please trust me, I mean you no harm.'

As he spoke, his words seemed to enter her ears, flow through her body and tug at her soul in a most pleasurable way. Her body responded to his request without her realising, allowing him to quickly lead her into the next street and through the door of a cottage. Once inside, the man shut the door, locked it, and led Mariette down into the cellar through the trapdoor in the main room. The door was quickly shut above her, leaving the cellar pitch black and cold. She felt a sudden rush of fear as she believed she had just been imprisoned, but the stranger did not light any lamps and, as she sat on the hard dirt floor, tears streaming silently down her face, she soon heard the mob's angry shouts grow louder and then pass, fading as they hurried to the edge of the town.

Once he was sure they were gone, he lit a candle and opened the trapdoor.

'You're safe for now, but I have no doubt they'll return.'

'It is okay, I will stay down 'ere.'

'No, it's fine. I'm sure we'll hear them coming.'

Mariette looked up at her rescuer, examining him for the first time. His face was round, kind, and young, only a few years older than her own. He had a mess of curly white hair, which was a little wild, and the beginnings of a beard and moustache. The whiteness of his overall appearance made Mariette wonder if he was from her world at all.

He put out his hand, making her jump.

'My name is Alain du Maurier.'

Well, it was certainly a Noir Eternalan name. She eyed his hand suspiciously before slowly reaching out her own. 'Mariette le'Chuse.'

'Pleased to meet you, Miss le'Chuse.' He had one of those smiles that could make your heart dance even in your darkest moments.

Alain helped her out of the cellar. 'Please, make yourself at home, you are most welcome. I'll get you some clothes and a nice hot mug of chocolate, and then you can tell me your story.'

He disappeared into another room as Mariette took in her surroundings. It was obvious his power lay with words;

the sparsely furnished room was covered in loose sheets of paper, stacks of clean paper, pencils, ink stains and ink wells, and, surprisingly, even loose words, written in black, just laying on the floor, or attached to the wall, or jumbled up in a big ball. She didn't know of any other Wordmaster that could make words appear like that. Curious, she picked up the closest sheet of paper and read what was on it, becoming so engrossed she didn't notice him return with the clothes and two steaming mugs.

When anyone, usually Jean-Luc himself, came looking for Mariette over the following weeks, Alain used his power to talk them into searching elsewhere and eventually they stopped searching altogether. Mariette stayed in Alain's house until she gave birth to her son, Luc, who was instantly recognisable as a vampire.

'He won't be able to come with us,' Alain told her quietly, looking at the wailing baby in despair. His arms were still covered in blood from having delivered the child himself. 'I've been to every world along this Highway and they all have daylight.'

Mariette looked at the child in her arms, tears falling down her cheeks. 'I know.'

They were silent for a moment. Even Luc stopped crying.

'It is best zat 'e stays 'ere,' she finally said. 'Zen 'e will never know zat 'is mozer was ze Freak of Reine.' She looked up at Alain and gave him a sad smile, which he did not return.

'We'll find him a good home,' he promised.

True to his word, Alain found Luc a home with one of his neighbours (a retired brothel worker, unable to have children due to too many years performing the wild acts of her profession) who gladly took the child in with no questions asked. Then, on an exceptionally black day, Alain and Mariette packed up their few belongings, wrapped themselves in dark cloaks, and hurried out of the town.

Two days of travel took them to the Pleu Forest at the base of the Parangon Montagne Range. There, they fled through the Noir Eternalan rift – a large shimmering hole in the air framed by glittering black rocks – and travelled along the Highway Between the Worlds to the neighbouring planet of Varatalé.

Present Day – Varatalé

Dressed in a pink dressing gown and pink slippers, her long blonde hair up in its usual high ponytail, Mariette le'Chuse shuffled sleepily across the manor's polished floor to the kitchen. A wave of earthy aromas engulfed her as soon as she opened the door; the garlands of herbs and dried flowers hanging from the wooden beams mixing with the smell of toast, coffee, and fruit.

'Good morning, Alain, Arrahbella,' she greeted, cheerfully.

'Good morning, Mariette.' Alain du Maurier was sitting at the long wooden kitchen table, eating a croissant while reading the village newspaper, *The Luc'can Local*. He was dressed in the same ensemble he wore every day; a white shirt, partly open at the top revealing a triangle of pale white chest, white pants, and brown boots. The morning sun was pouring in through the large bay window, shining on his back and hair, giving him an angelic glow. 'We've made the front page this morning.'

Mariette giggled as she sat down. 'We always make ze front page when we perform in Luc'ca.'

'True, but it's nice to know that they still love us, and there are some great comments about the new routines. A lot of them reckon it's our best show yet!'

Mariette smiled broadly as Arrahbella placed a plate of Noir Eternalan-style toast and sugared strawberries in front of her.

'Mmm, Arrahbella, you are a goddess,' she said, inhaling the scents wafting from her plate.

'No, just a mind reader,' Arrahbella replied, her ice-blue eyes twinkling. Like her husband, she, too, was dressed in her usual style; an ankle-length patterned skirt, flowing, silk and lace, mystic-style top, and a pair of faux leather cowboy boots. Her long, wavy, black hair was loose, snaking all the way down to her waist.

Mariette laughed at the well-worn joke and picked up a strawberry. 'I cannot believe it is our fourz tour,' she said to Alain. 'Ze time seems to 'ave gone by so quickly.'

'I know. It feels like only yesterday I was travelling the Highway in search of troupe members.'

Arrahbella sat across from Mariette and watched with cool amusement as the two began to reminisce about the years spent building the circus from a simple idea to a reality, Alain almost bouncing up and down in his seat with enthusiasm. Daintily biting into a poppy seed biscuit, she marvelled once again at how the fates had worked to bring them all together, starting that very night in Reine, all those years ago.

Not far away, in the small village of Luc'ca, Melody Bell and Chester from the Apricot Meadows were walking arm-in-arm through the main street as the villagers went about their daily business. Luc'ca sat nestled among the rolling green hills and farmlands of Neapania; a large region under the rule of King Benico, which sat in the west of Varatalé. The apricot-coloured houses were small and square, their windows framed with brightly painted shutters and flowerboxes.

'Mmm, smell that bread,' Melody said, referring to the mouth-watering aroma that greeted the Luc'cans every morning. They were heading toward the bakery where a line of people already trailed out of the door, waiting to be served.

'You and your bread,' Chester teased. His voice had a strong nasal quality to it that was less seductive than Alain's deep tones, but just as spine tingling.

'What? Bread is the food of life.'

'It's a little boring.'

'Says he who doesn't like chocolate.'

Chester made a face. 'That's because chocolate is just weird.'

Melody laughed. 'Chocolate is romantic.'

'So you keep telling me, but picture this.' He stopped walking and adopted a dreamy tone. 'I'm lying on the bed,

29

and you break off a piece of creamy dark chocolate, put it in my mouth... and I throw it up on you.'

'Eww, Chester!'

Chester grinned and kissed her.

'For that, I think I'll have a chocolate roll for breakfast.'

'Then I just won't kiss you for the rest of the day.'

Melody pouted. Chester's heart fluttered at the adorable picture she created. She was wearing blue, Varatalian pants (wide-legged, with laces criss-crossing on the outer sides from hem to mid-calf, and various designs embroided around the legs and waist), and a pink, short-sleeved, low-cut top that laced up at the front. Her brown ringlets were loose, falling to her shoulders, and her plain but not unattractive face was bathed in morning sunlight, making her pale green eyes twinkle.

'You know I actually love the fact that you don't like chocolate, don't you?' she assured him. 'It makes you unique. In all honesty, I'm not that fond of the stuff myself. Just the romance of it.' A sneaky look crossed her face. 'You know what Alain and Arrahbella do with it.'

'No, you know what Alain and Arrahbella do with it... and they only do that so they can re-enact how they met. We use honey, and honey is fine with me.'

'It's sticky.'

'That's what the cream's for.'

Melody rolled her eyes. They reached the bakery and joined the end of the queue, only to be pounced upon by the person standing in front of them, an elderly woman named

Dalia Heath.

'Well, look who it is,' she said, loudly, prompting everyone in the line to turn and face them. 'I just loved your show last night. You two are so effortless together. It was as though you were flying, Melody.'

Melody and Chester smiled at this for Melody had, indeed, been flying while on the trapeze. She had a set of small, blue and white wings, which Izan kept invisible at Alain's request and much to Chester's disappointment. The jester reached a hand up and discreetly stroked her left wing, making her shiver.

'Thank you, Mrs. Heath. We're glad we could entertain you for a while,' Melody replied, hoping the shiver would go unnoticed. She gave Chester a light whack on the back in warning. Chester stroked her wing again.

'Well, you'll be entertaining me again tonight, my dear,' Dalia went on, completely oblivious to their antics. 'I've already bought another ticket.'

'Wonderful. We'll be sure to look out for you.'

The line shuffled and they stepped up into the shop. The smell of bread was even more potent inside, with faint traces of flour, honey, and chocolate noticeable as well. The glass counter displaying the various rolls, cakes, and pastries glowed warmly beside them, luring people into indecision. As Dalia placed her order, those who had already been served stopped by Melody and Chester to shower them with their own praise before heading off to start their day.

Patrizio, the baker, a short but muscular, goateed man, smiled broadly when he saw them. 'Good morning,

Chester, Miss Bell. Didn't expect to see you up and about so early. Doesn't Alain let you sleep?'

'Usually he does,' Melody explained. 'But we have to get the train packed so that we can leave for Toulon straight after tonight's show.'

'Ah, fair enough. Well, no doubt you're hungry after all that energy you used. What will you have?'

'One chocolate roll, please, and a jam roll, and an almond square.'

'And I'll have a honey twist.'

As Patrizio turned to fill their order, his daughter, Eona, appeared from the back room.

'Chester!' she squealed, her pretty face lighting up.

Chester smiled pleasantly. Being renowned throughout just about every world along the Highway as one of the most incredible looking creatures in existence, he was used to this kind of reception.

'Hello, Eona.'

She flicked her long brown hair back over her shoulder. 'Oh, hi Melody.'

Melody waved and gave a polite smile, her arm still wrapped around Chester's. She watched Eona chatter away happily, flirting unreservedly, feeling a familiar tingle of pride at the fact that this girl wanted her man. Her eyes went from Eona to Chester, taking in his flawless features: his short but toned stature, dressed today in black Varatalian pants (the male version of which did not have laces on the side), and a purple shirt which accentuated his purple eyes; his sandy-brown, slightly messy short hair; his porcelain skin; and, his

32

most exquisite feature, his mouth – soft luscious lips that made everyone who saw them go weak at the knees. He had just celebrated his twenty-sixth birthday, making him eight years older than his girlfriend.

Chester, sensing Melody watching him, looked at her and smiled. Eona's endless babble faltered.

'Here you are,' Patrizio interrupted, as he returned with their breakfast. 'Tell Arrahbella I'll have her order ready by lunchtime.'

'Thanks, Patrizio, will do. Bye Eona.'

Eona's shoulders slumped as she watched them walk away. Once outside, Melody lost no time in tucking into her warm, gooey chocolate roll, making Chester laugh when she shivered with pleasure.

Back at the manor, Alain was walking up the grand polished wooden staircase to the third floor, which belonged solely to Izan Bell and his very large ego. The Wordmaster knocked on the bedroom door and, when there was no response, opened it slowly. Seeing the mound under the covers, he wrote the word "awake" in the air and pushed the white smoky substance toward the bed. A groan followed.

'Morning, Izan. Time to get up, there's work to be done.'

'What time is it?'

'Ten o'clock.'

'Sweet Mythos, Alain. Is the sun even up this early?'

Alain went over to the window and pulled open the black curtains, sending shafts of sunlight into the room which bounced off of the numerous gothic-style mirrors lining the walls and desk and spread out over the bed.

Izan groaned again.

'Apparently it is.'

'Oh, very funny.'

'Come on. We need to get the train packed before the show tonight. Breakfast is waiting, so get up, get dressed, and come downstairs.'

Izan freed his arm and pointed at the window. The curtains shut instantly and the arm disappeared once more as the magician sunk further down under the covers.

Alain tapped his foot. 'Just because you're one of the most powerful beings along this Highway, Izan Jaraimah Bell, that doesn't mean you can sleep in while the rest of us have to work.'

He was answered by a snore.

Alain sighed, walked over to the bed, and threw back the covers.

Down on the ground floor, in a room just off of the manor's grand entrance foyer, sixteen-year-old Sora Mai was sitting at her dresser, pinning her long, sleek, black hair into a bun. Her slim build was poised perfectly on the chair, her olive skin accentuated by the black satin corset and short skirt she was wearing. She had just put the last pin in place and was inspecting her work when someone knocked on her door.

'Come in.'

A young girl with waist-length red hair entered the room. She was wearing a red sundress and carrying one of the costumes she had worn in the show the night before.

'Oh, hey, Asseniah,' Sora said, turning to face her friend.

Asseniah placed the costume on the dresser, spread it out, and pointed to a tear along the side.

Sora frowned. 'How did you manage to do that?'

The thirteen-year-old shrugged, her face void of expression.

'Oh well, it's easily fixed.'

Sora took the costume over to her sewing machine in the corner of the room, sat down, and set to work. Asseniah sat on the bed and watched with wide eyes; eyes that were hypnotic in the way they constantly moved, the green swirling around the black pupils like mist.

For a while there was only the sound of the sewing machine working away and the birds warbling outside the open window, but then Asseniah heard the faint tinkling of a piano being moved. With astonishing speed, she leapt up and raced out of the room into the entrance foyer where Oleg Fyzek was carefully carrying a small, battered piano toward the front doors.

'Oh, there you are,' he said, when she stopped in front of him. He was a small giant, only three inches taller than Alain's six-foot-one-inch and twice as broad around the girth. He had deep green eyes and black hair that started growing halfway down his head, falling to his shoulders and leaving him bald on top. The only item of clothing on his muscular body was an animal-hide wrap (the feel of which was similar to that of an ox's coat), covering from waist to knees.

Asseniah frowned and pointed to the piano.

'I'm sorry, but I couldn't find you before. Am I treating her properly?'

Asseniah studied him for a moment then nodded satisfactorily.

'Good.' He continued on, heading outside with Asseniah following closely.

The dirt road that led to the village began at the manor's double oak doors, slicing the large grassy area in two. The sweeping views of the surrounding hills and farmland were today interrupted by the sight of a long colourful train made up of nine intricately carved caravans and one driving cabin. Perched on, under, or inside the train, making sure that all was in working order, were the five dwarves.

Oleg and Asseniah disappeared into the final caravan just as Melody and Chester returned from the village.

'Heads!'

The pair ducked quickly as a hammer flew past them.

'Watch it, Fenton!' Chester called up to the dwarf sitting on the roof of the fourth caravan.

'Sorry! Sorry! Flew out of me hand, she did.' At fifty-four, Fenton was the oldest of the dwarves and, therefore, the unofficial team leader. He had a rough attractiveness about him with a lined face, a full head of thick black hair and a small black beard. His eyes were also black, but then, so were those of everyone else who had been born on the planet Terrenvale. 'Mind throwing it back?'

Melody picked up the hammer and flew up to the roof, much to Chester's delight.

'Thank you, Missy.'

'Maybe you could ask Izan to enchant them so they don't slip?'

'Will do.'

Hearing their voices, Asseniah jumped down from the caravan and hurried over to Chester.

'Here you go,' he said, handing her the jam roll as Melody returned to the ground beside him. 'Is Sora inside?'

'Nope, I'm here,' the seamstress said, stepping out of the manor. Chester handed her the almond square while watching Asseniah ravenously attack her breakfast. 'Thanks. You took your time.'

'Sorry. Everyone kept stopping us to say how much they enjoyed the show.'

Sora swallowed a mouthful, then smiled. 'It went really well, didn't it? This tour is going to be great.'

'Indeed it is, Sora,' Alain said, joining them on the grass with Mariette and Arrahbella close behind. 'I can't wait to be on the road again. And now that you're all here, we can get to work loading this train.' He raised his voice slightly. 'How's she looking, Fenton?'

'She's good to go, Alain,' the dwarf replied, hooking his hammer on to his belt and climbing down the nearby ladder.

'Every bolt is bolted and every nail is nailed,' agreed Grent, the youngest of the five at twenty-one, sporting a long blonde plait, and a chubby face.

Phan, who looked almost like Grent's twin but with spiky hair, climbed out from underneath the train. 'She hardly needed anything done to her. Built to last, she is.'

'Excellent,' Alain replied, as Dell and Cravel joined the group, looking hot and sweaty. Dell was the shortest of the group but stood out with his red hair and beard, while Cravel had brown colourings. Most of the dwarves had an earring or two, and all of them wore a tee shirt and overalls which varied in pattern and colour.

'I've moved the last of the furniture, Alain,' Oleg told him, stepping out of the third caravan.

'Thank you, Oleg. Could you go with Arrahbella into Luc'ca to help her carry back supplies? And, perhaps, the dwarves could go as well. As for the rest of you... wait, where's Izan?'

The magician stumbled out of the manor, shielding his grey eyes quickly from the bright sunlight. His tall, thin physique was dressed completely in black, the cloak he hardly ever took off swirling around his legs as he came to a stop next to Chester. His black hair was perfectly combed, a silver streak running smoothly down one side.

'I'm here, O Great Leader.'

'Where did you get to last night?' Chester asked, his arms wrapped around Melody.

'You remember those girls I was talking to after the show?'

'The blondes?'

'Yep. Well, they were from Ramola. I figured it was only polite to show them around.'

Melody sighed as Chester grinned.

'Well, I hope they were grateful.'

Now it was Izan's turn to grin. 'Veeeery grateful.'

Alain cleared his throat. 'Izan, I warned you last night that we had to be up early to pack this train, so if you don't mind I'd like to get cracking, now that it can no longer be considered early and we have a show to do in less than ten hours.'

'Absolutely, my good man.' He turned to the others and clapped his hands. 'Come on, people, let's not stand around jabbering. You heard Alain. Chop chop.'

Alain shook his head and sighed as the majority of the troupe hurried back inside to collect all they would need for the tour. Arrahbella patted his arm before heading off with Oleg and the dwarves to the village.

Now alone, Alain looked at the train once more, remembering how nervous he had been before they had set off on their first tour, three years ago. He was still somewhat nervous now, but that initial tour had ironed out the major problems and they had only had to deal with minor issues since. So, on this, their fourth tour, Alain was confident there was nothing Cirque du Phantastique couldn't handle.

'Don't just stand there, man,' Izan said from the doorway, his enchanted possessions floating before him in a straight line, dutifully heading toward the train. 'You want us to do all the work?'

Alain smiled and went inside to pack.

CHAPTER 2

MELODY AND IZAN

Present Day – Varatalé

As the train headed out of Neapania and headed toward the neighbouring region of Oregaine, Alain was in the kitchen / dining car, waiting for a pot of water to boil so he could make some tea. The caravan looked like a plainer version of the manor's kitchen: a long wooden table in the centre; stove, benches, and cupboards along one wall; and a stardust-powered refrigerator near the door that led to the practice room. The sun was streaming in through the two windows, filling the large space with a warm glow and combining with the rocking motion of the train in such a soothing way that Alain began to feel quite sleepy.

The door opposite the practice room opened and Melody entered, smiling when she saw Alain.

'Hello, Melody.'

'Hi.'

'How's that poem of yours coming along?'

She sighed. 'It's stuck at the moment. I'm having trouble thinking of the right word to describe something.'

Alain nodded in mock seriousness. 'Those somethings

can be tricky to describe.'

Melody smiled. 'Well, I can't explain the something to you if I don't know the word for it.'

Alain chuckled. 'Well, if you need help feel free to ask.'

'Thanks, Alain, but I need to work it out for myself. Besides, it's too easy to ask someone who has words running around their bloodstream.'

'I may have words in my bloodstream, Melody, but that doesn't make it any easier. There are so many of them, and they're in thousands of different languages.'

He turned back to the stove as the pot boiled. Melody reached up, standing on the tips of her toes, and took down a couple of mugs from the cupboard.

'Tea?' he asked her.

'Yep, but it's okay, I'll make it. I have to make Chester's as well.'

'One teaspoon of honey and a dash of milk, right?'

'Right. Well done.'

'Well, it's the same way you have yours,' he said with a wink. 'And Arrahbella has two teaspoons. How you can stand it so sweet, I don't know.'

'I don't know how you can have yours so strong.'

'I'm just a Noir Eternalan at heart.'

Melody frowned. 'No, you're not, you're a Varatalian at heart.'

He laughed. 'True. Noir Eternalan blood, then.' He finished making the teas and handed one to her before blowing on his own. 'We should be in Toulon in a couple of hours. Izan and I will go straight to King Duozo and let him know we've arrived. Will you be coming?'

Melody shook her head. 'Probably not. I saw him last month when Chester and I were there, and I know that you men like to have a chat without me hanging around occasionally.'

Alain frowned. 'That's not true.'

She smiled. 'Maybe not for you.' She blew on her tea. 'It's okay. I'll go into the market with the others.'

'Alright.' He picked up Arrahbella's tea. 'Come on, we'd better take these through before they get cold.'

Melody picked up the remaining mug and followed Alain through to the adjoining caravan, which was shared by Sora, Asseniah, and Mariette. All the caravans were magically bigger on the inside than they appeared from the outside but, even so, it was still a bit of a squeeze in the girls' room. There were two double beds, two wardrobes, two dressers, and a desk, all fashioned in the style of Sora's home planet, Ormance; dark mahogany wood with numerous carvings of snake-like dragons. Asseniah had no furniture in her corner, just a hammock of red material hung amongst a few other red strips. Her clothes were in Mariette's wardrobe and her piano was down in Oleg's caravan at the end of the train. The young girl was currently lying on her back, on the red carpeted floor, next to the CD player, her fingers mimicking the convoluted piano arrangement coming from the speakers, using the air as her instrument. Thanks to Arrahbella, the troupe had quite a large CD collection, Asseniah's favourites including the works of Tori Amos, Coldplay, and Sarah McLachlan – musicians who could use a piano just as skillfully as Alain could use words.

The Earthling artist (Tori, in this case) began to sing, and Asseniah's hands fell still, her whole body listening intently, as though she were being told all the secrets of the universe. Sora began to softly sing along as she mended a corset while Mariette, sitting at the dresser trying out a new make-up design, tapped her foot.

'Ah, now there's a song I haven't heard for a while,' Alain said, stopping in the middle of the room and looking at Asseniah.

'For about a year, in fact,' Melody agreed.

'You obviously don't go up to the Northern Tower very much, Alain,' Sora said.

Asseniah had rolled onto her stomach so she could blink at them all.

'No, that's quite true,' Alain replied. 'I think I only really ever go up there when Asseniah decides to sleep in on rehearsal days.' He narrowed his eyes at her.

The silent girl lost interest, flopped onto her back again, and turned up the volume.

Alain looked down at Melody, shook his head, then continued on towards the door that led through to Izan's caravan. Melody giggled and followed. Before they could leave, however, the CD player started skipping and jumping. Asseniah sat bolt upright and looked at the machine as though it had just sprung to life.

'I don't remember the song ever doing that before,' Alain said, to no one in particular.

Asseniah leapt to her feet and raced from the room, barely avoiding knocking the mugs of tea from Alain's hands. When she returned, she was pulling Arrahbella after her, only letting go when they were both standing in front of the player (which was still stuck on the same word) so she could point at it frantically. Arrahbella quickly knelt down and stopped the CD.

'It's okay, Asseniah,' she said. 'They do that sometimes. You just have to stop them and start again.'

Asseniah put her hands to her head and mimed some horns.

'No, honey, there are no pixies in there,' the psychic assured her, with a serene smile.

Asseniah looked unconvinced.

'It sounded like pixies,' Alain pressed.

'Trust me, it's very common for a stereo to do that. Asseniah does use it a lot and Earthling devices aren't always built to last. CD players aren't used much at all on Earth anymore. They're a dying breed.'

Asseniah's eyes widened in horror.

'No, I didn't mean it like that; "dying breed" is an expression used for living and non-living things.'

The teenager frowned. Arrahbella blew on the CD, wiped it with her skirt, and placed it back in the player. She skipped to the same track and everyone listened with baited breath until the song had successfully played past the troublesome point.

'See? Working fine now,' Arrahbella said, but Asseniah continued to bounce up and down anxiously, watching the

44

player as though it were a baby with its first fever.

'Tell you what, why don't you use the player in our room for now, and Alain and I will use this one, and when we get to Tokinov's Inn we'll see if any traders have a new one, okay?'

Asseniah nodded vigorously.

'Alright.' Arrahbella took the offending player out of the room and returned with another, similarly designed unit. Asseniah examined it carefully for a moment before delicately pressing play and lying down once more. Only once she had closed her eyes did the others smile at each other and shake their heads in loving amusement. Alain held Arrahbella's now tepid tea out to Sora who produced a fireball in her palm and warmed the mug from underneath until the liquid was steaming again, then he handed it to his wife and they left the room as Sora gave Chester's tea the same treatment.

A short while later, the countryside gave way to vineyards, which were soon replaced by apricot-coloured houses when the train reached the outskirts of Toulon, Oregaine's main city. Once they had pulled to a stop in a large grassy area, Alain and Izan set out for the castle while the others went into the market and Oleg stayed with the train for security.

'Asseniah and I will be over at the cloths and silks,' Sora announced, when they had reached the edge of the market. She took Asseniah's hand and quickly disappeared amongst the throng of people.

Cravel spotted a stall selling a range of masks and pointed. 'Look, friends.'

The other dwarves made various exclamations of delight before running over and purchasing a ghastly expression each. The four humans watched with amusement as the dwarves put on their masks, hid behind a nearby fountain, waited for an unsuspecting pedestrian, then jumped out, scaring the wits out of them.

'There are so many people here today,' Melody observed, as the dwarves hid once again. 'You're going to have to walk behind me, Chester.'

'Easier said than done. We can go and do something else if you like.'

'No, I love the market, and I want to go to Luigi's bakery.'

'We'll stand on either side of you, Melody,' Arrahbella assured her, and moved to stand on Melody's left while Mariette stayed on her right. In this formation, they continued into the bustle, getting bumped and jostled constantly, but without too much damage to Melody's wings.

The market was a large network of streets and lanes lined with food vendors and tables shaded by silk canopies. As they moved further in, the air became heavier with the heat of a mass of bodies, the warm sun, and the scent of spices, perfumes, and pastries. Sellers shouted over the endless chatter and laughter, trying to tempt anyone who walked by.

As they passed a stall selling a range of silverware and trinkets, Melody spotted a small silver box carved with roses. Tiny silk butterflies no bigger than a fingernail flew in a halo above the box, occasionally settling on the rim to form a crown, then jumping up and dancing once again. 'Oh, look at this!' she exclaimed, picking it up carefully and examining the artwork.

Arrahbella looked over her shoulder. 'That's pretty.'

The elderly woman sitting behind the stall watched Melody closely for a moment before standing and whipping the box out of her hands, causing the butterflies to jolt violently.

'I know you, you're Callinna Canero's daughter,' she hissed.

Melody stared indignantly as the other three narrowed their eyes at the woman.

'I don't want your cursed hands touching my wares.' The woman spat on the ground, making her black head scarf shift slightly with the force.

Chester felt Melody's wings beat in anger as he stepped forward and leant across the table. 'Hey, Melody is not cursed.'

'Is too. And she should be for what her mother did. Seducing one of our greatest men and then killing him.'

Melody's face went hot. 'My mother loved my father and he loved her.'

'Don't worry about it, Melody,' Arrahbella said softly, putting a hand on Melody's arm. 'Let's just go.'

Knowing there was nothing she could do, Melody turned and walked away with Arrahbella and Mariette. Chester glared at the woman a moment longer, breaking through her hard exterior and making her blush, much to her annoyance. Smiling his perfect smile, he put a hand over a group of mirrors sitting to one side of the table, preparing to magically smash them to pieces.

'Chester. Don't.'

He lowered his hand, turned, and walked over to Melody.

'Spoil my fun.'

'They can't help it. They really do believe we're cursed. You don't need to go and take away her livelihood,'

'She shouldn't have said what she said.'

'I know.' She smiled and kissed him. 'Thank you, though.'

'You're getting as bad as Izan, Chester,' Arrahbella sighed.

'Why, thank you.'

'I didn't mean it as a compliment.'

'I know.' He looked at Melody. 'Are you okay?'

'Yeah.' She wiped the tears from her eyes and put her arm through his. 'Come on, let's go to Luigi's, I'm hungry.'

Twenty-three Years Ago – Varatalé

Duke Alcino Rockford Bell, well-respected enchanter and best friend of King Fello, had travelled to the small village of Pizane to interview a potential university lecturer. The candidate, Kootol Canero, was a tall, dark man with a deep voice and almond shaped brown eyes. His range of magic was impressive and Alcino left the small cottage already writing the report in his head to give to Fello. With his thoughts elsewhere, he didn't see the young maiden turning out of a side lane and walked straight into her, sending her basket of apples crashing to the ground and shiny red orbs rolling away in all directions.

'Terribly sorry,' he muttered, as he gathered the apples. 'Completely my fau...' His voice trailed off as he looked at her for the first time.

She was plain but pretty with loose light brown hair that fell down her back in lazy ringlets. Her eyes were a soft, pale green and her nose was lovely and slender. Her fitted green and white dress showed a divine set of curves outlining her petite body. Alcino was instantly smitten, and her quiet, almost scared demeanour did nothing to prevent his heart from turning to a pile of mush.

'I do apologise, my lady, I hope you aren't hurt,' he managed to say.

'No, my lord, I am unharmed. I must apologise for being so clumsy. Please, forgive me.' She bowed her head, aware that his well-dressed figure meant he was of great importance.

'I will not forgive you because it was entirely my fault. It is I who needs forgiveness.' Alcino bowed to her and she blushed. He was a handsome man; tall and thin, with grey eyes, silver streaked hair, and a pointed nose.

'Thank you, sir.' Unsure of what to do, for forgiving a rich man was not something she felt herself worthy of, the maiden nodded nervously and continued walking, shifting the basket of apples under her arm to a more comfortable position.

'Please, my lady, before you go, may I have your name?'

She stopped, turned around, her eyes lifting to meet

his. 'Callinna, my lord,' and then she was gone.

Alcino stared after Callinna for a long while. From that day on there was never a moment when Callinna was not on his mind.

He returned to his villa where he wrote up a glowing report for Kootol, then, he sent his page boy to deliver it to the King, giving him a few extra coins to find out what he could about a girl called Callinna who lived in Pizane. Once the page boy had left, Alcino lay on his day-bed and dreamed about her, saying her name over and over as though it were some delicious delicacy he was savouring on his tongue.

The page boy woke Alcino in the late afternoon, bowing when the duke quickly sat up in anticipation.

'My lord, the King thanks you for your report and wishes you to know that he has sent a messenger to the subject inviting him to the castle for a second interview. He also wishes you to join him for dinner if you have no other plans.'

'Yes, yes, but what about the girl, man?'

'Miss Callinna Sarista Angelo is a milkmaid in the Pizane village, under the employment of Master Dougray Vento. She is an only child, daughter to Lorena and Davide Angelo. She is twenty years old and will wed her betrothed, Master Kootol Kallidean Canero, on her twenty-first birthday.'

Alcino stared at his page boy for some minutes, making the poor lad shift uncomfortably.

'Repeat that final part, please,' he finally said, his voice cracking a little.

'She is twenty years old and will wed her betrothed, Master Kootol Kallidean Canero, on her twenty-first birthday.'

Alcino nodded slowly, thanked his page boy and dismissed him. He did not attend dinner with Fello that night, saying he was ill, which, in all honesty, he was, but the next morning he got up and continued life as usual, his heart aching painfully.

Kootol underwent his second interview at the castle, where the University was situated, and King Fello told him he would start in the new term. Kootol and Callinna married before Callinna's twenty-first birthday so they could then pack up and move to Toulon to live in the University's teaching quarters.

Over the next few months, Alcino saw quite a lot of Callinna as he helped Kootol settle in. They ran into each other at functions, around campus, and whenever Alcino visited Kootol in his apartments. Over time, Callinna became more relaxed around Alcino and slowly fell in love with his reserved countenance and extensive range of knowledge. He treated her with respect and had such an obvious love for her that she felt protected and safe in his presence. Kootol was a harsh lover and often beat her. She knew he got impatient with her shyness around the other university staff.

An affair followed, then shortly after, a pregnancy. Kootol was teaching when Izan was born, giving Callinna enough time to call on Alcino who magically altered his son's grey eyes and, later, the silver streak that began to show in his dark hair.

But, just as inevitable as the affair was the discovery.

One day, when Izan was three years old, Kootol realised he had left a book he needed for class back in his apartment and he left his students in the midst of essay writing to fetch it. Opening the door, he found Callinna and Alcino locked in a passionate kiss and flew into a wild rage.

'What in Mythos' name is this?!' he cried.

Callinna leapt from the couch and ran over to him. 'Kootol! I'm sorry, it just happened-'

Kootol knocked her to the ground without even glancing at her and stormed over to Alcino.

'How dare you treat like her that!' Alcino rumbled. He tried to skirt around Kootol and get to Callinna, listening to his heart rather than his head and only realising his error when a jolt of magic froze him in place. Callinna gasped. Alcino gave her a look of apology then screamed as Kootol's magic hurtled through him painfully, transforming him into a large blue bird.

This was the customary punishment for adultery in Varatalé. The majority of magical beasts lived in their own regions, particularly the giant bird race as they were too large and caused too much mess to live in the cities, and so the offending couple would be forced to live apart forevermore. The spell could not be reversed by the one it had been cast upon and King Fello was powerless to intercept because Kootol was well within his rights.

This did not stop the lovers, though. The journey from the bird region, Palero, took Alcino a week one way, and so, each month, Callinna and Izan would sneak out to the forest on the edge of the city and find him waiting for them in a well-hidden cave. The young boy had a fit the first time he saw the giant creature. Magic exploded out of him as he wailed and cried, bouncing off the cave walls and transforming Alcino back into his human self, much to his and Callinna's delight. The rays of the setting sun saw the Duke reverting back to bird-form, but Izan was able to repeat the same trick each month before promptly leaving his parents to do the icky adult stuff and going into the forest to play.

Callinna soon became pregnant again and gave birth at the end of the year. This time, Kootol was around for the birth and when Melody was born with a set of tiny blue and white wings he beat the confession out of his exhausted wife while the nurse cowered in the corner clutching the still gooey and squealing Melody. Alcino was due to meet his lover the next day because Melody had not been due to arrive for another two weeks, so Kootol went along in Callinna's place.

Alcino didn't have a chance.

Kootol paralysed him then plucked his feathers out one by one before finally setting him alight and watching as he squawked and died.

Kootol stayed with Callinna but barely took any notice of the two innocent children. Whenever Callinna took them anywhere they were frowned upon because everyone knew they were the product of an affair. Their father's once well-respected name did nothing to gain them any goodwill, but Alcino's friendship and favours to Fello at least allowed them to stay in the city and remain untouched. To add more problems to the sorry situation, Izan had a lot of magic and no idea how to harness it at such a young age, especially when no one was willing to teach him. He caused quite a number of accidents in the city and had others linked to him, which he may or may not have been responsible for, including a few unexplained deaths, so, the people soon came to believe that the children were cursed, deciding that the main Varatalian God, Mythos, was frowning upon them for being created in such a sinful way.

Present Day – Varatalé

Sora and Asseniah were looking through the cloth stalls in the eastern end of the market.

'Let me know if there's anything you like, Asseniah. You haven't had a new outfit for a long time.'

Asseniah showed no sign that she had heard but Sora was used to that.

The stall owner watched them both suspiciously. Although Sora was a frequent visitor to this part of the market, she hardly ever bought anything; the stall sold some of the finest material in Varatalé and her funds were limited.

'These silks are beautiful,' Sora gushed, running her delicate fingers along a roll of deep red shiny silk. 'This one would be stunning on you, Asseniah.'

Sora held the cloth up to Asseniah's face to see the contrast, but Asseniah wasn't interested. Instead, she pointed to a far corner of the table. Sora gasped when she saw the material her friend was pointing to. Setting the red cloth down gently, she hurried around to the other side of the table to run her fingers over a pink silk embroided with small white flowers.

'Oh, Asseniah, it's absolutely stunning,' she exclaimed. Then, remembering that Asseniah had seen it first, she said gently, 'But, you know you can't wear pink; not with your hair.'

Asseniah shook her head. She held the silk up against Sora's face and nodded, satisfied.

'Oh, you meant for me?'

Asseniah nodded again.

'You really do know me very well, sweet one.' Her smile faded as she looked again at the silk in her hands. 'But, I can't afford it.'

Asseniah put a hand on Sora's shoulder and stared into her eyes.

'Alright, I'll ask him,' Sora said, quietly. She turned to the stall owner who had forgotten his suspicions and was watching the silent girl with great fascination. 'Excuse me, sir, would you mind holding this silk until I come back later?'

The stall owner hesitated momentarily before agreeing. 'But, if you're not back by three o'clock, I'll have to put it back on sale.'

'Thank you, sir, that's plenty of time.' Sora clapped her hands happily and turned to Asseniah, whose blank face didn't betray how amused she was that her friend could get so excited over a piece of cloth.

Thirteen Years Ago – Varatalé

'Mariette, I found this incredible book today that explained an Earthling concept known as a "circus,"' Alain babbled excitedly, as soon as he had walked through the door of the small house they had lived in since fleeing Noir Eternale four years before. Mariette was in the kitchen – which, right now, resembled a war zone – cooking dinner for them both, filling the air with the aroma of tomatoes and oregano. 'They have these travelling shows where people perform a range of acts that the average Earthling finds remarkable. And, of course, they are, because Earthlings don't have magic.'

He paused to read some of the notes he was holding in his hand.

'And what's even more fascinating is that they originally started out as "freak shows," a horrible term, but it was a place for people who didn't belong.' He looked up at her with a large grin. 'They're basically a family of people who have been shunned from society who tour the world and bring a touch of magic to the people. It's brilliant.'

'It sounds interesting.'

'I'm going to see if I can find any more information on them. Just think of it – what if we could start our own circus and travel the Highway? Wouldn't that be something?'

Mariette giggled at his boyish excitement, bringing him out of his thoughts.

'I'm sorry, I should be helping you with dinner.'

'It is okay, Alain, it is almost ready. You can get out some plates if you like.'

Alain put his notes down and made his way to the cupboard, carefully avoiding the tomato juice and small piles of flour on the floor.

'How was work today?' he asked her.

'Good. I just wish I did not stand out so much. The Varatalians 'ave such lovely golden skin and ours is so white.' Due to their genetic make-up, Noir Eternalans remained as white as snow, no matter how long they lived in the sun.

'I know, but I don't think the Varatalians care too much.'

'But I care. When we arrived 'ere, I felt like I 'ad come 'ome after a long journey. I feel like a Varatalian, but every time I stand next to Jala and Saran, I am reminded zat I am not.' Mariette worked in a clothes store just down the street from their house; a job she enjoyed a lot more than her last profession. Jala and Saran were her co-workers.

Alain turned Mariette to face him and looked her squarely in the eyes.

'Mariette, you're a wonderful human being no matter which planet you're from. Jala and Saran enjoy your company as do all our friends so don't you worry that you aren't a native Varatalian, the point is that it's your home now and you love it here.'

Mariette nodded. 'I know. I'm sorry.'

'Don't be sorry.'

'Well, why don't you tell me more about zis circus while we 'ave dinner?'

The next day, Alain was at work in his rooms in the castle. He worked as a scribe for the King; translating, writing poems and songs, copying texts, finding lost words. Fello had grown to like him and his stories of the adventures he had had in other worlds, making him somewhat of a reluctant party favourite at the frequent royal feasts the King held. As a result, the name Alain du Maurier was now recognised throughout all four corners of the globe.

Realising he needed a book from the library, Alain put down his pen and set off down the corridor. It soon became apparent that something rather gossip worthy had happened as there were clusters of people talking in low voices and hurrying about.

With his curiosity aroused, Alain entered the large sprawling library, looked around, and headed toward a pair of lecturers who were whispering frantically beside the Earthling section. Stepping into a nearby row, Alain used his magic to grab hold of the words they whispered and bring them to his ear. Above him, the eyes of Mythos' attendants peered down from the painted dome ceiling.

'I can't believe that Callinna Canero suicided,' the shorter of the two said. He had a rather high-pitched voice that Alain had heard the students parody frequently.

'Well, she has never been the same since Alcino's death,' replied the other in a voice that was permanently heavy with disdain.

'She shouldn't have strayed from her marriage in the first place.'

'Jumped from the cliff, I hear.'

'Yep, wanted to fly like a bird.'

'Disgraceful.'

'What about the children?'

'Left them at home.'

'Should have taken them with her, cursed little creatures.'

'And can you believe that His Majesty has said that he'll take them in until something can be done for them.'

'He wouldn't?!'

'Well Kootol doesn't want them and the King still feels he owes it to Alcino.'

'But the people will protest. He'll be thrown from office!'

'He's not keeping them forever, just until he knows what to do with them.'

'Kill them is what I say.'

'I agree.'

Alain completely forgot about the book he had come for. Frowning, he hurried out of the library and walked the maze of corridors that led to the King's chambers, so lost in thought he didn't notice the people that greeted him along the way.

'I need to see the King urgently,' Alain said to the guard at the King's chamber door. The guard disappeared, leaving Alain to pace until he returned moments later and ushered him in.

'Alain du Maurier,' Fello greeted, as Alain fell to his knee in a bow. 'I'm afraid I cannot talk for long. You have probably heard about the unfortunate event that happened this morning?'

Alain got to his feet. 'Yes, sir, that is why I am here. I

wish to take the children into my care.'

Fello stared at Alain for some long moments. Alain held his gaze. The King had intense blue eyes that were highlighted all the more by the fact his hair was completely grey, like two raindrops falling from a thunder cloud.

'You what?'

'I believe they need a home and I'd like to give them one.'

'Why in Mythos' name would you want to do that?'

'I believe the young girl has wings and the boy has magic?'

'Yes.'

As Fello listened with interest, Alain explained the idea for the circus that he had and how he could train the children to use their magic for entertainment purposes.

When he was done, Fello studied him for a moment before saying, 'Alain, you're a well-respected man. You do realise that you'll be giving up that respect if you take these children in, don't you?'

'Yes, sir, I do.'

The King smiled and shook his head in wonder. He walked over to the large open window and looked out over the castle grounds, stroking his beard as he pondered Alain's proposal. A good five minutes passed before he spun around elegantly in a swirl of cloak and faced the Wordmaster once more.

'Alright, Alain, the children are yours, but on one condition. You must take them away from Toulon, perhaps even to another region. It'll be a shame to lose you and your talents but it's the only way to keep the people happy.'

'That's fine, sir.'

'You should also know that Alcino had a vast amount of wealth to his name. When he was murdered, that wealth came to me and I let the public believe it would be going to the university, which some of it has, but I also kept a substantial amount in case the children should need it. This idea of yours sounds like it could use a fund behind it-'

Alain was rather shocked. 'Sir, I never intended-'

Fello held up his hand and Alain fell silent. 'I know. I know. You're a good man, Alain du Maurier. I know you aren't doing this for the money. The money belongs to the children and as you are now their guardian it goes to you. But, the fact it goes to you will remain between you and me… and the four guards standing in this room, who are in this room because I trust them with my life.' He looked around at each of the statuesque guards in turn as if daring them to defy him. None of them so much as blinked.

'Of course, sir,' Alain assured him. 'You have my word.'

'Well, coming from a Wordmaster I should think that means something.' He smiled.

Alain returned the smile and nodded. 'Based on one very painful experience I can tell you that breaking my word also means breaking a bone. And it doesn't heal until you have mended the word.'

Fello winced as he reached out to shake hands with Alain.

'Well, I suppose you should meet them, then.' He

waved a hand to the nearby guard who disappeared further into the chamber, returning with the two children.

'Hello there,' Alain said, as he squatted down to their level and smiled kindly at them. Izan, who was nine at this time, had his arms crossed and his nose in the air. Melody was half hiding behind him, one hand gripping his shirt, the other hand in her mouth so she could suck her fingers. At five she already had a mass of brown curls and the green eyes of her mother, but Alain found himself drawn to her wings; white with blue edges, giving the impression of a tiny angel standing there in front of him. Knowing she was scared, Alain wrote the word "angel" in the air and pushed it toward her. She couldn't suppress a giggle as the word danced in front of her. Izan still had his nose in the air but was watching the interaction between his sister and this stranger out of the corner of his eye.

'And what might your name be?' Alain asked. Of course, he already knew but he wasn't sure what else to say.

Melody found his deep soothing voice too calming to be afraid of. 'Melody Castlereigh Bell.' She said this with her hand still in her mouth.

Izan frowned at her but she wasn't watching. She was rather intrigued by this strange man's wild white hair.

'It's a pleasure to meet you, Miss Bell,' Alain told her with a nod.

Melody released her hand from her mouth and offered it, still wet, to Alain. Touched, the Wordmaster looked up to Izan for permission.

'You've come to take us away?' Izan asked.

'Yes.'

'Where?'

'We'll have to move to another village. You and your sister may live with me and my friend, Mariette, if you wish.'

Melody had dropped her hand again, picking up on Izan's disapproval.

'Why do you want us? Nobody else does.'

'I wish to teach you, help you learn how to use your magic properly, and, if someone doesn't take care of you, you'll most likely be put in prison or killed.'

Fello was a little stunned at this bluntness, but Izan seemed to appreciate it. He already knew what people were planning to do to them but only because he had been eavesdropping.

'How do we know *you* won't kill us?'

'I have other plans for you, but I'll tell you about them later in more detail.'

Izan looked down at his sister, who was smiling up at him with that disgusting cuteness she had, and nodded. She reached out her hand once more and Alain shook it gently.

'Excellent,' Fello exclaimed, a broad smile on his face. 'Andreno, tell the nurse to pack the children's belonging's together.'

As the guard hurried off, Melody giggled again and Alain almost melted right there on the King's polished marble floor.

The four of them moved into a small house in the village of Luc'ca where Alain began to teach them to hone their skills for entertainment. During this time, King Fello, with his son Duozo, would make monthly visits to Alain's house to check on their progress, health, wellbeing, and to teach his son to accept them for the good people they were. In this way, Duozo and Izan became good friends and the children learnt their true story.

Present Day – Varatalé

When everyone arrived back at the caravan train that afternoon, they were buzzing with stories. Izan was the only one missing, having gone straight from Duozo to an inn with a woman he had met in the corridors of the castle.

Melody and Chester had bought pastries for everyone from Luigi's bakery and the troupe tucked into them as soon as they were handed over: chocolate éclairs for Alain and Mariette; a strawberry tart for Arrahbella; doughnuts for Izan, Oleg, and Sora; a bag of cookies for the dwarves; a honey log for Asseniah; and cream filled wafers for themselves, one vanilla, one chocolate. Everyone secretly kept an eye on Asseniah as she took the first bite of her honey log, smiling when a look of pure ecstasy washed over her.

They had taken some chairs outside on to the grass to enjoy the sunshine for a short while before they had to set up the tent, when Sora glided up to Alain to ask him about the silk.

'Alain,' she said, after waiting until he had finished telling Arrahbella about his conversation with Fello. 'Asseniah and I saw the most beautiful material in the market today. It'd look incredible as a corset with some white lace and ribbons, and it's not even all that expensive compared to the others in the stall, and I wouldn't need very much. I was wondering if maybe Arrahbella or you could come and look at it and see how much it is and... oh, it was just gorgeous, Alain!'

Alain smiled with amusement and looked at Arrahbella, the main keeper of the finances, who gave him a nod. He then nodded at Sora who let a very out-of-character squeal of delight escape her before throwing her arms around the Ringmaster, making him chuckle. Arrahbella went inside to get the money, then, the two of them, accompanied by Asseniah, returned to the market.

When they were gone, Alain turned to Melody and beckoned. She uncurled herself from Chester's lap, walked over, and stood in front of him.

'Arrahbella told me that there was some trouble in the market earlier,' he said, taking her hands in his.

'Yeah. But it's okay, Alain, I know that some people are just never going to like us.'

'Well, Izan did cause some disasters with his magic...'

'I heard my name. What's going on?' Izan asked, walking up behind Melody.

'Some woman in the market was giving Melody a hard time over your parents,' Chester told him.

Izan's expression darkened. 'Which woman? Take me to her.'

'Calm down, Izan. You aren't going anywhere. I've told you before that there's nothing you can do. They already think you're cursed and scaring them with magic isn't going to help. The same applies to you, Chester.' Chester frowned. 'We don't run into many of them anymore so you just need to leave it alone.'

'But the things they say about our parents...' Izan fumed.

'I know, I know. Your parents were good people and they loved each other and it was a matter of poor timing, but they did commit adultery, and Izan you did kill a few people, even if it was an accident.'

Izan kicked the grass. 'I don't understand you, Alain. You created a circus so that people who had been cast out of society had a place to belong and then you go and stand up for the people that cast us out.'

'I'm not standing up for them. I'm saying you need to understand where they're coming from.'

Izan muttered under his breath and sat down. Alain looked up at Melody again.

'You know what, though? We're about to play three shows to the people of Toulon and it'll be a full tent every night. Most of the people love us, so don't let it get to you, okay?'

Melody nodded. Izan continued to mutter. Alain stood and wrapped his arms around Melody, habit instructing him to avoid her wings.

'You know you're not cursed, Melody Bell.'

She looked up at him. 'I know. If Mythos really didn't like me then I wouldn't have people like you, Chester, and Izan around me, would I?'

Alain and Chester smiled while Izan frowned and muttered something along the lines of 'corny' and 'sickly sweet.'

Alain released his hug and stepped back, looking at Izan with mock concern. 'Do you need a hug?' he asked.

'Hug me and I'll smite you to smithereens,' the magician replied.

Melody ran over and threw her arms around her brother, planting a big kiss on his cheek.

'Get off. Get off,' he complained, pushing her away.

Alain laughed and clapped his hands together. 'Right, you lot, time to get this tent set up.'

CHAPTER 3

ARRAHBELLA AND ASSENIAH

Present Day – The Highway

As soon as they had performed their final show in Toulon, Cirque du Phantastique headed out of the Varatalian rift and began the month-long journey along the Highway Between the Worlds to Earth. It had been nighttime when they had left, so most of the troupe were asleep, all except for Fenton who was in the driving cabin, singing to himself as he steered.

In the du Maurier's caravan, Alain had only just drifted into a dream – where ships made from crystals glided across a sea of words – when he was woken by noise and movement. He sat up, blinking a few times in the soft lamplight before realising where the noise was coming from; Arrahbella was tossing and turning next to him, muttering something incoherent, clutching the quilt as though it were a lifeline.

'Arrahbella?' Alain said, quietly, resting a hand on her arm. 'Arrahbella?'

She cried out again, a cry of pain and torment.

'Bella, wake up,' he said, more urgently.

Arrahbella opened her eyes and sat up suddenly,

shaking violently.

'Bella, what is it?'

Her fear-filled eyes softened as soon as they met his, the realisation that she was awake and safe sinking in quickly. Alain stroked her hair as she swallowed a few times and tried to catch her breath.

'There was this wall of white light,' she said, her voice quiet and unsteady. 'Then blood, lots of blood, and a girl screaming.' She paused. 'And I was in so much pain, my head felt like it was on fire.'

She flinched at the memory. Alain continued to stroke her hair, unsure what else to do. The lamplight flickered slightly as they went over a small bump in the road, causing the shadows in the cluttered room to jump and dance across the numerous bookcases lining the walls, the towers of books on the floor, and the nine pairs of cowboy boots sitting in a row by the antique wardrobe. The small fountain sitting on the large desk amid the mess of papers and books bubbled away in ironic serenity. Incense perfumed the air.

'Are you alright?' he asked.

She nodded. 'Yes.'

'Do you think it was a premonition?'

'I don't know.' She forced herself to smile. 'No use worrying about it, though, not unless there's more information. It was probably just a dream.'

Alain nodded, not entirely convinced. They lay back down, Alain putting his arms around her as she snuggled into his chest, and soon they fell asleep once more.

Six Years Ago – Earth

Alain was walking through the streets of Glastonbury, England, his head bent against the fierce wind, white shirt whipping around him, trying to free itself from his body. Wrapping his arms tightly around his chest, he hurried down the main street, passed the famous Abbey, and crossed the road to the tiny café on the opposite corner, the door jingling as he opened it.

Inside was deliciously warm. Only half of the handful of tables were occupied, including one by the window where a woman named Arrahbella Forester was sitting on her own, eating a baguette and reading a novel. She froze as Alain entered, her psychic powers picking up on the strange vibes he carried with him.

Unaware of the reaction he had caused, the Wordmaster walked over to the counter where a young woman with an eyebrow ring and pink-streaked black hair was putting some scones in the display case.

'Hi,' he said, cheerfully. 'Can I have one hot chocolate, please?'

'Sure. With marshmallows?' Her heavy accent forced Alain's magic to automatically switch from English to Irish in order to understand her.

'Absolutely.'

'Take a seat and I'll bring it over.'

Alain thanked her, paid the money with practiced ease, then sat at the table nearest the serving counter, facing the other patrons of the café. He took out a notebook and pen from his pocket and started scribbling down some lines while he waited. Words always bombarded him here, there was so much inspiration and so many ideas wherever one looked. Plus, he could hear the words of all the writers that had lived there over the centuries; snatches of Shakespeare, lines from Lewis, and reams of Rowling, all their creations sitting in the hills and rivers of England's chocolate box landscape, waiting to catch humans and pull them out of reality for a while. This was the reason he had come to England; to discover more about the natural magic of Earth. The rift to the Highway opened down in Adelaide, Australia, but Alain had been to Earth a few times now and so he was well versed in planes and travel. He had used his power with words to secure himself a passport and had seen nearly all the countries that were easily accessible. England, however, remained his favourite place, being much like the magic strewn, castle dotted worlds he was used to.

'Here you are, sir,' the waitress said, interrupting the river of words rushing through his brain as she placed his drink in front of him.

Alain thanked her again before drowning the marshmallows in the creamy-brown liquid and stirring. He tapped the spoon free of drips and rested it on the saucer, then, he lifted the mug to his lips, blew, and took a sip. The sweet liquid coursed through his icy body, reaching into every crevasse and warming him from head to toe. Alain savoured the moment, closing his eyes briefly, before taking another mouthful.

It was in that moment, with his insides already gooey

with pleasure and his tastebuds swamped with chocolate and sweet marshmallow goodness, that Alain's eyes fell on Arrahbella. It was, possibly, the most exquisite moment of his life. She was wearing a black skirt and a forest-green, silk and lace top with transparent bell sleeves. Her black hair was like a waterfall of cascading waves down her back, falling in a pool on the seat of her chair. She was deliciously curvy, leaning to the heavier side (which Alain always preferred), of average height, and she had a pretty, round face. She looked to be in her late thirties, as he was at this time, and she had an incredible air of mysteriousness about her, which is perhaps what Alain found the most alluring.

After some moments he remembered to swallow, but his brain didn't get as far as telling his hands to put the cup down and he held it and the saucer in mid-air as he watched her take a sip of her tea, then bite into her baguette and wipe the crumbs away with a napkin. His eyes went to the cover of the book and registered it as *Nectar* by Lily Prior, a novel he had read some years back.

Then, a peculiar thing happened.

Arrahbella was reaching for her tea once more when, suddenly, she froze. Her eyes shot up to the kitchen doors behind the serving counter and an anxious look crossed her face. Alain hadn't heard anything that might warrant such behaviour. None of the other patrons seemed to have either.

Perhaps she is still waiting for something to be brought out, he decided.

A loud crashing of plates reverberated through the café, quickly followed by a short bout of swearing. The diners fell silent as every head turned toward the kitchen doors and the waitress hurried out, looking flustered.

'Terribly sorry, everyone. Everything's alright, just a few plates lost. Please go back to your meals, terribly sorry,' and she disappeared back into the kitchen.

Alain was shocked. Looking at Arrahbella once more he saw her anxious expression had changed to an almost guilty one, as though the crash in the kitchen had somehow been her fault. She was staring at the table, over the top of her book, fidgeting with its pages.

No more than two minutes had passed when she froze again. This time, her eyes darted sideways to a table in the front window where a young couple had been sitting for quite a while; kissing, cuddling, giggling. They had been sharing a pizza, the remains of which still sat on the circular tray between them. Alain's eyes flicked from Arrahbella to the couple a few times until he saw the young male drop his fork, taking care to position it near his girlfriend's chair from which her handbag was dangling, its zip wide open.

Surely he's not going to steal from her handbag? Alain thought.

The boy knelt down as the girl took a sip of her Coke, looking out of the window at a group of tourists lining up to enter the Abbey, struggling against the wind. The boy pulled a small, neatly wrapped present out of his shirt pocket and, with a shaking hand, dropped it into his girlfriend's bag. He even zipped it up afterward before returning to his seat, remembering to pick up his fork along the way.

Filled with wonder, Alain turned his attention back

to Arrahbella, shaking his head ever-so-slightly.

Arrahbella knew the strange man had been watching her and, as she looked away from the young couple, she couldn't resist finally sneaking a glance in his direction. Their eyes met, only for a second, but in that second, she was hit by a barrage of dark and disturbing images; vampires, drunkards, werewolves, a world where darkness was eternal, a world that was not Earth.

Frightened, she began to collect her things in a hurry. Realising that he had spooked her, Alain quickly moved over to the empty chair at her table before she had even put her book away.

'Hi,' he said, and held out his hand. 'Alain du Maurier.'

If she hadn't been so scared she would have noticed what a lovely, if strangely accented, voice he had. It was like auditory chocolate. She dropped her gaze to eye his outstretched hand suspiciously, still with one hand on her blue velvet bag, the other holding the book above it. He pulled his hand back, gesturing at the book as he did so.

'That's an exquisite book. I read it a few years ago. Prior knows exactly how to use the right combination of words to awaken her reader's senses, don't you think?'

Arrahbella was beginning to calm down a little, thinking that, obviously, this man was from Earth, no one could be from anywhere but Earth. She was even taking notice of his appearance, attraction seeping in and threatening to weaken her guard. A mental kick managed to stop a blush moments before it reached her cheeks.

Get a grip, Arrahbella, she told herself, sternly. Those weird vibes he's carrying have got to mean something nasty.

Curious, and to see if he really was going to harm her, she looked into his eyes a second time and opened his mind, barely registering the shiver he gave as their minds connected. This time, she not only saw Noir Eternale in all its seedy glory but also Mariette, Melody, Izan, Varatalé, the Highway, and pieces of the other worlds he had visited and the adventures he'd had. There was no doubt he was not from Earth and Arrahbella drew out of his mind in a fearful hurry, grabbed her things as quickly as she could, and dashed out of the café, shaking with fear.

Alain followed, not wanting to lose her. 'Please, don't be frightened. I just want to talk to you. I mean you no harm.' He was faster than she was, quickly catching up to her.

'Stay away. I'll call for help,' she warned and, despite the threatening tone, Alain was struck by how lyrical and pretty her voice was.

He couldn't bear letting her go, or the thought of never seeing her again and so, reluctantly, he switched on his powers.

'Stop, lady, calm down. I will not harm you.' His voice was so soothing, so calming, so safe and protective. It flowed over her like sweet nectar, caressed her heart and wrapped its calmness around her until she had to stop walking out of sheer giddiness.

She turned, looking into his eyes once again. He was standing quite close to her now, so close that, had the wind not been so strong, their breath would have mingled. This time, she saw her own future in his eyes, not in detail, but she instantly knew this was the man she was meant to spend the rest of her life with. All the fear left her as though the wind had simply blown it away.

Alain saw her relax and smiled. 'I'd really like to talk to you,' he said.

'I have to go back to work. My lunch break is over,' she said matter-of-factly and Alain's heart sunk.

'Oh, of course.' Now what was he supposed to do?

'You can walk with me if you like. It's just up the street.'

Alain beamed. 'Alright.'

Arrahbella turned and started to cross the road. Alain looked to the sky and silently thanked Mythos a thousand times over before following.

Together they walked past the shops that lined the main street, stopping about halfway up at a small gift shop that sold statues of Arthur and Guinevere and fairies frozen in dance poses, gem stones and tarot cards, daggers, dream catchers, and other such items.

'This is it,' she told him, stopping by the window front.

A question formed itself in Alain's mind, but, when he opened his mouth, his powers jammed and the words fell out in a babbling mess. 'Do you think, I could, perhaps, maybe, take you to dinner tonight, possibly?'

Arrahbella smiled serenely and a wave of calm washed over him.

'Alright. But you'd better come to my house, I have a

feeling the things we're going to talk about won't go down too well in a public restaurant.'

Alain nodded. 'True.'

She gave him her address, said goodbye, and disappeared into the shop.

Alain returned to his little Bed & Breakfast cottage and passed the rest of the afternoon in painful impatience, writing down words and poetry to describe the woman he had just met, picking the sentences up off of the page and letting them float around him, whispering in his ear as they passed. After looking at the clock for the millionth time, he got fed up and decided that the Time Pixies must be playing tricks on him, before remembering that Time Pixies didn't exist on Earth any more.

The wind calmed itself sometime around sunset, though the air remained bitterly cold, and it was finally time to leave. After some roaming and wrong turns, he arrived at her small semi-detached stone cottage, which sat hidden behind a garden full of flowers and herbs and a little wooden gate. Smoke poured out of the chimney, spilling secrets out into the wind.

'Sorry I'm early,' he said, when she opened the door. 'I'm still getting used to Earthling addresses.'

Now there was an apology she had never heard before. The night was going to be an interesting one.

'Not a problem. Come in.'

Through the main door was the sitting / dining room, a cosy area with the kitchen off to one side. The first things that Alain noticed were the two long bookcases against the far wall, both almost bursting at the seams, and some beautiful, large dream-catchers hanging on the walls and above the stone fireplace. Then, something glinted in the firelight, catching his attention, and he turned to find a mahogany case sitting open on the sideboard, inlaid with velvet and showcasing about eight beautifully decorated daggers of all shapes and sizes. He looked at Arrahbella with renewed awe and wondered how much more fascinating she could become.

'I forgot to ask if there was anything you didn't eat,' she said, as she poured them both some wine from the bottle Alain had brought with him. 'So I went with pasta.'

Alain smiled. Pasta was the most consumed food in Varatalé. 'Perfect,' he said.

Over dinner, they learnt about each other and Arrahbella was educated about the Highway and the other worlds.

'So, this Highway joins worlds together?'

'That's right. The worlds belong to parallel universes and when those universes rub against each other they create a wasteland of planetary matter and stardust, like when two land masses come together they create a mountain range, well, the universes form a Highway.'

'And from the Highway you can get into other worlds?'

'Yes. Worlds that are near the edge of their universe, the ones closest to where their universe rubs against another, develop a rift, like a tear in their outer casing.'

'So, can we humans get from Earth to, say, Jupiter along this Highway?'

'Not along this Highway, no. Jupiter is part of your solar system, it's still in your universe, so you have to travel through space to get to that one, but, every world is rubbing against others in parallel universes, to my understanding, so once you were on Jupiter you would most likely find a rift leading to a different Highway and a new set of worlds.'

Arrahbella shook her head. She understood, but it was a lot to take in. In a way, she was relieved because she had always believed that there were others out there. In a universe as big as the one Earth was in, there simply had to be other life forms, and the fact there were possibly thousands of other universes as well meant endless possibilities. She suddenly felt very small.

'So, along this particular Highway, Earth is at the end?'

'That's right. Earth is at the eastern most end, then it's a month's journey to either Kartan or Ormance, then Varatalé and Icecess, followed by Noir Eternale and Terrenvale, with Landau, Arelia, and Da'Laarwick up the western end. I'm pretty sure the Highway continues on past Da'Laarwick but there's either nothing else along there or there's a great distance until another world because I don't know of anyone who's ever gone there and found anything.'

Arrahbella pondered this for a moment.

'The rift on Earth opens down in Adelaide?' she finally asked.

'Correct.'

'How come humans aren't always walking into this rift and finding the Highway, or there aren't more beings from other worlds coming here?'

'Well, first of all, I think you're referring to people from any world but Earth as being non-human. I'm as human as you are, but with a bit more magic. I'm a Noir Eternalan and you are an Earthling.'

'Sorry,' she said, a little shyly.

'Oh no, it's okay. Sorry, I didn't mean to sound like I was being authoritarian.'

Arrahbella giggled at this. Alain flushed a little and smiled awkwardly.

'Go on,' she told him.

Alain fiddled with his empty wine glass, cleared his throat, and continued. 'Earth used to be a very magical place, and, some of it still is, like here in Glastonbury; not only the place itself, but the fact that the Abbey claims to hold King Arthur's grave links back to a very magical time. Somewhere along history's timeline, Earthlings stopped believing in magic, or chose to ignore it, or wiped it out. According to Earthlings, magic doesn't exist; they don't even think of the natural world as being magic, everything can be explained scientifically, which is, of course, a form of magic in itself, but anyway...'

Arrahbella held up her hand to interrupt. 'Now, it is I who must correct you. You're making it sound as though *all* Earthlings have done away with magic.'

'You're right. I apologise. Most Earthlings don't believe in magic, yet, they keep craving it, through their movies, books, games, and holidays. Anyway, there are a couple of reasons as to why Earth doesn't get many foreign visitors. The first is the distance. Most people are content to stay in their own worlds and those that do venture out can't be bothered making the month or more journey. We're also taught from an early age about Earth and its strange ways. It really is a fascinating place, but the emphasis is always on the fact that magic isn't welcome. Many of the worlds along the Highway, especially Noir Eternale, cannot abide the thought of a planet without magic. You only have to look at Mariette's story to see what I mean there.'

Arrahbella nodded. She had been appalled at Mariette's treatment when Alain had recounted his own story earlier.

'So, although many people are fascinated by Earth, they tend to stay away. They also know it's a hard place to get around and has so many different worlds inside the one; like Asia. Asia is a completely different world to Europe while Europe is different again to Africa, and even within those you still have vast differences and speak different languages. That confuses people and puts them off, but, see, that's what I find so intriguing about Earth.' He paused to take a sip of the wine that Arrahbella had just refilled while she smiled in amusement at the excitement he was showing over her home planet.

'We experience quite a bit of your world anyway,' he continued. 'There are a number of traders that go between the worlds and though there are strict laws about taking anything *in* to Earth, there are plenty of objects that find their way out, especially books. I have quite a collection of Earthling authors, I find them remarkably entertaining.

'Earthlings don't find themselves wandering through

81

the rift because it's very difficult to find unless you know where it is, and every rift is closely guarded by rift guards, none so much as Earth's rift, which is guarded by a mix of foreign guards and Earthling guards who have been magically forbidden to speak about it to any of their fellows. If someone does find themselves walking aimlessly out of the planet then the guards have them back through and on another road fast and the person finds themselves unable to remember the last ten minutes of their life.'

Arrahbella shook her head again.

'But, enough about the Highway. I want to know your story.'

'Oh, it's not that interesting.'

'Every story is interesting. To me anyway.'

She smiled. 'Well, I was born in London, but adopted at birth, and brought to Glastonbury. My birth name is Annabella but I used to write my name in cursive when I was little and my 'n's looked like 'r's.' Alain smiled. 'I liked how it sounded so I kept it. I added the 'h' later when I started doing psychic readings.'

'What do your parents do?'

'Mum was a teacher and Dad was a gardener. They were killed in a car accident about fifteen years ago.'

'I'm sorry.'

They were silent for a moment. Then, Alain asked, 'Do you have any brothers or sisters?'

'My parents had a biological daughter, Serena, when they adopted me. We never got along, though. She always thought I'd been brought home to replace her, even though

Mum explained to her constantly that it was because they couldn't have another child naturally. And I freaked her out with my psychic episodes. She moved to the USA when they died and she hasn't spoken to me since. I know she blames me. She thinks I should have been able to see it coming and prevent it.' She looked away.

'Psychic powers are some of the hardest to control,' Alain said, softly.

She smiled. 'I know.'

They continued talking until the early hours of the next day when they became so delirious with tiredness, wine, excitement, and information intake that they fell asleep on the rug by the fire, Arrahbella's head resting on Alain's chest, her hand in his.

The next day was spent packing Arrahbella's things together, including the CD player and a collection of albums which now, mostly, belonged to Asseniah. By late afternoon, the two of them were leaving for Adelaide, Alain using magic along the way so that no trail was left.

The police were baffled by Arrahbella's disappearance, putting her down as a missing person in a case that would never be solved. They contacted Serena who felt a faint pang of something in her chest as she listened to the news.

'They think she's been kidnapped,' she told her husband, after putting down the phone. 'She was last seen hurrying out of a café with a guy chasing her.'

'And she didn't see that coming either?' he said, not looking away from the TV.

Serena laughed and the pang in her chest was forgotten.

Present Day – The Highway

At the end of the second week travelling the Highway, with no stops along the way, Izan was kneeling on his bed, looking out of the window in anxious anticipation. The Highway was a barren place; vast stretches of short, patchy grass, and rocky ground spread out on either side of the road, with the occasional small mountain adding variety to the horizon. The light was weak, like twilight, no matter what time of the day it was, the sky a murky mix of pink and grey.

'Come on, come on,' Izan whined, chewing on the end of a straw of talooey – a peppermint-flavoured, beige-coloured plant that was the Terrenvale equivalent of candy. He turned away from the window and checked himself in the nearest of the seven mirrors that lined his caravan walls. The caravan was mostly decorated in black and silver, what little furniture there was was gothic and elaborate, the bed up one end, the lounge down the other. Heavy, thumping, Earthling music blasted out of the stereo, making the floor vibrate.

The train slowed and he whipped around to face the window again, yelping in delight when he saw a cluster of trader wagons lined up on the side of the road. Not even waiting until the engine had stopped purring, he jumped down from his caravan and strutted toward the Inn, his cloak billowing out behind him.

Tokinov's Inn was a large grey block that looked almost as unimpressive as the Highway. The wooden sign above the doorway was splintered and fading and almost came off its chains when Izan whacked it with his hand as he passed underneath. The few travellers who had decided to sit at the decaying tables outside gave him disapproving stares for his arrogance, but Izan didn't see them. He didn't feel they were worthy of his attention.

Once inside, the magician's grey eyes adjusted quickly to the dim light as they searched the smoky room, passing over the fifteen people dotted around the tables until they eventually settled on one of only two females in the entire Inn. His mouth curved into a smile as he watched her deliver drinks to a table. Her blonde hair was pulled back in a bun and she wore a white dress that fell off her shoulders. She wasn't particularly pretty and was a little on the skinny side but to Izan she was beautiful.

'Sasha, my darling girl, how are you?' he said, approaching her as she returned to the bar.

Sasha's opal-coloured eyes shot up at the sound of his voice and a large, brilliant smile that displayed her crooked teeth lit up her face.

'Izan!' She threw her arms around him and kissed his cheek. Tokinov, Sasha's father, cleared his throat at this outburst, shaking his head when Sasha looked at him.

'What time do you get off?' Izan asked her.

But Tokinov overheard. 'She works until close, Izan. You'll have to wait a while.'

The rest of the troupe walked through the door at this point and took up various positions around the Inn; Chester, Oleg, and Alain sat at the bar, in a position where they could keep an eye on the train, while the girls took up a table in the corner, and the dwarves another on the far side of the room.

Izan leaned close to Sasha's ear. 'If I don't have you right now I'm going to die,' he whispered.

Sasha whimpered with longing and looked at the clock behind the bar.

'Father, I haven't had my lunch break yet.'

The Innkeeper sighed. He couldn't argue with that, even if a train load of fourteen customers had just walked through his doors.

'Alright, but make sure you're back by two.' He walked over to his daughter and lowered his voice. 'And don't forget to eat some lunch. I don't want you coming back faint with hunger and exhaustion.'

Izan flashed him an innocent smile. 'Don't worry, sir, there'll be plenty of time for her to rest. I only need her for fifteen minutes.'

Alain groaned and shook his head as Izan and Sasha ran off, disappearing behind a door at the end of the room. The other patrons had been watching this episode since Izan had entered, but now they went back to their meals, drinks, or games, some frowning and muttering, others snickering. Tokinov maintained a calm composure as he walked back along the bar to stand in front of Alain, Oleg, and Chester. He was a beefy man with a black handlebar moustache and large mouth.

'I must apologise for Izan,' Alain said, sincerely. 'We've tried to teach him some manners but he doesn't listen.'

'It's alright, Alain, I know what he's like. I just wish my daughter showed a little more restraint.'

'Ah, I wouldn't fear for your daughter's reputation,

86

sir. Izan once managed to bed a man who was well known for intensely disliking same-sex couples. We think it may be part of his power; that he can seduce anyone he wishes.'

Tokinov nodded sadly. 'How he lasts on that train of yours for so long is beyond me.'

'It's beyond us too,' Chester agreed.

'What will you have, friends?'

Alain ordered lunch for all but the dwarves, who liked to take care of themselves, and Tokinov got busy serving stew and drinks. His wife, Mishkan, had entered from a back room not long after Sasha had left and she took over serving, stopping to chat to the female troupe members for a while.

Izan and Sasha emerged at exactly two o'clock, by which time five of the patrons had left and most of the others were lazily smoking and playing cards. Positively glowing, Sasha bounced over to the bar and proceeded to serve Izan some stew and a drink, which he downed at an alarming rate. When he was done, he turned in his seat so his back was leaning against the bar, stuck a straw of talooey in his mouth, let out a satisfied sigh, and clapped Alain appreciatively on the shoulder. Alain just shook his head.

While Arrahbella and Mariette continued to talk to Mishkan, and Sora and Melody went outside for some fresh air, Asseniah headed back outside to Oleg's caravan. Closing the door, she walked past the mattress, closet, and table, past the easel where the giant liked to spend the countless travelling hours painting, and sat at her piano in the corner of the room. The instrument was housed here mainly for spatial reasons, but also because there were four caravans between this room and the room she shared with Sora and Mariette – the dwarves' room, the store room, the practice room, and the kitchen / diner – which meant that whenever her roommates got tired of the endless stream of CD playing, Asseniah could wander down to the end of the train and play in peace. Oleg was always happy to have her.

As the weak Highway light shone through the window, warming the brown wood of the instrument, Asseniah played a few notes and, when the song had chosen itself, she put both hands to the ivories and played passionately. The song was one from Tori Amos' repertoire which meant it had lyrics. Asseniah always tried hard not to sing, but as the music flowed in through her ears and connected with her soul, mixing with the vibrations coming through the floor, her heart swelled gloriously until she was so overcome that she was forced to open her mouth and softly let the words come out in an exquisite voice that could have been an instrument all on its own. By that time, she was lost, nothing else in the world existed except for that song and the feelings that it provoked, taking her away on a river of ecstasy until the very last note had faded.

After taking a moment to come down from her music high, Asseniah wiped her tearful eyes, closed the lid... and froze. Someone was watching her. She looked up quickly, saw Oleg standing in the doorway that led through to the dwarves' caravan, and let out a breath of relief. Oleg was the only other person who knew about her secret voice, having walked in on her one day, last year, when she was mid-song.

'You have a beautiful voice, Asseniah,' he told her, not

for the first time. 'The others would love to know about it.'

She shook her head frantically.

'It's okay, I won't tell. It's your secret.'

Asseniah climbed off of the piano stool, walked up to him, nodded once in thanks, then continued through to the practice room where she got lost in her aerial silks.

Three Years Ago – Tokinov's Inn

Cirque du Phantastique had been on their very first tour when they had found Asseniah in Tokinov's Inn. Returning from their performances on Earth, they parked the train, turned off the engine, and entered as a group, grateful to be off the road for a while.

'Alain du Maurier,' Tokinov called in hearty greeting. 'Back already?'

'Hello again, Tokinov,' said Alain, cheerfully, as he sat at the bar. Arrahbella sat next to him while the others dispersed to sit at various tables.

'How was Earth?'

'Not too bad at all. There were a few problems but we managed. The Earthlings are a great audience.'

'Ah, but you have to say that,' replied Tokinov, winking at Arrahbella. 'You're married to one.'

Alain chuckled but shook his head. 'No, they really are great. You can put magic right in front of them and they still think there's a trick.'

Tokinov laughed and looked around the room. 'Where's that daughter of mine got to?'

'I'm afraid we may be to blame for that,' Alain explained. 'It's Izan, again.'

Tokinov threw down his tea towel. 'She could have asked me first.'

'Sorry, Tokinov.'

'No, no, you're not to blame.' His expression changed from annoyance to excitement. 'We've had an addition to our staff since your last visit and I can't wait for you to meet her. I'm sure she's going to be someone of high interest to you, Alain du Maurier.' He winked and headed for the stairs that led to the bedrooms. Alain was pleasantly surprised and highly intrigued by Tokinov's words. He looked at Arrahbella with a boyish grin.

A few moments later, Tokinov returned followed by Mishkan and a young girl whose dead-straight, waist-length hair was the colour of a deep red theatre curtain, positively radiating in the dark room. Both Alain and Arrahbella were instantly captivated and they watched her intently as she walked behind the bar after Tokinov. When she finally looked up at them with her unreadable expression both gasped at her incredible, swirling eyes. Alain had no idea which world she might be from but it certainly wasn't any he was familiar with.

'Alain du Maurier, meet Asseniah,' Tokinov introduced them, smiling with satisfaction at the expected reactions of his friends.

'Hello,' Alain managed to say.

Asseniah just stared.

'She doesn't speak,' Tokinov explained, quickly.

'Hasn't said a word or uttered a sound. We only know her name because she wrote it down.'

'Where is she from?' Alain asked, feeling a little rude for talking about the girl as though she weren't there.

'No idea,' Tokinov replied. 'You've heard of Merek, the space traveller from Landau?'

'I have.'

'Well, he was up in Earth's space last week and he found her sitting on a star, all alone, just sitting with her knees tucked up under her chin, silent, and seemingly unfazed. We have no idea how long she was there for or why, but obviously Merek's not the only one who can survive out there unaided. He left her with us because I needed another waitress while Sasha was ill.'

Arrahbella had to nudge Alain discreetly to stop him from staring at Asseniah in mystified awe.

Seemingly bored with the attention, or perhaps just a dedicated worker, Asseniah left to serve a customer. Tokinov waited until she was out of ear shot then leaned in close to Alain and Arrahbella who followed suit and leant across the bar.

'She's a little odd, Alain. She likes to be up in the air.' When the Ringmaster gave him a puzzled look, he continued. 'We showed her to a room and told her she could stay in it while she worked here but she took one look at the bed, pulled the cover off it, then somehow managed to string the sheets up like a hammock. She climbed up into it and went to sleep! Whenever she's not working, she's up in the rafters and – this is what I think you'll love, Alain – one day, Mishkan walked in on her doing amazing things with the sheets. She'd rigged them up so that one end was around the roof beam and the rest was hanging down to the floor and she rolled herself up in it then tumbled down until the sheet caught her, inches from the ground. Mishkan nearly had a heart attack.'

Alain could barely contain his excitement. He looked again at the young girl who was now staring blankly at the troupe as Sora, Mariette, and Melody exclaimed over her hair and eyes.

'I don't suppose I could go and talk to her now?' he asked.

Tokinov was thrilled to have found something for Alain's insatiable curiosity to feast on. 'Well, it's fairly quiet today and you're the only ones left to be served, so if you want her for a few moments, I think I can spare her.'

'Excellent.' Alain leapt up and hurried over to her.

Within a few minutes, they had told the bewildered ten-year-old about their circus and asked her if they could see what she could do with the bedspreads. Dazed by all the sudden attention, though still stony faced, Asseniah led them up the stairs to her room.

A network of sheets had been slung among the wooden beams that held up the roof, giving the impression that a giant spider had been through and woven a very thick web. Asseniah left them standing in the doorway, hoisted herself up one of the sheets as though it were a ladder, then proceeded to show them what she could do within the limited space she had between roof and floor. She tumbled and twirled, always catching herself in the sheet at the last minute, sometimes dangling by just her ankles or her neck.

Alain watched in amazement, his mind already working on ways this act could be expanded and spruced up to suit the circus' needs. When Asseniah had finished and stood on the floor looking at them without any hint of expression whatsoever, he looked at Arrahbella who smiled back at him and gave a single nod.

'Why don't you come outside and have a look at our train, Asseniah?' he asked, and the girl nodded.

The train was one caravan shorter at that time as Melody and Chester weren't yet a couple and Chester was sharing with Izan. Alain was a little worried about space, Melody and Mariette already had to share a bed, but Asseniah pointed to the ceiling and indicated she would very happily sleep in a hammock.

'So, Asseniah,' Alain said, once he had thrown the others out of the kitchen and sat across from her at the table. 'Do you think you might like to join our circus?'

She stared at him for some moments, her swirling eyes almost putting him in a trance. Then, she nodded.

Alain smiled broadly. 'Excellent. Welcome to Cirque du Phantastique.'

They shook hands and she had been a mystery to them ever since.

CHAPTER 4

Present Day – The Highway

As evening closed in around Tokinov's Inn, Asseniah (who was now the proud owner of a sparkling new CD player, thanks to one of the traders) was helping Arrahbella prepare teas in the train's kitchen. Tokinov made tea, of course, but he didn't have quite the range of flavours, or the skill, that Arrahbella had.

'You can do the peppermint teas for Mariette and Sora, and get your own,' Arrahbella told her, as she took six mugs down from the cupboard. 'I'll do the others. Can you please get me the Griffinseed, the ginger, and the Earl Grey?'

Asseniah did so, taking the canisters from their position on the long counter and carrying them back to Arrahbella two at a time.

'Only a pinch of each, remember. Mariette likes hers slightly stronger than Sora's, but you only need a few leaves.'

Arrahbella watched as Asseniah carefully prepared the teas, smiling when the young girl frowned in concentration.

They carried the teas back to the Inn where the troupe was scattered about, sleepy and relaxed after dinner.

Asseniah set one mug down in front of Mariette, who was playing poker with Melody, Chester, and Oleg, then took the remaining two over to where Sora was playing a board game with the dwarves and settled in next to her friend. Arrahbella gave Melody her tea before sitting next to Alain who was in the next booth. The Wordmaster was watching the poker game while he wrote down words, pulled them off the page and played with them, finding the best order before linking them together and replacing them on the paper. Melody loved watching him do this and, as a result, found herself losing poker terribly.

'How's the Griffinseed supply going?' Alain asked, setting down his pen and picking up his cup.

Arrahbella smiled her cool, serene smile. 'Fine. There's plenty there and I've got more stored in the storage room. There should be enough to last us until we reach Ormance.' Alain nodded as she took a sip of her tea, his eyes on Melody and Chester. 'You know I'd give you plenty of warning before it runs out. I always do.'

'I know. It's just that, with the amount of travelling we're doing, they're spending more time in bed.'

Griffinseed was a native Varatalian herb which acted as a natural contraceptive and was highly traded among the worlds. Arrahbella used it nightly in Melody's tea. Sora had also started on it a few months ago, when she had turned sixteen, but she took it in biscuit form as the tea didn't agree with her.

'A full house. Wait, does that mean that I finally won a hand?'

'Yes, Melody, well done.'

Melody grinned and gathered up her reward (a pile of matchsticks) as Chester kissed her cheek and Alain smiled with amusement.

Six Years Ago – The Highway / Da'Laarwick

Two months after leaving Earth, Alain and Arrahbella were sitting at the bar in Karantale's Inn. Situated between Terrenvale and Landau on the southern side of the road, Karantale's was the busiest of the four Highway inns, servicing the numerous traders and travellers from at least four of the ten worlds. The Innkeeper had been listening intently as Alain recounted the story of how he and Arrahbella had met.

'My dear girl,' Karantale said to Arrahbella, raising his booming voice slightly over the buzz of chatter. 'You are very welcome. To think that you could be on different planets and still manage to find each other. Amazing.'

Karantale was a Varatalian by birth but had lived in Arelia for most of his life, taking over the Inn with his partner, Bray, only four years ago. He was a ruggedly handsome man with black hair, beard, and moustache, chiselled features, and toned arms from wiping numerous glasses and lifting barrels of mead on a daily basis.

Bray, who was standing nearby, overheard this and put an arm around Karantale. 'Ah, but you and I are from different planets and we found each other,' he said, his orange eyes glowing brightly in the smoky atmosphere. He was also handsome but his features had a slightly more feminine appearance.

'True, true,' Karantale agreed with a smile, 'but to find her on Earth!'

'Have you been to Varatalé yet?' Bray asked Arrahbella.

The Earthling opened her mouth to reply, but a wave of nausea made her close it again, one hand shooting to her mouth as her eyes closed in a grimace. The poor girl looked almost as pale as a Noir Eternalan.

'She's not feeling too well,' Alain explained, his voice soft. He reached out and stroked her hair. 'I think it's all the travelling we've been doing; the Highway can take a lot out of a first-time traveller, especially one who didn't know such a thing existed until two months ago.'

Karantale and Bray looked at Arrahbella with concern.

'I took her back to Varatalé for a while after we'd left Earth so that she could see the place and meet Izan, Melody, and Mariette,' Alain continued. 'She wanted to see more of the Highway though, so we're off to Arelia to search for troupe members, then we'll return home for a while.' He took a sip of his mead.

'Will you be going to Da'Laarwick?'

Alain shook his head. 'No, I don't think there's any need. The Da'Laarwickans don't have any desire for a circus and it's dangerous territory.'

'I'm surprised. After hearing the legend, I thought you of all people would have been determined to go there, Alain du Maurier.'

'Legend?'

Karantale smiled at Bray who returned the smile before leaving to serve a customer.

'You haven't heard about the outcast?'

Alain shook his head and wiped some drips from his moustache.

'Even the Da'Laarwickans have an outcast of society. Sel was telling me about it just before you came in. He's on his way to Da'Laarwick right now to trade.' Karantale looked around the room until he spotted a thin, beaky man sitting hunched in a corner. 'Sel, come 'ere a sec.'

The man that approached the bar appeared to be Kartanian with his brown hair, brown eyes, and olive skin, but he also looked weary, sporting large shadows under his eyes.

'Sel, this is Alain du Maurier and Arrahbella Forester. Tell them about the outcast of the Burtock Clan.'

Sel remained expressionless as his eyes slid from Karantale's face to the travellers. He sat on the stool next to Alain, setting his tankard on the bar.

'As you know, the Da'Laarwickans are a giant race, but, there is one who is smaller than the rest, only a fraction larger than a normal human man. He was born in the Burtock Clan, in the Gruston area, but when they discovered he was different they tried to kill him and he ran away. Even his parents didn't want him, but they were killed for bearing such a monstrosity anyway. Now, it's believed that he lives in a cave on the outskirts of Gruston. His name is Oleg Fyzek.'

Alain looked at Arrahbella with raised eyebrows.

'Do you know much about his personality?' Alain

asked, turning back to Sel.

Sel shook his head. 'No, none of the traders have met him and the Da'Laarwickans don't talk about him. There are rumours, of course, but it's useless telling you those because there's no evidence.'

'And I don't suppose you know if he has the same Da'Laarwickan strength as the rest of them?'

Again, Sel shook his head.

Alain nodded thoughtfully, his curiosity awake and hungry. 'It may be worth checking him out,' he said to no one in particular.

'Even if it's not safe for travellers?' Arrahbella said, her voice barely more than a whisper. She was slowly regaining colour in her face.

Alain nodded.

'I don't like your chances, friends,' Sel told them. 'Only traders are welcome, especially in the Gruston area.'

'Would it be better if they had a trader with them?' Karantale asked.

'They'd certainly get to the clan unhindered, but then they'd have to get to the outcast's cave on their own. No trader would take them there.'

Alain knew where Karantale was going with his question and took over.

'Would you take us there?' he asked Sel.

Sel let the question linger as he took a swig of his mead. 'I can take you to the Burtock Clan and I can wait there for you but that is all.'

'Thank you, we appreciate it. Thanks, Karantale.'

Karantale smiled at them before moving away to serve another customer. Sel arranged to meet them in the morning then returned to his table in the corner.

'Are you sure this is a good idea, Alain?' Arrahbella asked when they were alone.

'Yes. I always trust my instincts, and they've been good to me so far.' He gave her a wink and she smiled. 'Besides, experience has taught me that outcasts are usually craving somewhere they can be accepted.'

'What if all these years of being alone have made him... angry?'

Alain kissed her. 'I have to go and see him, Bella. If he gets out of hand I'll just have to hope that my powers work on him. You can stay here if you like, until I get back.'

'Don't be silly, I'm coming. I'll keep my mind open and perhaps I can be of some help.'

Alain smiled and nodded. The more time he spent with her, the more he found to fall in love with.

The next morning, they began the four-day journey to Da'Laarwick with Sel, their wagon attached to his own while their horses joined Sel's up the front. Alain and Arrahbella sat in Sel's wagon amongst the various trade items; books, jewellery, urns, carvings, paintings, utensils, CD players and music from Earth, food, wines, teas, cameras, leather and wools, and a myriad of other odds and ends.

On the morning of the fourth day, Sel drove the wagon through the Da'Laarwickan rift and along the rocky landscape to the cluster of caves that was the home of the Burtock Clan. Alain and Arrahbella got out and stretched in the drizzling rain as the giants emerged from their caves to view Sel's wares. They were a fearsome sight. All the adults were twice or three times the height of a tall human and about as much again around the girth, their waists covered by an animal-hide wrap. They had bulging muscles and matted or wispy hair, large eyes with no eyelashes, and a clumsy walk. Arrahbella stayed close to Alain's side as they approached, scrambling over each other in their haste to get to the best items, which they traded for the rock carvings they were famous for.

'If you follow this path you should come to a secluded beach,' Sel told them quietly, unaware that one giant, a mountain of muscle named Kryk, was listening nearby. 'That's where the outcast is rumoured to be. If you're too long though, I'll have to leave. They won't like me hanging around.'

'Thanks, Sel,' Alain said. He turned to Arrahbella and wrote "speak Da'Laarwickan" in the air, pushing it toward her and watching her shiver as it sunk in. 'Can you understand me?' he asked in the giant's tongue, once she had opened her eyes.

'Yes. How come you couldn't do that in Varatalé?'

'Language commands have a time limit. You need to learn Varatalian properly if you want to speak it for more than two hours.'

'Of course I do.'

He took her hand and they began their journey along the dirt path. Kryk waited until they were some distance away before approaching them.

'You're looking for the outcast?' he asked Alain, suspiciously. He had a booming voice and horrible breath that smelt of rotten meat.

'Yes, we are,' Alain replied, his body tensing, one hand shielding his eyes from the rain as he squinted up at Kryk.

'What do you want with him?'

'We want to see if he wishes to come and live with us.'

Kryk looked them over. 'You want to take him away?'

'Only if he wishes to come.'

'Forever?'

'Possibly.'

'Do you have any powers?'

Knowing she was reading the giant's mind, Alain looked at Arrahbella for confirmation that he wasn't going to get killed for answering. Some of the Da'Laarwickans despised humans with magic because they hated the idea of being overpowered. When she nodded that everything was okay, he answered. 'Yes. I have the power of words and my companion is psychic.'

Kryk scratched his head as he thought, rain dripping down his nose. 'I'll take you to the outcast if you'll do something for me.'

'What exactly did you have in mind?'

'I should be leader of this clan. If I take you to the outcast, you must give me the words that will help me claim the leadership from Slivek.'

Alain looked at Arrahbella, not wanting her to think

less of him for agreeing.

'It's okay,' she said in his mind, her psychic voice even more lyrical than her speaking one. They had discovered they could speak to each other in this way the morning after they had first made love. 'I know there's no choice.'

'It won't last long anyway,' he replied. 'Someone else will take over soon enough.' He turned back to Kryk. 'Can you guarantee our safety out of here as well? We wish to return to the trader and leave with him.'

Kryk eyed him contemptuously but nodded. 'You have my word.'

'And you have my word.'

They shook hands, Alain trying not to grimace with the strength of Kryk's clutch. Kryk turned and continued along the path, leading them along the edge of a cliff, the humans hurrying to keep up with his massive strides. Below them, the vast grey ocean that surrounded the rocky land was crashing ferociously against the rocks, waves reaching up as though trying to pull the travellers down into their watery clutches. To their right, goat-like creatures called javviis (which, along with fish, were the only other living creatures on the planet) grazed on what little grass there was.

A good hour later, panting and sweating and wet to the bone, they found themselves descending the cliff, Alain assisting Arrahbella as they precariously stepped from rock to rock while Kryk clambered down easily like a spider. When they finally reached the sandy shore at the bottom, Alain looked up, wondering how they would ever manage to climb back up again. Deciding to think about that later, he looked around and saw they were standing in a small bay, the water rolling noisily against the shore, the rocks massive. At the edge of the bay, nestled a short way from the water, was a cave. Kryk walked to the cave's opening then stopped and turned his back on it.

'I will wait here,' he told them.

Alain nodded. He gave Arrahbella one last anxious look, then, together, they entered the cave.

'Oleg Fyzek?' Alain called, as their eyes adjusted to the dark.

There was an echoing clang, as though a brass object had just been dropped on the hard stone floor, followed by a shuffling noise. Alain could feel Arrahbella trembling and he squeezed her hand. It occurred to him, then, that Oleg may not be able to speak Da'Laarwickan, or indeed, any language at all, and he looked to Arrahbella for help once more.

'It's okay,' she whispered after a moment. 'He's listening and he understands you.'

Alain wondered how he had survived thirty-nine years without this woman.

'Oleg Fyzek, my name is Alain du Maurier and this is Arrahbella Forester. We have something we'd like to discuss with you. Could you please give us a moment of your time?'

There was a lengthy pause. Alain continued to stare in the direction that the sound had come from while Arrahbella took in their surroundings. The cave had been carved into beautiful scenes, mostly of family and group celebrations. The faces on the carvings had such fine detail that Arrahbella could read their expressions (the majority of which were happy ones) right down to their eyebrows.

Finally, a dark shape moved toward them and stepped into the light. He was much cleaner than the other giants they had seen and slightly bulkier, his bulging muscles more obvious due to their proper toning. He stopped in front of them, threw the remains of the javvii he'd been eating on to a pile of bones in the corner, and looked them over curiously.

Alain decided to jump right in. 'Oleg Fyzek, I have a home in Varatalé where I'm starting up a circus that will, hopefully, tour most of the worlds along the Highway.' He wasn't sure if Oleg knew about any other worlds, but he had decided from the outset to treat him as though he knew everything, as it seemed the politer way of doing things. 'I'd like to know whether you have any skills that we could use and whether you'd be willing to work in a team. We will provide food, lodging, clothing, anything you need if you wish to join.'

Oleg studied the pair for a moment.

'What is a circus?' he finally asked.

They flinched when he spoke, expecting something worse than just a question, but they quickly recovered.

'It's a show where performers do lots of tricks and athletic and magical feats to amaze the audience. It's a family of outcasts and so-called "freaks." The people that don't quite fit in with the world they've lived in and need something else, something more than everyday life. It's a world of its own and it brings magic and inspiration to all who see it. For the performers, it's total freedom.'

Again, Oleg looked at Alain closely.

'Do you have any powers or skills we could use in our circus, Oleg?'

'Like what?'

'Well, the Da'Laarwickans are known for their strength. Can you lift things?'

Oleg smiled at this. It was a pleasantly warm and friendly smile. He walked past them, out into the open air, making Kryk turn away in disgust. Oleg paid him no attention. He walked over to a boulder the size of a small Earthling car that was sitting a short way up the beach. Rubbing his hands together, he squatted, slid his hands underneath, and lifted effortlessly until the boulder was above his head. He took one hand away, balanced it there for a while, then gently set it down on the ground once more.

Kryk had been watching this from the corner of his eye and, when Oleg was done, he forgot about his disgust for the outcast, approached the boulder and tried to lift it himself. He got it into the air alright, but he couldn't take away one hand and consequently dropped the boulder, narrowly missing his toes and making the ground shake.

Alain was impressed. 'And is it true that a Da'Laarwickan's skin cannot be pierced?'

Oleg went back into his cave and returned with a long stone knife. He put it against the fur he was wearing and sliced off a small square to show them how sharp it was, then he put the blade against his skin. Arrahbella held her breath as Oleg pushed the blade hard into his chest but the knife didn't even leave a scratch.

The Ringmaster smiled. 'And how do you feel about

working in a team? Living with others? Travelling on the road in a caravan? Showing your skills to an audience?'

To Alain and Arrahbella's great surprise, Oleg's eyes started to water.

'Forgive me,' he sniffed, wiping away a tear. 'But I can't help feeling that this is all too good to be true. Are you expecting something in return? Are you just teasing me?'

He was very eloquent for a Da'Laarwickan, Alain thought, especially one who had had no apparent contact with another Da'Laarwickan-speaking individual. But, then, his manner was in complete contrast to his race too.

'I expect you to treat the other troupe members as family – no, closer than family – and I expect you to work hard. Nothing more. This isn't a joke, Oleg Fyzek. I've travelled from Noir Eternale to Varatalé to Earth to here and I'm now going to Arelia before returning to Varatalé where we'll train and prepare for a couple of years before touring. We'll welcome you if you wish to join us.'

Arrahbella looked at Alain. She was beginning to realise how trusting he could be; a quality that was admirable but something to be wary of.

Oleg really was crying now, much to Kryk's horror. He nodded while wiping his eyes.

'I would love to,' he said.

Alain walked forward and shook hands with the giant, surprised at how gentle his touch was.

Oleg gathered a few things from his cave, then he led the other three a short distance along the beach to a safer passage up the cliff. Alain noticed that Kryk stayed a few strides behind Oleg, obviously not wanting to get any closer to him than he had to.

When they approached the cluster of caves, they saw Sel leaning against his wagon, studying a rock carving. He was surrounded by giants, who were either leaning against rocks or cave openings or sitting on the ground, examining their new toys. As soon as they saw the outcast, however, they abandoned their possessions and started rampaging toward the group with surprising agility. The air was quickly filled with howls and grunts of anger, prompting even more giants to appear from their caves and join the stampede. Alain, Arrahbella, and Oleg stopped walking as Kryk continued on, trying to placate them.

'It's okay,' he shouted at them. 'They're taking him away.'

But no one was listening. Arrahbella clutched Alain's arm tightly as he stepped forward to shield her. Twenty or so Da'Laarwickans charged toward them, arms waving, the ground trembling with the force.

Alain closed his eyes, calling up a wave of power, which roared through his body and exploded out of his mouth in the form of the command 'Stop!'

The giants were frozen mid-stride, stunned and infuriated.

'They're taking the outcast away with them. Forever,' Kryk repeated. 'It was my idea and therefore I should be your leader.'

Alain tentatively took his command off of the group, relieved when they stayed where they were. They looked around at each other in puzzlement, muttering, then they broke into grunts and howls of celebration. Kryk was lost amongst the crowd as they gathered around to celebrate their new leader, ignoring Slivek's furious protests, which were soon silenced when Kryk knocked him to the ground and broke his neck.

Alain let out a long shaky breath and looked at Arrahbella, blushing when he saw her staring at him with wide eyes.

'Sorry, did that freak you out?' he asked, nervously.

She shook her head and said breathlessly, 'No. That was the most incredible thing I've ever seen.' Then, realising she was acting like a character in a romance novel, she cringed. 'I mean, that was pretty impressive.'

Alain beamed.

Sel was shaking his head in disbelief when he hopped onto his wagon and drove them away from the Clan. Once outside Da'Laarwick, Alain thanked the Kartanian graciously and paid him, then they unhitched their wagon and horses and he, Arrahbella, and Oleg crossed the Highway and headed toward Arelia.

Present Day – Tokinov's Inn

Alain wanted to get moving. Dawn had barely stretched and climbed out of bed as the Ringmaster rounded up his troupe in Tokinov's Inn.

'Come on, you two,' he said, as Melody and Chester bounced down the creaky wooden stairs to meet him at the bar. 'Let's get this show on the road.'

'Breakfast?' Chester asked.

'Arrahbella's making it.'

There was a bang as a door closed and Sasha entered the room, looking tired and grumpy.

'Good morning, Sasha. Is Izan still in bed?'

'No. He left last night.' There was a definite hint of disappointment in her voice but Alain didn't notice. He was going over the bill that Tokinov had tallied up for him.

'How did he get out?' Tokinov asked. 'I locked up when he was still in here.'

'Locks don't hold Izan. I'll check his caravan.'

'Thank you, Melody. I'll fix up the bill and then I think we're right to go, if we have Izan.'

Melody wandered out to the train, entered through her own caravan, then knocked on the adjoining door to Izan's room.

'Izan, you in there? Alain wants to get going.'

Izan answered the door with only a quilt wrapped around his naked body.

'Good morning, sister dear,' he said, cheerfully. 'Tell Alain I need five minutes.'

Melody shot a glance past him and saw one of the traders from the Inn pulling on his clothes.

'Sasha wasn't enough, hey?'

'Melody, we have been on the road for two weeks with another two to go before we reach Earth. All the traders in the Inn wouldn't be enough.'

Melody shook her head sadly and returned to the bar.

'He'll be five minutes, Alain.' She lowered her voice. 'He's got company.'

'That doesn't surprise me in the least.'

'What kind of company?' Sasha demanded, bobbing up from behind the bar where she had been stacking glasses.

Melody bit her lower lip.

'One of the traders, I assume,' Alain said, as he took the change Tokinov handed him.

Sasha grunted and folded her arms. The realisation that she was a little heartbroken finally dawned on Alain and he raised his eyebrows at Melody and Chester.

'Sasha,' Chester said. 'Don't lose your heart to Izan. He loves you completely when he's with you, but then he moves on and loves another just as completely.' It was a line the troupe had frequently had to use on various people.

Sasha sniffed. 'He'll have to settle down one day. Everybody does.'

Alain smiled sadly. 'The day Izan settles down in a long-term relationship will be the day Earthlings start believing in magic again.'

Sasha looked at the ground. Alain gave Tokinov an apologetic look before following Melody and Chester out to the train. A few minutes later, Izan's guest returned to the Inn where he found himself covered in hot porridge after Sasha "accidentally" dropped it while serving. Oblivious to the shouts inside, the train rumbled to life and continued on its way to Earth.

Six Years Ago - Arelia

Alain, Arrahbella, and Oleg arrived in Arelia shortly after leaving Da'Laarwick and checked into the Cherry Bear Hotel in the centre of Greensvale City. Arelia was a kaleidoscope of colour… grass could be blue in one area and red in the next, which meant that most first-time visitors had to take a day or two to adjust. So, leaving his companions alone with their headaches, Alain went to the palace where he was greeted by Queen Vaya's eldest daughter, Princess Prarny of Greensvale City.

'Welcome back to Arelia, Mister du Maurier,' she said, as she offered him her hand to kiss. 'Please forgive the absence of my mother, she is not well.'

'I am sorry to hear that, Your Highness,' Alain replied, taking the seat that was offered to him. 'I hope it is not too serious.'

Prarny's pink eyes looked at the ground. 'I'm afraid she will not recover. The doctors have done all they can for her.'

They were silent for a moment. A servant poured them tea from a porcelain and gold pot. The room was the very picture of opulence.

'What brings you to our world this time, Mister du Maurier?'

Alain explained about the circus and his quest for members.

'We have some fine performers in this city,' Prarny said, once he was done. 'The Greensvale City Players are some of the finest actors in Arelia. We are going to make them our official Royal Players very soon, in fact.' There was a strong note of pride in her soft voice. 'You are welcome to view them. There is a play at the end of the week being held here in the palace.'

'That would be wonderful, Your Highness. I'd be most honoured to attend.'

They continued to talk for a while, Alain asking about the current state of politics in the land and being educated on any changes that had happened since his last visit. Then, he returned to the hotel.

That Friday night, Alain and Arrahbella went to the palace once more to see the Players perform (Oleg had voluntarily stayed at the hotel as they knew he wouldn't fit comfortably into a theatre seat). Much to Arrahbella's surprise, the play they saw was Shakespeare's *A Midsummer Night's Dream*.

Alain laughed when she exclaimed in shock. 'The Bard's works have High Trading Status along the Highway,' he told her, and Arrahbella marvelled at the fact that Shakespeare could not only transcend generations but universes as well.

They took their seats and soon the house lights dimmed and the curtains opened. The Arelians were a vocal lot; heckling, shouting, cheering, and booing as the actors attempted to shout their lines over them.

When Act 2 began and the actor playing Puck walked on stage, prompting an even larger response from the crowd, Alain was instantly captivated. He had an incredibly unique, nasal voice and was disastrously good-looking, even with layers of make-up covering his face. More importantly, though, his acting abilities were so powerful he even managed to silence the audience. After that, there were no thoughts about where they were or why until the play had finished, by which time everyone in the theatre was on their feet in a standing ovation, throwing multi-coloured flowers on to the stage.

There was a lavish party held afterwards in one of the palace's great banquet halls, Princess Prarny leading the festivities in her mother's place. The party had been underway for a half an hour when the Players entered, earning a hearty cheer and applause, along with a number of gushing sighs from the adoring fans in the room. Prarny, whose bright pink hair was piled high on her head in an impressive design, greeted them publicly, showering them with praise, and then the party continued.

Alain and Arrahbella had claimed a corner of the room where they watched as Puck was mobbed by a bevy of females and backed into a corner, disappearing from view.

'Poor man. The Players can't go anywhere without being asked for autographs or photographs,' Alain said, with a shake of his head.

'It's just as bad on Earth.'

He looked at her in surprise and she nodded.

'He was good though.'

'He was astonishing. I'd love to have him in the circus.'

Arrahbella put her empty, crystal-made glass down on the nearby table. 'I received images when he walked on to the stage.'

'Really? What kind?'

'They came very quickly, and I didn't see many before I blocked them out.' Years of being barraged by unrequested images had made her learn to shut them out, she felt intrusive otherwise, and now she did it out of habit. 'I have no doubt he'll be a part of the circus, Alain.'

Alain smiled excitedly and looked toward the mob. Arrahbella bit her lower lip, thinking, then, she put a hand on Alain's shoulder, making him turn to face her once more.

'I also saw images of him and Melody together.'

'Melody?'

She nodded.

'But she's only twelve and he's got to be at least eighteen!'

Arrahbella shrugged. 'Like I said, I blocked them out before I saw too many, but they were certainly more than friends.'

Alain frowned and fiddled with his beard.

Just when they were beginning to wish that they could leave, Prarny finally approached them, bringing most of the Players with her.

'Mister du Maurier, Miss Forester, allow me to present the Players of the Greensvale City Theatre. Players, this is Alain du Maurier and Arrahbella Forester, they are in Arelia searching for recruits for a circus. I'll let Mister du Maurier talk to you.'

'Thank you, Your Highness,' Alain said. The Players gathered around him so he didn't have to shout over the music and chatter of the party.

Arrahbella's eyes found the actor who had played Puck. Now she was closer, she could see his features resembled those of a clown, in a way, which is perhaps what made him such a fine character actor, but he was the most handsome clown, and man, she had ever seen. His shining purple eyes were highlighted all the more by the eyeliner and mascara he had not yet taken off.

'Thank you all for a very entertaining evening. That was one of the best shows I've had the privilege of seeing in all the worlds along the Highway.' Alain continued, telling them about the circus and its current members, his plan, and why he was there. The Players listened intently. 'So, if you, or anyone you know, have something to add to Cirque du Phantastique then please come and see me. I will be at the Cherry Bear Hotel until the end of next week.' Alain smiled, nodded his appreciation, and stepped back.

There were a lot of interested faces but their interest was only in the idea as many of them approached Alain only to offer him luck. Puck had disappeared as soon as Alain had finished and neither Alain nor Arrahbella could see him in the crowd, so, after thanking Prarny, they left the castle.

'Perhaps his fans recaptured him and he'll come and see us during the week?' Arrahbella suggested, as they walked past the guards and out into the balmy night.

'I knew that it was going to be hard to find any members in Arelia,' Alain replied, thoughtfully. 'Most of them are happy with their way of life and don't wish to leave, but, if you saw him in Cirque's future, then I'm sure he'll come and find us.'

'Excuse me,' said a unique, nasal voice from behind them.

They turned to find Puck walking toward them. Obviously, he had been waiting by the entrance hall so he would see them come out and could talk to them in private. He was wearing simple dark grey pants and a black shirt in Arelian style (loose and voluminous), the top laces undone to reveal part of his smooth, hairless chest.

'I'm interested in joining your circus.' His speaking voice was much more boyish than the dramatic tones he had used on stage.

Alain smiled, discreetly squeezing Arrahbella's hand. 'Excellent. Why don't we go and have a drink and discuss it?'

The Player shook his head. 'I'm afraid I can't. It's impossible for me to go anywhere in this city without being harassed; it's one of the reasons I wish to join you. I'm sick of it. I'm also not too keen on the idea of becoming the Royal Players. Everything will change then. There'll be even more commitments. No. Just tell me when you're leaving and I'll meet you at the rift.'

Alain nodded in understanding. 'Well, if you have any concerns or questions, you know where to find us. And you'll have to ask Prarny's permission.'

Puck nodded.

'I must warn you though, we'll be touring Arelia, so your fans will still be able to see you. Prarny has told me, however, that we will have the use of some Royal Guards, should one of her Players decide to join us.'

'That's fine. I don't mind fame in small doses. It's just when you have to live with it every minute that it burns you out. And I don't like it when it follows me into my house.'

'You'll be left alone in Varatalé.'

'Then I'm in.'

'Just one more thing. Apart from being a very fine actor, do you have any other skills?'

The Player looked at Alain for a moment before throwing himself into a series of back flips, somersaults, handstands, rolls, and tumbles. Then, he stood still and smiled at their impressed faces.

'I also have magic, but no one's ever told me how to use it, so I'm not sure how much I have.'

Alain nodded and looked at Arrahbella with a satisfied expression. He would have liked to have had a drink with the man and got to know him more because of what Arrahbella had said about Melody being in her images, but, he could certainly tell that Melody was going to fall head-over-heels for him and he had to trust that all would be well. He reached out his hand.

'Alain du Maurier.'

'Chester from the Apricot Meadows.'

'The Apricot Meadows? Where is that?'

'In the country, a fair distance away.'

'Do you have family?'

'Yes, my mother, Caraia, and my father, Warwick, both work for the Queens' sister.'

'Duchess Tella?'

'That's right. She lives on an estate in the Apricot

118

Meadows. Mother is her physician and Father is the head chef. My brother, Brillon, also works in the kitchens now, but I always had a passion for performing. I performed for the Duchess a few times, with the Apricot Meadows' Theatre Group, and she referred me on to the Greensvale City Players. I've lived here since I was sixteen, so, about four years.'

'Will they mind if you leave and live on another planet?'

'I doubt it. They're used to me living away. And I'll still be able to visit them, won't I?'

Alain nodded. 'You will. Let them and Prarny know that you're leaving and we'll see you at the rift next Friday morning.'

Chester nodded then turned and headed back inside.

'What's wrong?' Arrahbella asked, seeing Alain's thoughtful expression.

'He obviously comes from a wealthy background, and he's not an outcast.'

'He may not be an outcast but that doesn't mean he's not looking for a place to belong.'

Alain looked at her thoughtfully, then smiled. He reached out his hand to her and bowed. 'My lady.'

Arrahbella curtsied before taking his hand and letting him lead her out of the castle grounds.

CHAPTER 5

Present Day – The Highway / Earth

'Right, troupe, we'll be arriving at the rift shortly, so I just want to remind you all of the importance of blending in.'

'We know, Alain, we have been there three times before.'

The troupe was gathered in Melody and Chester's caravan, spread about the place on the two red velvet lounges and numerous piles of multi-coloured silk cushions. The last few days of travelling had dragged by, leaving them all a little irksome, especially Alain, who was having trouble with a particularly mischievous poem that had decided it would rather stay stuck in his bloodstream than flow out onto the page. It could be quite painful at times.

'It's not like it matters, Alain,' Izan argued. 'Even if we do use magic they still don't believe it. It really is quite incredible.'

'But, we aren't going to use any real magic, are we?' Alain insisted. 'Well, not obvious magic anyway. We've been through the adjustments to each act and it's important that you stick to those adjustments.'

'But my act is so boring without magic,' Sora complained. She was playing with one of the coloured veils that hung randomly from the ceiling as Asseniah braided her hair. The whole caravan looked like the inside of a genie's bottle, provided that the genie liked reading and playing guitar; one wall was entirely devoted to bookcases, which held both Melody and Chester's books as well as overflow from Alain and Arrahbella's room, and a rather fanciful looking stringed instrument (which was known either as a shria or an elaborately decorated guitar depending on whether you were an Arelian or an Earthling) sat in the corner on an iron stand.

'Throwing knives at Mariette isn't boring for an Earthling audience,' Alain explained to Sora. 'Producing fire out of your palms, and making knives dance around you would freak the poor things out.'

'Isn't the point of Cirque du Phantastique to bring magic to people's lives?'

Alain massaged his brow. 'Yes, Izan, and we are, just in doses that won't bring the Earthling's very knowledge of their existence crashing down around them.'

'Earthlings are weird. No offence, Arrahbella.'

Arrahbella smiled. 'That's alright, Izan, the feeling's mutual.'

Melody and Chester snickered. They were laying entwined on the circular bed that sat on a raised dais in the corner.

Izan frowned. 'Oh well, it won't be too long before they wipe themselves out anyway. You'd think they'd have learned after they destroyed the other eight planets they lived on. They've seen images of Mars, right?'

'They're doing their best. The world is constantly changing and trying to improve itself.'

Izan muttered something inaudible.

'If you're done denouncing the Earthling race, Izan Bell, do you think we can get to work on changing a few appearances?'

Izan sighed and strode over to the bed, sitting on the edge with a flourish of cloak. 'Of course, O Great Leader. Who's first?'

'Asseniah?'

The young girl uncurled herself from the cushions and sat in the bedside chair.

Izan looked into her swirling green eyes. 'I've tried to change them before, Alain. It doesn't work,'

'I know. You haven't thought of anything else that might do it?'

'Well, there is this.' Izan waved a hand over her unblinking eyes and she closed them quickly.

'Careful, Izan,' Alain said, standing up quickly and taking a step forward. Izan looked mystified. 'Asseniah, are you hurt?'

Asseniah opened her eyes again, which had not changed at all, and shook her head. She ran her fingers up Izan's arm to indicate it had merely tickled.

'See? I wouldn't hurt her,' Izan protested.

Alain sat back down, glaring at Izan.

'She'll just have to wear my sunglasses again, while

we're in the city,' Arrahbella said, resting a hand on Alain's arm. 'And they won't be able to see her eyes from the audience.'

Izan moved on to Chester. A simple wave of his hand and Chester's bright purple eyes became a shade of pale blue.

'That looks odd,' said Melody.

Chester stared at her intently.

'Stop it. It's freaky.'

He leapt up and chased her around the room.

'Enough you two,' Alain said, quietly.

Arrahbella took her turn next, her hair shortening to her shoulders and changing to a deep red, her ice blue eyes darkening to green.

'Do you want to be taller?' Izan asked.

'No, that hurts.'

He shrugged. 'Only for a moment.'

'She's fine,' Alain assured him, watching as she walked toward him and sat down again. 'Even I can barely recognise her.'

Arrahbella smiled serenely.

'Ah, now that I recognise.' He kissed her. 'I agree with Melody though, it is rather odd.'

Arrahbella played with her new hair. 'Well, I quite like it. I look like Asseniah.'

Asseniah nodded in approval, not looking up from Sora's braid.

The door that led to Alain and Arrahbella's caravan opened and Cravel stepped into the room. 'Alain, Phan needs you to show your papers to the rift guard.'

'Thank you, Cravel. Right, everyone, go and get ready. I'll only be a moment.'

The troupe dispersed quickly, eager to leave the train. When Alain returned he found them all ready and waiting, dressed in their most Earth appropriate clothes.

The train was too big and out-of-place to enter the rift so it sat outside on the Highway with Oleg and the dwarves. Neither would have looked out of place on Earth, but the dwarves didn't particularly like the Earthling way of life and Oleg stayed to protect them and the train. Leaving them to clean the caravans, the other eight troupe members walked a short way along the Highway, past the rift guards, and, one by one, they stepped through the shimmering rift.

Thick, heavy, dry heat enveloped them instantly.

'Blimey,' said Izan, once they were all standing beside him on the footpath. The street and cars in front of them were fuzzy with haze. 'What's with the weather?'

'This isn't unusual for Adelaide,' Alain explained, shielding himself from the harsh sun with his hand.

'I don't remember it being like this before. How do they stand it?'

'In various ways,' Arrahbella said.

They had been in the heat before, of course – Varatalé was warm for eleven months of the year and they had performed on the desert planet Kartan – but the Australian heat is not to be matched; it sucked their energy straight from their bones, cracked their lips, hung to their eyelids, pulling them closed, and turned their brains to goo.

'We're going to have to change,' Melody told Alain,

and Sora nodded in agreement. The Ringmaster sighed and led them back through the rift.

Alain, Chester, Izan, and Arrahbella stayed in their usual everyday clothes but Melody traded her long pants for a skirt of Sora's while Sora changed out of the corset she had been wearing and into a very loose, very sheer, flowing top. Asseniah wore a netted top and shorts, while Mariette donned a short pink dress. Once they were ready they returned to Earth and set off along the café lined street.

'Okay,' Alain panted, as they entered the cool interior of one crowded eatery. 'You wait here while Arrahbella and I go and find the organisers for instructions.'

They headed off as the others went to the counter and bought various drinks.

'Now I understand why they have this air conditioning thingo,' Melody sighed, as she slid into a chair at a table near the front window.

'I still do not see 'ow it can work wizout magic,' Mariette said, shaking her head. 'I mean, outside it is searingly 'ot and in 'ere it is almost cold enough for a coat. Zat 'as to be magic of some kind.'

Chester shook his head as he greedily sipped some Coke, one of his favourite things about Earth. 'Nope. It's pure invention and technology.'

'But isn't that magic?' Sora asked. 'It still takes imagination, creation, and the Earth's resources.'

'Perhaps the fact that they don't use any magic to help them with all of this stuff is what makes it magic,' Melody suggested. 'I mean, look at them talking to people that are miles away on those weird rectangular devices they've all got, and then there's those big metal things outside there...'

'Cars,' Chester provided.

'Yeah, and the fact that they can fly through the sky in them as well.'

'The cars don't fly, that's planes.'

'Whatever it is, it's pretty incredible that they've made it all without magic helping them. Maybe that's because it's a kind of magic in itself.'

'But, zey are killing ze planet in ze process. Zat is not magic.'

'Why not?' Sora asked. 'Izan and I have killed people and wiped out a city between us and we didn't mean to. Da'Laarwickans will wipe themselves out with all the fighting they do. Noir Eternale doesn't really take care of itself...'

'Yes, but zat is ze people, not ze planet itself. Zose races do not try and kill ze natural environment.'

'I tell you, these Earthlings are strange,' Izan repeated, as he watched the petite waitress behind the counter. After another two weeks on the road, it was taking a mammoth effort for him not to run over to her and whisk her off to the nearest locked room.

They were silent for a moment, then Melody put her head in her hands.

'How are we going to perform in this heat?'

'It's not that bad,' said Chester.

Melody gave him a withering glare. 'Well, you don't feel the heat, do you, because you're Mr. Perfect.' She was beating her wings as much as she could without taking off

126

from the chair in an attempt to cool herself down, prompting the patrons sitting nearby to puzzle over the sudden breeze.

Chester smiled a perfect smile at her.

'Don't do that, I'm trying to cool down.' But her pretence of being annoyed was ruined when he laughed and kissed her.

'You two are nauseating,' Izan told them, before his attention was diverted to the window where a couple of young women dressed in short skirts and tank-tops were walking past. 'Well, at least there's one good thing about this furnace; everyone strips off as much as possible.'

Chester laughed again while Melody, Sora, and Mariette rolled their eyes. Asseniah, looking somewhat like a strange bug with Arrahbella's sunglasses on, had finished her water and was now leaning heavily in her chair.

'It's a good thing we're only here for a couple of nights,' Melody said.

'Yes, why do we travel all this way for only two shows?' Izan asked.

His sister rolled her eyes. 'Because if we did any more we'd draw too much attention to ourselves.'

'Why do we come to Earth at all, then?'

'They deserve some magic as well. And it's Arrahbella's home planet. Don't you ever listen to Alain?'

'I don't have to. I have a sister who hangs on his every word.'

Melody kicked him under the table but it just made him laugh so Chester zapped him with magic, which started a discreet war between the two until Mariette told them to stop because they were beginning to draw attention.

When Alain and Arrahbella finally returned, Alain looked rather worse for wear. He despised the heat, but would never complain about it in front of his troupe. Arrahbella, however, remained as cool as ever, for, even though she was from a cool climate herself, she, like Chester, always seemed to maintain a constant body temperature.

'We're all set. Let's get moving,' he told them.

'Why don't you both have a drink first?' Melody suggested, not wanting to leave the air conditioning just yet and concerned about how warm Alain looked.

The Ringmaster shook his head. 'We stopped on the way back and bought one and we have to get the tent set up.'

'Did you tell the organisers they're insane for holding a festival in this heat?' Izan asked, as they left the cool of the café and headed back down the street toward the Parklands. The festival he spoke of was known as the Adelaide Fringe. Held every February/March, it attracted hundreds of performers from Australia and overseas, making it the perfect set up for the small circus to attract audiences and keep a low profile. The Fringe Program listed Cirque du Phantastique's state of origin as Glastonbury, England.

'No, Izan, I didn't. Apparently, the city is experiencing a heatwave and it's going to continue for a few days yet.' He didn't tell them it was a record breaking, once-every-three-hundred-years heatwave where the mercury stayed stuck to the 39C mark for eight days straight.

'Yuk,' Izan replied, before his attention wandered to a

128

group of young men that were walking past.

They grew sluggish as they walked along, everyone but Chester and Arrahbella finding it very hard to pick up their feet. There were a lot of people around, some happy to be in the warmth, others visibly sweltering in their long sleeves and trouser pants.

When the troupe arrived at the train, they entered through the practice room and collapsed onto the floor mats.

'Come on, everyone, we must get this tent set up,' Alain panted, his white shirt sticking to his chest.

'Alain, we can't go out in that heat again,' Melody complained, weakly.

'What are we meant to do, Melody? We can't leave it any longer or it won't be ready for tonight. We have to do sound, light, and safety checks, and props... I'm sorry but we have to go now.'

'Tell you what, Alain,' Izan suggested. 'Why don't we relax this no-magic-on-Earth rule? Then I can go with you and set it up nice and discreetly and we'll be back in no time at all?'

The others looked at Alain hopefully.

'I'm sorry, Izan, as much as I trust you, you know very well that we must set up by hand so safety is assured. I do appreciate the offer though.' Izan opened his mouth to protest but Alain quickly continued. 'Come on everyone, the show has to go on and the sooner we set up, the sooner we'll have the shade of the tent to work under.'

So, the troupe pushed themselves up off the floor,

splashed their faces with water, put bags of ice in their clothes, and followed their Ringmaster back into Adelaide.

They didn't work too badly, having a task to focus on helped take their minds off the weather a little, though the shade provided by the tent was hardly more comfortable. Izan put a coat of magic over the colourful marquee so it cooled a few degrees but the task of putting up Melody's trapeze and Sora's tightrope soon had them sweating again. Without the help of the dwarves and Oleg, it was not light work; hefting spotlights, rigging sound systems, securing poles and platforms. Although they were careful to do things properly, knowing that things had to be safe, they took their frustrations out on each other; shouting, arguing, insulting, until Alain roared at them, threatening to command them all into silence if they weren't quiet. The bags of ice soon melted, becoming warm and cumbersome. Izan, Sora, and Melody stripped down to their underwear to work, but, even so, Izan became so hot that magic began to ooze out of him. Alain noticed this when the feet of those standing closest to him suddenly disappeared and Izan swooned.

'Izan, go backstage now and cool down.'

'How am I meant to do that, O Great Leader?' His voice was weak, the usual irony it dripped with had melted away.

'Just lie down. You'll have to have that magic under control by tonight.'

'There could be a lot of dead Earthlings by the end of this,' he muttered on his way out.

'And some dead troupe members,' Chester said

quietly, looking at Asseniah who had been growing steadily paler for the last half hour.

Alain heard but didn't say anything.

They finished setting up and checking the tent as the sun was lazily melting away for the night. This did little to cool the earth but it was a relief not to have its heat and light bearing down on them. They left the tent under the watch of a pair of Earthling security guards while they trudged up the street to find somewhere to eat.

'It's so busy,' Sora observed, as they passed a large restaurant window. The tables and chairs on the footpath were overflowing, the buzz of chatter and cutlery filling the night air.

'People will be grabbing something to eat before heading off to the various shows, I presume,' Alain replied.

'Why would anyone *choose* to be out in this weather?' Melody asked.

'A lot of Australians don't mind it,' Arrahbella told her. 'Life goes on.'

'There's some tables in here, Alain,' Sora announced, stopping by a shop front that was mostly glass and polished wood and peering in at the brown couches and cosy interior.

Alain shook his head and pointed to the sign. 'Nope, it specialises in chocolate. We aren't going in there.'

'Good,' Chester breathed, but nobody complained. Chocolate was the last thing on their minds.

Finally, they found a vacant table at a place halfway up the street, by which time they were all very tired and quite sick of the trek. None of them felt very much like eating

– except Chester, who always had an appetite – so they pretty much stuck to salads.

Alain looked around at his troupe as they played with the food on their plates. He hoped the excitement of performing would liven them up. He hated putting them through this but cancelling the show never even crossed his mind. At least being in the air conditioning again (as artificial and flu-inducing as it was) was giving them a bit of colour back. Asseniah, however, remained frighteningly ill-looking. Her skin had gone from white, to pale, to slightly green and she hadn't eaten a thing. Eventually, she pointed a shaky finger at the toilets and wobbled off in their direction.

'Alain, I really can't eat this,' Melody mumbled. She tried to sit back in her chair but it was the wrong design for her wings so she leant forward again, resting her head on her hands.

'Okay, as long as you can perform properly then do what you want,' he finally said. All but Alain and Arrahbella put down their forks. Chester had finished long ago.

Asseniah returned looking even worse.

'Asseniah, are you alright?' Alain asked her.

Asseniah nodded, then quickly put a hand to her head. Sweat was running down her neck. Alain bit his lower lip and looked at the young girl with concern. He closed his eyes for a moment as he called up some of his power.

'Come on then, troupe,' he said, with more energy than he had. 'It's the weather; it's a natural process that we can't do anything about. What we can do is give the audience an hour's solace and take their minds so far out of this world that they'll forget whether it's Summer or Winter, day or night. They'll feel rewarded for having braved the heat to come out and see such a memorable show. And, more importantly, they'll believe in magic for a while.

'I want this show to sizzle. Everybody gets lustier in the heat, so let's play with that. By the time the audience leaves our tent they'll be so turned on that they *will* need to cool down. Izan, Chester, you'll perform bare-chested. Girls, you'll wear your most revealing outfits. Melody and Chester, you'll close the show and I want that audience so fired up that they're almost leaping onto their neighbours. We've been given heat so let's use it to our advantage. The audience thinks it's hot outside? We'll show them hot!'

Lust wasn't usually the motivating factor behind the circus' performances – magic was, escaping reality – Alain only used it now to remind his troupe of the ecstasy of performing, to get them fired up, and it worked. He had their attention. They were on the edge of their seats, being seduced by his voice, turned on by his words, wanting desperately to make an audience feel the same way. Even some of the patrons at the nearby tables had been caught up in Alain's motivation and were looking longingly at the troupe. Only Asseniah seemed unmoved by her Ringmaster's words.

'Well, come on, man, pay the damned bill so we can get going,' Izan demanded.

'You all head to the tent. I'll pay and follow.'

They were gone within seconds, Asseniah slowly following, a hand clutched to her stomach. Arrahbella saw this and quickly followed her while Alain went to the counter to pay.

A short while later, Alain opened the show with a speech that really did make the audience forget about the heat, even though it was a full house. He introduced Mariette then stood in the wings to watch as she danced to a piece of music recorded on the CD player, her muscles so warm she was more agile than ever, moving like a river of flesh and pink feathers.

Once Mariette had finished and Izan was on stage, shirtless but still wearing his cloak, Alain watched anxiously as Asseniah weakly climbed the ladder to her silks. He had made her lay down for the beginning of the show, worried she might pass out if nestled in the bundle of material for too long.

Izan's act was entertaining but fairly standard for the Earthlings, even when he cut Mariette in half and showed them her neatly divided insides. He made things disappear and reappear all over the tent, swapped the clothes of two audience members, guessed the right card every time, and then he annoyed Alain by bringing a young boy up on stage and turning him invisible right in front of everyone. The boy then ran up to his mother and hugged her, making her scream, before being turned visible once more. Alain was worried he would have to go into damage control but the audience clapped and the mother laughed as though she had been silly for believing such a thing. Izan bowed, said a few words, then walked off stage. Alain grabbed his arm as he passed.

'I want you to wait here in case you need to stop

Asseniah from falling,' the Ringmaster said.

Izan nodded and waited for the scolding.

'Don't do that again.'

'That's the beauty of children, Alain. You can use magic on them without them needing therapy. And the mother *knows* it's not real.'

Alain would have argued back but he had to go on stage to introduce Asseniah.

The young girl tumbled into view and performed flawlessly despite the conditions, moving fast, trying to catch a breeze as she spun and fell. The audience gasped and applauded a number of times as their eyes followed her through the air, swinging from her neck and ankles, twisting herself up in a cocoon then spiralling down toward the stage. When she finally planted her feet on the ground, she gave a shaky bow and almost ran off as Alain walked on to introduce Sora's tightrope act. When the Ringmaster returned to the wings, he found her slumped on the floor, Izan waving a damp cloth over her face.

'Are you alright?' he whispered over the music.

Asseniah blinked a couple of times, then nodded slowly.

'You don't have to do manipulation,' he told her. 'Sora and Melody can do it on their own, or we can omit the act altogether, it's fine.'

Asseniah frowned and shook her head, then wished she hadn't as the room spun.

Chester took to the stage as Sora did a costume change. Asseniah struggled out of her wet leotard and into

135

her manipulation costume as well, then sat down again as Mariette took over fanning her.

Alain watched with bated breath as the three girls cartwheeled into view and took up their first position. He could see Asseniah trembling and dripping with sweat and he cursed himself for letting her go on. Manipulation was pretty much as the name suggested; three young girls manipulating their bodies in ways that should not be humanly possible. They had just moved into their third pose, each supporting the other in a complicated arrangement of arms and legs, when Asseniah fainted, causing all three of them to tumble to the ground in a heap.

'Mythos!' Alain cursed. 'Chester, close the curtain. Mariette, hold the audience.'

As soon as the drapes were drawn, Alain, Izan, and Chester hurried on stage where Sora and Melody were climbing out from underneath Asseniah. Mariette's voice filtered through the curtain as she tried to keep the audience entertained.

Alain felt Asseniah's forehead, checked her breathing and pulse. They seemed okay, if a little fast.

'Izan, can you take her to the back room?'

The magician nodded, lifted Asseniah's body magically off the stage, and floated her to one of the backstage rooms.

'Melody, Sora, are you hurt?' Alain asked. The girls shook their heads. 'Okay, Melody and Chester, you'll have to go on now, alright?'

They nodded and hurried to get into position. Alain waited until they were ready then he signalled to Mariette to come off, relieved to see that no one had left their seats. Once Melody and Chester were swinging from the trapeze, Alain hurried back to attend to Asseniah. She had regained consciousness but wasn't focussing well, the swirling part of her eyes moving rapidly in all directions. Izan was dipping a towel in water to mop her brow while Sora kept tipping water into her mouth and fanned her with one of Mariette's pink feather fans.

'Asseniah, are you alright?' Alain asked quietly, then felt rather silly for doing so because, obviously, she wasn't. 'I mean, are you in pain?'

Asseniah shook her head slowly.

'Just the heat?'

She nodded.

'Okay, honey, just stay here for a few more minutes until Chester and Melody finish the show, okay? Then we'll all go back to the train. Can you do that?'

Asseniah nodded weakly and closed her eyes. Alain closed his eyes, too, for a moment, letting out a breath of relief, then, he returned to the wings to watch Melody and Chester.

They were certainly sticking to the hot theme. It had been a fantasy of theirs to make love on the trapeze for quite a while now, but Alain had forbidden them from ever doing so for two reasons; safety (in all honesty, he wasn't entirely sure it was even possible, but it certainly sounded dangerous), and their desire to do so made their act much more intense. The eyes of the Earthling audience followed intensely as the pair stroked each other, slithered over each other, flew back and forth, twisted around the bars, hung from each other's legs, and danced through the air. Even Alain loved watching them, mesmerised by a world he would never be a part of.

They finished their piece and alighted to the stage, holding hands, and bowed. Then, all the performers, except Asseniah, walked out and bowed together. They left the stage as Alain thanked the audience for coming. Then, they closed the curtains, gathered their things, left the tent in the care of a new pair of security guards and headed to the train, Izan carrying Asseniah.

Arrahbella was ready for them, predicting that at least some would be in a sorry state. 'There are re-hydrating teas and water on the counter,' she announced, as soon as they had all walked through the kitchen door. Then she saw Asseniah in Izan's arms. 'What happened?'

'She collapsed,' Alain explained, sinking into a chair at the long wooden table. 'She's okay.'

Arrahbella wasn't surprised that she hadn't received any images of Asseniah collapsing; the mysterious girl seemed to be the only troupe member immune to psychic powers.

'Give her to me. Oleg, you'll have to serve dinner.' She left the giant to dish up the salads as she took Asseniah through to her room and placed her in Sora's bed.

The troupe had recovered their appetites after performing and cleaned their plates quickly. Only Alain left his untouched, feeling suddenly weary. Later, when he was alone with Arrahbella, he all but collapsed in her arms.

The next day, Asseniah stayed in the cool of the Highway while the others braved the heat once more to go into Adelaide and catch a movie at the cinema, something they found rather incredible (cameras could be found in Kartan and Arelia, but no one had quite yet figured how to make moving pictures the way Earthlings could). Unfortunately, the excitement of such a novelty meant that they had never quite grasped the concept of remaining silent and Alain ended up having to mute their voices after more than one Earthling had expressed their displeasure.

The show went well that night and this time Arrahbella joined them, offering readings to any interested people once the curtain had closed.

'We're going to explore the city, Alain,' Izan announced, once they had packed up. 'Will you be joining us?'

'No, thank you, Izan, I'll wait for Arrahbella. Have a good time and please be careful.'

'Aren't we always?'

'No.'

Izan shot him a wide cheesy grin. Alain shook his head as Melody and Chester exited the tent, dressed once more in casual wear.

'Come on, you two, I'm dying here,' Izan whined.

'We have to wait for Sora,' Melody told him.

The magician groaned. 'You people are insufferable.'

'Why don't you go ahead? We'll follow. You're just going to leave us eventually anyway.'

'Brilliant idea.'

Alain grabbed Izan's arm as he turned to hurry off.

'No, Izan, I want you all to stay together. Somebody needs to keep an eye on you.'

Izan tapped his foot impatiently. 'The faith you show in me confounds,' he said, dryly.

Sora appeared from the tent, putting the last pin in her hair. 'Mariette and Asseniah are going to a café, so we can go.'

'Finally.' Izan looked at Alain who released his hold and watched as the four headed up the street in search of a bar.

They found a place across from the cinema they had been in earlier, brimming with people, the air full of noise and music.

'It's not much cooler in here,' Sora observed, as they stood inside the doorway looking around.

'It'll do,' Izan replied, as his eyes roamed the crowd hungrily. 'Right, don't wait up, kids.' He disappeared amongst the throng and resurfaced at the bar next to two girls who seemed to be on their own.

'Looks like we're staying here, then,' Melody sighed, and moved toward the bar. Due to the proximity of the crowd she had to brush past a few people, making them jump as they felt feathers tickle their skin.

Sora laughed. 'I love watching their faces when you do that, Melody.'

'I don't do it on purpose.'

They sat at the bar and ordered some drinks, watching the Earthlings around them and talking in low voices. Izan and his girls disappeared for a while before returning to sit at a table in a corner and continuing to make out.

Chester was drawing a lot of interest from both men and women. A group of girls standing at the end of the bar had been eyeing him and flirting unreservedly since he had walked in. Having learnt to keep to themselves, the foreigners ignored them, until one of the group walked over and positioned herself right between Chester and Sora.

'Hi.' She was an attractive girl but with an air of arrogance about her. Her long brown hair would have looked better in a shorter style to suit her round face.

Chester smiled politely. 'Hi.'

'Do you want to buy me a drink?'

'No.'

'Why not?'

'Because I'm not interested.'

'Right. And which of these two are you interested in?' She barely glanced at Melody and completely ignored Sora.

Chester smiled. 'Depends on the day.'

Melody tried to cover a laugh with a cough.

The girl looked at him for a moment before snorting in disbelief. 'Well, if you've already got two, what's one more?'

'No thanks.'

'Shame. I could give you a better time than these two ever could.'

'I doubt it.'

The girl licked her lips in annoyance before shaking her head and returning to her friends. After a moment of furious discussion, the group of girls all turned to look at the trio with withering glares. Chester smiled at them, put a hand to Melody's cheek, and kissed her passionately. The girls turned away in disgust. Sora smiled with amusement.

'Be careful, Chester,' Melody told him when their lips had parted. 'Earthling hearts break easily.'

'I know.'

'That's because they're obsessed with beauty,' Sora said.

'So are the Arelians,' Chester pointed out. 'It amazes me that they still come over when I'm obviously with someone.'

Melody ran a finger over his porcelain skin. 'It's because they don't believe that such a gorgeous looking guy like you could be with a plain looking girl like me.'

Chester frowned at her. 'Personally, I think you're the prettiest girl in the room.'

'But I'm not, and everyone but you can see that, so they think you're free for the taking.'

Sadness appeared in Chester's eyes. 'I wish you wouldn't talk like that, Melody.' He leaned in closer. 'If I really am as good looking as everyone thinks I am, and I can have any girl I want, then I want you because you are the most beautiful to me, inside and out.'

Melody grabbed him and kissed him tenderly. Sora smiled but then turned away as a pang of loneliness hit her hard in the stomach.

CHAPTER 6

Present Day – The Highway

As the train rumbled along the Highway toward Ormance, a week after leaving Earth, Izan was in the practice room, testing his magic. Even after twenty-two years he was still learning how to use it properly. Today, he wanted to practice his ability to transform things. A long line of objects stood on the table in front of him, ready to become something else entirely.

Closing his eyes, Izan looked into his well of power. Searching and sifting through the many, many strands, he found one he couldn't remember seeing before and stopped in surprise.

'I wonder what that is,' he pondered out loud, before calling it up. The power hurtled through him at an astonishing rate and exploded out of him, knocking him backwards.

'Woah.'

He sat up and shook his head. When he looked up, he saw Asseniah standing very still in the kitchen doorway.

'Mythos,' he cursed, as he hurriedly picked himself up and ran over to her. 'Asseniah, what do you think you're doing?! I'm experimenting here.'

Asseniah's swirling eyes slowly turned to meet his, then she leapt at him, passionately kissing him on the mouth. For a moment, he was too shocked to move, but then he recovered and pushed her away, trying to restrain her as she struggled against him, attempting to kiss him again.

'Oh dear,' Izan breathed. Then, he shouted, 'Hey, anyone?!'

Sora heard him from the kitchen car where she had been searching for her friend.

'What's going on?' she asked, poking her head through the doorway.

'Sora, thank Mythos. You need to get Alain.'

Sora watched as Asseniah tried desperately to break free of Izan's grasp.

'What's wrong with her?'

Asseniah turned around, looking for the source of the voice. When she saw Sora she tried to wriggle free, arms outstretched in her direction.

'Just get Alain, please, hurry.'

Sora disappeared as Asseniah bent forwards, flipping out of Izan's grasp, almost kicking him in the face.

'No, Asseniah, come back.'

But she was gone from the room, pursuing the Ormancian. Izan cursed then followed.

Sora burst into Melody and Chester's room where everyone but Oleg and the dwarves were gathered.

'Alain, you have to come quickly. Izan's enchanted Asseniah. I don't know how but she's...'

She was cut off as Asseniah whisked her around and kissed her while the troupe watched on in stunned silence. Sora pushed her friend away but Asseniah caught sight of Chester and was on top of him in a second, kissing him just as passionately as she had kissed Izan and Sora. Melody watched with a mixture of amusement and surprise as Alain firmly grasped Asseniah by the shoulders, pulled her off of Chester, then looked at Izan with an accusatory expression.

'What did you do?' he asked, as Asseniah attempted tirelessly to kiss her Ringmaster.

'I don't know. I wasn't trying to do anything-'

'I don't care what you were *trying* to do,' Alain interrupted. 'I want to know what you *have* done and I want you to fix it.'

'That's just it, Alain, I don't know what I did. Don't get angry at me. I told everyone I was practicing and she just came into the room.'

'I think she must have been in the bathroom when Izan told us,' Sora explained.

'I think I can fix it,' Chester said. 'It should be a simple power depletion spell.'

Izan and Alain looked at Chester doubtfully.

'I don't know, Chester. We don't know what Izan actually did to her.'

Poor Asseniah was crying now as she desperately tried to kiss anyone in reach.

'Can you do it?' Alain asked Izan.

'I don't know. It may be worth giving Chester a try. A power depletion spell has to be cast by someone other than the person who put the power there in the first place.'

Alain wasn't sure if that made any sense to him but he sighed. 'Alright, Chester, but be careful.'

'I wouldn't do it if I thought it would hurt her.'

Alain nodded.

'Perhaps throw in some memory eraser as well,' Izan suggested.

Melody gave her boyfriend a hard look. 'You can erase memories?'

'Can we just hurry, please?' pleaded Sora. 'It's heartbreaking seeing her like this.'

'Alain, you'll need to let go of her. Izan will freeze her.' Chester looked to Izan who gave him a nod.

'Alright.'

'Ready... now.'

Alain released his grasp on Asseniah and she leapt up to throw her arms around him. Izan froze her in midair as Chester threw a strand of purple magic over her like a lasso, followed by another. The colour shimmered over her body, making her shiver from head to toe, then, the light dimmed. Izan retracted his magic, planting Asseniah's feet gently back on the floor, and both men stood back.

Asseniah blinked a couple of times then looked blankly around at the faces watching her.

'I think it worked,' Izan said.

Alain breathed a sigh of relief. 'Alright, Izan, you are now permitted to lock the room whenever you or Chester are practicing. Sora, can you please take Asseniah to the practice room and make sure all her skills are normal?'

Asseniah looked at Alain, frightened and confused. 'It's okay, Asseniah, you're okay. Go with Sora, she'll explain everything.'

Sora put her arm around her friend's shoulders and they left together. Izan returned to his room to try and work out exactly what magic he had wielded. Melody gave Chester an impressed kiss before they left to get themselves some tea.

When all but Mariette and Arrahbella had gone, Alain massaged his brow. 'How long until we reach Ormance?'

'Still another three weeks,' Arrahbella replied, patting him on the shoulder.

Six Years Ago – Varatalé / Ormance

After staying a while to see how Oleg and Chester got on with the others (especially with Melody, but as she was only twelve at this time she was blissfully unaffected by any romantic feelings), Alain ventured out on to the Highway alone, heading for the wealthy desert planet, Kartan.

Kartan had offered him a fourteen-year-old girl named Hanar who could do all sorts of tricks on trampolines and springboards. Unfortunately, Hanar had wanted to be *the* star of the show and when Alain brought her back to the manor she was nothing but trouble; she hated Melody with a passion for no other reason than the fact she existed; she flirted constantly with Chester; she teased Mariette for her forgetfulness; and she argued with everybody. So, Alain and Oleg had dragged her kicking and screaming back out onto the Highway and left her at Haaj's Inn where she talked her way into a job as a waitress, hoping someone would come along and take her away. Alain then returned to Kartan to inform Hanar's parents she wasn't coming back and found he couldn't really blame them when they looked more than a little relieved.

Alain had been back for a day when he was in his office, up in one of the manor's towers, sitting in the large leather armchair as Arrahbella massaged his shoulders.

'Where will you go this time?' she asked him.

'Ormance,' he replied. 'It should be my last stop.'

'What about Terrenvale, Icecess, and Landau?'

'Not many Icecesseons can leave their planet. Part of their magic is being able to survive in freezing temperatures so they can't actually physically leave. Only those who have more magic, like Tokinov and his family, can survive away from it. Some of them go to Noir Eternale but find it too dark after the brilliance of their home. I will go to Terrenvale eventually. The dwarves' magic lies in music and we'll need a band and helpers when we go on the road, but that can wait a while.'

'And Landau? I know you love Landau.'

'That's true.' Alain had once managed to save Landau from almost certain destruction when his first visit there had taken a rather drastic turn. As a result, the Landaus now considered him somewhat of a hero and always treated him like royalty. 'But they're having a war again. Nobody's allowed in or out when there's a war.'

'Didn't they just finish a war?'

Alain smiled sadly. 'Yes, they did. Landau is almost

always at war. This one is between King Somerset and King Hudson. Somerset owns Hamptonsvale, the largest realm in Landau, and Hudson owns Sudbury, the smallest. Hamptonsvale's kings are always trying to claim Sudbury as their own.'

This battle was resolved by the time Cirque du Phantastique went on their first tour. Hudson came out victorious, but, like the kings before him, was content with his small realm, so, Somerset retained his realm and agreed to leave Sudbury alone for the rest of his reign.

'I'd love to see it sometime,' Arrahbella said. 'From what you've told me before, it sounds like the kind of world Earthlings usually write about in their fantasy novels.'

'Definitely, it's got it all; unicorns, dragons, griffins, mermaids, fairies, wizards, stunning landscapes.' He sighed. 'But, we won't be going there for a while, so Ormance it is.' He turned and pulled Arrahbella gently around to the other side of the chair and into his lap. 'Then, I can stay home and finally spend some time with you.'

Arrahbella smiled and rubbed her nose against his.

So, Alain journeyed to Ormance, entering the rift into the empire of Kutiko and the city of Kutiko-mi.

'Welcome to Kutiko,' the large beefy guard greeted, somewhat gruffly. There were at least ten guards standing around the rift and another five hovering around inside a small wooden pavilion that sat beneath a canopy of cherry tree branches. 'Every visitor is required to see the Empress before they do anything else. An Empirial guard will be appointed to you to ensure the peace and tranquillity of the city is kept.'

The guard waved a finger and another beefy man hurried out of the pavilion and stood at Alain's side. Alain was used to this, having been to Ormance on a number of occasions, but that never stopped him from feeling slightly intimidated by these unsmiling hulks of muscle.

'Follow me,' his guard ordered, and set off down the street.

Alain breathed in the incense and peach scented air as he walked among the wooden houses and buildings. Thin windows made from paper and wood opened outward into the street, letting in the cool air but magically keeping out the rain that fell lightly. Trees grew along the streets or sometimes in the middle of the street, their roots lifting up the stones. Small dragon-like creatures known as yamuis scuttled around the place, searching for food, uttering small bleating noises. The guard didn't say a word but Alain was happy listening to the peaceful sounds of birds, yamuis, trees, and rain; the lyrics to the melody being played by the wind chimes that tinkled in the wind.

Despite all this calm, Alain was hit by a sudden pang of emotion. He had spent so much time with Arrahbella lately that being away from her now was quite hard to handle. He just wanted the search for members to be over so he could get started on training them all.

'We're here,' the guard informed him, bringing him out of his thoughts. They were standing at the circular wooden gates that led into Empress Setana's palace. 'What's your name?'

'Alain du Maurier from Varatalé.'

The guard nodded and led him through the gardens, leaving him to wait by the throne room door while he announced his arrival. He had just enough time to check his appearance was neat before the guard ushered him in.

'Master du Maurier, welcome,' Setana said, once Alain had knelt in front of her and bowed so low that his head touched the ground.

'Empress Setana, I hope you're well.'

'Thank you, I am.' The twenty-four year old Empress was sitting on her wooden, gold-and-red throne, which sat on a raised platform. She was wearing yards of silk and cotton in an elaborate design, her long, sleek, black hair was piled high on her head as though it were a crown itself, decorated with red ribbons and tassels, and her pretty face was painted, giving her the appearance of a porcelain doll, which Alain always found wickedly deceiving. Beefy guards surrounded her like stone statues and more doll-like ladies sat around the room, strumming instruments, painting, pouring tea, attending to their Empress.

'We haven't seen you for a while, Master du Maurier. You do not travel as much anymore?'

'Not as much as I used to, Your Highness, but it's always lovely to come back to your world.'

'Ormance is the most beautiful world along the Highway.'

Alain smiled politely.

'My sister's birthday is approaching, Wordmaster. I'd like you to write another poem for her. She loved the one you composed for her sixteenth.'

Alain bowed. 'I'd be most honoured, Highness. I shall bring it to you tomorrow.' He was, in fact, a little thrown by this request. Writing a poem for Setana's sister, Raika, had been nerve-wracking enough the first time. To do it again, and at such short notice, was near terrifying, even for someone who had the power of words.

'Good. Now, what brings you to my city this time?'

Alain put the poem out of his mind and returned to the business at hand. 'Empress, I am planning to create a circus that will tour and perform the worlds along the Highway. I have come to Ormance to see if your empire would be interested in seeing the show once it is ready and whether you have any performers to offer.'

Once he had explained what a circus was, the Empress sat back in her throne to think for a moment. Alain kept his eyes lowered while she did so, as was required. He was worried a circus might be too hectic for Ormance. Her answer, then, pleasantly surprised him.

'I think it sounds like something the people of Kutiko-mi might enjoy, but perhaps a trial would be a good start.' Alain gave a nod. 'As for a performer, I am not sure what you are looking for. You are welcome to roam the city and view the people as they attend their sessions but if any of them take your fancy or wish to leave with you, please come to me first. I am reluctant to lose any of my citizens and I would be surprised if any of them wished to leave.'

Alain bowed. He was assigned another guard, a large, bald man named Sutoto, and the two of them walked out onto the streets once again. They passed very few people, most of them tourists, but Alain wasn't surprised; the people of Ormance stuck to strict regimes of work and lessons during the day. The women would attend the mass sessions in the mornings while the men worked on the farms and businesses, then they would all have lunch together with their families before swapping in the afternoons. The sessions were held in large paved squares that sat around the city and it was to one of these that Sutoto was now leading Alain.

'Here we are,' Sutoto announced, as they reached a circular wooden gate set into a long stone wall. He pushed the gates open and stood aside so Alain could enter. Rows and rows of Ormancian women dressed in red-and-gold robes moved in complete poetic unison, standing out like motes of dust in the sunlight against the sunken grey square. Elaborate wooden pavilions and statues of the Ormancian God – a four-armed, hedgehog-like being named Furo – surrounded the square. Four masters stood at the front, facing the group, leading them through a combination of fighting stances and meditative poses. Not a sound was uttered; no grunts of exertion, no commands from the masters, not even a peep from the children, of which there were plenty.

Alain watched, impressed and mesmerised. They came to the end of their poses and picked up the swords that lay on the ground next to them. Then they began the same thing all over again, this time controlling the blades as they flew around them.

'What do you think?' Sutoto asked Alain, a proud smile on his broad face.

'Superb. Very impressive,' Alain replied, and Sutoto nodded. 'But, I wonder, is there anyone who's better than everyone else? Someone who stands out from the crowd? Someone who's different?'

Sutoto studied Alain for a moment, knowing he was looking for someone to take away with him. 'There is one,' he finally said, and pointed toward the farmland and mountains that surrounded the city. A small, square house could be seen sitting amongst the fields, dwarfed by the great mountains behind it, isolated from everything else. Sutoto closed the gates on the square and started walking down the street as he told Alain about the girl who lived there.

'Her name is Sora Mai. When she was little, she seemed ordinary, taking part in the practice sessions like everyone else and helping out on her parents' farm. But, as she grew older, she began to refuse to do the same things as everyone else. She could command swords and knives, but she would make them do what she wanted to do, fly in all sorts of patterns, rather than adhere to what her master told her. Same with fire. She can produce fire out of nowhere. She would receive the normal punishments that a disorderly child would get but they only seemed to make her want to rebel even more. If she were an adult she would have been locked away, or killed, but the Empress believes that children can change. Mistress Mai wouldn't though.

'About three or four years ago there was a fire that wiped out nearly a quarter of the city. Thirty-three people were killed, including Mistress Mai's parents and siblings. Everyone believes that she started the fire but nothing has ever been proven and she was only eight years old at the time.

'Then, there's the comics she draws; they're violent and gruesome. No one wishes to read them and many believe now that she really did kill her parents on purpose and that she's evil and intends to kill us all. They're scared of her. That's why Empress Setana had to make her an outcast. She still lives on her father's farm but she keeps to herself. If she does come into the city, she's ridiculed. She makes her own clothes too and they can be quite different to what we wear. Quite... revealing.'

Sutoto fell silent as they approached the house, but Alain had become rather excited by all he had heard and he couldn't wait to meet the strange girl.

Before Sutoto could knock, however, they heard noises coming from behind the house; a soft swishing noise combined with a girl's voice. The men looked at each other before slowly venturing around the back of the small building.

Standing in the field directly behind the house was a young, pretty girl dressed in a red silk top with flowing triangular sleeves and long, loose black pants. Her black hair was straight and loose and her face was painted in the traditional Ormancian doll-like way. Around her, small kitchen knives were flying in a variety of patterns while she performed fighting stances between them.

Sutoto was unnerved by this display but Alain watched with boyish excitement, taking care to remain as unnoticeable as possible, not wanting to startle her.

The performance ended when the girl sent all five

knives sailing through the air at top speed to land in a wooden fence post, embedded up to their hilts. She bowed before walking to the fence to pull the knives out and it was then that Alain cleared his throat to signal their presence. The girl whipped around quickly, taking up a fighting stance, then, realising she was in the presence of an Empirial Guard, she stood up straight again. From the information Sutoto had just given him, Alain deduced she must have been about ten or eleven years old.

'Sora Mai,' Sutoto began. 'This is Alain du Maurier from Varatalé. He would like to speak to you.'

Sora bowed to them both, her face maintaining a passive expression.

'Welcome to my home, Empirial Guard and Master du Maurier. I would be honoured if you would allow me to serve you some tea.'

Alain was surprised by this custom show of courtesy, after hearing how individual and non-conforming Sora was, he had expected her to be a little fiercer. He followed this surprise with a mental kick, realising he had fallen into the trap of judging her before knowing her.

'Thank you, Mistress Mai. We'd be delighted.'

Alain knew Sutoto wasn't the least bit delighted, but *he* certainly was, and he bounded after Sora as she led them into her small house.

Inside was unconventionally messy: scattered around the square, open, sparsely furnished main room were towers of paper, some clean, some full of writing; drawings decorated the walls in a disorderly manner; quills and ink sat on the desk, table, and floor, stains appearing here and there like bruises. What space was left was covered with scraps of material, sewing tools, and a few potted plants that were growing extremely well, almost swallowing up the nearby furniture with their tendrils.

Alain felt quite at home amongst all the creative clutter but Sutoto was crinkling his nose in disgust, or, perhaps, in interest, Alain couldn't tell which.

Sora walked into the small area designated as the kitchen to prepare tea while Alain and Sutoto stood in the main room unsure what to do with themselves. She hadn't indicated that they could sit yet so Alain took the time to discreetly examine some of the drawings. Sutoto had not been exaggerating about the violent and graphic pictures but they were exquisitely done, full of detail, and Alain felt his appreciation for the young girl double.

When the tea was ready, Sora carried it through on a tray, setting it down on the low table in front of the men, not bothering to move the sheets of paper already there. Then, she daintily crossed her legs beneath her and poured the tea. The men quickly fell to the ground on the opposite side of the table to accept the cups she offered them. Alain could hardly believe this was the same girl they had just witnessed playing with knives outside. She was the very picture of elegance and courtesy.

Finally, Sora lifted her pretty brown almond-shaped eyes to Alain's own and he recognised the cue to start. She listened attentively the whole time, her expression blank, her eyes not leaving his, her hands lifting her tea to her lips every now and then. When Alain had completed his speech, she set her cup down and looked at the table top.

'Thank you, Master du Maurier. I will consider your offer and give you my answer later. Are you staying in the city?'

Her answer managed to catch Alain off-guard, but, he had been planning to stay anyway so it didn't matter, it was a rather life changing decision. 'Yes. In the Kutiko Inn. You'll find me there for the next three days when I'm afraid I must leave.'

Sora nodded and stood up, signalling it was now time for the men to go.

'What an intriguing girl,' Alain mused, as he walked down the path back to the city with Sutoto.

The guard shivered. 'A creepy girl.'

Sora stood in the middle of the main room and looked around. It only took her a few moments to make a decision, then, she went to her bedroom, pulled on her most conservative clothes, put her hair under a short black wig, and headed into the city. As it was not quite lunchtime yet she was able to move through the streets undetected, walking fast and keeping her head down out of habit. She stopped outside a small store selling fruits and vegetables, checking to make sure no one was watching before hurrying inside.

'Sora Mai, what brings you here in the middle of the day?' Kenjiro, the owner of the store, asked in surprise. This small, middle-aged man was the only resident of Kutiko that had any kind of good feeling toward Sora. He sold her produce to the unknowing citizens and gave her ample profits.

'I'm leaving Ormance,' she said.

'Are you now? Where will you go?'

She told him about Alain and his proposition.

'What kind of a man is this Alain du Maurier?' Kenjiro asked with a frown, as he stacked apples into wooden boxes.

'I'm not sure yet, but I can protect myself if need be. That's the problem, Kenjiro, I need someone to take over my farm but I'll need to come back to it if things don't work out.'

Kenjiro smiled. 'Not to worry, my dear. My daughter has a suitor. I was going to have him work for me but he can take your farm and you're welcome to have it back if you need it.'

'Thank you, Kenjiro.'

'You take care of yourself, Sora Mai. I hope they treat you better in Varatalé.'

Sora bowed to him and left, heading back to her home. After tidying up the place and gathering together all she wished to take with her, she said farewell to her plants, took a good look around the property once more, and headed into town.

The streets were suddenly alive with people as the city bells signalled the lunch hour. As Sora walked past them, dressed in a violet-coloured corset and short black skirt, despite the rain and cool breeze, she was met with stares and snide comments.

'There goes the witch-whore,' a boy not much older than herself said loudly to his group of friends.

'Kill anyone recently, witch?' spat another.

One of them picked up a rock, preparing to throw it at her, but a guard stopped him, reluctantly muttering something about keeping the peace.

Sora put her chin in the air and walked on without even glancing at the youths.

Alain was delighted to see her. They went to see Setana as soon as Sora had dropped her belongings into Alain's room.

'Alain du Maurier, back so soon...' Setana's voice trailed off when she saw who he had brought with him.

'Your Highness, I have asked Mistress Mai if she would like to join my circus and live with me in Varatalé.'

There was a moment's pause.

'Would you like to go, child?'

Sora raised her eyes to meet the Empress'. 'Yes, Your Highness.'

With steely eyes that did nothing to betray her feelings, Setana only hesitated out of traditional courtesy before giving her permission for Sora to leave.

'Very well, Mistress Mai.' Sora bowed. 'And you, Master du Maurier, shall be bestowed with the Empirial emblem for,' she hesitated again, her eyes flicking to Sora, 'for services to the Empress.' She flicked her fingers ever so slightly and a guard hurried off, returning moments later with a wooden box, which he handed over to her.

Alain was shocked. This was an honour given only to heroes and the highest masters of the Furo temples. He knew he was getting it for taking Sora away, ridding the city of the outcast, and this made him rather annoyed, but, he would only be killed for refusing, so he bowed his head to the floor, deciding to think of it as a reward for the poems he had given her.

'Your Highness, I am most honoured.'

Setana took the emblem (a red butterfly on a gold background) out of the box, rose, walked toward Alain, and placed the gold chain around his neck.

'This allows you to enter my city without a guard, Master du Maurier.' She returned to her throne, sitting down with perfected elegance. 'Do you have my poem for me?'

'Yes, Your Highness.' He handed a roll of parchment to the nearest guard who gave it to the Empress.

Setana read it through, closing her eyes briefly at the end. 'Thank you. When you and your circus are ready, please come and visit us.'

Alain and Sora bowed again. Two hours later, they were on their way to Varatalé.

CHAPTER 7

MELODY AND CHESTER

Present Day – The Highway

One evening, three weeks after leaving Earth, Izan and Chester took to the practice room to work on Chester's magic and alleviate their boredom, this time making sure that they locked the doors.

'So, where did we get up to?' Izan asked, as he studied his black nail polish.

'Invisibility,' Chester reminded him, patiently.

'Ah, yes, then, when you and Melody are living alone together in many years time and I'm off visiting my fans in another world, you'll be able to keep her wings hidden.'

'She may not want her wings hidden. I know I don't.'

Izan shot him an exasperated look. 'If you're still in the circus then Alain will. I'm being hypothetical anyway. Now, let's see if you can de-visualise this ball.' Izan held up one of his juggling balls, turning it in his hand before placing it on the table.

Chester looked at the colourful ball and waited. Izan had gone back to studying his nails. He wasn't a bad teacher, usually, but there were times when the vast amount of magic in his body pulsed so painfully he couldn't think straight. It didn't help that Sasha had feigned illness when they had arrived at Tokinov's the week before, and the only two traders there had left an hour after the troupe's arrival. For the last five days, the magician had been pacing up and down the train trying to expend his energy, wreaking havoc by bringing inanimate objects to life, turning things invisible and not making them reappear, transforming things, and generally giving the others headaches.

'What exactly am I meant to do?' Chester prompted.

Izan blinked at him blankly a couple of times before realisation dawned. 'Oh, sorry, let me demonstrate.'

He gave the ball a hard stare, waved his hand (with a perfected flourish) and the ball was gone. When he waved his hand again, the ball reappeared. He frowned at Chester.

'I'm not exactly sure how I do it. I guess you just concentrate on the ball and on what you want it to do. Like everything else we do.'

'Okay.' Chester did as he was told. The ball stayed visible.

'Give it another try. It's probably not going to happen straight away.'

Chester tried again while Izan watched him closely. His eyes strayed to Chester's porcelain skin and luscious mouth and he turned away quickly, focussing on his nails again, trying to ignore the unwelcome images now flashing through his mind.

'Hey, I did it!' cried Chester.

Izan looked at where the ball had been sitting on the table top. He waved his hand across the surface and they heard the ball bounce onto the floor.

'Well done,' he said to Chester, who punched the air and did a back flip.

As Chester was perfecting his skills with invisibility, Sora was at the other end of the train, watering the plants in Alain and Arrahbella's room. Alain was playing with a poem Melody had just written while Arrahbella tended to her knife collection. The mood in the room was lazy and peaceful, the small fountain trickling away serenely in tune with the Celtic music floating out of the CD player, the lamps giving the room a cosy feel.

'Sora, could you come here a moment please?'

Sora put down her watering jug, stroked the happy plant's leaves, and went over to Arrahbella who was crouched on the floor. The collection of daggers was impressive. Arrahbella had twelve altogether now; eight of them from Earth, two from Varatalé, and two from Ormance. She was hoping to buy another when they arrived in Kutiko-mi. Each one was a different design, all crafted from different woods and metals; some had opals or jewels encrusted in the hilt, one was inlaid with gold, most of them had blades shaped in ways that were painful just to look at, and each had been named after an Earthly goddess or mythological female; Diana, Hera, Venus, Aphrodite, Eve, Virgo, Freya, Morgana, Guinevere, Athena, Izanami, and Anu. Arrahbella loved them as though they were her children.

'Diana needs sharpening,' she said, once Sora had knelt down in front of her.

Sora gently picked up Diana, Arrahbella's favourite dagger, and studied her carefully. Diana was the simplest in design but she had also been the first dagger Arrahbella had ever purchased. She had a simple straight silver blade that was engraved with Celtic designs, and a polished wooden hilt inlaid with mother of pearl that shone like the moon.

'Sit back.'

Arrahbella did so as Sora let go of Diana, letting her fly around them, checking how easily she cut through the air. Alain had finished playing with Melody's poem and was watching this display from his armchair. Even though he trusted Sora, human instinct couldn't stop him from being on high alert when there were razor sharp blades flying around his loved one.

Once she had soared around the room, Diana came to rest back in her place beside Venus and Hera.

Sora shook her head. 'Not yet. If we sharpen her now she'll be slippery. Give her a couple more practice sessions.'

Arrahbella nodded.

'How's Aphrodite?' asked Alain.

Arrahbella picked up the knife in question. Alain had bought it for Arrahbella as a wedding gift. She was one of the Varatalian knives and the most intricate in design with a wave-shaped, twisted, silver blade, a polished oak hilt inlaid with gold and opal, and bronze knuckle guards.

'She's magnificent,' smiled Arrahbella.

'She hardly ever needs sharpening, Alain,' Sora added.

'She glides through the air so smoothly.'

Alain nodded with satisfaction. He lifted his pen to write "perfection" in the air. The word hovered in front of him in white smoky ink, then it floated over to the case of daggers and dissolved into them. The girls smiled.

'Well, I suppose I should go and make some teas,' Arrahbella said.

'I'll help,' Alain said, rising from his chair and stretching.

'May I put them away?' Sora asked.

'Of course.'

Arrahbella and Alain left for the kitchen as Sora carefully packed away the knives in their mahogany and velvet case, placing them back on the chest of drawers where they glinted splendidly in the soft lamplight.

The next day, Alain was in the dining car, fixing some freshly squeezed juice, when he heard a yell from the practice room where Melody and Chester had been for the last hour. As he approached, he heard them arguing, but by the time he had knocked and opened the door they were standing with their backs to each other.

'What's going on?' he asked.

Melody whirled around angrily. 'Chester dropped me.'

'I did not. You slipped.'

'No, you were holding me and you let go. That means you dropped me.'

'You fell about thirty centimetres. Onto a mat.'

'That's not the point.'

'Hey, hey, calm down, both of you.' Alain was standing between them now. 'Melody, are you hurt?'

'No.'

'Because you barely fell.'

She gave Chester a cold look. 'That's not the point. It's not that you dropped me, it's that you weren't concentrating. Something's been on your mind lately and you won't tell me what it is. That's why I'm upset.'

Chester chose to look at the ground instead of answering. Melody sighed impatiently and stormed out of the room. Alain watched her go before he turned to Chester.

'Is that true?'

Chester finally looked up, his shining purple eyes meeting Alain's own blue ones. It was one of those rare moments when Chester looked his full twenty-six years.

'You know I'd never put Melody in danger. It was an accident.'

'I know.'

They were silent for a few moments. Chester was now looking at the trapeze behind Alain while the Ringmaster continued to study his jester.

'Chester, even though Melody can seem a little... childish at times, she can also be mature beyond her years. If anything was worrying you, she'd understand. She understands a lot more than we give her credit for.'

Chester smiled. 'I know.'

'And, you know that, despite my being as close to Melody as I am, I wouldn't tell her anything you said to me in confidence.' He paused. 'Well, unless your life or hers were in danger, but we're not talking about anything that drastic, are we?'

'No.'

'Good. Well, my door is open.'

Alain waited a moment longer, then he turned to leave.

'Alain?'

He faced Chester again. Chester pulled up one of the cylindrical stands that Izan used for his act and sat on it, then, with one hand, he magically closed the practice room door behind Alain as the Ringmaster pulled up another, slightly taller, stand and sat across from him. He had to wait a few moments before Chester spoke and even then Chester kept his eyes pretty much on the ground throughout his speech.

'Melody didn't have any boyfriends before me.'

'That's right.'

'I worry sometimes that she wants to be with people her own age, or that she should be. I mean, most of the time the age difference isn't a problem, I hardly ever remember that she's younger than me, but, sometimes I'll see her watching Sora and Asseniah, or looking at a group of people her own age when we're in a town and I wonder what she's thinking.' He shuffled on his stool, put a fist to his mouth and cleared his throat. 'I mean, don't get me wrong, I love Melody, I'd be broken if she did leave me, and I know she loves me and it sounds silly saying it out loud, but I worry sometimes that one day she'll realise I'm older than her and see it as a bad thing. And I wonder if she really is in love with me? I remember when I had my first girlfriend, I thought I was in love with her but I realised after we broke up that I wasn't. What if Melody only thinks she's in love with me because I'm her first boyfriend? It's silly, I know.'

He looked up at Alain now, feeling slightly uncomfortable from his outpour.

Alain thought for a moment before answering, finding the right words. 'Chester, I understand what you're saying and it's perfectly human to have doubts about a relationship. I know that Arrahbella loves me but I still can't help those moments when I worry that I'm not making her happy. And she and I are the same age. Those worries come with being in love and you just have to push through them, knowing that you trust your partner. As for you and Melody, I wouldn't exactly say that you act your age most of the time, Chester, and Melody doesn't act hers. You kind of balance each other out, I think.'

'That's because she's been around you most of her life, Alain. She's learnt a lot about the world from you.'

Alain smiled. 'Well, I don't know about that. I think she had to grow up fast when she and Izan were left on their own. It's always been her nature. Nevertheless, I'm sure that if she were having doubts she'd tell you. She's not one to keep her feelings hidden for long.'

'What if she didn't want to tell me because she thought it might break up the troupe or cause problems?'

'I think Melody would know that, if she were unhappy in the relationship, it would be better to talk to you about it rather than keep that unhappiness bottled up knowing it would cause problems anyway, like it did when you had feelings for her but hadn't yet revealed them.'

Chester looked unconvinced.

'Or, she'd come and ask me for advice, and she hasn't.'

Chester managed a weak smile.

'You just have to trust her.'

'I know. I do.' He sighed. 'Thanks, Alain.'

Alain patted Chester on the shoulder before standing and walking out of the room. He finished making the juices and carried them back through the caravans to his room where he found Arrahbella sitting in her armchair and Melody curled up in his, her eyes downcast. He gave one glass to Arrahbella, giving her a small smile in answer to her knowing expression, then he set his own glass down on the small round table between the two chairs, looked at Melody, folded his arms across his chest, and cleared his throat.

'Ahem. I believe you're in my seat, Miss Melody.'

She looked up at him sadly. 'Did you talk to him?'

'Come on, up you get.'

Melody slowly uncurled herself, rose, and dragged herself to the door where she stopped, holding it slightly open.

'Go on, scoot. You and Chester need to go over those moves so he doesn't drop you again.' He smiled at Arrahbella who smiled back, but when Melody turned to face them, she had tears streaming down her cheeks.

'Is he okay, Alain?'

'Hey.' Alain's expression immediately changed to one

of concern and he reached out his hands to her, beckoning her over. When she was standing in front of him, his fingers lightly brushed the edges of her wings as he drew his hands in to take hold of hers. He looked up at her, his heart aching slightly at the sadness in her eyes.

'Melody, do you love Chester?'

That worried her. 'Why? Does he think I don't? Why would he think that?'

Alain gave her hands a squeeze and she stopped.

'Melody, do you love Chester?'

'I do, Alain, so much. You know I do.' She was whispering now.

'Then everything's going to be okay.' He smiled at her. 'Don't cry, sweet one.' He gently wiped her tears away with his thumbs.

Melody sniffed and nodded.

'Come on.' Alain stood and pulled Melody's head to his chest where he cradled her, careful not to crush her wings. Arrahbella's heart swelled with the sincerity of the moment.

'You know, I think you should show Chester that poem you wrote last night.'

'He won't want to read it right now.'

'I think he will. Here.' He handed Melody her poem from where it had been sitting on the table. She looked it over.

'You can't swap "lips soft as rose petals" and "creamy, silken skin" because then the above two lines won't... oh, you've changed them too.'

'It reads better that way.'

Melody read through the poem and her shoulders slumped. 'Oh, you're right.'

'They're the only bits I changed, Melody.'

She sighed. 'I know.' She walked to the door but stopped and glanced at Arrahbella. 'Men,' she said and left. Arrahbella chuckled.

When the door had closed behind her, Alain heaved a sigh and looked over at his wife. He reached out his hand, which she took, rising from her chair to stand in front of him. Alain wrapped his arms around her, brushed some hair out of her pretty blue eyes, then, he kissed her, squeezing her gently. When they broke away, he rested his head against hers, eyes closed.

'I love you,' he whispered.

Her heart tingled. 'I love you too, Ringmaster.'

Melody placed her poem on Chester's pillow and walked back through Izan's deafening metal music and Asseniah's softer piano melodies to the silent kitchen car, where she knocked gently on the practice room door before entering.

'Chester?'

Chester was still sitting on the cylindrical stand, his face wet with translucent purple tears, the wetness making his eyes shine like amethysts. When he saw her, he attempted to stop crying and wiped his tears away on his sleeve, leaving small purple stains on the white fabric.

'Melody.'

'Chester, what's wrong?' She hurried over to him, putting her hands to his face. Chester hardly ever cried. It

172

just wasn't in his nature. It worried her even more when he broke down at her touch, pulled her toward him, and cried into her chest. Melody fought back tears herself as she stroked his hair and hushed him.

After some lengthy moments, Chester pulled back, stood up, and walked away a few paces, trying to get himself under control.

'Chester, darling, what is it?'

He sniffed a few times before he turned to face her, smiling. 'I'm sorry,' he said. 'I'm just being silly.'

She went over and threw her arms around him. He kissed her hair and stroked the wings he couldn't see, making her shiver. When she looked up at him, he kissed her passionately, then she rested her head on his chest.

'Melody,' he asked after a while. The crying had made his nasal tones even rumblier. 'Do you ever wish you were... with people your own age?'

She looked up in astonishment. 'No. Why do you?'

'No, no. I just worry sometimes that you do. Like last week at Tokinov's Inn, when Sora and Asseniah were flirting with that boy and you were watching them as though you wanted to be having fun with them.'

'Oh, you silly boy! Is that what this is about?'

'I know, it sounds ridiculous, I just...' he faltered. 'I don't know.'

'I was looking at Sora and Asseniah thinking how glad I was that I don't have to play that silly game or worry about impressing every guy I meet. I felt sorry for the poor boy, he looked so uncomfortable. Oh, Chester, you know I love you. I hope you know I love you.'

'I do. I'm sorry. I just wait for the day that you'll realise I'm old.'

'Chester, you don't exactly look or act your age. If I didn't know how old you were I'd guess you couldn't be a day over twenty.'

'That's what Alain said. He said we balance each other out.'

'And he's right. Besides,' she added with a sly smile. 'Maybe you being older is one of the things that attracts me to you.'

He smiled but it quickly vanished as he looked away, absent mindedly fiddling with her feathers. He swallowed hard. 'I am your first boyfriend though. What if you only... think you're in love with me?'

Melody's eyes widened in surprise. 'If this isn't love then I don't particularly want to know what love is because what I'm feeling is already unbearable. All I know is that I feel incredibly deep emotions for you and couldn't imagine being with anyone else. I want to experience your life with you and for you to share mine. I don't want to be apart from you. My heart leaps every time I see you and tingles every time I think of you. I love everything about you. Sometimes I feel I can't get enough of you. All I want is for you to be happy with everything you do in life. If that's not love... if what I'm feeling isn't the deepest it gets, then frankly I'd be terrified of ever being in love because any deeper and I'd melt or explode or... I don't think the human body could handle it. I believe that I'm in love with you. And I don't want to be with anyone else.'

He was tearing up again. That was exactly how he felt about her.

She kissed him. 'You don't have to worry about me. If I ever had any doubts or was worried, I'd tell you.'

He nodded. 'As would I.'

'So, you're okay?'

'Yes.'

They kissed again.

'You know, there's a trapeze over there,' Melody said, slyly.

'And it's off limits.'

'Alain wants us to practice so that you don't drop me again.'

'And we both know that you'd never defy him.'

Melody dropped her seductress act.

'You're right, I wouldn't.'

'Though I do have permission to lock the door.'

'No, Izan does. Come on, we'll just have to go to our bedroom.'

They walked back through to the girls' room and on to Izan's room. The magician was at his favourite mirror (the one that showed him in the best light) preening himself.

'Great Mythos!' he shouted over his music. 'There's been more traffic through here today then there is on the Highway.' He noticed their intertwined hands and smiles. 'Ah, I shall be staying out of your room for at least the next hour.'

'That's probably wise, Izan dear.' Melody ran over and

kissed her brother's cheek, much to his annoyance.

'Ugh! Now I have to readjust every hair, sister.'

She giggled. Chester leapt to Izan's side and ruffled his hair until the magician ducked away and stood up.

'Oh, you'll pay for that, jester!'

He lunged forward, but Melody stood in his way.

'Uh-uh. You can't have him until I've had my way with him.' Melody took Chester's hand and they hurried out of the room leaving Izan to sit back down at his mirror and study his now messy hair.

'I hate it when they're all loved up,' he muttered.

When they reached their bed, Melody quickly pulled the poem off of Chester's pillow and put it on the bedside table.

'What's that?' he asked.

'Read it later,' she replied, pulling him down on top of her. 'Now, I'm going to show you that you have nothing to worry about.'

Thanks to Izan's loud music, the sounds of the couple's lovemaking were drowned out on that side of the train, but Alain and Arrahbella weren't so lucky.

Alain put down his novel and sighed. 'And everything returns to normal,' he said.

Six Years Ago - Varatalé

With the troupe expanding at a steady rate, Alain purchased the manor and they all packed up and moved in a few days after Chester and Oleg had arrived in Varatalé.

On the fifth night in their new home, Chester found himself unable to sleep. He tossed and turned for the umpteenth time before deciding to get up and go to the kitchen to make some tea. There, he was surprised to find the young Melody sitting at the long table, drinking a tea herself, reading a book which Chester (glancing at the front cover) noticed was called *Halliday*, written by an author named Kruitar Vabonn (Melody's favourite author; a Varatalian who wrote gothic-style histories).

'Hi,' he said.

'Hi,' she replied. She seemed surprisingly awake for the late hour. 'Everything okay?'

'I couldn't sleep.'

'Me neither. I think it's the new place. It can take a while to adjust to a new home. You should have some Milksap tea. Arrahbella swears by it. Alain hardly ever sleeps, being a Noir Eternalan, so Arrahbella gives him Milksap before bed and he's out to it. Ironic thing is, it tastes bitter and you have to add heaps of milk. I'll make you some.' She leapt up from her chair and bounced over to the row of canisters containing the teas and herbs.

'Oh, thank you.'

Chester sat at the table. He was bare-chested, wearing only white pants and an open dressing gown, which he did up quickly while Melody's back was turned. Melody was wearing only a loose, white night gown.

Chester searched for something to say. 'Is it true that you have wings, Melody Bell?'

Melody sat across from him, handing over his mug

of tea. The liquid was very white, reminding him of the reflection of the moon on a lake.

'Yes. Izan keeps them invisible.'

'Why?'

'Partly because Alain wants them hidden for the show when we do it, and partly because the people here know about my brother and I and if they see my wings they point and mutter.'

'I know that feeling.'

'Because you were famous in Arelia?'

Melody blushed as Chester looked at her.

'I'm sorry. I overheard you talking to Alain.'

'It's okay.'

They were silent for a moment.

'So, what colour are your wings?'

'White with blue edges.' Melody recognised the look that was now crossing Chester's face. 'Do you want to touch them?'

Even though he had been wondering what they would feel like, Chester was a little startled by this question, but Melody was already moving around the table to sit beside him.

'Most earthbound people want to touch wings when they see a creature that has them. It's another reason Alain wants them kept invisible, because otherwise people keep touching them and they get all damaged. Of course, having them invisible also means people don't know they're there and they brush against them anyway, but oh well. Alain and Izan never forget they're there, when they hug me or pat me on the shoulder, but Mariette always forgets. It does make people jump, though, when they touch them and they can't see them, or when a feather falls out and turns visible again.' She giggled.

Chester watched her with fascination.

'Go on,' she said. She took his hand and placed it on top of her right wing. Chester gently stroked the soft feathers. They felt like velvet. Melody shivered, not unpleasantly.

'What does it feel like?' he asked, quietly. 'Like someone stroking your arm?'

'No. My arm has meat and is strong and is used to being touched. My wings are soft and vulnerable, like touching my stomach or my breasts.'

Chester quickly withdrew his hand.

'Oh, I'm sorry,' she said, her shoulders drooping a little. 'I forget to tell people that before they touch them. Some people feel a bit weird after knowing it's like touching my breasts. I don't go around letting everyone touch them, only the troupe because then they don't want to touch them again. It gets it out of the way.'

'It's okay.'

Melody yawned. 'Well, I think the Milksap is finally melting my brain. I'm gonna go back to bed. 'Night Chester.'

'Goodnight, Melody Bell.'

His purple eyes followed her as she gathered up her book and mug and left the room.

So, the troupe expanded and practiced together over two years and Alain taught them the various ways of the worlds they would be visiting, and they became fluent in every language they would need to use. Then, they toured for the first time.

Just before they left for their second tour, Melody turned sixteen.

Alain, Arrahbella, and Izan arranged a small party for her, inviting the few friends that she had made in Luc'ca. Being her sixteenth, they made it a little more special than her previous birthdays.

The last few guests had arrived and everyone was chatting away happily when Melody made her entrance. No one had ever seen her in anything but her loose pants and tie-up tops, so when she walked down the manor's main staircase, dressed in a long green satin dress with corseted bodice and pink ribbon trimming that Sora had made for her, her brown curls up in an elegant mess, tied with pink ribbon, with a few loose ringlets dangling by her neck, her wings visible, everyone was quite amazed. Chester, however, went warm all over, felt short of breath, and forgot where he was.

Melody, bursting with happiness on the inside at the stares of amazement, glided down the stairs and floated over to her group of friends who were now bubbling with compliments.

'Whoa,' said Izan, who had appeared beside Chester unnoticed, a glass of mead in his hand. 'When did my little sister get a pair of those?'

It took Chester a moment to realise what Izan was talking about. Melody's corset was displaying her set of petite breasts rather more fully than her strict leotard or casual tops usually did. Chester couldn't remember them being so noticeable before now either.

'My little baby sister's all grown up.' Izan clapped Chester on the shoulder before heading off to refill his glass and tease his sister.

Chester stayed in the room for as long as he could, his eyes hardly able to leave Melody's image, unaware that Alain had been watching him for a while. Eventually, though, he had to go outside for some air. He excused himself from watching Melody, Sora, and their friends give a rousing rendition of a Varatalian song and hurried out of the open double doors into the night. He kept going until he was around the side of the manor where he leant against the stone wall, just out of reach of the yellow light flooding out of the sitting room window, trying to breathe.

'Oh, this is not good,' he whispered.

After Melody's party, problems started. Chester thought if he revealed his feelings to Melody she wouldn't return them and then there would be complications with working together. If she did feel the same way and they started something which didn't work out, would that cause problems too? What about Alain? Would he approve? And Izan, his closest friend? Was he too old for her? His feelings certainly didn't think so.

And what were his feelings anyway? Was it just lust? It had been a while since he had been with anyone, and even that had been just a casual fling with a woman from a neighbouring village. Perhaps these feelings would pass in a few weeks. Yes, he would keep quiet, live life as usual, and hope the feelings would disappear.

They didn't.

As the weeks passed, Chester found more and more to fall in love with. Unfortunately, the suppression and confusion of feelings made him grumpy, frustrated, and snappy, and he began to work badly with the others, finding cause for argument and not concentrating properly. Alain kept quiet for the time being, hoping things would resolve themselves.

It wasn't long before Chester was accompanying Izan into Bologn, the town next to Luc'ca, to pick up girls (none of the troupe had any romantic relations with anyone in Luc'ca as a general rule, they were too close to them all). This didn't help to ease his temper, however, and the rest of the troupe watched with growing unease as their beloved jester erupted day after day over the smallest of things.

About a month after Melody's party, Chester ran into her one night in the manor's foyer.

'Hey Chester,' she said, stopping at the bottom of the stairs she had been about to ascend.

'Oh, hey Melody.' He tried not to look at her. She was wearing purple pants and a yellow tie-front top, her bare arms looking delicious in the light from the chandelier, her hair loose and half dry from a shower she had taken a while ago.

'Where are you going?'

'Out.'

'Out with Izan?'

'Yeah.'

'Don't go, Chester,' she said quietly.

'Why?'

'Because, you've been going out a lot lately and it's... well... just don't.'

'What do you care if I go?'

'I do care. Something's changed in you recently and none of us like it.'

Chester felt irksome. He hated that he was disappointing her. He hated how he had become. He hated how she was standing there on the bottom of the steps, looking all gorgeous and caring and he couldn't touch her.

'Melody, I'm fine. Don't worry about me.'

'It's not just me, everyone's worried about you. Even Izan.'

'Well, everyone can just mind their own damn business.' He stormed out.

Melody sighed and turned. She saw Alain standing at the top of the stairs, watching with furrowed brow.

'What's happened to him, Alain?'

'I'll talk to him.'

'Are you going to ask him to leave?'

'Not yet. I think he'll be okay.'

She nodded and continued on up the stairs past her Ringmaster.

The next morning, Alain barged into Chester's room, threw open the blinds, and waited with his hands on his hips as Chester moaned at the sudden onslaught of noise and light.

'Chester, wake up.'

'What in sweet Arelia's name is going on?' he asked,

as he covered his eyes with his hand and tried to sit up.

'You're drunk.'

'No, I was drunk last night. Right now, I'm hungover.'

'Even Izan doesn't get drunk the day before a rehearsal, and if he does, he still turns up on time. You, sir, are late.'

'Fine. I'll be there in a minute.'

Alain's tone changed. 'Chester, we need to talk.'

'Does it have to be now?'

'Yes, it does.' He sat on the edge of Chester's bed as the actor rubbed his eyes and squinted at him. 'We're concerned about you, Chester, all of us. Lately, you've been behaving in a way that isn't who you really are.'

'How do you know who I really am?'

'The Chester we've known for the last three and a half years is fun, willing to work in a team, and always happy, always wanting to make other people happy. Now, you're a marvellous actor, Chester, but three and a half years is a long time to put on an act if that's not who you really are.' Chester didn't say anything. 'No, this change in you has been recent and it's obvious that something is troubling you. I like you, you're a good man, and I think you're perfect for our troupe, but if you don't resolve this problem in the next few days then you'd better be willing to leave. Your problem is risking the safety of the others and I can't have that.' Chester fiddled with the bedcovers. 'I don't want you to leave and I'm sure you don't want to leave either, so please try and resolve whatever it is. I'm willing to help with that if you feel you wish to talk to me.'

Chester looked up at Alain, holding his gaze for a moment, knowing that if it were any other girl on his mind he'd tell Alain in a heartbeat, but, then, if it were any other girl he wouldn't have a problem. So, he nodded instead.

'I'm sorry, Alain, I'll work it out.'

'Good.' He patted him on the shoulder and stood up. 'Now, get dressed and come to rehearsal.'

Chester groaned. 'Does Arrahbella have anything for hangovers?'

Alain turned at the door. 'Yes, but you don't get out of it that easily. You get drunk the night before a rehearsal, that's your own fault.' He left the room, closing the door behind him.

Chester remained quiet for the rest of the day, mulling over his decision. He worked well with the others during that rehearsal and everyone relaxed, feeling happier without him snapping at them.

In the evening, when they all sat down together for dinner, Chester remained lost in thought. Not even the fact that Arrahbella had made his favourite meal, an Arelian dish known as Honeymesh (which resembled Earthling teriyaki) could help to brighten his spirits. He didn't even notice what he was eating, moving the fork to his mouth in robotic style.

After dinner, the troupe hung about in their favourite sitting room, doing individual things, tired from the day's rehearsal, sleepy from the meal: Alain and Arrahbella were in the plush armchairs, reading, next to the fireplace which hardly ever needed to be lit; Oleg and Mariette were playing chess (Mariette was never a good chess player and always lost but she enjoyed it so it didn't matter); Sora was illustrating one of her new comics; Melody was sprawled out at Alain and Arrahbella's feet, also reading; Asseniah had retreated to her tower to converse with her piano; Izan was at the village Inn, or someone's house, or in Bologn, no one really knew; the dwarves were still in Terrenvale but would be arriving soon for the tour; and Chester was on the lounge, facing the fireplace. He was thinking, watching Melody as she swung her legs back and forth, looking up at the other troupe members, looking into the fireplace once more.

Eventually, Alain closed his book and quietly told Arrahbella he was going to do some work up in his office. Chester waited about five minutes after he'd left and then followed, knocking quietly on the heavy wooden door.

'Come in.'

Chester opened the door and looked in. 'Alain, could I have a word with you?'

'Of course. Come in, Chester.' The Wordmaster put down his pen and sat back in his chair as Chester closed the door, pulled up the red leather armchair so it was in front of Alain's desk, and sat down. The beautiful mahogany desk was the feature of the small circular room, taking up most of the cluttered space. The large window behind Alain was almost always kept covered to avoid the room getting too hot. Objects from every world dotted the shelves, including a rug from Kartan with patterns that constantly swirled and changed, a large framed photograph of Canada's Lake Louise from Earth, a vial containing pure music (a sparkling, colourful, misty substance) from Terrenvale, a crystal container holding one of Duke Alcino Bell's blue and white feathers, and another crystal container housing a pen made from Alain's own flesh – the result of a rather unfortunate meeting with a witch in Landau.

Alain waited patiently as Chester looked around the room, nervously.

'I'm going to have to leave,' he finally said. 'I'm sorry. I've thought about it and it's for the best. I'm only sorry I have to leave you so close to the tour.'

Alain paused before answering.

'The problem can't be resolved?' he asked.

'I don't know. I've tried to think of how it might be, but I don't think I can risk staying here in case it can't.'

'And you're sure you don't want to talk about it?'

'Yes. I think it's better for everyone if I just go.'

Alain nodded thoughtfully, his mind working fast. After a moment, he stood up and reached out his hand. Chester took it firmly.

'Alright. You'll be missed, Chester from the Apricot Meadows. You're a good man and an excellent performer and I've no doubt you'll do well in life. Thank you for everything you've done over the years, it's been a pleasure.'

'Thank you, Alain du Maurier. You've got a good thing going here. I hope it continues to be a success.'

Alain smiled sadly. 'Where will you go?'

'I don't know. I don't particularly wish to go back to Arelia. Right now, I'm going to the Inn. I'll stay there tonight.'

'You're welcome to stay here until you make other arrangements.'

'Thank you, but I need to go tonight.'

Alain decided that fate needed a helping hand at this point.

'Chester, if it's about a woman...' He paused to judge Chester's reaction. When the actor didn't protest he continued. 'And, you feel you can't reveal your feelings to her, for whatever reason that may be, my advice would be to try telling her anyway. People tend to like being told that they're loved, it's one of the greatest compliments of all, and, even if they don't reciprocate the feelings, they'll generally let you down gently. If you never tell them, you'll always be wondering if they feel the same way, you won't be comfortable loving another, and bottling it up can have serious consequences. Could you live with all that turmoil?'

Chester had been biting his lower lip during this speech, but then he seemed to melt with anxiety and the need to release the thoughts that had been going around and around in his head for weeks was so great that he opened up.

'But, if I tell her, it could ruin our friendship. I don't want to lose that. I mean, do you tell them and risk never seeing them again, or do you keep it in and at least have the pleasure of their company and friendship?'

'Love is a powerful emotion. It's brought down kingdoms, spawned worlds, killed. It can do damage if it's ignored. Sometimes telling the person helps you to get over them, if you can't have them. At least then they know, so if ever there was a time when things change or they feel unloved in their life, at least they'd know that somewhere, someone loves them. And if something were to happen to you tomorrow, at least you've told them. It doesn't have to get in the way of friendship either. But, kept inside, it creates all sorts of problems.'

'There are other factors involved, Alain, and if it meant that those other factors remained unaffected then I'd rather be the only one in turmoil than risk hurting others just so that I can sleep at night.'

Alain knew he could say no more so he nodded slowly and smiled understandingly.

'Please tell the others I say goodbye,' Chester added. He gave Alain a final nod and left the room.

Alain played with his beard while he thought, then, he, too, got up and left, headed in Melody's direction.

Sora had gone to the practice room to use the tightrope but the others were still in the sitting room, Melody now in the armchair that Alain had vacated. He walked over to her, tapped her gently on the arm, and motioned that she should follow him out of the room. Melody closed her book and did so as Arrahbella watched them in her serene way over the top of her own novel, fully aware of what was evolving.

'Melody, Chester's decided to leave us,' Alain told her, once he had closed the sitting room door.

She looked crestfallen. 'Really? Why?'

'He has his reasons. I'd like you to talk to him.'

'Me? Why me? Shouldn't Izan talk to him?'

Alain shook his head. 'Izan's not too good at serious

talks and he gets distracted too easily. No, this is something I'd like you to do.'

Melody looked unconvinced. 'Okay, Alain, but I really don't know what I can do.'

He put a hand on her shoulder. 'Trust me.'

'Don't I always?'

He smiled. A wave of emotion suddenly swept over him and he gathered her up in an embrace, catching her by surprise. When he released her, she gave him an amused expression.

'You'll find Chester at the Inn. He's planning to sleep there tonight.'

'Oh, that means I have to go get dressed up,' she complained, and went back into the sitting room to collect her novel.

Once Melody had left, looking suitably attractive in another Sora-made dress, this time in pink, Alain returned to his armchair in the sitting room. He gave Arrahbella a glance that told her everything and squeezed her hand. She squeezed his in return.

Chester was sitting at the Inn's bar, slouched over, drinking. Not even alcohol was helping to numb the empty, painful feeling that had taken up residence in his chest since he had left the manor. He half-noticed someone sit on the stool next to him but didn't look up from his glass.

'Good evening, Melody,' Giorgio, the barman, greeted heartily in his booming voice.

Chester looked up quickly. There she was, sitting next to him, smiling her gorgeous smile. He felt the familiar sensation of wanting to reach out, pull her to him, and kiss her, then, the pain that always followed.

'Hello, Giorgio.'

'What will you have tonight?'

'Umm, just a lemon and lime, thanks.'

Giorgio turned his broad back to prepare the drink as Melody turned on her stool to face Chester. He was dressed in black Varatalian pants and a purple Varatalian shirt which, when combined with the strange lighting of the Inn, made his purple eyes shine brighter than ever. His porcelain smooth cheeks were a little flushed from the mead and the stuffy room, and, possibly, from seeing her.

'Hey.'

'Hey,' he replied, completely stupefied as to why she might be there.

'Alain tells me you're leaving us.'

'He's right.'

'He didn't tell everyone, just me.'

Chester didn't say anything.

'He sent me to talk to you but I don't know why 'cause I don't know what your reason is.'

Chester stared at her for a moment then turned back to the bar top, shaking his head as realisation came to him. He began to laugh.

'What's so funny?' Melody asked, amused.

'Alain sent you?'

She nodded.

He laughed again but looked at her. He figured he had to tell her now, he was leaving anyway, so it couldn't do him any harm, and, he just had to get it off his chest. Alain had been right.

Melody was beginning to think Chester had had too much to drink. 'Are you alright?'

Chester stood up, moved closer to her, looked into her eyes for a moment, placed a hand to her head and stroked her curls before gently pulling her head to his and kissing her softly. Then, he pulled away, watching to see how she reacted. Her cheeks had turned a soft pink and she looked a little surprised but he took this as a good sign and kissed her again. This time, she put her arms around him and returned the kiss, so he kissed her more passionately, feeling months of love and longing explode out of him. Melody was just as passionate; looking at Chester's delicious mouth was one thing, kissing it was quite another. Chester felt so overwhelmed with relief that he had to stop kissing her to rest his head on her shoulder, all the time stroking her wings, her hair, feeling her shiver with the contact, her chest rising and falling next to his as they tried to catch their breath. After a moment, when the emotions had calmed slightly, he raised his head to look at her.

'I love you, Melody.' He could barely speak.

It took her a moment to find her voice as well. 'And you were going to leave rather than tell me?'

'I was scared I was too old for you and I didn't want to upset Izan and Alain. I didn't know what to do. I've been watching you while we rehearse, while you read, every moment, just longing to tell you. I've tried to forget the feelings by drinking or sleeping with other women, but all

I do is close my eyes and pretend they're you. I can't sleep, I can't eat, I can't think...'

'Oh, Chester, you really are messed up about it,' she said, compassionately, brushing some sandy-blonde hair out of his eyes. He was still holding her shoulders, both of them unaware that Giorgio and everyone else in the Inn were watching on with amusement.

Melody kissed him again. She didn't think she'd ever be able to get enough of those lips.

'So, you're okay with it?' he asked.

She seemed to melt. 'Chester, I've been in love with you since the day we met.'

Chester could have died with happiness, right then and there on that mead-stained floor. He gathered her up in his arms and kissed her again. This time, they kissed so passionately and for so long that Giorgio, who could see hands roaming and things heating up, cleared his throat. When they looked at him he was holding out a key to one of his rooms upstairs and motioning that they should head up there because the other patrons were beginning to cheer. Chester reached for the key but Melody stopped his hand with hers, shaking her head.

'Follow me.' She pulled him along after her as she hurried out of the Inn before Chester stopped, dashed back to Giorgio, slapped some money on the bar top, gave him a huge grin, and ran out after her once more.

The two of them kept running through the village then along the road that led to the manor. It was a fair distance but they were young and fit and pumped full of happiness.

'Where are we going?' Chester asked her.

'Just follow me,' she replied, and Chester was relieved to see her go past the manor's main doors and around the side. He didn't particularly want to face the others just yet.

The manor's surrounding farmland was owned by Alain, but, as he didn't have much need for it, he let the neighbouring farmers use it for free. Melody led Chester to the nearest field where one of the farmers had erected a barn that housed horses. Running into the barn, she fell back on to one of the piles of hay, pulling Chester down on top of her. Chester could barely contain himself, the run had helped occupy his body but now that they had stopped and he was lying on top of her, feeling her chest rise and fall against his, all that desire came flooding back and it took a mammoth effort for him to pull away from her, take a few breaths, and look down at her seriously.

'Are you sure you want to do this? We can wait if you want?'

She paused for a moment, but when she replied with, 'I'm sure,' he knew she meant it.

Still, he asked again. 'Absolutely sure? You're not going to wake up in the morning and regret it?'

Melody grabbed his shirt, pulling him down to her again. 'Shut up and kiss me, boy.'

He did.

In the morning, when neither of them turned up for breakfast and still hadn't appeared just before lunch, Alain knocked on both their bedroom doors, then, when only silence answered him and he opened them to find their beds empty, he went into the village to see Giorgio. Giorgio gave him a detailed and exaggerated account of what had occurred, so Alain went to the barn, knowing it was a place Melody often liked to escape to when she was feeling cramped in the manor of eight other residents. There, he found the pair snuggled up in the hay under a horse blanket, their clothes in a pile next to them, hay and feathers strewn through their hair. Alain smiled and left them.

A short time later, Chester and Melody returned to the manor. They pretended everything was as usual for the afternoon, though they couldn't resist giving each other glances or brushing against one another. No one else knew that Chester had told Alain he was leaving and because Alain had given them the morning off (predicting that Melody and Chester would need it) none of them really noticed that they had been missing or that anything was different, except perhaps that the general mood was lighter and happier.

They rehearsed all that afternoon and into the evening. When Alain casually suggested that Chester might like to learn the trapeze, the pair enthusiastically agreed.

After dinner, Chester, once again, went to seek out Alain, finding him in the sitting room alone with Arrahbella.

'Chester, good to see you back,' Alain said, cheerfully.

'Well, it seems the problem has resolved itself. I just hope it stays that way.'

Alain nodded. 'I'm glad.'

Chester hesitated before asking, 'How did you know?'

'Ah. When you walked onto the stage in Arelia on the night we met, Arrahbella had images of the two of you together, happy images, but she blocked them before she saw too many... And it wasn't too hard to notice the way you've been looking at her lately.'

Chester nodded. 'Well, thank you. I promise I'll take good care of her.' He paused. 'I love her.'

Alain smiled. Arrahbella watched with serene amusement.

'I'm sure you will.' Chester nodded and turned to leave. 'But, Chester, remember that if you ever make her unhappy you'll not only have me to answer to but Izan as well.'

Chester felt a small wave of anxiety hurdle through him, even though he had known this fact for a while. He nodded and left.

Alain looked over at Arrahbella.

'They're so cute,' she said, scrunching up her nose adorably.

Alain smiled, sadly.

'You're worried.'

He sighed. 'They spent the night together.'

'Of course they did.'

'She's just so young.'

Arrahbella squeezed his hand. 'She's a smart girl. Chester's smart too, and he's a good guy, he'll look after her.'

'I know, but they're so full of lust at the moment. All afternoon, they've had that look in their eyes like they want to devour each other.'

'Like the one you still give me?'

'Yes, that's the one,' he said with a smile. 'I guess I'm worried that Melody tends to think with her heart most of the time.'

'That's why she needs you, because you're her head.'

Alain leaned closer to her. 'Well, maybe now Chester can be her head and you can have all of me.'

She rubbed her nose against his. 'I already have all I need of you. You've got so much to give that other people get pieces of you too.' She kissed him. 'But that's one of the things I love about you, Alain du Maurier.'

He kissed her tenderly.

'Besides,' Arrahbella said, casually. 'She's been taking a contraceptive since she turned sixteen.'

Alain blinked at her. 'I didn't know that.'

The Earthling shrugged. 'There are some things you don't necessarily need to know, Alain.' She smiled sympathetically. 'I know Melody tells you everything, but she obviously didn't feel you needed to know that and, now that she's with Chester, there will probably be a lot more that she won't want to share. I very much doubt she'll tell you about last night.'

Alain's eyes went to the floor as he pondered this. Arrahbella watched him, smiling serenely.

'You know,' he eventually said. 'I always knew she wouldn't be with us forever, it's just that it's always seemed so far off in the future. But, it's beginning now, isn't it?'

Arrahbella nodded. 'There will be times in her life when she'll get hurt, Alain, and there will be nothing you can do except to let her get hurt.'

He closed his eyes for a moment.

'You can't keep her wings invisible forever.'

A smile played at the corners of Alain's mouth.

'Too corny?' she asked.

'Just a tad, my dear.'

She giggled.

'It wasn't half as bad as this book, though,' he assured her, despairingly, looking at the Arelian novel in his hand. 'I've tried to persevere but it really is quite nauseating.' He flopped it onto the floor and picked up another from the table beside him.

Arrahbella returned to her own novel, but a few minutes later she noticed Alain's gaze had drifted from the page to the window, his thoughts somewhere else entirely.

CHAPTER 8

Present Day - Ormance

Four weeks after leaving Earth, the train came to a stop in a field on the outskirts of Kutiko-mi. Alain set off for the palace as soon as the engine had come to a halt, Izan hurtling out of the train after him.

'I'm coming with you, Alain,' he said, tying his cloak around his neck.

The Wordmaster sighed. 'Izan, the Empress will never succumb to your advances.'

Izan put his nose in the air. 'You don't know that.'

'Setana knows that love can bring down empires. She has never had a lover and she never will have one.'

'But that's exactly why I want to love her,' he whined. 'She looks so lonely.'

'She is also a very proud woman and thinks you only sleep with people for physical gratification, and, if she did give in to you, she fears you would become bored with her and no longer pay her any attention.'

Izan looked offended. 'I do not only sleep with people for the physical side of things. I love loving people. Everyone should feel loved. I love every person I've ever slept with equally. And I certainly wouldn't get bored of her. I don't get bored of anyone. I've gone back to some people at least twenty times. I just think she's a lonely woman who could use some love and I want to see what adventures under the covers such a powerful woman can give me in return.'

Alain stopped walking and looked at his magician. 'I know that, Izan, you don't have to explain yourself to me. I also know that you only use your magic on a small scale and so it's imperative to your wellbeing that you let off steam somehow. But, unless you can prove that to Setana, which you have no way of doing, then you'll never have her.' He smiled pleasantly.

Izan kicked a loose rock and watched it roll away to the side of the road. 'I've never met anyone I couldn't have, Alain.'

The Ringmaster leaned in closer and lowered his voice. 'That's not true, Izan; you can't have Arrahbella or Chester, and I certainly don't want you.'

Izan made a face. 'You're like a father to me, Alain, so that thought is just gross. And as for Arrahbella and Chester… troupe members don't count.'

Alain studied him for a moment more before turning and continuing on down the road.

Inside the throne room, the men fell to their knees before Setana. Today, the Empress was dressed in blue and gold and looking just as magnificent and deceptively doll-like as she had the day that Alain had met Sora. The usual ladies and guards were seated or standing around the room, looking at the newcomers with unreserved curiosity, though, in truth, most eyes were on Izan, some of the ladies blushing under their heavy makeup.

The performers kept their heads bowed to the matted floor until Setana addressed them.

'Cirque du Phantastique has arrived then has it, Master du Maurier?'

Alain looked up. His shirt, as always, was partly open, revealing the Empress' emblem hanging around his neck. 'It has indeed, Empress Setana. We hope we can provide you with a few nights of entertainment.'

'As do I. I look forward to seeing you tonight. Your show is always exciting.'

'Thank you, Your Highness, you're very kind.'

Setana's narrow black eyes turned to settle on Izan's still bowed form. 'And I see Master Bell is with you... as usual.'

Izan raised his head and gave her his most handsome smile. 'Your Highness, I would never pass up the opportunity to be in your presence.' He would have loved to have kissed her delicate light brown hand, but he knew that if he took so much as a step closer to her, even by accident, he would be set upon by all the guards in the room. Instead, he contented himself by giving her a look full of meaning. The other ladies in the room giggled behind their elaborately decorated fans or looked on with longing. Setana's eyes flicked to her ladies, her courteous smile still on her face, and they instantly fell silent.

'Master du Maurier, you must be proud of such a

complimentary young man.'

Alain knew by her tone that she was in a good mood, but, even so, he had to choose his words carefully. 'Izan certainly has a way about him, Madam,' he replied.

'You are partly responsible for his upbringing, are you not?'

'It is true, Your Highness, that when Izan and his sister were orphaned, I and my friend, Mariette, took them in, but Izan was already a young man at this stage and was...' He shot a sideways glance at Izan, 'past being brought up.'

Izan's eyes had never left Setana and at Alain's words he gave her such a wide, cheesy grin that the ladies were set off into a fit of giggles once more. Setana raised her eyebrows.

'But,' Alain continued. 'Izan is a good man and dearly loved by all the troupe.'

She nodded. 'Well, as usual, Master Bell, you will need a guard.' She raised her right hand, moved her fingers ever so slightly, and the nearest guard stepped forward to stand beside the magician. Ever since Izan had managed to seduce some of the Kutiko priestesses, resulting in them having to repent heavily and painfully, Setana had ordered that he be escorted. This didn't stop him bedding the other women of the city though, especially since the Ormancian women were usually so repressed that they went wilder than most when they were with him. 'And, as usual, Master du Maurier, you and the rest of your troupe are free to travel at leisure provided that the peace and respect are kept.'

'Thank you, Your Highness,' Alain replied with a bow. 'We always enjoy the tranquillity of your beautiful city.'

'Do you need any guards for your train?'

'If one or two could be spared, I would be most grateful, ma'am.'

Setana flicked her fingers again and two more guards stepped forward.

'You will accompany Master du Maurier to his train and watch over it for him. You are to do his bidding.'

The guards bowed before taking up positions on either side of Alain.

'Before you go, could you give me a word?'

'Which word would you like, Empress?'

'Any word you wish. You are the Wordmaster.'

Alain had to think for a moment, this was a bit of a challenge. Deciding on the obvious, he wrote "solace" in Ormanican script in the air with his finger and, when Setana smiled, he pushed it toward her. The white smoky word floated delicately over to the throne where it rested in Setana's hands, solidified, and took on a form that resembled black lace. She pressed it to her heart and it sunk into her soul, making her shiver briefly. Izan shot Alain an envious look.

'Thank you, Alain. Until tonight.' She nodded.

The men bowed and left with their guards.

Once they were outside the palace, Izan practically ran down the street toward the city's centre, heading for the local ladies, forcing his guard to stride quickly after him while issuing a series of reminders about keeping the tranquillity.

'See you tonight, Alain,' he called back with a wave.

'Don't wear yourself out before the show,' Alain called back, then he sighed; Izan never wore himself out, he just kept going.

Back in the caravan train, the troupe were getting ready to stretch their legs about the town.

'Right, everyone,' Alain announced, once he had stepped into the girls' bedroom. 'I want you all back two hours before the show. We will probably be invited to a gathering at the palace afterwards but I want you to make sure you have a healthy dinner anyway, please.'

'Alain, it's Ormance. It's impossible to have an unhealthy dinner,' Sora pointed out.

'Well you know what I mean. I don't want you all so weighed down by noodles that you can't move.'

'But Alain,' Melody whined, teasing. 'That's what we're here for. Sora, Asseniah, Chester, and I are off to the Red Snake for lunch.'

'Well, fill up for lunch then have lighter meals later.'

'Alright,' they sighed and left.

'We're going to visit the Furo Temple,' Fenton said. 'We'll be back mid-afternoon to help set up.'

'Thank you, Fenton.'

'Oleg and I are going to 'ave lunch at ze small 'otel on... what is ze name of zat street?'

'Willow Street?' Oleg suggested.

'Oh, yes, of course. Ze small 'otel on Willow Street. Would you like to join us?'

Alain looked at Arrahbella.

'No, thank you, Mariette. I think Arrahbella and I will spend some time alone.'

The giant offered his arm to the dancer and escorted her out of the caravan.

'And where do you wish to go, my dear?' Alain asked, taking Arrahbella's hands in his.

'I think I'd like some tea and then I'd like to buy a dagger.'

Something about that sentence was wonderfully erotic for Alain.

'Then it's tea and daggers you shall have,' he said.

The pair walked out onto the street, still holding hands. Alain nodded to the guard standing on that side of the train, then he and Arrahbella walked lazily into the town centre to their favourite tea house. Ormance made the finest tea along the Highway, but it was unavailable in any other world as it had to be used the day it was picked.

Not far away, Chester, Melody, Sora, and Asseniah were walking slowly through the pretty streets, admiring the eternally glowing paper lanterns that floated magically above them while yamuis scrambled about their feet or flew up into the trees. Because it was lunchtime, the Ormancians had finished their morning routines and were now filing into the eateries as the clouds burst forth again and sprinkled them with rain. Some were wearing their red and gold robes, others were dressed in normal Ormancian wear – long sleeved, wrap around tops, and loose pants. Those they passed would glare at the quartet and make comments to their companions.

'It's shameful that the Empress allows them to walk around without a Guard,' they would say.

'That girl is a disgrace to the Ormancian name,' said

others, eyeing Sora with disdain. 'It's lucky she doesn't live here anymore or I'd petition for her death.'

Sora ignored them as she strode past, revelling in the chance to be free of Ormancian rule by wearing a deep red dress with a neckline that plunged to her waist, revealing a large "V" of her bare olive chest, and slits from ankle to hip. The long sleeves were see-through and the trim was gold. It was one of her most expressive creations.

'Here we are,' announced Melody, as she stopped in front of a small, flap-covered doorway sitting under a tiny veranda. This was the Red Snake Noodle House, the place they always went to eat when in Kutiko-mi as it was run by Hato Hiro, one of the few locals who treated them with courtesy.

Ducking through the entrance flaps, they entered and stood in the doorway, inhaling the aromas of fresh vegetables and sesame oil as their eyes adjusted to the dim interior. The buzz of conversation died slightly as all eyes turned to look at them.

'They're all men,' Melody whispered.

'The women eat with their families until they're married,' Sora reminded her. 'And then they cook for their husband at home. These men are single or engaged.'

'Oh yeah.' She looked at Chester. 'Don't expect that to happen. I can't cook to save myself.'

Chester grimaced. 'I know. It's a good thing we live with Arrahbella.'

Melody stuck her tongue out at him. Chester smiled and stroked her wing.

Picking a path carefully through the cramped and crowded room, they headed toward the eating bar that separated the dining room from the open kitchen. A glass display case sat to one side showcasing samples of the meals available, the only source of colour in the otherwise brown and white room. The hiss of steam from the kitchen tried to outdo the calming music filtering out of an old CD player.

'Uh-oh,' Chester said quietly, looking at the man behind the counter. 'It's Tanuto.'

Tanuto was Hato's brother and quite the opposite in personality.

'Maybe Hato's out the back?' Melody replied.

'Hey, there's Izan,' Sora announced, pointing to the counter. Izan and his guard were sitting with their backs to the room, hunched over their meals, Izan's cloak flowing down the back of the stool and touching the spotless floor. The others took up the seats next to him.

'What are you doing here?' Melody asked him. 'I thought you'd have been holed up in a bed somewhere.'

Izan slurped up some noodles. 'I've already been there and done that, sister dear. Then, I realised I was famished, so I'm here for some lunch while my dear lady feasts with her family, then I shall return to her side.' He grinned at them then turned to his guard. 'May I introduce Empirial Guard Eriko.'

Eriko looked at them but gave no sign of acknowledgement, even when they nodded and said hello.

They had barely made up their minds as to what to order when Tanuto stormed over and glared down at them from behind the display case, his large, round face like a thunder cloud ready to burst forth with a downpour.

'I don't want your kind in my restaurant,' he growled. 'Remove yourselves.'

The buzz of the restaurant died as every pair of eyes turned to see if an argument was about to erupt.

'Hato always welcomes us,' said Chester, politely.

'Hato no longer runs this restaurant, I do.'

Melody frowned. 'What happened to Hato?'

'He moved to Tamayuma. Three months ago.'

Sora eyed the watching crowd, giving them deathly stares. Nobody turned away.

'We love the food here,' Chester said, still trying to remain polite and calm. 'We'd just like to eat, that's all. We won't cause you any trouble.'

Tanuto's temper had been bubbling under the surface but now it boiled over. 'I don't serve freaks and murderers,' he snarled. Sora turned in her stool to give him a look full of loathing.

Izan moved to stand up, about to defend his friend, but Eriko put a hand on his arm, pushing him back into his seat, as he stood up slowly.

'Master Hiro,' he said. 'You have no right to remove these people from your house, they are friends of the Empress and have done nothing to disturb the peace. If you feel differently you are required to notify an Empirial Guard and it will be up to him to determine whether they should be removed or not.'

Eriko was right and everyone knew it. Izan looked

at him with renewed appreciation. Tanuto looked at him as though he would very much like to strangle him.

'They are disturbing the peace,' he said in a low voice. 'Nobody's eating anymore and you're an Empirial Guard so do something about it.'

Eriko sat back down. 'I don't think they are, Tanuto. You may serve them now.'

A vein pulsed dangerously in the chef's forehead. He turned to Chester and through clenched teeth he spat, 'What can I get for you, sir?'

'You know,' Chester said with disinterest. 'I don't think I want to eat here anymore. Do you girls?'

'No,' said Sora and Melody. Asseniah shook her head.

'From memory, there's a nice little place a couple of streets away,' added Sora.

'You're right, mistress,' Eriko said. 'The Black Pig.'

'Sounds good,' said Chester, getting off the stool and walking toward the door.

'Give our regards to your brother,' Melody said to Tanuto, who had turned red, looking very similar to the snake on the sign outside.

Izan and Eriko followed the other four out of the small building. As soon as they were on the street they heard bursts of glass shattering as the entire display case exploded. This was quickly followed by shouts of anger and surprise and the patrons of the Red Snake quickly filed out into the street, hurrying away in all directions. Sora, Melody, and Chester looked at Izan suspiciously.

'What?' he asked, genuinely offended. 'It wasn't me this time.'

They looked at Asseniah who shrugged innocently. Eriko was unimpressed.

Izan smiled broadly and patted the guard on the shoulder. 'Innocent until proven guilty, my good man. You were quite inspiring in there.'

'I was simply reminding Master Hiro of the law.'

'Ah, but you did it with style. I'm going to buy you dinner for that.'

'He's a horrible man,' Melody scowled. 'I'm going to miss Hato, he was the only one who treated us like humans in this place.'

Asseniah saw some of the Red Snake patrons standing nearby, glaring at them, so she gave them a wide-eyed stare and they fled at the sight of her swirling green eyes.

Chester laughed. 'Well, I suppose we don't make it easy on ourselves, do we?' He took Melody's hand. 'Come on, I'm hungry.'

Despite the cold reception they received during the day, the tent was always full at night. Humans were odd creatures. But, the people of Ormance were just like any other audience, all looking for a short escape from reality, and Cirque du Phantastique treated them as such. The tent was a world all of its own after all, a magical place where anything was possible.

After the show, the troupe was standing outside in the cool night air as the dwarves packed up loose equipment inside and Arrahbella held readings. Empress Setana glided up to Alain, flanked by guards, looking as calm as if she had just been soaking in the Kutiko Hot Springs, not spent an hour in a small, crowded tent.

'Marvellous show, Alain,' she said. 'As always.'

Alain bowed. The others followed his lead.

'Thank you, Your Highness. It is our pleasure.'

'It would be my pleasure if you and your troupe would join me at the palace for a feast tonight. No doubt you are all hungry after such an energetic show. You will be my guests of honour.'

'Empress, you are very kind. We would be delighted to attend. My troupe will just get changed into more suitable clothing and then they will hasten to your palace. I'm afraid that Arrahbella and I will be a little later as we must wait for her to finish her readings.'

'Of course,' she smiled. 'You are welcome whenever you can make it.'

The Empress and the Wordmaster bowed to each other, then, Setana swept around and sailed away.

'Damn, she's gorgeous,' Izan breathed, once she was out of ear shot.

Alain turned to face his troupe. 'Indeed, Izan, the Empress is a stunning woman.'

'And, out of your league,' Chester added.

Izan zapped him.

'Ow!' Chester tried to zap him back but Izan blocked it before it could hit him.

'You're too predictable, jester,' he snorted.

211

Chester folded his arms and smiled. 'Izan, look behind you.'

Izan turned to see a fireball quickly making its way along the ground toward the hem of his cloak. Yelping, he leapt aside, freezing the flames with a bolt of ice at the same time. The others laughed – all except for Asseniah, who got down on her knees and examined the frozen flame with fierce curiosity.

'Taking sides now, are we?' Izan grumbled at Sora.

She shrugged innocently as Alain held up his hands. 'Now, now, children, that's enough. Go and get changed and hurry to the palace.'

The feast was held in one of the palace's long spacious rooms and was already well under way by the time the troupe arrived. One of the walls had been slid aside, revealing the leafy garden behind it. Lamps floated just below the ceiling, giving everything a golden glow, while dragonflies darted around the guests in a brilliance of colour. Long tables piled with trays of food and drink lined the walls and at one end of the room, a small group of musicians played traditional Ormancian drums and stringed instruments. There was a crowd of people, Setana had invited the wealthy as well as the most respected citizens – teachers, priests, former guards, and the like.

The Empress was standing a short distance away, talking to a tall, thin man, laughing elegantly when he made an amusing comment. When she saw the troupe, she excused herself from him and floated over, two guards stuck to her side.

'Welcome, welcome. Please help yourself to as much food and drink as you'd like and enjoy yourselves.'

They bowed in unison and she moved away to welcome more arrivals.

'I'll be over there,' Izan announced, and with a swirl of cloak, he disappeared among the crowd, bee-lining for a couple of ladies who were standing in a corner.

'We'll be eating,' announced Chester, taking Melody's hand and dashing off toward the tables. A number of female eyes were instantly drawn to Chester as he moved through the room, looking ever so delicious in a simple white shirt and black pants, and they lingered on his form until their male partners cleared their throats. Melody had undergone one of her transformations, changing from her trapeze outfit into a beautiful purple silk dress that she had bought in Varatalé. It was fitted well around her torso but moved and floated freely around her legs.

'Oleg, would you like to dance?'

'Thank you, Mariette, I'd love to.'

He hooked his arm through hers and led her to the area in front of the band. Some of the couples already dancing decided it was time to take a break when they saw the giant bump his way into their midst, unaware he was actually as delicate on his feet as he was with a paintbrush.

'Let's check out the band,' Fenton suggested to the other four dwarves. 'Ormancians have such strange instruments.' The five of them scurried off, ducking and darting between people's legs.

Asseniah pointed to the band as well. She was wearing

a dress that Sora had made for her a number of months ago. It was deep red, like her silks, reflecting their style; a halter neck that snaked down her small body in folds and cascades. Her hair was long and straight, as always, making her stand out strikingly against the sea of dark Ormancians, just like Mariette.

'Okay,' Sora nodded, and watched as Asseniah skirted the dance floor to take up a chair next to the dwarves, leaving her alone in the doorway. She was wearing a deep blue dress that looked as though she had simply taken a piece of the sea and wrapped it around her lithe form. Thin straps held it up, criss-crossing at the back, and the skirt was in messy strips with a mix of pale blue to create a two-tone effect.

The Ormancian looked around, unsure of what to do. More people were entering behind her, forcing her to move out of the way. Deciding to get herself a drink, she headed over to the tables. With a glass of heatberry juice in one hand and a piece of vegetable slice on a small napkin in the other, she scanned the room, eventually spotting an empty chair along the far wall. She walked through the crowd and claimed it, setting her drink on the floor just beside the front leg of the chair. As she ate, she watched her friends dancing, eating, talking, and, in Izan's case, tongue wrestling. Alain and Arrahbella arrived, dressed neatly but casually, and spent some time talking to Setana.

Turning to watch Asseniah and the dwarves staring in awe at the band, Sora noticed a boy of about her own age watching her from the opposite side of the room. When their eyes met and the boy blushed and looked away, she took the chance to study him. He was handsome, with typical black hair and brown almond-shaped eyes, tall, and athletically built. He didn't seem to be with anyone or doing anything, just leaning against the wall with his hands behind his back. He was wearing black pants, a white shirt that overlapped itself to button up on the side, and slipper-style, silk shoes. His eyes flicked up again and when he saw her still looking in his direction he gave her a guilty smile. Sora looked away, not sure yet what to think about him.

As the night crept on, Sora kept her eye on the boy, noticing that he kept an eye on her too. Finally, when the chair next to her emptied, the boy gathered up his courage, walked over, and sat down.

'Hi,' he said.

'Hi,' she replied.

'You're Sora?'

'Yes.'

'Is it true you can command fire?'

'Yes.'

'And you make clothes?'

'Yes.'

'Did you make that dress?'

'Yes.'

'Who taught you to sew?'

'I did.'

'You taught yourself?'

'Yes.'

'That's pretty cool.'

There was a moment's silence.

'I'm Taran,' he said, putting out his hand.

Sora studied it for a moment, noticing a number of scars, before shaking it.

Across the room, Asseniah had left the band and had taken the seat next to Melody and Chester. When she noticed Sora talking to Taran, she nudged Melody who followed her pointed finger and giggled at the sight, nudging Chester until he looked as well. Izan had moved over to sit next to Chester, still lost in his two ladies (and drawing a number of disapproving stares and warnings from guards).

'Izan,' Melody said.

Her brother broke from kissing only long enough to ask, 'What?'

Melody gave an impatient sigh as Chester reached out and grabbed Izan's chin, pulling the magician's face away from the girl so he was looking in Sora's direction.

'Look at Sora.'

Izan raised his eyebrows. 'Well, well, I didn't know she had it in her.' He nodded approvingly before disappearing in his girl again.

Melody and Chester looked at each other and rolled their eyes.

'How long are you in Kutiko-mi for?' Taran asked.

'Five days. It's a big city and we've just been on the road for two months so Alain likes us to stay here a while.'

'He's your Ringmaster? The one who found you?'

'Yes.'

'So, is he like your father?'

'No, he's like my Ringmaster, like the one who gave

216

me a home, a place to practice my crafts.'

Taran nodded and looked around. 'Your friends are staring at us,' he told her.

'They do that. It doesn't bother me.' What did bother her were the disapproving stares she was getting from the other people in the room who didn't like her talking to one of their own.

'Do you want to get some fresh air?'

Having relaxed a little and deciding that he seemed like a nice, nervous guy, Sora nodded. Taran took her hand and led her out into the night. They walked out of the lush, manicured palace gardens (lit by floating lanterns and strange chipmunk-like creatures called charipos that glowed in the dark) and out on to the quiet streets.

'My grandfather is one of the High Masters,' Taran told her, as they strolled along. 'He teaches the Empress all her fighting skills. My father was an Empirial Guard, but he was killed when someone from Namiji tried to assassinate her. He saved her life.'

'Wow.'

'Yeah. I want to be an Empirial Guard too. I start training soon.' He fell silent for a while. 'What about you?'

'Oh, there's not much to tell, really. I live in Varatalé with my friends and we take our show to some of the worlds along the Highway. That's all.'

Taran smiled, taking the hint that she didn't really want to talk about herself.

They walked down one of the empty streets, bordered on one side by a stone wall. When the wall ended abruptly, the side of the road gave way to a grassy bank that sloped down to the edge of the Kutiko river. They walked down the bank, stopping at the edge of the water which shone silver in the moonlight. Sora found herself shivering a little as a slight breeze turned the glassy surface to ripples.

'It's a shame you don't live here anymore,' Taran said, quietly. He seemed to be studying the ground very hard as he drew circles in the grass with his slipper. The grass was damp but the slipper had been enchanted to cope with such conditions.

'People don't want me here,' she replied, simply. 'And I don't particularly want me here. I like Ormance itself but the people give me the shivers.'

'Why?'

'Because nobody wants to be different.'

'You're right,' he agreed, almost gruffly. 'It gets ridiculously boring.'

This surprised Sora and if she had thought about it she would have realised that it rather contradicted his ambition to be a guard, but, she was a little too taken in by now, standing by the river under the clear night sky, feeling pretty and knowing Taran thought so. She had only had two small relationships, the last ending three months ago, but living with five very loved up people had given her more than enough education in such situations.

'Why don't you leave?' she suggested.

Taran looked at her. Instead of answering he moved closer, put one hand around her waist and the other to her cheek, pulled her to him, and kissed her. 'May I have you,

Sora Mai?' he asked, adhering to Ormanican custom.

Sora hesitated. She didn't like the idea of lying with a stranger, but she'd been feeling so lonely lately, and when they were on the road for such a long time it was hard to get to know anybody properly.

'Yes,' she finally whispered, not hearing the small voice in her head that was shouting warnings.

Taran kissed her again, his hands becoming friendlier. He led her up the bank until they were behind the wall, out of view of the road, and laid her on the grass.

'How do you take this dress off?' he asked, after a moment of fumbling with straps and ties.

'Do we have to undress completely?'

'I want to love you properly, Sora, I don't want to just lift up your skirt and get it over with.'

Sora's heart did a small flip. 'Are you going to undress too?' she asked.

'Of course.'

Sora moved around to undo her dress as Taran rolled off her to fiddle with his own clothes. When they were both completely naked, he climbed back on top of her, taking her dress from her to set it aside.

'Be careful with it. It's delicate.'

Taran had been about to put it on the grass but he smiled and put it under her head as a pillow instead. Sora grabbed him and kissed him.

When they were done, Taran rolled off of Sora and they lay side by side, panting, beaded with sweat, looking at the stars. They lay that way for about five minutes before

Taran propped himself up on to his arm, leaned over, smiled, and kissed her.

'I'll be back in a minute,' he said.

'Where are you going?'

'Just over to those bushes. I had quite a few glasses of heatberry juice earlier.' He stood up. 'Don't get dressed. I want to have you again when I come back.' He disappeared into the darkness.

Sora lay still, feeling pleasantly tired all of a sudden. Then, her mind kicked into gear. She couldn't remember Taran having a drink in his hand at all while he was talking to her. She wondered why he had made such a fuss about shedding all their clothes when he had barely taken the time to actually "love" her at all. She was cooling down, thinking more clearly. There was something about the way he had said that this city was boring, it had been almost hateful. She stood up and reached for her dress.

Just as her fingers brushed the material, eight teenage boys ran out from the bushes, whooping and calling out, and formed a half circle around her, trapping her against the river. Taran, still naked, appeared from behind them and took his place among the circle, directly in front of Sora, sneering.

He's not all that good looking, really, she found herself thinking.

'We have you cornered, witch,' Taran spat.

'You couldn't have cornered me before you screwed me?'

'Hey, I drew the short straw, I may as well have enjoyed myself – not that you were any fun, you lay like a

220

wooden plank. I'da had more fun with a corpse. I'm surprised actually. I mean, you dress like a whore.'

'Well, you didn't exactly give me much to work with, did you?'

The other boys laughed and jeered. Taran looked murderous.

'I want to see you bleed, witch,' he growled.

Sora had just enough time to scream silently in her mind before they attacked her.

Back at the palace, Arrahbella stopped dead still, grabbed Alain's arm with a gasp, and went into one of her trance-like states. Alain, knowing what this meant, waited impatiently until she came back to herself. They had only just noticed that Sora was missing.

'What is it?' he asked, once Arrahbella's eyes had refocused.

'It's Sora. She's being attacked.'

Alain hesitated in surprise only for a moment then he took Arrahbella's hand and dashed through the crowd to Izan.

There were a number of river banks in the city that looked like the one Arrahbella had seen in her mind and by the time the three of them arrived at the correct one, Sora was badly beaten, lying bruised, bleeding, and trembling beneath the group of boys who were still hitting, kicking, spitting, and scratching her while calling her names like "witch," "whore," "murderess," "enchantress," "freak," and so on.

Alain was about to command them to stop, but Izan was faster, barely glancing at the scene before bowling them over backwards with a wave of his hand, sending them sprawling onto the grass. Arrahbella made a move to run to Sora, but Alain reached out his arm, holding her back. They watched as Sora stood up shakily and gave the boys a look full of loathing, blood dripping from her lips and the cuts on her face.

'Sora?' Alain called.

'Hold them still, Izan,' Sora said thickly through a mouth full of blood.

Izan raised his hand to do her bidding. The boys were picked up off the ground and floated magically into a straight line, side by side, their feet hovering a few inches above the grass. Their bodies were paralysed, their expressions fearful as they followed Sora with their eyes.

'She doesn't have the strength, Alain,' Arrahbella protested.

He looked at her with sad eyes. 'I know, Bella, but she won't rest until she's had some sort of revenge.'

Arrahbella bit her lower lip and watched Sora anxiously.

Sora hesitated only to make sure that all of her limbs were still under her control, knowing that if she paused for too long she would start to feel the pain and exhaustion, then she hobbled over to the first boy in the line. For the next few minutes, she fought her way through every one until they were knocked out cold, passing out while still standing straight up, unable to fall to the ground in a huddle thanks to Izan's spell. When the last boy had fainted, she returned to Taran. He had regained consciousness and was now bleeding from the lip as well. Sora looked into his unfocussed eyes, her naked body inches away from his own.

'Sora,' Alain warned, knowing what she was capable of.

But Sora smiled evilly, ignoring the pain it caused, as she produced a ball of fire in her hand. Taran's eyes widened in fear. Arrahbella gasped and clung to Alain's arm. Izan turned the other boys on an angle so that those who were conscious would be able to watch. Sora lowered her hand and the fire leapt on to Taran's most sensitive area. The fire was instructed to burn painfully but to leave no damage to his skin. Under Izan's spell, Taran couldn't even scream; instead, he silently gasped in pain until he passed out again. Sora kept the flame going, hoping that it was causing his organ unhealable damage. She could have stayed there all night, or until she collapsed.

Alain and Izan had turned away at the sight and were only taking quick sporadic glances. Finally, Alain had to stop her.

'Enough, Sora, you'll kill him.'

'So?' she called back.

'Think about it, Sora,' Izan called. 'You kill him and he gets off easy.'

Sora closed her hand and the fire went out. She wouldn't have really killed him, of course, but Taran didn't know that. She stumbled back to the bank. Arrahbella hurried to her side to catch her but Sora pushed her off and continued on to pick up her dress then she walked to where Alain and Izan were standing. Izan let the boys drop and they hobbled off, half conscious, half pulling the barely alive Taran after them. Izan took off his cloak and threw it around Sora.

'Thank you for holding them,' Sora whispered, looking up at him.

'Don't mention it.'

Alain tried to examine the extent of Sora's wounds but she pushed him aside as well and kept walking up the grassy slope.

'Sora, stop, you need to stop,' he said, as they followed.

'I'm fine, Alain,' she replied stubbornly.

When she reached the side of the road her legs finally trembled and gave out and she was forced to stop, collapsing in a heap and bursting into tears. Arrahbella crouched down, wrapping her arms around her, hushing her. Annoyed at herself, Sora brushed her tears away and choked down her sobs. Then, wobbling, she stood up again and walked in the direction of the train.

Alain switched on his power. 'Sora, stop! Now!'

Much to his relief, she was so tired, she didn't even protest. Izan picked her up and carried her the rest of the way.

Once inside the train, the men waited in Izan's room while Arrahbella helped Sora into bed. As she attempted to sip some tea, Arrahbella sat on the edge of the bed, opening a container of balm; a mixture of flowers and herbs, giving off a strange, sweet and savoury aroma.

'How are you feeling now, honey?'

'It's starting to hurt.'

Arrahbella nodded, taking the mug from Sora as she slowly lay down again, wincing. There was silence as the Earthling massaged the gooey concoction into the wounds on Sora's arm.

'It's not fair, Arrahbella,' she said, tears welling. 'This is why I promised myself that I'd never lie with strangers. He seemed so nice.'

'I know, honey. You can't tell sometimes, you just can't.'

'I can usually pick them, though, but I just... I get so lonely sometimes. I see you and Alain together, or Chester and Melody, and Izan's always got someone, and it's hard. I just want someone to love me.' Tears rolled down her face and onto the pillow. 'I couldn't even fight them off. There were just too many of them.'

Arrahbella stroked the top of her head, trying to calm her.

'You'll find someone, Sora. I know it seems impossible sometimes, but love has a way of finding you, usually right when you've given up hope.'

Sora tried to smile.

'Go to sleep now, you're exhausted.' She kissed the top of Sora's head and the girl closed her eyes, falling asleep almost immediately. Arrahbella waited until her breathing had deepened before she went into Izan's room.

'She's asleep,' she told them.

Izan leapt up. 'Right, then, I guess you don't need me anymore.'

Alain was sitting in the chair by the dresser, his head

in his hands. 'No, thank you, Izan.'

'Well, I'll be heading back to the palace to pick up my girls and then I'll be in a bed somewhere.'

'Just be careful on the streets, please.'

'Yep.'

Izan took his cloak from Arrahbella and was out of the door in a flash.

'How is she?' Alain asked.

'Disappointed, hurt, hating all men.'

Alain nodded. 'Poor Sora.'

'I'm going to go sit with her, in case she needs anything.'

Alain followed his wife back into the girls' room and watched her take up a chair beside Sora's bed then hold the sleeping girl's hand in hers.

'I should go and get the others.'

'You should.'

'I'm reluctant to leave you two here alone.'

'There are guards outside.'

'I know, but they may not be enough. There's only two of them, it's dark, and this is a long train.'

'I don't think they'll be coming back, Alain.'

'You don't think they'll want revenge?'

'No. Not tonight anyway.'

Alain looked unconvinced so Arrahbella stood up again and went over to him, putting her hands to his cheeks.

'Go. We'll be fine.'

He took her hands and held them. 'I may get held up;

I'll have to speak to Setana and thank her.'

'Will you tell her about this?'

He shook his head. 'Not tonight. Not while she has guests.'

Arrahbella nodded.

'I wouldn't feel so reluctant to leave if Sora was up to fighting but you're pretty much on your own.'

'Alain, I'll be fine.' She was smiling that serene smile. She kissed him lightly.

'Alain?' came a weak voice from the bed.

He hurried to Sora's side. 'Sora? I thought you were asleep.'

'I'm in too much pain to sleep.'

'You should try to sleep. You need sleep.'

'I look worse than I feel, Alain.' This was a lie. 'Go and get the others. I'll be awake until you get back.'

'I can't ask you to stay awake...'

'Alain, if you don't leave now I'll chase you out with a fireball.'

Arrahbella giggled.

'You would too,' he said with a smile.

Sora nodded as best she could.

'Get out,' she said.

Alain squeezed her hand and walked to the door.

'I'll send Oleg back as quickly as I can,' he told them. 'If anything happens, or you feel suspicious or threatened in any way, no matter how small, you let me know.'

Once he had closed the door, Arrahbella returned to the chair by the bed and took hold of Sora's hand.

'I'm going back to sleep now,' the injured girl whispered.

Arrahbella nodded.

Outside, Alain had stopped to talk to one of the guards who was standing like a statue just outside the door to the kitchen car.

'One of my troupe members was attacked tonight, by a group of teenage boys. She's in there now with my wife and they're alone. I need you to guard this train with your life, please, until I get back.'

'Sir,' replied the guard, his eyes looking over Alain's head into the darkness. 'The Empress told me to watch over your train, therefore, I have been guarding it as though my own wife and child were inside since my shift began and will continue to do so until my shift ends.'

'Thank you. And your comrade?'

'Sir, we are members of the Empirial Guard. Some guards don't take that responsibility as well as they should but I consider myself good at what I do. I know my fellow guard well and I can assure you that he is too. You have nothing to worry about, Master du Maurier.'

Alain squinted at him, his Noir Eternalan eyesight corroded from so many years in the sun. 'Sutoto?'

'Yes, sir.' Sutoto gave a small smile.

Alain's attitude changed dramatically. 'I didn't recognise you in the darkness. I feel much better knowing it's you guarding my train.'

'Thank you, sir.'

'Good, well, I'll go and get the rest of my troupe and

I'll be back as soon as I can. Come to the train sometime when your off duty and we'll have a drink.'

'That would be good, sir.'

Alain walked a short distance away then turned, wrote "protection" in the air, sent it toward the train where it settled and disappeared, then he continued on toward the palace. He was almost there when, dodging some scurrying yamuis that were chasing lanterns in the middle of the road, he ran into Asseniah.

'Asseniah? What are you doing out here on your own?'

The young girl looked like she was falling asleep on her feet and she blinked at him a couple of times before pointing in the direction of the train.

'Oh, honey, it isn't safe for you to be out here alone right now. You're going to have to come back to the palace with me while I round up the others, okay? I'm sorry, Asseniah, you know I don't like pushing any of you when you're tired. It'll only take a few minutes.' He hoped so anyway.

Asseniah shook her head and continued walking.

Alain sighed. 'Asseniah, please?'

She stopped, turned, gave him a glare that told him she was more than capable of looking after herself, and headed back towards the palace. Alain closed his eyes with relief and followed.

The feast had diminished in size, but was still going strong despite it being almost midnight.

'Can you go and get Melody, Chester, and the dwarves for me? I'll get Mariette and Oleg and then say goodbye to the Empress.'

Asseniah headed off in Melody and Chester's direction, finding them in a different set of chairs, looking sleepy but happy with Melody's head on Chester's shoulder, his head resting on hers. The dwarves were sitting next to them, picking away at some food, as they discussed Ormancian history.

'Oh, hey, Asseniah. I thought you went back to the train,' Melody said.

Asseniah pointed to where Alain was speaking frantically to Oleg and Mariette, then she took Melody and Chester's hands and pulled gently.

'What's going on?' Melody asked, as they all stood up.

Asseniah shook her head, fighting to keep her eyes open, and led them over to the others.

'Oleg, I need you to go back to the train immediately,' Alain was saying. 'The rest of you stay here, stay together. I'm going to say goodbye to the Empress and then we're all going back to the train together.'

'What's happened, Alain?' Melody asked him, as Oleg dashed off, concern making her grip Chester's arm tightly.

But Alain was already disappearing through the crowd. 'I'll explain everything when we get back. Just wait here, please,' he called back over his shoulder, the peaceful tune coming from the band conflicting with his anxious tone.

'What do you suppose has happened?' Phan asked.

'Sora disappeared with that guy and then Alain,

Arrahbella, and Izan left,' Melody said quietly. 'I hope everyone's okay.'

'We saw Izan come back and get those girls,' Chester reminded her, rubbing a hand over the lower part of her back. 'I'm sure he's okay and if the other two hadn't been then he wouldn't have come back looking for a good time.'

Melody nodded. Asseniah stumbled forward as she struggled to stay awake.

'Oh, you poor thing,' said Chester. He picked her up and she fell asleep instantly.

Alain returned to the group and indicated in the Empress' direction. They saw her looking at them, bowed together, then, Alain hustled them out.

Together, they hurried down the street. Melody had taken up Mariette's hand in the absence of Chester's, Alain following behind, looking around them in every direction nervously. They didn't speak again until they had reached the train.

'Go into the dining car,' he instructed them, nodding to Sutoto as he passed.

Melody, Mariette, and the dwarves sat at the table while Alain softly knocked on the adjoining door to the girls' room and opened it. Oleg was there, with Arrahbella, but he left when he saw Alain, joining the girls in the kitchen. Chester entered with Asseniah, gasping when he saw the cuts and bruises on Sora's face. Arrahbella quickly put a finger to her lips, nodding in Asseniah's direction and he fell quiet. He set the silent girl on her feet as Arrahbella walked over to help her undress and climb into her hammock. Chester then returned to the dining car with Alain who shut the door behind them and sat down across from those already seated. They watched him anxiously as he stared at the table top and took a few breaths.

'Sora was attacked tonight,' he said, and waited while they responded with shock and concern. 'I can't tell you what happened until I've spoken to her. It's her story and she may not want it told. But, I do want you all to know that there are a few people we meet on our tours who don't like us very much and Ormance seems to have some who would rather attack us than just ignore us.' He looked at them all sternly. 'We will stay as planned, if Setana is happy for us to do so, but I want you all to be extremely careful and alert whilst walking these streets over the next few days, especially at night or when it's quiet. Try not to go anywhere alone, okay?'

'Is Sora going to be alright?' Mariette asked.

'Yes. She's a strong girl, I think her pride hurts more than the injuries.'

'Is Izan okay?' asked Melody.

'He's fine. He seemed to enjoy himself, actually.'

She smiled sadly.

'Will the Empress be able to do anything?' Fenton wanted to know.

'I doubt it. Her role is to protect the citizens of Kutiko and Sora is no longer one of them, but I will tell her anyway. She needs to be aware of it.'

Fenton nodded. 'Will we come back next tour?'

'We can talk about that later, but it's most likely. The people of Kutiko may not like us but they do love our shows.'

There was silence for a moment as they thought this over.

Alain clapped his hands together. 'Alright, off to bed with all of you. Try not to look at Sora as you go through.'

There was an abrasive scratching of chairs as they all stood up.

'Do you need me any further, Alain?'

'No, thank you, Oleg.'

Oleg headed toward his room with the dwarves as Mariette and Chester left in the opposite direction. Melody was left with Alain who looked very tired all of a sudden.

'Are you and Arrahbella okay?' she asked, as he leant against the table and rubbed his face with his hands.

'Yes,' he replied with a sigh. 'Just a bit rattled.' He studied her for a moment. 'I'm so glad you have someone like Chester,' he said. 'I'm glad you're not out flirting and having one-night stands, and that you're with a man who loves you.'

'Sometimes it seems too good to be true,' she replied. 'I'm so happy.'

Alain gave a short humourless laugh and nodded. 'Being human is strange, isn't it? Even when we're deliriously happy... we can't be happy.'

Melody chuckled. 'Something like that.'

Alain gathered her up and squeezed her tightly. 'Wait until you have children,' he said, quietly, referring to the whole troupe, not just her. 'You'll never think of your own happiness again.' He released her.

'One thing at a time, thank you, Alain.'

He smiled. 'Go to bed.'

'You too.'

She waved a goodnight then left him alone in the room. She waved to Arrahbella who was preparing to leave Sora's side by gathering up her mugs and balms, closed her eyes at the sight of Sora's bruised and now swelling face, and hurried through to her own room.

Alain was staring at the wall when Arrahbella entered the dining car. He watched while she put the mugs in the sink and made Melody's nightly tea, then she walked over to him and put her arms around his waist, her head on his warm chest. They held each other for a moment, then walked through to their caravan, depositing the mug of tea to Melody on their way through.

CHAPTER 9

Present Day – Icecess

From Ormance it was a two-day trip along the main Highway and then a further three days along the side road that led to Icecess.

As Phan drove the train toward the rift, he noticed something rather unusual. Frowning, he pulled the small lever that rang a bell both in Alain's room and the dwarves' room, and within seconds the Wordmaster was standing beside him.

'Yes, Phan?'

'Something's up, Alain. People are speaking to the guard and turning away. Only a few have gone through.'

Alain looked out of the large front window and watched as wagons pulled up at the rift, stopped a moment, then turned away.

'How interesting.'

'Should I stop and ask someone what's going on?'

Alain played with his beard while he considered this. 'No. Continue on. It may just be that the resort is closed for some reason.'

'Sure thing.'

When they reached the rift, the two guards on duty signalled for them to stop and Alain jumped down from the cabin to speak with them. Both were young and typically Icecesseon; large and beefy with white skin, fair-coloured hair, and opal-coloured eyes.

'Alain du Maurier?' asked the younger of the two, as he shuffled through some papers.

'Yes.'

'You're allowed to go through, sir, but I must warn you that you do so at your own risk.' The guard looked rather nervous, which was not typical for his race.

'What's happened?'

'One of our villagers, Kristav Brolegvak, has overthrown the council and is running the place on his own.' He was whispering as though he was afraid those inside the rift would hear him. 'He believes Icecess should be run by one person and wants us to accept him as our King. He's happy for tourists to come through still because they bring money, and he wants all the money to go to him, but those that go in don't want to stay long when they see what he's done to the place. You can go through, Mister du Maurier, but I caution you strongly.'

Alain wasn't sure what to make of all this. 'Thank you,' he said. 'We'll continue on. People are expecting us. Perhaps if we are allowed to perform, we can help to ease people's worries for a short time.'

'The people of Icecess always enjoy seeing your show, sir.'

Alain nodded his appreciation and climbed back into the driving cabin.

'Continue on, Phan,' he told the dwarf. 'And park in the usual spot.'

Phan restarted the engine and drove through the rift as Alain walked back through to the girls' caravan where everyone had gathered. They were all dressed in the special white furs that Sora had individually designed for them, Izan's incorporating his cloak and Melody's accommodating her wings. The fur used was from an animal known as a leffelai; a small fluffy creature, native to Icecess, which resembled a polar bear.

'Everyone, Icecess has apparently had some changes to its ruling structure and we may no longer be welcome here.'

'What?' exclaimed Melody. 'What about Rustinov and the council?'

Alain shook his head. 'I'm not sure. I think we should all go into the village together and see what's going on.'

Phan entered the room, looking nervous. 'It's dead out there, Alain. There's a real bad feel to the place.'

A few of them turned to look out of the nearest window but all they could see were the snow-capped mountains that formed a ring around the edge of the world, and the grey sky.

Alain frowned. 'Thank you, Phan. Is everyone ready? Stay together, please.'

They nodded. Alain took Arrahbella's hand and led them out into the snowy plain. Below them, sitting directly in the middle of the world, was the one and only village.

'It's so quiet,' Arrahbella said, her voice barely more than a whisper.

'You're right, Phan, it is different,' Sora agreed.

Unconsciously, Melody, Mariette, and Arrahbella huddled slightly closer to Chester, Oleg, and Alain.

Alain took a deep breath and began to walk toward the village, passing a number of the beautiful ice sculptures (carved into a myriad of things from other worlds; roses, dragons, castles, dolphins, birds, waterfalls, and trees among them) that dotted the landscape. The oversized log cabin that acted as the world's ski resort was almost completely deserted and those handful of people that were on the slopes weren't making a noise.

Asseniah tugged on Sora's coat and pointed to something.

'What is that?'

Fourteen pairs of eyes squinted into the distance, watering in the freezing air.

'It looks like a row of giant lollipops stuck in the snow,' Melody said.

'They aren't lollipops,' Izan said gravely, using his magic to see better. 'They're heads.'

'Heads?'

'Heads on stakes. Icecesseon heads.'

Everyone stared in stunned silence.

'These people need help, Alain,' the magician told him.

Alain didn't say anything. He felt sick, but he swallowed hard and continued on toward the village, his

238

hand gripping Arrahbella's even more firmly.

They passed very few people as they walked the cobbled streets. The windows and street lamps were still emitting golden light, but instead of being warm and inviting they somehow looked ghostly. The once pretty stone cottages seemed cold and dull. The cheerful shop fronts were dark and abandoned. The villagers walked quickly, glancing around them as though they were being followed.

'Should we be doing zis, Alain?' Mariette whispered.

Alain was about to answer when they heard the sound of a fiddle and a man's booming voice talking and laughing. They followed the noise silently, holding their coats tightly around them, until they came to a tavern in the centre of town. Alain held up his hand and the troupe stopped. The light from inside made his flushed face glow as he peered in. Snow began to fall down softly.

The tavern was crowded inside but nobody, in Alain's view, seemed very happy to be there. Most eyes were staring at a large man – Kristav, presumably – who was sitting at a long wooden table near the large open fireplace. No one spoke, not even the children. Serving girls dressed in small dresses and oversized boots brought him tankards of ale and plates of food while he laughed, talked loudly, and waved his drink around.

Alain looked around at Arrahbella who had been peering in the window next to him. Behind them, Izan had made part of the wall transparent so that the rest of the troupe could see the scene inside. Arrahbella shrugged. Alain took a deep breath. At least the air hadn't changed, it still smelt of pure snow and wood fire smoke.

'Right, troupe, let's go.'

He pushed open the wooden door and stepped inside.

The noise of the tavern ceased instantly as all eyes turned toward the troupe, surprise registering on their faces as they recognised them for they had forgotten that such a happy thing as a circus existed. The Icecesseons that had once formed the council, including Rustinov Darlinski, a long-time friend of Alain's, were seated alongside Kristav, looking as though they would rather die than share a table with the man.

'What have we here?' Kristav asked, rising from his chair. His bushy red hair was tied back in a ponytail with a dirty gold ribbon that matched the one threaded through his plaited beard. Black furs and strings of gold chain were thrown around him in Icecesseon fashion, adding more bulk to his already large frame. His beady eyes were yellow (though they had, perhaps, once been green) and had a coldness about them that sent shivers through the troupe.

Alain sent a silent prayer to Mythos then smiled pleasantly, adding magic to his words so they wouldn't betray his nerves. 'Alain du Maurier, sir, and my troupe, Cirque du Phantastique. We are scheduled to perform tonight.'

A few of the council members were discreetly shaking their heads at Alain but the Ringmaster kept his eyes on Kristav, as did Oleg and Sora. Izan had one eye on the scene and one eye on the pretty barmaid standing behind Kristav.

'Ah, yes,' said Kristav. 'The circus.' He set down his

240

drink. 'You may have noticed that there have been some changes to Icecess since your last visit, Mister du Maurier. There is no longer a council. I am in charge. My name is Kristav Brolegvak.' He reached out a hand to Alain who reluctantly let go of Arrahbella's and shook it. 'Come and join us for a drink.' Kristav waved a hand at the long table before sitting down once more.

'Thank you.' Alain looked around at his troupe and nodded. They dispersed to sit in various places around the tavern, their eyes still on Kristav and Alain as he and Arrahbella sat next to Rustinov, only a few seats down from the red headed man. Melody, Chester, Sora, and Asseniah sat at an empty table by a window on the far side of the tavern, while Izan leaned against a stack of ale barrels behind them, took out his nail file, and started filing away while he watched Kristav, and the barmaids, carefully. Oleg and Mariette sat together on the other side of the room, as did the dwarves.

The du Mauriers were now facing the rest of the room and, as she looked around at the terrified expressions of the Icecesseons, Arrahbella's psychic barrier suddenly gave way and thoughts filled her mind with an almost overwhelming force.

'Stop! Get out of here!' some were saying.

'Help us!' others cried, desperately.

'He's going to kill us all.'

Arrahbella shut her eyes, despair and helplessness making her giddy.

'So, Mister du Maurier,' said Kristav, as he took a leg of meat and bit into it greedily. 'You wish to entertain our small village?'

'If we're still welcome here, then it would be an honour, sir.'

'Of course you are welcome. This place could use some cheering up; it's been ever so dreary lately.'

'Why might that be?' Izan asked in a low voice, not looking up from his filing.

Alain glared at him. The Icecesseons froze in horror as the tension in the room increased dramatically.

Kristav gave him a cold look. 'The people are adjusting to the new way of things, young man. They'll cheer up as time goes on.' He turned back to the table. The council members looked down sadly. 'Give us a tune minstrel. We need some music for our guests.'

The small weedy looking man (who looked like anything *but* an Icecesseon) that had been playing the fiddle before the troupe entered put his bow to the strings quickly and began to play once again, the lively tune contrasting jarringly with the heavy mood.

'Come.' Kristav stood, taking one of the barmaids by the hand. 'Let's dance, my sweet girl. Mister du Maurier, you and your troupe may eat and drink to your heart's content... as long as you pay for it, of course.' He laughed raucously, spinning the barmaid on to the open floor in the centre of the room. She did a very good job of appearing happy about this treatment.

As soon as Kristav was out of ear shot, Alain leaned closer to Rustinov. 'What's going on here, Rustinov?' he asked, as quietly as he could.

'It's not good, Alain. Kristav's a monster.' He spoke so quietly that Alain had to magically grab his words as they were breathed out of his mouth and force them to reach his ear. 'We can't so much as breathe without asking him first. He rules everything we do. People are getting sick, no one ever used to get sick.' His opal eyes never left Kristav, his forehead and his balding head glistened with sweat.

'Hasn't anyone tried to do something about it?'

'Of course we have. We've had our biggest and strongest go against him. He welcomes it, but they've all lost, and he has their heads skewered on spikes on the edge of the city so we know just how much power he has over us. We've lost some of our best men to Kristav. Get out of here, Alain. Get your troupe out of here as soon as you can. I fear our world is doomed.'

Alain didn't know what to say. He looked over at Izan and saw that he had also been listening to the conversation by magical means and was giving Alain a look full of pleading, bursting to take on Kristav right then and there. Alain gave him the slightest shake of his head. The magician frowned, violently tucked his nail file away in his shirt, and stormed out of the tavern, unable to watch the miserable faces of the Icecesseons a moment longer. Arrahbella had taken up Alain's hand again and was clutching it tightly under the table, trembling with the psychic fear she was experiencing. Chester had his arm around Melody.

'Rustinov, come and dance, my man,' Kristav called over the music and nervous laughter of the barmaid.

Rustinov glared at Kristav before rising slowly. With

a limp (the result of an encounter with a leffelai) and the aid of a cane he hobbled on to the dance floor.

'Dance, man, dance,' Kristav commanded, with an evil smile.

The room watched with pity as Rustinov tried his best to dance, wincing in pain, his cane acting as support. Kristav took one hateful look at the cane before kicking it out from under him, sending Rustinov crashing to the floor. As Kristav roared with laughter, Rustinov's wife, Mayazna, ran over to help him up, but when Kristav saw her he stopped laughing and slapped her hard across the face with the back of his hand.

'Get away from him, witch. He can get up on his own, he's not an infant.'

The fiddle player had stopped again. Everyone held their breath. Rustinov looked furious. He was trembling with fear, or rage, or both, as he put his hands to Mayazna's face where tears were mingling with the large red mark growing on her cheek.

'Get up, cripple,' Kristav yelled, turning almost as red as his beard, his yellow eyes rolling wildly, creating a frightening image. He kicked Rustinov in his injured leg making the man moan with pain and turn a shade of white that matched the snow outside.

Arrahbella had to look away. Alain could see Izan pacing the pavement outside the window. The magician could still hear what was going on inside and was furiously trying to restrain himself. With a heavy heart, Alain quickly wrote "stay" in the air under the table and sent it out on the breeze to Izan. Nobody saw it, but Izan gave Alain a deathly glare through the window when it hit him. Alain turned away to see Chester, Oleg, and the dwarves almost jumping out of their seats too. He wrote more commands and sent them out as well. Chester tapped the table top impatiently and frowned at Alain. The dwarves hid their anger by taking long swills of their ale. Despite the evil looks he was getting, Alain couldn't help feeling rather proud of them all, always wanting to help those in need.

Kristav was now delighting in kicking Rustinov each time the man tried to get up. Mayazna was sobbing loudly but had moved out of the way. When Rustinov fell down again and stayed down, knocked out cold from the pain, Kristav turned on the poor fiddle player who jumped clean off the ground when the tyrant's eyes fell on him, trembling so fiercely his fiddle hummed.

'Why have you stopped playing?' Kristav roared, droplets of saliva flying out of his massive mouth. 'Did I tell you to stop playing?'

The fiddler attempted to shake his head but he was barely in control of himself.

Arrahbella closed her eyes again as the psychic pleas got stronger. The people were desperate to leave but too afraid they would be killed if they moved, their flight response in turmoil as they tried to sit still. She was also being drawn into the fiddler's mind, she could feel his fear, smell Kristav's breath on the fiddler's face, feel his insides turn to mush inside him as fear sent him paralysed.

Alain felt her hand grip his so tightly she nearly broke

his fingers and looked at her. She was breathing fast and swaying slightly, her forehead glistening in the firelight.

'Arrahbella,' he whispered into her ear, trying to call her back to herself. When her eyes remained closed and her breathing intensified, he pushed up the sleeve of her coat and sweater and lightly pinched her arm. With tremendous effort, Arrahbella's mind fought through the voices to the pain in her arm and she was able to shut them out completely. She opened her eyes and slumped weakly into Alain's arms.

'You're useless,' Kristav said quietly to the fiddle player. Rustinov had regained consciousness and was now crawling over to his wife. 'I don't need useless people in my community. And we have other fiddle players. You're an embarrassment to this society. What must out guests think of you?'

Alain started as Kristav waved a hand in his direction. Melody's hands flew to her mouth as a sob escaped her.

'Alain,' Arrahbella whispered.

But it was too late.

'Your days are done,' Kristav said.

The fiddle player suddenly found his voice. 'No, please, Kristav, sir, no, no, I beg you.'

Every Icecesseon in the room closed their eyes or looked away. Only Alain, Oleg, Fenton, Dell, Phan, Asseniah, and Izan watched as Kristav grabbed the fiddle player's bow and rammed it down the small man's throat until only the tip of it was showing out of his mouth. The man's head was forced backward at a horrible angle so he was staring at the ceiling with eyes that eventually popped slightly out of their sockets. A spine-tingling choking noise filled the room as the man stumbled about before finally suffocating, falling flat on the floor, and lying still, his head propped up, looking straight at Alain with those ghastly protruding eyes.

Arrahbella opened her eyes and was about to turn around but Alain put a hand to her head and kept it on his shoulder. His eyes went from the fiddle player to Kristav. The man looked euphoric and manic.

'Well, Mister du Maurier,' he said, gleefully. 'I hope you weren't looking for a sword swallower for your circus because I believe he failed the audition.' Kristav broke into hysterics and sauntered back over to his seat. Alain watched him carefully through narrow eyes, trying to remain calm, his mind racing.

Kristav took a swig of ale. 'Sorry you had to see that. I'm trying to stamp out the scourge of our society so that Icecess is filled with only the best specimens.'

Alain forced his voice to work. 'The fiddle player wasn't giving us a negative view of your society, sir. In fact, I was admiring his talent.'

People were looking at the body in the middle of the floor now. Distressed cries escaped some of the women as children started crying.

'Quiet!' Kristav roared and they choked back the sobs. He smiled unpleasantly at Alain. 'Oh well, my mistake. Doesn't make any difference now, though, does it?' He raised his tankard to his lips and drank, his yellow eyes not leaving Alain.

Sensing the tyrant's growing impatience, Alain decided it was time to leave. He stood up, pulling Arrahbella with him.

'Well, if you'll excuse us, sir, we must go and set up our tent if we are to perform for you tonight. Thank you for your... hospitality.' Alain nodded to Kristav and turned to leave, praying he was going to let them walk out alive. The rest of the troupe stood up and headed to the door.

'Of course,' Kristav called. 'We look forward to seeing you. Please, enjoy your stay, and if anything displeases you, you be sure to let me know. I'd be only too happy to dispose of anything that you find less than satisfying.'

Alain nodded to Kristav again, glanced at Rustinov and his wife, then swept out of the room and closed the door behind him.

'Sweet Mythos, Alain,' cried Izan, when they were halfway down the street, out of earshot of the tavern. 'Why did we just stand there and let him kill the man?! We could have stopped him. We could have killed Kristav right there and then and put the whole town out of its misery.'

'Have you ever killed a man, Izan? I mean, on purpose?'

Izan kicked the nearest lamp post. 'No. You know I haven't.'

'Then perhaps you'll understand that I'm trying to find a way to help the people without anyone, especially one of you, getting killed in the process.'

'So, you agree that something should be done?'

Alain finally lost his cool, making a good number of them jump. 'I don't know.' He kicked the snow furiously. 'I don't know what to do. I don't know whether we should go back in there and blast Kristav to smithereens or whether we should mind our own business, perform, and get the Mythos out of here and hope dearly that things resolve themselves. I mean, Landau's in constant war, but nobody goes in and tries to resolve that, do they? No. Why? Because it's not their world.'

'So, it's not our problem, they can work it out for themselves. Is that what you mean? Even though Rustinov clearly told you that they'd sent their finest men to resolve it and they're heads are all decorating the village perimeter now.'

'Did Rustinov ask us for help?'

'Would you ask someone for help if you thought they'd die in the process or that you'd die for asking? No. We have magic, Alain.'

'So do they.'

'What, surviving in sub-zero temperatures and making pretty ice sculptures? Reeeaaal helpful.'

'They have other powers as well.'

'Not as much as all of us combined.'

'Izan, if we were to fight Kristav it would be you, me, Oleg, and Chester. Not all of us.'

There were protests about this, mainly from Sora.

'The more of us that fight, the better chance we have,' she argued.

'You see?' Izan said, waving in her direction.

Alain glared at them all. 'Tell me honestly, Izan, you would send your own sister, whose only power is the ability to fly, to fight that?' He pointed to the Tavern.

249

'Hey,' Melody protested.

Izan tapped his foot impatiently. 'If she or Sora wanted to fight then of course I'd let them, because as Sora pointed out, we're stronger in numbers. Sora is one of the most powerful weapons we have. We're a troupe, Alain, we do things together, and if all of us were against that one man, we'd win, though I could take him on my own all the same.'

'You're right, Izan, we are a troupe, a *circus* troupe, not a fighting gang. Besides, we don't even know what his power is.'

'It doesn't matter Alain, we could beat him.'

'Izan...'

'No.' Izan walked up to Alain, stopping close enough for their boots to be almost touching. 'Do you know what happened in there, Alain? Kristav used us as an excuse to kill a man and you could have stopped him. You could command the wind if you wanted to, Alain du Maurier, so there was nothing stopping you from commanding that bastard to back down. It would have shown Kristav you weren't afraid to take him on and you would have saved a poor man's life. But, you just sat there because it's not our problem. You killed that man, Alain, not Kristav.' Izan turned and walked a short distance away, seething and muttering curses.

Alain ran a hand through his hair and turned away as well, guilt making him feel ill. The words in his blood stream raced around his system, demanding to be expressed. He took a few deep breaths, trying to settle them, as his mind whirled. The snow fell a little harder as though trying to aggravate him further. He turned back to his group.

'Everyone, we're going to go back to our train and set up our tent on the snow field, together. Then, we're going to come back into town and have dinner. Now, we'll probably be forced to eat with Kristav and I know most of you won't feel like eating in his presence, but Arrahbella and I didn't plan any dinner in the train tonight because the locals here are usually so much fun to eat with and have always welcomed us warmly. So, we'll just have to do our best. We are guests here, and we will act as guests like we do in every world we visit. If, and only if, Kristav lays a finger on any of you, or, if he starts reducing the Icecesseon population by the hundreds, then we will act, but, until then, we are simply guests, here to entertain and to try to bring the people a small amount of cheer, and then we are passing through because we have a schedule to keep. We stick together, we watch out for each other, and we work together to try to bring smiles to these people's faces, to help them forget their troubles for a while.' He looked at each of them. 'Do you all understand what I'm saying? Will you all trust me on this and refrain from fighting him?'

They were silent for a moment so he prompted them.

'Oleg?'

'Yes, Alain.'

'Mariette?'

'Of course.'

'Melody?'

Melody looked at Izan, torn between the two. Her shoulders slumped. 'I'm sorry, Alain,' she said, looking at the ground. 'If Izan fights, I'll have to help him.'

Alain's eyes closed briefly. 'Chester?'

'I'm with Izan.'

'Sora?'

'I'd fight too, Alain.'

'Asseniah?'

Asseniah nodded once. She was with Alain.

'Dwarves?'

'We do as you say, Alain,' Fenton answered.

'Arrahbella?'

Arrahbella hadn't been expecting him to ask her. 'Of course I'm with you, Alain.'

Alain looked at Izan. 'Izan?'

The magician stopped kicking the lamp post and straightened up. 'You don't control us, Alain. You found us, you gave us a home, a place to express ourselves and to do what we love, and we thank you for it, but you don't control us. You forget that sometimes. No one in this troupe has to do as you say outside of performing.'

Alain looked hurt.

'I'll go back with you and help set up,' Izan continued. 'But I can't guarantee that the next time I see that heartless bastard I won't smite him to smithereens.' He turned and headed up the street.

Alain took a deep, shaky breath and did the same, his troupe silently following. Arrahbella stayed back with Mariette and Oleg, watching Alain walk to the train alone, desperately wanting to go and comfort him.

When they arrived at the train they entered through

the store room. For the entire afternoon they worked in silence, setting up the tent for the show, only speaking to give the occasional "Watch out!" or "Raise it higher" or "That cable's come unstuck." Arrahbella and Melody would glance at Alain occasionally and see him lost in his own thoughts as he mechanically helped rig Sora's tightrope or helped Melody hang the lights.

Once the majority of the work was done, Alain decided it was safe to retreat.

'Right,' he said, a little too cheerfully. 'I'm ducking into the train for a bit. Come and get me if there are any problems.' And he left. The troupe gave each other a look before continuing to set up.

Once they had gone through the safety check and a sound, lighting, and equipment test, the thirteen of them stood together in the middle of the stage.

'Well, this is ridiculous,' Izan snarled. 'I'm outta here.'

'Nobody goes anywhere until Alain says so,' Arrahbella told him.

'Did you not hear me, Arrahbella dear? Alain doesn't control us.'

'He's your Ringmaster, Izan.' Her voice was low but serious. 'He gives you a job and he can kick you out if he wants. He kicked Hanar out, didn't he? And he was prepared to kick Chester out.'

Chester looked at the ground.

'You might try and show him some respect,' she continued. 'You know he's doing this with your interests in mind and your cutting him down just so that you can show everyone how powerful you are and be the hero of Icecess, and, perhaps, get us all killed in the process. You know that Alain is waiting for the opportune moment to put Kristav in his place, but you, all of us, come first.'

Izan didn't respond.

'I'm going to find him and see if he's okay and then we'll all go to dinner. Everyone go and get ready.'

They slowly moved off as Arrahbella walked closer to Izan. 'We need you to stay with us in case we need protecting, okay?'

He gave a non-committed nod and she turned to walk away.

'Arrahbella?'

She stopped and turned.

'I do respect Alain. You know I do.'

'I know, Izan, but sometimes you act as though you don't and it makes him worry that he's doing something wrong.'

She left him alone on the stage.

Arrahbella found her husband lying on their bed, one arm over his eyes, boots hanging off the edge. When he heard someone enter, he moved his arm slightly and, when he saw that it was her, he sat up. Words – random words, strings of words, half-written words – were floating around the room or lay scattered on the floor and furniture where they had landed after exploding out of their creator.

'Is everything set up?' he asked, his beautiful deep voice a little husky.

Arrahbella nodded, deliberately stepping on an inky black "Kristav" and narrowly missing an "Izan". 'They're all getting ready to go out again.'

'All of them?'

'All of them.'

Alain stood up. 'I guess we should as well.' He waved a hand and all the loose words disappeared.

'Where *do* they go?' It was a question a few of them had wondered before and each one had different ideas on the matter. Alain smiled and studied Arrahbella for a moment. He seemed more relaxed, which made her relax as well. He put his arms around her, kissing her sweetly, though it was a kiss of need rather than desire.

'I'm worried about being here,' he said.

'I know.'

'Am I doing the right thing?'

'I think so.'

They held each other for a few moments longer.

A short time later, all fourteen troupe members headed back into the village together. The sky had been transformed from the grey of the day to a paintbox of colours as the sun slowly climbed down for the night, turning the mountains into lovely shades of purple and pink. The snow was still falling but only gently and half-heartedly, stopping now and then for a rest.

Alain desperately wanted to find a quiet place for them to eat in peace, but they soon found that all the other taverns were closed. So, reluctantly, he led them back to the one they had been in earlier.

Kristav was still there, though he was a little less energetic now. The plates had been cleared away and he was smoking a thick cigar, his chair pushed back a bit from the table, his legs stretched out close to the blazing fire. The crowd and the barmaids had changed and the fiddle player's body had been cleared away. The council members were still around the table looking tired and worn. As he glanced around the room, Alain noticed many of the people were getting much thinner than what their bodies were used to and he wondered how much longer they would survive.

'Ah,' said Kristav when he saw them enter. 'The circus has returned. You'll be wanting some dinner, no doubt?'

'If it's no trouble,' replied Alain, glancing at the tavern's owner, Farinov, who was wiping glasses behind the bar with hands that shook. Farinov looked at Alain but gave no sign of acknowledgement.

'Of course it's no problem. Sit down. Farinov, prepare our guests some dinner.'

The troupe stayed where they were.

'If you don't mind, sir, my troupe has special requirements before a show. I'll need to talk to Farinov about which meals we have.'

Kristav gave Alain a look that plainly showed that he thought this was a ridiculous idea but he grunted an approval.

'Thank you, sir.' Alain and Arrahbella moved off to speak with Farinov while the rest of the troupe separated and sat in the available spaces around the room.

When they were seated, a barmaid came around with

a tray of tankards, serving them to the troupe, whether they wanted ale or not. She was a pretty girl, still full figured, with a mane of blonde hair that was pulled back into a bun. When she served Izan, she caught him looking at her with his hungry eyes and gave him a timid smile.

Kristav noticed the exchange. 'You there, boy.'

Izan turned his head to look at Kristav coolly. Melody and Chester, sitting across from Izan at the same table, felt their hearts begin to race even harder.

'You have a liking for that woman?'

'I have a liking for all women, sir.' The "sir" dripped with irony.

Kristav gave a short laugh. 'Well, by all means, have her.'

The barmaid had stopped in the middle of the room, looking nervously at both men. All eyes in the room turned to Izan to see how he would respond.

'With respect, sir, unless you are her father I don't think you have a say in the matter.'

If the room had been still before, it was deathly so now. Alain and Melody almost stopped breathing as they turned to Kristav, but the man simply lost his smile.

'She's an Icecesseon, boy, and as I am the ruler of Icecess I have a say in what all my people do.'

Izan remained cool and calm. 'Where I come from, sir, that is not how a world is run. Where I come from, that is called tyranny and tyranny always ends in disaster.'

'We're not in your world, boy!' Kristav reminded him, powerfully, without even raising his voice. 'You're a guest here and you'd best remember that.'

'You're quite right. However, being a guest doesn't mean I have to follow your rules or do as you say.' Kristav looked furious. 'It does mean that I must respect your rules and so I shall. Though, I must also respect my own morals and so I would still prefer that the lady decides what she wishes.'

Kristav looked at the barmaid, his face red, on the brink of explosion. 'Go on,' he said roughly. 'Say he can have you, then he can have you right here on the floor and give us all some entertainment.'

Alain fought the urge to throw up.

Izan got annoyed. 'I didn't mean she had to answer right now. And I prefer to talk to my women and get to know them first, so, if you don't mind, sir, she will continue on with her duties and I will continue on with my drink and we will have no more meddling in a person's private affairs.' He took a sip of ale, looking away from Kristav for the first time.

The tyrant continued to stare at him with wild eyes for some moments, breathing hard, as the Icecesseons watched on in horror. When Kristav's gaze finally did leave Izan and swept around the room, they held their breath, praying that the cold yellow eyes wouldn't settle on them. Alain saw the colour drain from their faces and he wished Izan had kept quiet.

Kristav's gaze came to rest on Mariette who had been forced to sit at the table closest to his chair. Her eyes were glued to the table top as she fiddled nervously with her tankard. Within a matter of seconds, Kristav had leapt from his chair, grabbed Mariette by the arm, pulled her to him, and had a knife at her throat. Mariette screamed as a collective gasp filled the room.

Alain stepped forward.

'Don't move,' the tyrant roared, fury making his voice shake. He turned to Izan. 'I think your boy needs to learn some manners.'

Izan set his drink down and stood up slowly. 'Then it's me that you should be teaching, not her.'

'If I teach you, then you won't learn, but if I kill one of your friends,' he pressed the knife harder into her neck, 'you might think twice before being rude again.'

Mariette's eyes were darting rapidly between Izan and Alain. Sora focussed on the knife, waiting for Alain's word but not wanting to draw attention to herself.

Luckily, Izan was thinking along the same lines. 'Do we have your permission now, Alain?'

'You had my permission as soon as he touched her, Izan.'

Sora connected with the life in the weapon, finding it as stubborn and cruel as its master. Putting all her strength behind her magic, she ordered the blade away from Mariette's neck. The knife protested for a moment before weakening under her power and giving in. It flew out of Kristav's grasp, shocking him so violently that he stepped backward and loosened his grip on Mariette. Without hesitation Oleg leapt up and grabbed him by the arms, twisting them behind his back, as Sora hurried to control the blade before it could plunge into any one. When it got within reach, she clasped the handle tightly and held it close to her chest, feeling it buzz with injustice. Alain walked forward to stand beside Izan as Mariette fled to stand beside Arrahbella who was still behind the bar with Farinov. Izan raised his hand, wanting to finish Kristav right then and there, but the tyrant stopped him.

'Wait. This isn't fair. In Icecess we settle a dispute by wrestling out in the snow fields. At least give me that.'

Izan looked to Alain who looked to Rustinov. Rustinov consulted the other council members with a look, but when most of them turned their attention to the table top he turned back to Alain with a look of defeat.

'It is a law of ours that an Icecesseon may be given a fair duel with no magic used. Kristav is an Icecesseon so he's entitled to that right. You may choose one of your own to wrestle him in the snow fields.'

As Kristav smiled evilly, Alain nodded and looked at Izan who lowered his hand and sighed. He turned to Oleg.

'What do you think, Oleg?' Alain asked him.

Knowing he was the only choice, Oleg nodded. He released his hold on Kristav who straightened his furs, stuck his red, bulbous nose in the air, and walked out of the tavern, giving Izan a smug look as he passed. Everybody followed him out in a hurry, now suddenly animated with hope. Surely the strongest Da'Laarwickan was enough to finally rid them of their oppressive leader.

As they walked through the deserted streets, the people from the tavern knocked on doors and shouted for people to come out and watch the duel. Soon, there was an enormous crowd.

Kristav led them to the edge of the village where the

snow stretched out to the mountains and more glittering ice sculptures dotted the landscape. The villagers formed a ring, making an arena of snow where Oleg and Kristav took off their coats and primed themselves. The severed, bloody heads watched the action from their tall spikes with lifeless eyes.

'Is this a fight to the death?' Alain called to Rustinov over the noise.

'Yes,' he shouted back.

Kristav looked ready to kill the whole village.

Alain walked up to Oleg.

'You're happy to do this, Oleg?'

'Not happy, but prepared.'

The Wordmaster clapped him on the shoulder affectionately. Oleg saw his worried expression and ceased his stretching.

'Don't worry, Alain. I'm going to give him everything I've got, and if he wins, you know Izan's going to finish him off whether the villagers think it's fair or not. They're free, whatever happens, and if I die, I'll die knowing that.'

Alain nodded, reluctantly.

'Come on, giant, let's go,' Kristav called, jumping up and down with impatience.

Oleg looked at each of his fellow troupe members in turn. They each smiled, nodded, or held back fear. Then, Oleg moved into the arena. Rustinov walked into the centre, between the two men, and raised his trembling hand. Alain held Arrahbella, Chester held Melody, Izan folded his arms across his chest, Mariette clung to Sora while Asseniah watched blankly and the dwarves shuffled around excitedly, calling out encouragement and wishing they could take bets.

Rustinov gave the signal and quickly moved out of the way. Kristav charged at Oleg, skin meeting skin with a smack. Everyone had hoped that Kristav would be killed in an instant, but the tyrant proved to be equal in strength to the giant, both having trouble overpowering the other. They were chest to chest, arms wrapped around each other, feet spread in wide stance, occasionally moving back and forth as they tried to twist the other to the ground. Finally, they broke apart, danced around, and came together again with a clash that would have broken a weaker man's ribs. The cheers grew louder, although there were now cries of fear as well as support.

Watching without emotion, Alain turned to Izan and shouted over the noise, 'Not even an Icecesseon should be able to match a Da'Laarwickan in strength, even if Oleg isn't a typical Da'Laarwickan, he's certainly the strongest.'

Izan nodded. 'I was thinking the same thing. I can only assume that Kristav is a "freak" himself.'

Rustinov heard this. 'Kristav's father was Icecesseon but we don't know who his mother was. His father had more magic than most and so left Icecess as a trader for a while. When he came back, he had a son with him. He could very well be part Da'Laarwickan. That would explain his strength and size, but they don't usually cross breed and so he'd be the only one of his kind or one of very few.'

Izan looked thoughtful. 'Does that mean that he wouldn't be susceptible to Icecesseon law?'

Rustinov shook his head while Alain watched Izan

closely. 'No. Kristav is still part Icecesseon and has lived in Icecess his entire life. That makes him one of us, I'm afraid.'

Izan's eyes returned to the fight. Alain watched him for a moment longer before returning to the fight as well.

Oleg was looking for a way to get an advantage over Kristav. He saw Kristav's long ponytail and quickly manoeuvred his hand around to grab hold of it and yank Kristav's head back. Kristav howled but did not release his iron grip on Oleg. His neck was in an awful position but Oleg had to be careful not to lose his grip around Kristav's chest or he would be done for. He couldn't keep holding the ponytail so he let it go. Kristav's head sprang back, his yellow eyes glaring furiously. They broke apart then ran together once more. This time, however, Oleg bent down at the last moment, threw Kristav over his head, and quickly turned around. The man landed with an earth-shaking thud. He was on his feet again in a moment but Oleg was ready before him, grabbing his arms, twisting them behind their owner's back. Kristav kicked backwards and Oleg was forced to let go. Kristav was furious now and not thinking clearly. He charged at Oleg with his head low, aiming to ram him in the chest but Oleg stuck out his hand, giving Kristav a sickening whop on the back of his head, dazing him. After that blow, Oleg was able to overpower him easily, wrestling him to the ground, beating him near senseless and then preparing to finish him off by putting his hands to Kristav's head and twisting. One flick of his wrists and Kristav's neck would be snapped.

Kristav was still conscious, however, and he opened his rapidly swelling eyes until they focussed on Oleg.

'Please, sir, I beg you,' he said, breathlessly, through bloodied teeth and lips. 'Don't kill me. You win. I'll go to prison, but, please, spare me.'

Oleg hated that he'd said that; he couldn't kill a man who begged for his life, no matter what threat he might be. He dropped his opponent to the snow and turned away. There was a collective flurry of angry words from the crowd.

'Sir, this is a fight to the death. You must finish him,' Rustinov protested.

Izan stepped forward quickly. 'Oleg,' he said, looking at the panting man still in a heap on the ground. 'Do I have your permission to finish him off?'

Oleg had reached Alain who was handing him his coat.

'I'm not going to give you my permission to kill a man, Izan.' He finished buttoning up his coat and wiped an arm over his brow. 'I am finished with him, though, so you don't need my permission.'

Izan smiled. 'Rustinov, do I have your permission?'

'Yes, sir, you do.'

'Izan.' Alain warned.

But the magician wasn't listening. He turned to the crowd, his arms raised. 'Icecesseons, do you want this man dead?'

A hearty cheer erupted.

Kristav looked frightened. 'No, no,' he began, but Izan had an unsympathetic look about him.

'Silence!' he yelled, and with a wave of his hand Kristav's mouth was sealed shut.

'Alain,' Arrahbella cried, clutching her husband's arm. 'You can't let him do this. He's not a killer.'

He looked down at her and she saw fear in his eyes. 'I can't stop him, Bella.'

Her eyes widened. 'Yes, you can. Just command him to stop!'

He shook his head and turned away. 'It's his decision.'

Tears fell from Arrahbella's eyes, turning to crystals in the freezing air and dropping onto the snow. Sadly, she turned back to Izan. He had lifted Kristav into the air and was now walking him away from the crowd a few yards, a stream of black-coloured magic flowing out of his hands and encasing the tyrant.

Melody watched with fascinated horror at what her brother was about to do. She broke from Chester's grasp, running forward until she was in front of the crowd who had now all surged forward to watch. The rest of the troupe followed.

'This is your end, Kristav,' Izan called. He turned his head to call over his shoulder, 'This is going to be messy, I wouldn't let your women or children look.'

The parents in the crowd shielded their children's eyes, but only a small number of the women looked away; everyone wanted to be a part of this historic moment. Arrahbella buried her head in Alain's coat, Mariette into Oleg's, Sora continued to watch, and Asseniah would have too if Alain hadn't seen her and pushed her back behind him into Oleg's grasp.

Izan began to tear Kristav apart from the inside out.

He reopened his mouth and the world was filled with his bloodcurdling screams of pain and torment.

Alain tightened his grip on Arrahbella, bracing himself for what was sure to come next, then he noticed Melody. She looked like a child, standing there, lost and confused, unsure of what to do. Chester was trying desperately to turn her away but she was struggling against him.

'Melody, turn around!' Alain commanded in a booming voice, realising too late that he had just unleashed most of the power he wanted to use on Izan. Melody cried out as the force hit her, her breath momentarily taken away, then she turned rapidly, falling to her knees under the weight of the command. Chester dropped down and flung his arms around her, cradling her head to his shoulder, but not before she had managed to give Alain a look full of hurt. Ignoring the ache in his heart, Alain returned his gaze to Kristav in time to see the man explode. The pieces that scattered themselves in the snow steamed as heat met ice.

Izan lowered his arm as the Icecesseons cheered. They crowded around the magician or hurried to look at Kristav's scattered innards. More Icecesseons had come out of their homes to see what all the noise was about. The entire world, the resort workers, and tourists were all standing in the snow field now. Only the troupe stayed behind, watching without emotion, except the dwarves, who were cheering. Melody had started to cry and, though Alain's command had worn off, she remained buried in Chester's arms. Asseniah was the first to move, she wanted to ponder the poetry of a man's insides lying scattered in the purity of the snow. Alain felt too drained to stop her.

Izan was splattered with blood but the crowd still hugged and patted him with praise. He finally turned to look at the troupe, but if he was affected by their expressionless, non-smiling faces, he didn't show it. A group of men proceeded to take down the wooden stakes so that the heads atop them could finally be buried properly with the bodies they had once belonged to and all memory of Kristav could be erased. Leffelais appeared in the distant mountains, smelling the blood, waiting until the humans were gone so they could approach and eat the remains.

'Silence!' Rustinov roared, and word was passed around to hush up. 'There will be a feast in the town's square in two hours time.'

Another cheer and then a surge of movement as people left to get ready for the feast. Rustinov approached Alain.

'I hope you will join us at the feast, Alain, all of you, and perhaps you could perform for us there instead of in your tent? We'll still pay you handsomely.'

'We'd be delighted, sir,' Alain replied, though he sounded anything but delighted.

Rustinov smiled happily and clapped Izan on the shoulder. 'And, you, sir, shall be our guest of honour.'

Izan bowed. 'I am humbled by your kindness.'

'Nonsense, dear boy, you've just saved our lives – our world, in fact.' He beamed and headed into the village with his wife.

Alain watched him go, the field now eerily quiet.

'Come on, troupe,' he said quietly. 'Let's go prepare.'
They walked back to the train in silence.

Once they were there, Alain ran through what would have to be modified for a street performance. The main changes were that there would be no trapeze and no tightrope, nor any aerial silks. They would have to settle for manipulation, daggers and fire, and Izan, Oleg, Chester, and Mariette's usual performances, though shortened and adjusted. They changed into costumes that were better suited to a street show, then they gathered their props, locked up the train, and headed back into town to join the feast, though none of them were very hungry, not even Chester. Their tent sat silently in the cold, snowy landscape, its bright colours making a mockery of the white surrounding it and of the troupe's dark mood.

The large town square was bursting at the seams with people. Strings of lights and crystals hung between buildings while garlands of fake flowers and leaves decorated the tables and doors. When the troupe arrived, a mighty cheer erupted.

Rustinov smiled broadly and opened his arms to greet Izan. 'Mister Bell, we have a place at the head of the table for you, and you, Mister Fyzek, we haven't forgotten you, you have a place next to him. Come, come.' Izan and Oleg were whisked away to the main table where the other council members were already seated with their wives and families. Alain smiled sadly and led the others to the area where they would be performing.

The troupe felt drained but the excitement of the village combined with the excitement of performing soon had them feeling a little more like themselves. The crowd was full of praise for their help in ridding them of their tyrant and so the show was one of their most well-received ever. Once they had completed their show and Alain had had the entire population silent with rapture as he told them a story, the troupe found their appetites – they hadn't eaten since mid morning, after all.

When Asseniah and Arrahbella began to fight to stay awake, Alain announced they must be leaving and rounded up his troupe, leaving Izan to continue basking in glory and eventually go home with the barmaid.

As Arrahbella got ready for bed, Alain walked through to the adjoining caravan in search of Melody.

'She's in the kitchen,' Chester told him, stripping off his shirt.

'Is she alright?'

The jester shrugged. 'She says she is, but I'm not sure.'

Alain nodded and continued through to the kitchen where he found Melody sitting at the table, her hands wrapped around her mug of Griffinseed tea. She was lost in thought, only looking up when he pulled out the chair across from her and sat down.

'Are you okay?' he asked.

She shrugged. 'Yeah, I'm not worried about Izan.'

'Really? Because you look worried.'

She gave him a half-hearted smile. 'I was just thinking about how you had to kill a man when you were Izan's age in order to save Landau and you've got to be the very definition of the word "good," Alain.'

He frowned. 'Well, I don't know about that.'

'You are. And that's rubbed off on Izan. I mean, he'd killed a few people – accidentally, of course – by the time he was nine, our mother committed suicide, leaving us behind, and all of Toulon had us convinced that we were so evil that even Mythos didn't like us.'

Alain's gaze dropped to the table. He had forgotten how much Izan had been through in his short life.

'Before you and Mariette took us in,' she continued, 'Izan was angry all the time and he often talked about killing Kootol and other people who insulted us. If you hadn't have taken us in, and if they hadn't have killed us, then I reckon he'd have turned out bad.' She paused. 'But, after only a year with you, he'd stopped all that, and now he's always joking or being sarcastic and he channels a lot of his magic into loving people.'

Alain rolled his eyes. 'Does he ever.'

'I know you don't think he looks up to you, Alain, but he does, and King Fello and Prince Duozo as well, and with the three of you as mentors, he'll be alright. Besides, he's had plenty of opportunities to kill Kootol over the years and he hasn't.'

'That's true.'

Her expression turned thoughtful again. 'I suppose when you think about the other people along this Highway who have as much magic as he has, they're all using it on a grand scale every day; helping kings, healing the sick, or fighting in magical wars, and he's making juggling balls disappear.' Alain smiled and nodded. 'So, when he saw the situation here today, he saw an opportunity to use the magic he's been given to help people. Whether it was right to kill him rather than help the council take him to prison like you would have done depends on where your head is at, but, I believe that he killed Kristav because he wanted to help the people.'

'You're quite right, Melody. I, too, believe that Izan's intentions are good. It's just that having good intentions doesn't always result in the rightful actions.' He frowned. 'And it was more like watching a performance than an execution.'

'Well, he's Izan. You didn't just teach him how to be good, Alain, you taught him to be a showman, to give the audience what they need, and the Icecesseons needed Kristav to go out with a bang. That way, they feel as though they've got their revenge and they know for sure he won't be coming back.'

Alain studied her for a moment, then smiled sadly and nodded. Melody took a sip of tea. The faint sounds of the distant feast punctuated the silence.

'Alain, I didn't mean to side with Izan,' Melody said, after a few minutes. 'I agreed with you, but I meant that if Izan was fighting for his life, I'd have to help.'

'I know.'

'You didn't have to make me look away, though.'

'You didn't need to see that.'

'I've seen people die before, you know.'

'I wasn't talking about Kristav exploding.'

'Just because I didn't see it, doesn't mean it didn't

happen,' she whispered.

'No, that's true, but you and Arrahbella are my definition of what's good, Melody Bell, so forgive me if I want to keep you free from the sights of evil for just a little longer.'

She smiled and nodded understandingly.

Alain dropped his eyes to the table once more and traced his finger over the pattern in the wood. 'I am sorry if I hurt you, though,' he said, guiltily. 'I didn't mean for the command to be so strong.'

She shook her head. 'It didn't hurt. It just felt like my insides were going to explode.'

He cringed. 'Sorry.'

She gave him a small, reassuring smile. Alain waved her over and stood up so he could wrap his arms around her, hugging her so tightly that some feathers were dislodged, then he kissed the top of her head.

'You should go to bed,' he said, once he had released her.

'I'm not going to sleep just yet. All this fear, relief, and excitement has left me feeling rather in need of some love. What about you... do you feel in need of some love?'

Alain smiled. 'I must admit, I do feel a strong desire to go and protect and love someone, but as that someone is fast asleep I shall settle for watching her while she dreams.'

Melody smiled again. 'Goodnight, Alain du Maurier.'

'Goodnight, Melody Bell.'

She disappeared back into her room.

Alain walked through the caravans, checking that everyone had gone to bed and making sure all the doors were locked, his mind on a roller coaster of thoughts. Then, he walked quietly back through the dark rooms, too distracted to notice Melody and Chester rolling about under the covers, and into his own room where a single lamp glowed softly to welcome him. Usually, Alain slept wearing only a pair of loose white cotton pants, but tonight he stripped off his performance clothes and climbed straight in. He put his arm over Arrahbella and watched her breathing deeply until he fell into a sleep plagued with dreams that were a combination of both beauty and bloodshed.

CHAPTER 10

TERRENVALE

Present Day – Terrenvale

Five days after leaving Icecess, the train pulled into the Toufaun Creek region of Terrenvale, the home of the dwarves.

'Right, everyone,' Alain announced, when they had all gathered together in the kitchen car, 'I'm going to see Derk to let him know that we've arrived. Amuse yourselves until mid afternoon.'

'Great,' Izan said with sarcasm. He found the lack of available partners in Terrenvale to be an annoying inconvenience. He would have gladly taken a dwarf partner, of course, but no dwarves would take him, as they were fiercely loyal to their own race. He looked over at Sora. 'Sora, my dear girl, pile me with comic books.'

'Nonsense, Izan,' Alain said, cheerfully. 'It's a beautiful day, I want everyone out in the fresh air.'

'Then I shall read outside, my good man,' Izan replied.

Alain chuckled and left with Fenton to go and seek out Derk, the leader of the Toufaun Creek Clan. The other four dwarves followed, heading off to see their families for the first time in four months: Cravel (who had recently moved to Toufaun Creek from the neighbouring Telln Clan) went to see his heavily pregnant wife, Verna, and their children, Quenta and Flak; Phan left to see Della (his wife and Dell's sister) and their son, Jak; while Dell went to see Frima – his wife who also happened to be Derk's cousin. As Grent was only betrothed, he still lived with his parents in the Phoot region, so he went along with Dell for company.

'Here you are, Izan,' Sora said, returning from her room with her latest comic.

'Thank you, my dear.' Izan grabbed a chair and took it outside.

The train had been parked in a large grassy area known as Toufaun's Blanket. Each of Terrenvale's eleven regions had a Blanket, one forest, a number of hills, and a lake. Some also had a beach. No other trees grew outside of the forests; the only exception being the one which sat in the middle of the Telln Blanket, inspiring all sorts of legends as to why it was there. The air was pure music (the same sparkling, colourful, misty substance as the one sitting in a vial in Alain's office back at the manor), creating a constant flow of soft tunes and melodies that kept the listener's soul in eternal rapture. As Izan set his chair up next to the train and began to read, the others dispersed to various areas around the Blanket with their own activities. Asseniah, who felt very much at home in Terrenvale, hurtled out of the train ahead of the others, stopping in the middle of the Blanket where she promptly fell down to lie on her back and watch the music swirl and tangle around her.

An hour later, having returned from Derk, Fenton led Arrahbella and Mariette back to the cluster of grassy mounds that were the homes of the dwarves. These Turf Huts, as they were known, looked like small hills with little wooden doors set into their sides. The door that Fenton knocked on was opened by a very rotund dwarf who had a mop of red hair and bulging arm muscles.

'Fenton, my good fellow, is it that time of the year already?' His voice was high pitched and squeaky.

'Hello, Herb. Yes, I've brought the circus with me, I have. Thought you could use some entertainment.'

'We certainly could. I can't believe it's been a whole four seasons since you were all here last.'

'Time flies, Herb, that it does. You remember Arrahbella and Mariette?'

'Of course I do. Welcome ladies, welcome.' He took their hands and shook them enthusiastically as they said hello.

'Might we trouble you for some supplies?' Fenton asked him.

'Of course, come in, come in.'

Herb stood aside and they entered the hut, the two women having to duck quite low in order to fit through the door.

Inside looked just like a small cottage: the dirt floor, which was just as colourful and full of music as the air outside, was covered in rugs; bookcases and dressers lined the walls, crammed full of trinkets and books; armchairs sat beside a small fireplace, which was always lit; there was a wooden table and chairs, carved with native designs; and the lovely smell of earth and grass mixed with an aroma of baked bread and cookies.

'Bread is what you're wanting then, is it, my dears?' Herb asked.

'Yes, thank you,' Arrahbella replied, still bent almost double, her hair touching the roof. 'About four loaves and two batches of rolls please.' Some Terrenvale food tasted slightly odd thanks to its music-enriched ingredients, but the troupe was used to that by now, and one couldn't really afford to be fussy when on the road. If you had asked them what music tasted like, you would have received fourteen totally different opinions, which would have only changed the next time you asked them anyway.

'I've just taken some cookies out of the oven, I has. Chocolate and peanut,' Herb ventured.

'Then we'll have some of them as well.'

The baker smiled broadly. 'This way.'

They followed him further into the hut, winding through the long tunnels that went on for miles in all directions, to his bakery where he loaded them up with goodies.

Back at the train, Chester was strumming away on his guitar, Izan was in a deep discussion with Sora about her comic books, highly impressed by her graphic pictures, Oleg was painting the landscape, and Asseniah was still playing with music, so, Alain and Melody pulled up some chairs around the other side of the train and talked.

'I wrote a descriptive piece,' she told him.

'Let's see it then.'

Melody dashed into her room, returning with a single sheet of paper which she handed to Alain.

'Read it out loud. It'll sound better if you read it.'

Alain did so. Melody closed her eyes and listened. When Alain had her words in his mouth, Melody's soul was in raptures; those rich tones, the Master of Words reading her own creation...

The Bridge of Whispers
By Melody Castlereigh Bell

She stood on the Bridge of Whispers. All around, a sea of endless pink clouds; fluffy, soft. The last rays of the sun touching them, caressing them. The sound was sweet – a silence, but a golden silence, the sound of the clouds as they whispered to each other, speaking of what they had seen that day, of what secrets the wind had told them, of what the birds had sung, and of how the trees had sighed. The light played its own music, striking up an orchestra with the stars that were slowly appearing. The bridge was sturdy, it had carried many across it. Made of whispers, strung together, woven with promises and dreams. The girl wore a simple flowing pink dress, like a nightgown, which floated around her creamy white legs as the soft, warm breeze played with her loose ringlets. The air smelled of faraway places, fresh, clean, earthy. She had to cross the bridge before dark, so, taking a deep breath, inhaling all those scents, she looked around at the scene one last time, closed her eyes and took a step, disappearing into the clouds, hearing nothing but whispers.

Alain paused for a moment after finishing. Melody opened her eyes and looked at him with anticipation.

'Well?'

'It's good. I like it.'

Melody beamed, scrunching up her face in delight. Alain decided to play with her. He set the page down on his lap, looking at it intently. As Melody watched excitedly, her wings beating gently, Alain pulled an inky black sentence off the page, "the last rays of the sun touching them, caressing them," and let it float in front of them. He took the next line and gently tied their ends together, then, he took the chain and fastened it around Melody's neck. Next, he selected a few words, told them to jump into the air, and rearranged their letters to form different words entirely. The rest of the words flew up into the air, leaving a blank sheet of paper. Alain gathered them all up in his hands, scrunched them into a large black ball, then threw them into the air so that they rained down on Melody (there are, ironically, no words to describe the feeling of a torrent of words, especially words that you've written yourself, raining down on your head and skin, settling on your shoulders and in your hair, but it is a sweetly pleasant feeling and one Melody enjoyed very much). When the final word had settled itself, Alain directed them all into the air again and asked them to structure themselves so that they formed one of the piece's images in the air: the bridge itself. Melody clapped her hands in delight. Finally, Alain detached the string of words from around Melody's neck and sent every letter back onto the page in its exact original placing. Looking at the paper, you would never know they had left. Whenever Alain did this, he may as well have been holding Melody's heart in his hands; it was a strangely glorious, somewhat frightening and nerve-wracking, delicious experience that required the kind of trust they shared.

Inside the caravan, Arrahbella was doing a similar thing with herbs and spices in the kitchen while she prepared lunch. She had just returned from collecting the food with Fenton and Mariette, and, while the dwarf had gone off to finally visit his family (his wife, Krute, and his teenage daughters, Laun and Frida), Mariette was helping with the food preparation. Today it was burgers; red bean and carrot for Arrahbella (who was a vegetarian) and Alain (who had become one after meeting her), fish for Melody, Asseniah, and Mariette (who all ate red meat but liked a change occasionally), and steak burgers for Chester, Oleg, Sora, and Izan. The steak came from a small horned shaggy cow known as a dunt that roamed the Blankets of Terrenvale and mooed melodiously, creating quite the choir when done in unison.

''ow is Alain?' Mariette asked, while she peeled carrots. 'After what 'appened to Sora and zen in Icecess?'

'Oh, you know Alain,' Arrahbella replied, as she mixed up the mayonnaise for the fish burgers. 'Even if he were sick with worry he wouldn't let anyone know about it.'

''e let a little show when he was arguing wiz Izan.'

'I know,' she smiled sadly. 'He's okay. He always bounces back quickly, or hides his feelings, but, after talking to him, I'm sure he's okay. Both events just frazzled him a little, especially Sora being attacked. He, of course, feels responsible for that.'

'I zought 'e might, but 'e 'ad no way of knowing and she wouldn't 'ave let 'im protect 'er anyway.'

'I know. I think he's going to be a little more protective than usual for a while.'

Mariette nodded in agreement.

That night, after they had performed, the troupe joined the entire clan, made up of over one hundred dwarves, as they made small fires and sat out on the Toufaun Blanket in clusters to sing, play instruments, dance, eat, play games, and generally have a good time. It wasn't long before Izan had forgotten his loneliness and was laughing with Cravel over the antics of a rather comical dwarf while they chewed talooey. Mariette, Sora, and Asseniah were sharing stories with Krute, Laun, Frida, Della, and Frima. Oleg attempted to learn the guitar but found he didn't quite have the rhythm so he watched Dell play instead. Derk was telling stories to anyone who would listen, and dwarf children ran around the group playing Chasey.

Melody was snuggled up to Chester as he played the guitar with Derk's brother, Quell, watching Alain and Arrahbella who were slow-dancing lazily to the flutes and panpipes.

'Look at them, Chester,' Melody whispered. 'They're

so perfect together. Whenever I see them it makes me believe in true everlasting love.'

'And our relationship doesn't?' he teased.

'Of course it does. But when Alain first brought Arrahbella back from Earth, and before I knew you were in love with me, their relationship made me believe in it. I remember walking into the sitting room one time, when I was fourteen, and they were standing by the window, just looking into each other's eyes, and their eyes were kind of... fuzzed by beauty.' Chester smiled, though he had heard her recount the story many times before. 'And then they kissed, only briefly and softly, but it was such a heart caressing scene. They didn't even know I was there.' She paused. 'The entire world could fall to pieces, but their love will always exist. It's one of the constants of life.' She looked at Chester and kissed his cheek. 'And that's the kind of love I always wished for, and now I'm on my way to it.'

Chester stopped strumming to kiss her on the mouth for a prolonged moment, then turned his attention back to Quell. Melody turned back to the du Mauriers who were still oblivious to their audience, the misty air adding a dreamy veil to the scene. She recognised the signs of lust rapidly taking over and, sure enough, Alain eventually moved his mouth to Arrahbella's ear, his eyes closed, whispered into it, stood back to look into her eyes, which were as hungry as his own, then walked her toward the train.

'Chester,' Derk called. 'See if you can't strangle a tune from that guitar.'

All the dwarves within ear shot recognised the cue to

be silent. Even the pipe players put down their instruments and gathered around Chester who shook his head.

'Ah, no, sir, however, I will caress her and see what she sings for us.'

Derk laughed. Melody watched Alain open the door of their caravan for Arrahbella and keep hold of her hand as he helped her up the steps, then followed, closing the door behind them. She smiled and moved to sit next to Sora as Chester began to sing...

'There once was a princess,
A knight, and a dragon.
The knight loved the princess
But the princess loved the dragon...'

Not a unique story but much loved all the same.

Inside the du Maurier's caravan, Alain locked the two outside doors, the door to the driving cabin, and the door to Melody and Chester's caravan, then he walked over to his wife who was standing by the foot of the bed, scooped her up into his arms and laid her down gently. They were drunk with love, bursting at the seams with the need to intertwine their souls and bodies, be in that vulnerable position to show how much they trusted each other, forget that the world existed, and spend a few moments totally immersed in the one thing they loved the most. Both of them had powers that could enter other people, but no one could ever be as close to them as they were to each other in these moments.

A while later, when they lay in bed, side by side,

sleepy, happy, warm, delirious, Alain recited poetry then love-talked quietly, his calming, seductive tones washing over and through Arrahbella, making her feel warm and safe. She traced her finger lightly over his beard and moustache, around his eyes and lips, while he talked. Alain wrote "love" in the air and settled it on her bare chest where it shimmered and dissolved into her skin, making her shiver deliciously. He followed it with more words and pleasantries.

The troupe eventually said their goodnights and moved into the train. Phan, Dell, Cravel, and Fenton would spend the night with their families so they stayed outside until Derk called it a night.

Melody was talking to Sora on the floor of the girls' bedroom when Arrahbella came through, wrapped in a nightgown and dressing gown, almost floating with happiness. She bent down next to Melody, kissed her on the top of the head, and said 'tea time' in a melodious way.

'Would anyone else like a tea?' she asked.

'Yes, zank you, Arrahbella,' replied Mariette, who was taking off her show make-up.

'Sora?'

'No, thank you, I'm fine.'

'Asseniah?'

The flame-haired girl was up in her hammock, reading a comic of Sora's. She nodded.

'Come and help me then.'

Asseniah put down the book and climbed out of her hammock. The two of them went through to the kitchen car, Arrahbella humming some Earthly tune all the way.

284

After performing a second show in Toufaun Creek, the troupe moved on to Phoot.

Once Alain, Arrahbella, and Grent had returned from visiting Hirst, the Phoot Clan leader, Izan, Sora, Asseniah, Grent, and Dell decided to go for a walk along the beach before lunch.

'I'm surprised Alma wasn't home,' Grent said, not for the first time, as they strolled along. Soul-soaring music hummed in the air around them. Even the waves were playing tunes as they crashed against the shore.

'She wasn't in her hut?' asked Sora, picking up a seashell and examining it.

'No, which is odd because she knew I'd be here today.'

'Maybe she got caught up with something,' Dell suggested. 'I'm sure that she'll come and find you when she can. The train isn't exactly hard to miss.'

Grent smiled. 'I'm sure you're right, Dell.'

They walked in silence for a few minutes. The sun was full and having one of its rare warm summer days. Somewhere, far away in the distance, a dragon screeched, making Dell shiver.

'This sand is beautiful, Grent,' Sora said, letting a handful of pure white sand run through her fingers. 'It's perfect.'

'Yeah, we've got the best in any world along the Highway, we have... well, that I've seen anyway.'

'It's the kind you hear about in poems.'

'This is where I first met Alma,' he said, his memory

giving him a faraway look. 'I was fishing with my brother when she came walking along with her mother. The sun was setting and she was aglow with the reflecting rays. I fell in love with her instantly.'

Sora and Dell smiled.

''Course,' he continued. 'We'd known each other since we were bubs, being in the same clan and all, but it was that day I realised I was in love with her.'

Izan picked up a stone and threw it along the water, adding magic so that it skimmed the top until it was out of view.

'I'm surprised Melody and Chester aren't out here clicking away with that camera thingo,' he said.

'They're waiting for the sunset,' Sora said, matter-of-factly, not looking up from the sand. 'You can't take pictures if the light's flat.'

'Of course not,' Izan replied, without interest.

Asseniah ran into the shallows of the water and splashed around with her feet, making the others laugh at the rare display of animation.

They walked a bit further, stopping at a pile of rocks that interrupted the shore line. Nestled amongst the pile was a small but deep cave.

Izan was on the verge of daring Dell to enter first when, above the music of the waves, they heard soft sucking noises. Izan put his finger to his lips and they peered in quietly. The noise continued and was soon joined by soft moans, one in a female's voice, one in a male's. They seemed to have stumbled upon a couple of lovers, the sucking sound being that of some rather noisy kissing. Sora, Izan, Dell, and Grent grinned when they realised this and were about to turn away from the cave when the female voice said her lover's name in a long dreamy sigh.

'Bic.'

Grent froze when he recognised the voice, and the name, and a few seconds later his fears were confirmed when the male voice replied, 'Alma.'

The others had heard it too. All eyes slowly turned toward Grent. The poor man had gone as white as the sand, trembling from head to toe.

'Grent?' Dell said quietly, but the lovers heard him. They looked toward the entrance of their hideout, saw five faces looking at them, squealed, and leapt up quickly, their eyes on Grent.

'Alma?' he said weakly.

She knew she could not hide now and both she and her lover, Grent's cousin, walked out into the light. They stood before the dwarf with guilty faces. She wasn't particularly pretty, but she had a sweet face with a little button nose and pudgy cheeks. Her hair was brown and wispy and short. Bic was taller than Grent and far less attractive with lopsided, beady eyes, a large nose and spiky black hair.

'Alma?' Grent said again. Then, as his mind began to clear of the fog that had settled, 'What's going on?'

'I'm sorry, Grent,' Alma replied. 'I'm in love with Bic.'

Grent looked from Alma to Bic and back again, unsure of what to do. 'How long has this been going on?' he finally asked.

'Since your last tour. It just sort of happened.'

'Why didn't you tell me?'

Alma looked at Bic. 'We didn't want to hurt you.'

Grent finally put some force into his words. 'Didn't want to hurt me?! This *is* hurting me, Alma! Were you still planning on marrying me?'

Alma looked at the ground.

Grent shook his head. 'How could you have only just discovered this? We've known each other all our lives.'

'I know, Grent. We have known, really, in our hearts, for years, but I guess we just didn't realise it. Maybe because we've always thought about you.' She looked up at him. 'We're sorry, Grent.'

Although he had raised his voice a little, Grent still hadn't shown much anger. He seemed more defeated, looking from them to the ground and back again.

Bic finally spoke. 'You won't tell, will you, Grent? You know what will happen to Alma if they find out she was unfaithful.'

Grent nodded. 'Yes, I know.'

Dell had been trying to control his fury, but now he boiled over. 'Of course, he's going to tell, aren't you, Grent? Alma deserves to be locked away so that she doesn't ruin anyone else's life.'

Alma looked frightened.

'No, Dell, I'm not going to tell on her.' Everyone looked at him in surprise. 'We'll announce that we've parted ways and then Bic and Alma can wait for a moon before announcing their partnership.'

Alma was visibly relieved.

'Grent, you can't just let them get away with it.'

The young dwarf held up his hand. 'No, Dell, I love her and I want her to be happy. I wouldn't be able to sleep at night or live with myself if I knew I'd helped put her in a cage and brought the shame of the clan on her.'

'She's brought it on herself, she has.'

Grent faced his friend. 'I'm not going to turn her in and neither are you nor anyone else, okay?'

Dell scowled but nodded. 'Alright, if that's what you want.'

'It is.'

Alma squealed and rushed at Grent to throw her arms around him and kiss his cheek, but he pushed her away angrily.

'Don't! I don't want either of you to ever talk to me again. I'll move to Toufaun Creek. They'll welcome me there.' He looked at them for a moment. 'I still don't understand.' Then he turned and walked back along the beach, dragging his feet, his head low.

The others continued to stare angrily at Alma and Bic for a moment, Izan and Dell looking mutinous, but then they too turned and followed. Alma and Bic watched them go. Someone, possibly Asseniah, managed to conjure up a bit of wind, forcing a gust of sand to fly into the adulterous pair's faces. They ran back to their huts, wiping their eyes. Grent walked ahead of the group for the rest of the journey back to the train. No one spoke.

When they arrived, Alain and Arrahbella were setting out lunch on the grass, taking advantage of the nice weather, Melody and Chester were playing cards with Oleg and Mariette, and Phan, Cravel, and Fenton were giving the train a service. A few of them called greetings when they saw the group arrive but it quickly became obvious that things were not quite right when Grent walked straight past everyone without acknowledging them, threw open the dwarves' cabin door, and slammed it behind him.

'Is everything okay?' Alain asked Izan, when he had come within talking distance. The Wordmaster was, in fact, relieved to see them all return in one piece – Arrahbella had sensed something had happened but had not been shown exactly what.

'Nope. Grent just caught Alma cheating on him with his cousin.'

'Alma?! Is he sure?'

'Oh yeah, he spoke to her. He's an unhappy dwarf right now, Alain. He didn't even get angry.'

'And, he's not going to turn her in,' Dell told them, as the other dwarves climbed off of the train and gathered around. 'He's just going to let them get away with it.'

Fenton grunted. 'That's Grent for you.'

'It's outrageous,' Dell continued. 'She should be locked away.'

'I agree,' Phan said, using a rag to wipe grease off a spanner. 'Why don't we go and give her what for?'

'No,' Izan said, firmly. 'Grent didn't want to cause Alma any stress. He loves her and he's left them to be together because he wants her to be happy.'

'That's all very well,' Phan grunted. 'But he needs to be avenged and we can do that.'

'No,' Dell sighed, sadly. 'He was adamant that we don't do anything.'

The dwarves looked at each other with defeated expressions, though Phan remained unconvinced.

'Poor Grent,' Alain said. 'I'll go and talk to him.'

'It may be best if we leave him alone for a while,' Izan told him.

'I need to know if this is going to be our last show in Phoot.' Alain disappeared into the train. The others all sat down for a lunch of fish and chips, talking about the nerve of Alma and Bic. Sora, Phan, and Dell would have told the whole clan what they had done but the others understood Grent's decision. Asseniah was too busy playing with a misty strand of music to give her opinion.

When Alain returned, his face was etched with worry.

'Grent said that he'll still work on the show tonight, but he doesn't mind if we don't play here in the future and I don't think we will. The Phoot Clan have never seemed too fussed as to whether we play here or not. We've only ever come so that Grent's family can see his contribution. So tonight will be our last show here.'

Everyone agreed this was a good idea.

'He's going to ask Hirst if he can move to Toufaun Creek,' Alain continued. 'We'll go and see him after lunch.'

'He can move in with me for a bit,' Phan offered.

'Della won't mind.'

'That she won't, Phan,' Dell agreed. 'My sister has always had a heart bigger than the Toufaun Blanket.'

Alain smiled. 'Thank you, Phan. I'm sure Grent will appreciate it.'

That night's performance wasn't one of their best and as there was no after show gathering the troupe called it an early night.

In the morning, they moved on to Telln.

Having returned from seeing Ludo, the Telln Clan leader, Alain was in his caravan, going over facts and figures, when Arrahbella came hurrying in, looking more than a little flustered.

'Alain.'

He leapt up, his stomach plummeting to his feet at the sight of her worried expression. 'What is it?'

'We have a problem. Come into the kitchen.'

He followed her through the caravans to the kitchen car, stopping by the preparation counter where two of the herb canisters were sitting with their lids off.

Alain looked around for the emergency. 'What's the problem?'

'I was topping up the canisters and I noticed that two of them have been switched.'

Alain felt a surge of relief, which must have shown because Arrahbella frowned at him.

'I'm not talking about a minor incident, Alain. This isn't simply a case of the oregano being mixed with the thyme.'

'What is it then?'

'It's the Raven's Bark, it's been switched with the Griffinseed.'

A knot formed in the Ringmaster's stomach.

'And I don't know how long they've been like that,' she continued.

'What's the worst it could be?'

'I refilled it two weeks ago.'

'Two weeks?'

She nodded. 'And it wears off within a day or so if you don't keep taking it. And that's not all; the two are very similar in taste and appearance, but, ironically, one decreases fertility and the other increases it, among other things.'

Alain felt slightly ill. 'How did this happen?'

'I don't know. I've been trying to work that out. You know how careful I am with ingredients.'

He did know.

'Everyone has access to them, but they know to be careful with them too.'

Alain nodded, thinking. Arrahbella caught his thoughts.

'You think someone did it on purpose?' She stepped back, stunned he would even consider it of one of his troupe.

'I don't believe any of them would do such a thing, but I have noticed Chester looking rather longingly at any children we have passed in the last couple of months. I think he's getting a little paternal.'

'Chester wouldn't do this, though, neither would

Melody. They'd come and talk to us.'

'I think so too, but we'll need to speak to them about it and see what they say. I'm not sure how else this would have happened.'

She nodded.

'Have you checked the bags in the store room?'

'Not yet. I came straight to you.'

'Alright. I'll go and find them, you check the store.'

'Okay.'

Alain hesitated. 'It might be best if you talk to them.'

Arrahbella nodded again. 'That's fine.'

'I'll send them here.'

She froze as a vision came to her. Alain waited patiently until it ended.

'They're in the forest and they're getting undressed.'

Alain opened the kitchen door, looking toward the Telln forest across the road.

'In there?' he asked her.

'Yes. Not too far in, but hidden.'

Alain scrawled the word "stop" in the air and pushed it toward the forest before running out after it.

Nestled between a fallen log and a large talooey plant, only a few metres from the well-trodden dirt path, Chester and Melody were, indeed, half-naked and Melody's hands were working on Chester's pants while their mouths were locked in a passionate kiss. Their bodies were heating up, hormones running furiously through them, when suddenly they each felt an intense jolt and visions of their Ringmaster flashed through their heads. They quickly broke apart, staring at each other in stunned horror.

'Woah!' said Chester. 'Did something weird just happen?'

'Yes. That was Alain,' Melody replied, looking around. She tried to crawl off of him but found herself frozen from the neck down.

'Alain?'

'Uh huh.' She shuddered internally. 'Ugh! That was *not* good.'

'Damn right.'

They were silent for a moment, trying to get the feelings and images out of their minds.

They didn't have to wait long before Alain found them. He fought his way through a few branches and stopped beside them, hands on his knees, trying to catch his breath.

'Alain?' Melody prompted.

'You both need to come with me,' he panted. 'Arrahbella needs to talk to you.'

'Is everything okay?'

'We hope so. She'll explain.'

Melody cleared her throat to inform Alain that they were still frozen. He released his command on them and they were able to put their tops back on and stand up.

'Alain,' Melody said, as they walked out on to the path. 'Please don't do that again.'

'I had to, Melody. I didn't do it just for fun.'

'I know, but it was really weird, in a bad way.'

Chester nodded vigorously in agreement.

'Well, I'm sorry, but it couldn't be helped.' Alain was a little red in the face but whether this was still from running or whether he was blushing neither could tell.

They walked in silence to the train where Alain left them with Arrahbella in the kitchen.

'What's going on, Arrahbella?' Melody asked, as they sat across from her at the table.

'Melody, Chester, somehow the Raven's Bark has been swapped with the Griffinseed.' She waited for their reactions, watching the expected raising of eyebrows and tilting of heads. Under the table, Chester's hand took hold of Melody's. 'I don't know when it happened, it may have happened this morning and there may be no risk or it could have happened as long as two weeks ago, which means you've been fertile for a fortnight.'

The young pair looked at each other. Arrahbella couldn't read their expressions.

'How did they get switched?' Chester asked.

Arrahbella watched him closely while answering. 'I'm still trying to work that out.'

'You think it was us?' Melody asked.

Arrahbella's eyes lingered on Chester a moment longer before she turned to Melody.

'No,' she finally said, her usual air of mystery surrounding her. 'I believe you'd come and talk to Alain and I if you were thinking about children.'

'You're right, we would,' Melody assured her.

Arrahbella looked at Chester again.

'We would,' he repeated.

Arrahbella nodded, satisfied. 'Melody, have you been feeling okay? Does everything seem normal?'

'You mean, do I think I might be pregnant?'

'Yes, that's what I mean.'

'I don't know. But I don't think so.'

'It may be too early to tell. Let me know if you feel any different. You can always come and talk to me if you need to.'

'I know.'

'You too, Chester.'

Chester nodded. Something had come over him but Arrahbella couldn't work out what it was.

'You'll switch them back and put me on the Griffinseed again?' Melody asked.

'Of course.'

She hesitated. 'What if I am pregnant? If you switch me back onto the Griffinseed will it do any damage?'

'No. The Griffinseed works to kind of coat the female's egg so that no sperm can get through, as you know.' They nodded. 'So, if an egg's already been fertilised then your body is no longer producing eggs so it just goes through your system.'

Melody puffed out her cheeks as she thought.

'So, do you want us to lay off each other for a couple of days until the Griffinseed kicks in again?' Chester asked. His hand had relaxed its grip on Melody's.

'It does take a couple of days to settle in, yes, but I'm not going to sit here and tell you what you can and can't do. That's up to you, but you do know Alain's concerns, and I share them too, about the two of you bringing a child into the world at this stage of your lives, well, of Melody's life, and the circus' life.'

'Yes, we know.'

'And when we first talked to you about our concerns you shared them as well. I know it has been a while since then, and, Melody, you are an adult so you do what you wish to do, but I ask you to think carefully about everything. It'll only be three days before the herb kicks in again.'

The door opened and Mariette entered the room, stopping quickly when she realised there was a discussion going on.

'Oh, I'm sorry, I-'

'No, it's okay Mariette, we're done.' Arrahbella looked at Melody and Chester who nodded and slid back their chairs.

'Thanks, Arrahbella,' Melody said, and they left.

'Is everyzing okay?'

'Yes. Mariette, do you use the Griffinseed or Raven's Bark?'

'No. I tried ze Griffinseed once but did not like ze taste.'

Arrahbella nodded. She walked outside where Alain had taken one of Kruitar Vabonn's books (a book Melody had told him years ago that he should read and he had finally given in) having given up on the figures he was working on before. The book was in his hand, and open, but it hung limply by the side of the chair, his gaze in the direction of the forest though his focus was somewhere else entirely.

Arrahbella sat in the chair next to him, touching his hand lightly to get his attention.

'How did it go?'

'Fine. They were surprised but didn't seem too upset with the idea.'

'Hmm...'

'They didn't switch them, Alain.'

He nodded. 'Will you ask around?'

'I will.'

'Thank you for talking to them.'

'No problem,' she smiled. 'I have to go and make lunch.' She rose, bent to kiss him, and went back into the train.

Melody and Chester went to their room where they sat on their bed to talk. They were silent for a moment as they sat there holding hands. Finally, Melody looked into her love's bright purple eyes and started the discussion.

'Do you want children, Chester?' She thought he looked a little nervous, but she couldn't say for sure.

Chester was, indeed, slightly nervous. He shook his head. 'The question is, do *you* want children, Melody Bell?'

Melody wasn't sure why that was the question and she gave him a suspicious look before answering. 'I want to know what you want.'

He smiled. 'I want what you want. If you want children then I want children. If you don't, I don't.'

'That's not fair, 'cause then I'm just going to go through life not knowing if you're happy or not. You can't not tell me what you want, Chester. We have to know what each other wants if we're to make each other happy.'

'That is what I want – I want whatever you want and I'll be happy no matter what because I have you.'

'No. Because what if I say I don't and you do, or if I say I do and you don't, then we're going to have a problem.'

'No, we're not.'

She gave him a frustrated sigh. He had lost his nervousness and was smiling at her patiently.

'Chester, please tell me.'

He put one of his delicately carved hands to her cheek and stroked it. He could see that she was scared.

'Melody, do you want children now? I mean, if you were to fall pregnant tonight and in nine months time have a child, would you want that? You'd still be eighteen and I'd be almost twenty-seven.' He stopped for a moment, swallowing as the thought of being nearly thirty hit him. 'Do you want to be a mother by the end of the year?'

She thought about it. He watched her, his hands playing with her hair, stroking her hands, cheeks, and wings. Eventually, she looked up at him.

'No, Chester,' she said quietly. 'I'm not ready for children. Not yet.'

Chester swallowed again and nodded, smiling. 'Then we don't need to worry about it right now. We'll just stay away from each other for the next three days... which will be nice and hard.'

'We've gone longer than that before, you know. Quite a few times.'

'Yes, but I'm craving you right now and we're about

300

to hit the road again, and we have unfinished business since Alain stopped us. Mind you, I've still got his image in my head so that should be nice and off-putting for at least another ten years.'

'Ha! Yeah. That was weird.'

There was a pause.

'I could be pregnant, Chester, I mean, I really could be. If it has been two weeks then there's a very good chance I could have a child inside me right now. What if I do?'

Chester took a discreet deep breath. 'If you do, then you do.'

As his words sunk in, Melody felt a calmness wash over her. 'You know, you're right. If I'm pregnant, then I am. I guess we'll just have to wait and see. I was feeling a little off colour yesterday, come to think of it, and this morning, but my monthly's not due until next week so we'll know more then.'

Chester nodded, his porcelain skin taking on an even whiter shade of pale that Melody didn't notice as thoughts of motherhood went through her head.

'I don't know if I'm ready, Chester, but the thought that I may actually be pregnant doesn't feel as scary as I thought it might.'

Chester put his arm around her. 'Melody, let's just find out if you are or not. If you're not, then you keep taking the Griffinseed until you know whether you want children. If you are, well, then we'll think about the next step.'

'You mean, whether we give it away or not.'

'Yes, that's what I mean.'

'I don't think I could do that,' she whispered after a moment.

'You don't have to answer right now, okay?'

Melody nodded. Chester gazed at her for a moment, taking her in, before pulling her close and kissing her passionately. He briefly traced his fingers over her stomach and she quivered, then, he broke away and left the room without looking at her. He didn't stop until he got to the practice room, which he found empty, much to his relief, and he expended his energy by practising on the trapeze until lunch.

'The Griffinseed and the Raven's Bark were somehow switched,' Arrahbella told the group. They were gathered around the table in the kitchen, getting ready for lunch. 'Does anyone know anything about it?'

There was silence for a moment.

Arrahbella stood and walked over to the row of herbs, pointing to the canisters in question. 'These two.'

'That may have been me,' Phan admitted, guiltily. 'I accidentally knocked them over when I was reaching for the Raspberry Satin, just before we left Ormance. I refilled them though, but I must have swapped them. They look so similar. I was going to tell you but it was my turn to drive and I completely forgot about it afterward.'

'Phan, it is absolutely paramount that you tell me every little thing that happens with my herbs outside of the normal once a day use. Some herbs can be deadly if used in the wrong way. The Raven's Bark and Griffinseed are especially important.' The dwarves hadn't been told what the Griffinseed was for and had no idea that Melody drank it every night.

'I know, I'm sorry.'

Dell gave him a whack on the head for good measure.

There was no after show gathering in Telln that night either. The troupe ate their supper of baked potatoes with various toppings and an apple pie dessert then sat outside in the warm night air. Tomorrow they would leave for Landau, checking to see if it were open to tourists on the way (Alain had heard rumours that there was a war pending, which meant they may have to alter their plans). Only Asseniah went to her room, putting on a CD then climbing up to her hammock to listen, and Grent was still depressed so he went to bed straight after dinner, which, as had been the case the night before, he had eaten little of. Now, the other four dwarves were playing poker with Oleg and Mariette on a rug outside the train. Alain and Arrahbella were in chairs, reading, while Chester strummed his guitar across from them, and Melody combined reading with watching Chester and, sometimes, the stars, twinkling faintly so far away. There was no moon visible near Terrenvale and she found the night sky strange without one. Sora had brought her latest project – a corseted dress – outside and was working on that. Izan had been creating an extravagant magic display in the open Blanket in order to cope with the painful amount of unused power throbbing through his system, but, having tired of that, he now headed inside to listen to music, the thumping beats of his heavy metal album combining with the softer sounds of Tori Amos and the ever present Terrenvale music to create a strange orchestra.

Alain kept peeking over the top of Vabonn's novel, watching Melody and Chester. Once, when Melody had stopped reading to rest her head on Chester's shoulder, she caught him looking and raised an eyebrow at him. Alain smiled and returned to his novel. Melody looked across at Arrahbella, who had been watching Alain over her own book, and shook her head, making the Earthling smile. A moment later, the words in Melody's book danced around on the page for a few seconds. When she looked at Alain, he was reading intently, all innocence, though Arrahbella was giggling beside him. Melody closed her book.

'I think I'll go to bed,' she told Chester.

'Alright. Are you okay?'

'Mmm,' she nodded, but she was lying. She was feeling strange all of a sudden and though she usually complained when she felt unwell, the day's events made her keep her mouth shut. She stood up.

'Goodnight, everyone.'

The dwarves, Mariette, and Oleg all bade her goodnight but Sora began to pack up her things. 'I think you've got the right idea there, Melody,' she said, and stood up as well.

Melody walked behind Arrahbella's chair and gave her a hug.

'Thank you for looking after us, Arrahbella,' she said

into her ear.

Arrahbella kissed her cheek. 'No problem.'

Melody walked behind Alain and squeezed his shoulder. 'Stop worrying,' she whispered.

Alain put his hand on hers. 'Goodnight, Melody,' he said.

'You need to make him stop worrying, Arrahbella.'

Arrahbella gave a short laugh. 'Ha! You know that will never happen.'

'No.'

'He wouldn't be Alain if he didn't worry.'

'True.'

'I'm right here, you know,' Alain said, indignantly.

Melody squeezed his shoulder again. 'Goodnight, Ringmaster.'

She and Sora went inside and, a few moments later, both sets of Earthling music fell silent.

Arrahbella nuzzled her nose against Alain's cheek playfully.

'You do worry too much, you know.'

'I know, but somebody has to keep this lot in order.'

Arrahbella smiled. Alain studied her for a moment before tracing a finger down her nose. They returned to their novels.

After a while, Alain's reading was interrupted by Arrahbella's psychic voice informing him that Chester wished to talk to him privately. Alain closed his book and stood up.

'Chester, why don't you gather up the tea mugs and help me take them in?'

The jester put his guitar down and did so, following Alain into the kitchen and closing the door behind him.

Alain put his mugs in the sink, taking the others from Chester and doing the same. Then, he turned, leant against the bench and waited, arms folded across his chest. Chester didn't look at him.

'I know you're worried about this whole herb mix-up thing, Alain,' he finally said.

'Well, you know that I don't think Melody is ready for children. I'm not sure that the circus is either.'

'Melody doesn't think she's ready. We were talking about it earlier. Though, I don't think she knows if she wants any at all yet or not. And that's fine, she is young, and I know that. I wasn't thinking about kids at eighteen.'

'Well, I know, Chester, that, while Melody may not be quite at parenting age yet, you are. You have been for a few years, so I understand that you may be ready.'

The jester finally looked at him, turning from boyish to grown-up man in a split second. 'If Melody wants children then I'll wait for her, and if she doesn't then I'm fine with that too.'

Alain studied him. 'Which scenario would you prefer?'

'Why isn't anyone happy with that answer? I am.'

'Because I want to know what you want.'

'And I want what Melody wants.'

Alain narrowed his eyes.

Chester gave in. 'I want children with her, Alain. I love children, you know that, and I love Melody so much and I just...' he trailed off, rubbing a hand through his hair. 'To have a child that was part of her and part of me. I do want children with her, but, if she tells me she doesn't want any then I'll live with that because I'm completely happy just being with her. Having children would be extra wonderful.'

'You mean, you'd put her happiness before your own.'

'Well, I hadn't thought of it like that, but, yes, of course I would. And no, because I'm happy anyway.'

Alain nodded.

'I do understand your reasons for not wanting her to have any now, and I agree that now isn't the best time, but I do hope she wants some and I hope she wants some before I'm too old.'

Alain laughed. 'I don't think you'll ever get old, Chester.'

'Maybe not in mind and spirit, but my body will.'

'Not if you keep up the trapeze it won't.'

'I'm not sure what we'll do if she is pregnant now, though,' Chester said, tracing his finger over the tiles on the bench. 'She may want to give it up... and that's going to be a very hard thing for me to do.'

'I was under the impression that Melody is sure she isn't pregnant.'

'We're almost certain she's not, but there's still a possibility.'

Alain fiddled with his beard, the knot returning to his stomach. There was silence for a moment.

'Alain, do you think Melody is too young for me to

ask her to marry me?'

Alain's heart fluttered a little and he smiled. 'Do you think she's too young?'

'I don't think so, but I still can't help wondering if she'll change her mind about me in a few years and decide I'm too old.'

'Chester, we've been through this.'

'I know.'

'You can only ask her. If she's not ready, she'll tell you. You wouldn't lose her over it.'

'I know.' He paused. 'Do you have any objections?'

'You don't need to ask my permission, Chester, I'm not her father. And while I have some say in the children issue because I want you both in the circus a while longer, I don't have any say in anything else you do... as Izan very clearly pointed out.'

'I know that, but you're the closest thing Melody has to a father and she loves you more than anything.'

'That's not true.'

'Well, she loves me, but it's a different kind of love. Like how you love her in a different way to how you love Arrahbella... you know what I mean, Alain. Because Melody respects you and what you think, I want to make sure I have your approval too.'

'Chester, if I was scrutinising every male that Melody eyed, and if I had to give my permission to a man who wanted to marry her, if she did have a huge place in my heart and I cared deeply about whether she got hurt or not, then I would give you my approval, Chester from the Apricot Meadows, and say that there is no other man, in any world along this Highway that I would rather be by her side.'

Chester didn't know what to say.

'You love her, you'd put her happiness before your own, and I know that you'd do anything for her. I also know that she wants only to make you happy and loves you more than anything, more than me, more than Izan, and that you make her happy. And that's all I could ask for her.'

Chester's eyes were bright as he clapped Alain on the shoulder.

'Thanks, Alain,' he said, and the Wordmaster nodded. 'Well, I suppose I'll go to bed. Goodnight.'

'Goodnight, Chester.'

Chester walked to the door that led him back outside.

'And, Chester, you may want to consider asking Izan's permission as well.'

The jester nodded and exited the kitchen.

Alain stared at the floor for a while, lost in thought, stroking his beard. He wrote the word "happiness" in the air, considering it for a moment, then brushing it away. Finally, he walked outside to find the others had packed up and gone to bed. Returning to the kitchen, he locked the doors, turned off the main lights so that only the ever-present soft lamp glow was showing, and walked through to the girls' room where Mariette was just climbing into bed. He said goodnight to her before continuing on into Izan's room to find the magician in bed, snoring, obviously hoping that the sooner he fell asleep the sooner tomorrow would come and they could leave Terrenvale. Entering Melody and Chester's room, Alain found them tucked into bed as well. He had been in the kitchen long enough for Chester to have fallen asleep, or at least, he appeared to be asleep.

Alain went and sat in the chair beside Melody's side of the bed. The winged girl was on her stomach, fast asleep, visible white feathers scattered around her on the mattress and pillow. He sat and watched her for a while, thinking many different things, one of which was whether she was pregnant or not, what kind of mother she would make, whether the baby would have wings... Before he left he sent "sweet dreams" into her mind (watched her smile as it sunk in) then he closed the door behind him.

CHAPTER 11

ꡘNTERMISSION

Present Day – The Highway

'Alain. Alain. We have to stop,' Izan announced, as he ran into the du Maurier's caravan where the married couple were looking over the finances.

'Why? What's wrong?'

The magician bounced up and down. 'There's a group of people on the side of the road. They look stranded.'

Alain's concern dissipated. Arrahbella smiled and turned her attention back to the figures.

'I don't know, Izan, we're rather pushed for time.' Actually, they were right on schedule, but Alain couldn't resist teasing.

'But they're stranded,' Izan whined. 'They could die out there, Alain. Who knows when the next travellers will come along.'

'We're at the busiest end of the Highway, Izan.'

'So?'

Alain shook his head in disbelief. 'Are they Landaus?'

'I don't know. Does it matter?'

'Yes, if Landau is at war then no one is meant to be

leaving or going in. They could be fugitives.'

'They may not be either. Can't we at least take them as far as Karantale's Inn?'

'They may be going the other way.' The corners of Alain's mouth twitched as he tried to hide a smile.

Izan crossed his arms and tapped his foot. 'If you don't stop the train now you'll have to go back even further and we'll lose more time.'

'Oh alright,' Alain said, standing up. 'We'll have to make sure they're not bandits though.'

Izan jumped for joy and followed Alain into the driver's cabin. Cravel was driving and, at Alain's request, he turned the train around in a large circle until he was alongside the little group on the side of the road. The other troupe members felt the train's unusual movements and went to the nearest window to watch as Alain and Izan jumped down from the driver's cabin and spoke to the people on the Highway's gravel-strewn edge.

There were three of them, two girls and one man, ranging from their mid-twenties to early thirties at a guess. They had a bit of luggage with them and, after a few words had been exchanged, they picked up their packs and boarded the train, entering through the kitchen. Cravel took off the brake and they continued on their way.

'Welcome aboard our train,' Alain said, as the rest of the troupe filed into the room. 'My name is Alain du Maurier.'

'Am I right in thinking that we've just boarded the train of the famous Cirque du Phantastique?' asked the man.

He was tall and handsome with a mop of black hair, tanned skin, and deep brown eyes.

'Indeed you have, sir,' Alain continued, smiling. 'Might I also introduce Izan Bell, Fenton, Dell, Phan, Grent, Sora Mai, Asseniah, Mariette le'Chuse, Oleg Fyzek, Chester from the Apricot Meadows, Melody Bell, and my wife, Arrahbella du Maurier.'

'Pleasure,' the man said, gazing at Melody for longer than was necessary. 'I am Gabrion Callo and these are my sisters, Lota and Carna.'

Both girls were dark and voluptuous.

'You are Varatalian,' Alain commented.

'We are. Born and bred in Valaya.'

'Ah, yes. I've been to the Milanto region a few times now. It has some stunning scenery.'

The siblings nodded proudly.

'We hope to take the show there sometime in the future,' the Wordmaster continued. 'Once we work out how to get all of our equipment through the mountain pass.'

'Milanto borders Palero,' Gabrion reminded him. 'Some of the birds offer their services to travellers.'

Izan interrupted his game of exchanging suggestive looks with the girls to frown at Gabrion. 'Willingly?'

The man sniffed. 'Some are against it and find it degrading, but others are happy to do so if they get something in return.'

Izan cast a look at Melody who shrugged.

'Thank you,' Alain said, smiling politely. 'We'll be sure to look into that.' Then he psychically added to Arrahbella,

'Remind me to investigate the truth of that claim when we get home.' Magical beasts being used as slaves was a recurring problem in Varatalé. Alain had discovered a herd of enchanted centaurs being held under the spell of the university's head professor a few years back. He had gone straight to Fello who had made some enquiries and promptly thrown the offender in jail... but not before the centaur king had shown him what it was like to be a slave.

Arrahbella smiled at her husband's unquenchable thirst for justice and squeezed his hand. The gesture made him turn his head to look into her eyes and all else melted around him. Realising he wasn't about to surface anytime soon, Melody flicked the back of his shirt, making him look up quickly to see all pairs of eyes turned in his direction.

Lota broke the silence. 'I hope it's no trouble giving us a ride,' she said, her voice soft.

Alain cleared his throat as Arrahbella smothered a giggle. 'Not at all. I'm afraid we're limited for space though, so we can only take you as far as Karantale's Inn, and you'll have to sleep on the mats in the practice room.'

'Thank you, we appreciate it.' Gabrion's eyes slid from Alain's to rest on Melody once again.

Chester cleared his throat. 'Well, if you'll excuse us.' He took Melody's hand and led her back through to their caravan. Sora and Asseniah followed while the dwarves headed off in the opposite direction.

'Perhaps I can offer you a drink?' Alain suggested.

The travellers accepted refreshments, the girls staying long enough to be polite before following Izan back to his caravan while Alain, Arrahbella, Mariette, and Oleg chatted to Gabrion for a lengthy hour full of awkward silences. Gabrion flirted constantly with Arrahbella and Mariette who did their best to be polite while the men watched on with growing aggravation.

As Alain tried to turn the conversation away from how much the circus had earned already on its tour, Melody and Chester entered, on their way to the practice room.

'The practice room?' Gabrion said. 'That sounds interesting. May I watch?'

Chester looked to Alain for help.

'Unfortunately, Mister Callo, I don't allow anyone to watch my troupe rehearse.'

'Oh, of course.'

Chester thanked Alain with a smile and pushed Melody through the door ahead of him.

'I should probably start getting dinner ready,' Arrahbella announced.

'Alright. Mister Callo, why don't you go through to the girls' caravan and talk to them for a while. Mariette, would you mind escorting our guest?'

'Zis way, sir.'

Alain waited until they were out of the room before turning to Oleg. 'Would you mind sitting in as well? I don't want him left alone with them.'

Oleg nodded and left the room. His presence didn't help, though, Gabrion continued to flirt relentlessly with all the girls, even young Asseniah.

After practising, Melody and Chester went to shower.

Chester managed to come up with enough excuses to keep them away from Gabrion for a good couple of hours, but eventually, the excuses ran out and they talked to him until dinner time. He had Melody in a fit of giggles most of the time, even succeeding in making Chester smirk once or twice.

Finally, Arrahbella announced it was time for dinner and they all moved into the dining car. Due to a lack of seating, the dwarves ate in their caravan while Izan and the sisters took their plates back to Izan's room.

'So, your brother is a magician?' Gabrion asked Melody, rather unnecessarily. He was seated at the head of the table, opposite Alain.

'He is.'

'I know a bit of magic myself,' he said, and performed the age-old trick of making a coin appear from behind Melody's ear. Melody made the correct sounds of delight but Chester was unimpressed.

'That would be much more effective if we didn't all know how to do it.'

Gabrion shrugged and turned back to Melody. 'And you're the trapeze artist?'

'Yes, I am. And Chester, we do it together.' She turned to Arrahbella. 'May I have some more, please, Arrahbella?'

Alain almost choked on his vegetarian lasagne. Melody never asked for seconds, her father had been part bird after all.

'Of course, Melody,' Arrahbella replied, not batting an eyelid.

'What's it like up there?' Gabrion asked, shovelling another forkful of his second helping into his already full mouth. 'On the trapeze?'

'Exhilarating. Even more so when you're up there with the one you love because your life is in their hands, and that's exhilarating, erotic even.'

'She means erotic for the soul, not for the body,' Alain pointed out. 'Performing has a soul-soaring effect; a bit like when you're flying through the air on a griffin, or listening to a good piece of music.'

Asseniah nodded in agreement, her eyes not leaving her plate (where she had carefully dissected her lasagne, purged it of all mushrooms, viciously attacked the offending vegetables in case they had the nerve to re-invade her dinner, then re-built the slice once again as far away from the mushy remains as possible).

'That's right,' Melody continued. 'And every combination is different. Mariette's learning the trapeze, but when I'm up there with her it's different to when I'm up there with Chester, and it would be different again if Chester were up there with Sora.'

'Sounds like I should be in the circus,' Gabrion said, a little too enthusiastically.

Melody shook her head. 'Not just any circus. Only Cirque du Phantastique can make you feel like that. Cirque du Phantastique is all about bringing magic to people, inspiring them to believe that anything is possible, and that inspiration is arousing. And we all feel it, no matter what our weapon of choice; Asseniah and her aerial silks, Alain and his words, or Sora and her daggers or tightrope, it's all erotic, all exhilarating, because it makes the audience feel and there's a lot of trust between us and our tools and the audience. So, you can't join just any circus. You have to have a passion and you have to want to share that passion with the audience.'

Gabrion watched Melody, his finger tracing the rim of his wine glass.

Alain, seeing Chester's grip tighten on his fork, cleared his throat. 'But that's enough about us, Mister Callo,' he said. 'Why don't you tell us more about your father, the book trader.'

Melody took this the wrong way, thinking that Alain was unhappy that she had talked about their troupe in such a way to a stranger, and she looked down at the table. She suddenly didn't feel very well and pushed her half-eaten second helping away.

'I think I've told you all there is. He lives in Arelia and my sisters and I are visiting him for his birthday. He also trades magical tools.'

'Illegal ones,' Arrahbella said, psychically.

Alain was really beginning to wish he hadn't taken the trio on board.

'Excuse me, I think I'll go to bed,' Melody said, and stood up. 'It has been a pleasure talking to you, Mister Callo.'

Gabrion took Melody's hand and, much to everyone's surprise, kissed it. Melody finally realised he had been flirting with her all afternoon and bristled.

'And it has been a pleasure talking to you, Miss Bell.

318

Perhaps when you return to Varatalé we can talk again.'

'If our paths cross,' was all she said, then she left the room.

The black cloud above Chester's head was almost visible as he stood and collected up his and Melody's plates.

'I think I'll go too. Thank you for dinner, Arrahbella.' He walked to the sink.

'I'll do them, Chester,' Arrahbella said. 'Leave them there.'

Chester had been about to wash off their plates, but he put them in the sink and thanked her again. He was heading toward the door when Melody came bursting back in, threw herself onto Chester, who had to grab her legs as they wrapped around his waist, and kissed him passionately. Alain couldn't help smiling a little. Melody jumped back down off of Chester, took him by the arm, and led him out the door. Sora had also found this rather amusing and she watched Gabrion for his reaction. Rather to their disappointment, the man turned instantly to Mariette.

'So, Miss le'Chuse, do you have a partner?'

Asseniah had had enough. She gave Arrahbella a look that thanked her for dinner and left the table.

'No, I do not.'

'That's a shame. Such a beautiful woman as yourself should not be without a man to love her.'

'I do not want a man, zank you, I 'ave my friends to love me, zat is all I need.'

'Ah, it seems Miss le'Chuse has renounced all men, but, my dear girl, I hope you don't think we're all horrible;

319

some of us can be quite loving and attentive to our women.'

Mariette looked Gabrion squarely in the eyes. 'Mister Callo, as you can see, most of ze members of zis troupe are male and I zink very 'ighly of zem. Indeed, Alain is my oldest and dearest friend and I owe 'im my life. I 'ave also learnt from watching 'im and Chester zat men can be very caring, loving, and wonderful to women, but, I 'ave 'ad my fill of men and I am quite 'appy wizout one, zank you.'

Gabrion gave up on her. 'Fine, fine.'

Alain was smiling. So was Arrahbella.

'Well, I think dinner is over,' Alain said, rising from his seat. 'Mister Callo, you're welcome to follow my wife and I to our room to chat for a while or the dwarves would be delighted to have you for a round of cards or board games.'

Gabrion had become tired of the humans. 'I think some cards would be lovely.'

Alain was relieved to hear this. They all parted ways and whiled away the evening.

As Alain and Arrahbella walked through to their room, Melody was giving Chester another lecture on how he was silly to be jealous.

'He was flirting with you, Melody, and you were flirting back.'

'I was not. That's how I talk to everyone, if you haven't noticed. Do you think I flirt with everyone? I was just being polite. Really, Chester, you're being silly. I'm getting tired of reassuring you all the time.'

Alain smiled as he closed the door joining their rooms.

'Poor Chester,' Arrahbella chuckled, as she sat on the

edge of the bed.

'He does worry too much.'

'Well, Melody was being herself, but she does flirt when she's being herself, consciously or not.'

Alain sat next to her. 'That's true. Though I don't think she does it on purpose. She's just... innocent. She's always been like that.'

Arrahbella ran a finger up his arm. 'She flirts with you, you know.'

'She does, but in a purely platonic way.'

'Can you flirt in a purely platonic way?'

'Yes, because Melody's not physically attracted to me. But she trusts me, and it's the trust she flirts with.'

'Your words turn her on, when you're playing with her poems...'

Alain sighed. 'Arrahbella, my words turn everyone on.'

She laughed and hit him on the arm. 'Get over yourself, Wordmaster.'

He took her hand in his. 'I am the Ringmaster of a circus that thrives on being turned on. I turn all of them on with my words.' He stroked her hair. 'But you're the only one that turns me on.'

She kissed him.

Later that evening, Arrahbella went to make teas for the various people who wanted them. Alain was writing an account of what had happened in Terrenvale, thinking Arrahbella had been a while, when Asseniah came hurrying into his room, took his arm and pulled him up, pointing frantically to the doorway. Alain quickly followed her through the caravans to the kitchen where he found Arrahbella alone, looking a little white and staring at the floor.

'What happened?' he asked, hurrying to her side.

'Gabrion,' she said, angrily. 'He tried to kiss me and said some horrid things about what he'd like to do with me and his hands were everywhere.' She shuddered. 'When he saw Asseniah rush out to tell you, he left.'

Alain was furious. He took Arrahbella and Asseniah into the girls' room and left them there, then he continued through to the driving car to tell Grent to stop the train. Once the dwarf had done so, Alain went back down to the dwarves' cabin, threw open the door, and glared at Gabrion.

'You will leave this train, sir. Now.'

'What's the problem?'

'You know very well what the problem is. I took you and your sisters in as guests and you have tried, ceaselessly, to get every woman on this train into your bed, one right in front of her boyfriend, and another who happens to be married – to your host, no less! You are the very definition of rudeness, Mr Callo, and I cannot stand to have you on this train any longer.'

Five pairs of eyes turned to Gabrion as the dwarves watched what his reaction would be, the straws of talooey in their mouths swivelling as they chewed them. Gabrion threw down his hand of cards and rose so he was face to face with Alain.

'You don't seem to have a problem with letting that

boy of yours have his way with my sisters,' he spat. 'I just assumed that everyone on this train was free for the taking.'

'Your sisters seem to be having a rather enjoyable time with that boy of mine, whereas the women on this train have made it very clear that they're in no way interested in your advances, sir.' The last word was uttered through clenched teeth.

Gabrion looked as though he might hit Alain, but then seemed to think better of it when he realised Oleg had entered through the opposite door. The dwarves had put down their own cards and were frowning disdainfully at Gabrion. Gabrion pushed past Alain, stomping through to the practice room where he picked up his and his sister's packs, then he walked out of the practice room door that Alain had opened on his way through, and jumped out into the cold night.

Alain went through to Izan's room.

'Izan, the girls have to go,' he announced to the three forms under Izan's bed covers. Movement and muffled giggles stopped suddenly. 'Their brother is a sleaze and he behaved inappropriately to Arrahbella, Mariette, and Melody.'

Immediately, Izan sat up and kicked the girls out of his bed.

'Right girls, out you go.'

The girls scrambled to get dressed as they complained. 'Oh, but you don't have to punish us for our brother's actions.'

Izan held up his hand. 'Nope. If a member of this troupe has been insulted then I've been insulted. Off you go.'

The girls pouted as Izan pushed them out of the door. Alain accompanied them to the kitchen car where he opened the outside door and threw them out onto the Highway with their brother.

'I'm sorry, Alain.'

'It's my fault. I should have seen through them at the start.'

The train shuddered to life once more and they continued along the road, the sounds of Lota and Carna arguing with their brother growing fainter.

'Are the girls okay?'

Alain nodded and looked at Izan. 'At least you got a chance to relieve yourself, otherwise there would have been no living with you.'

'That's true. And what about you, Alain. When was the last time you indulged in some good loving?'

'Terrenvale,' Alain replied, matter-of-factly.

'Oh. Wow. You're very discreet.'

'Privilege of rank, Izan; we get the cabin that hardly anyone walks through.' He smiled.

'Ah yes.' Izan patted him on the shoulder and they walked back through to the girls' room.

Arrahbella and Asseniah returned to the tea making, then Asseniah went to the practice room. Alain waited for Arrahbella in their room and once she had set their mugs down he pulled her into a tight embrace.

'Alain.'

'Are you alright?'

'I'm fine. He wasn't going to hurt me.'

324

'I've never had to protect you from a man before.'

'Well, you did it very well, I thought.' She was smiling, making light of it, but she could see he was worked up about the event. She slid her arms around his waist. 'Hey, I'm fine. He's gone. Everything's okay.' She kissed him. Alain continued to hold her for a while longer.

The next morning, Chester awoke to the sounds of Melody throwing up in their bathroom. He was about to leap out of bed and rush to her side, but she was turning off the bathroom light and stumbling back to the bed before he had even sat up. She flopped onto the bed, closed her eyes, and moaned. Small beads of sweat covered her naked body. Chester continued to watch her, trying to suppress the hope rising in his heart.

'Are you alright?'

Melody nodded.

'That's the third morning this week that you've thrown up.'

She nodded again.

He had to ask. He couldn't hold it in any longer. 'Melody?'

She opened her eyes and moved her head so she could look at him, knowing what he was about to ask. He hesitated, looking down at her stomach, stroking her arm.

'Do you think... do you think you might be pregnant?'

'Yes, Chester, I'm pregnant.'

Chester's breath quickened. He could hear his heart

thumping in his ears.

'Are you sure?'

'I've been throwing up and then eating twice as much, my monthly hasn't come, and I just... know.'

His face lit up with excitement before he remembered that he didn't want to reveal his feelings. Melody gave a surprised smile as he tried to change his expression.

'You're happy,' she said. 'You do want children.'

'No, Melody, I don't just want children. I want children with you.'

Her heart fluttered. Something in her stomach did too.

'But, what do you want?' He was almost scared to ask. 'I know you said you weren't ready and...'

Melody put a finger to his lips.

'I know. But when I realised that I was pregnant, I felt really calm about it and I'm quite excited. And seeing your reaction makes me so relieved. I want to keep it, Chester.'

His happiness bubbled to the surface, lighting up his face once more, his mouth curving into a large smile. Melody took his hand and placed it on her stomach.

'We're going to have a child, Chester,' she whispered. 'You're going to be a father.'

He kissed her passionately, but she broke away.

'No, don't. I taste horrible.'

'You taste wonderful. You taste like someone who's pregnant.'

She let him kiss her. Then, they lay with their hands on her stomach.

'Do you think it'll have wings?' she asked.

'I don't know.'

'Would you mind if it did?'

'Melody, it could have wings, scales, two heads, and a tail and I wouldn't care. It's yours and mine and that's all that matters.'

They were silent for a while.

'We'll have to tell Alain,' Chester said.

'I know, but let's keep it to ourselves for a bit longer.'

'Fine with me. What about the trapeze?'

'What about it?'

'Shouldn't you stop, in case you fall off?'

'Chester, have I ever fallen off?'

'No.'

'And I have wings, remember? Even if I do fall off, I don't hit the ground.'

He narrowed his eyes at her.

'I'll be fine,' she assured him. 'Until I'm too big to move.'

Chester laughed. 'Hey, your breasts might get bigger. There may eventually be something there to squeeze.'

She whacked him on the arm. 'You won't be able to squeeze them, they'll start to produce milk, remember?'

'Oh yeah.' His hands were roaming now; one of them was stroking a wing while he kissed the breasts they were discussing.

'Will you be able to make love?'

'Well, I've heard your hormones rage when you're pregnant, so I could want you so much that you'll get tired of me.'

He looked at her with hungry eyes. 'Never.' He moved up to her mouth. 'Feeling better?'

'Much better.'

'Good.'

He devoured her.

That morning, just before lunch, the caravan train arrived at Karantale's Inn.

When the troupe jumped down from the train, they saw that it was, as usual, brimming with people. A few of the patrons sitting at the outside tables (tables that were in a much better condition than those outside Tokinov's Inn) recognised the troupe and called greetings which they returned as they walked past.

Inside, they split up – Chester (who was almost bouncing off the walls with happiness) and Melody went with Asseniah, Sora, Mariette, and Izan to a table by the wall while Alain and Arrahbella went to the bar to see Karantale and Bray. Oleg and the dwarves had stayed with the train as there tended to be some thievery in these parts. Karantale, who, along with Bray, was a huge fan of Chester's, waved to the jester before throwing his kitchen towel over his shoulder and turning to Alain.

'Alain du Maurier. I thought we might be seeing you. Bray went into Arelia last week and heard you were due to perform in Greensvale City soon.'

'That's right. We're scheduled to go to Landau first but we've heard rumours.'

'Yeah. You won't be getting through Landau's rift any

time soon. Prestonvale is trying to teach Kintore a lesson. You know why?' He leaned in closer. 'Kintore's prince, young Dryden, was discovered in bed with Prestonvale's Queen Kenora. Not good. Romantic, but not good. King Colwood wants revenge and he's got some of the most powerful beings in Landau on his side, cooking up a magical storm. Dryden's father, King Roberval, has his fair share of magic folk as well. That war is going to last a while, Alain, best make other plans.'

'Kenora and Dryden? Wow!'

'Yeah, it took everyone by surprise.'

'Best go straight to Arelia then,' Alain said to Arrahbella.

'That's fine,' she agreed.

He sighed. 'It's a shame. I do love going back there.'

Arrahbella patted his hand.

'Ah well. You're welcome to stay here for as long as you like.'

'Thanks, Karantale, but we'll just spend the afternoon and be on our way by nightfall.'

Bray came up beside Karantale and beamed when he saw the troupe.

'Hello, dear friends,' he said. 'Karantale you're being rude. You haven't offered our guests drinks or lunch and I'll bet they're starving after being on the road.'

'It's alright, Bray,' Alain said, with a hearty smile. 'We were talking business before eating.'

'Ugh! Something that should never happen. Not another word until you've eaten. I insist.' And he hurried to serve them all.

About half an hour after they had eaten lunch, Sora and Melody were discussing a new position they wanted to try out for manipulation while Asseniah traced the etchings in the wooden table with her finger. When shadows fell across the table, blocking out her light, Asseniah looked up and found that the rest of the troupe had gathered around the table, joined by Karantale, Bray, and a Kartanian trader.

'Happy birthday, young lady,' Karantale announced, placing a large, round cake with pink-icing and stardust flecks in front of her.

'It's not a honey log, but it is honey flavoured and has cream filling,' Alain explained.

Asseniah blinked at it. She looked at Alain, looked at the cake, looked at Arrahbella, then turned back to the cake once more. After a moment, she pushed back her chair and fled from the Inn, disappearing into Oleg's caravan. The troupe was used to this kind of behaviour – she had reacted the same way on her previous birthdays, too – and waited silently, smiling and shaking their heads at each other.

The sound of a piano being ravenously attacked filtered through the open door and windows, silencing the buzz of the patrons. She played for a good five minutes: a happy, bouncy tune, not slowing down for a moment. Then, just as suddenly as it had started, the playing stopped. Asseniah walked back into the Inn, plomped herself back in her chair, and stared at the cake.

'Okay?' Alain asked her.

She nodded once.

'Alright.'

He signalled to the others and they each broke into their native renditions of the Happy Birthday song, creating a multi-universal chorus, the Kartanian trader representing his world while Alain sang in Landau. Only Icecess was missing, which was a shame because its version was stunningly mystical.

Asseniah clapped her hands in delight, scrunching up her face and bouncing up and down on her chair. She reached out into the centre of the table, as though she could feel all their voices merging into one in that spot. The Arelian song was the shortest so Chester and Bray fell silent first, then Arrahbella, with Karantale, Melody, and Izan the last to finish.

Alain moved the cake closer to Asseniah. She looked at the candles and made a dramatic show of taking a deep breath in, preparing to extinguish them, but then she paused, exhaled softly, and blinked at the candle closest to her. Reaching out, she pulled it free of the icing and would have popped it straight in her mouth if Alain hadn't reached out and stopped her.

'Hey, sweetie, don't do that. They'll burn your mouth.' Then, he considered it for a moment. 'Well, actually, I have no idea if you can eat fire or not, but it's probably best not to, hey? Just in case.'

The silent girl sighed with disappointment and slowly blew the candles out one by one with little puffs. When only one was left glowing, she licked her fingers and clamped them over the flame before licking them again and sighing disappointedly once more.

Filled with wonder, Alain shook his head at Arrahbella, who was giggling away, picked up the knife, and cut the birthday girl a large slice. Asseniah attacked the cake, leaving the icing and cream untouched, then she cut herself another piece and devoured that too. The plate was then handed to Sora who gladly ate the remains.

As the others munched away on their own slices (all except for Fenton, who had been scared off of the dessert after hearing the Varatalian story that explained why the fairies had invented it in the first place), Asseniah went around the table and gave them all a tight hug. She would have hugged the Kartanian too, but knew it would go against his culture so she shook his hand instead. The now fourteen-year-old then skipped over to the serving bar, climbed up onto it, and swung herself up into the rafters where she stretched out on a wide beam and watched them all like a cat, even uttering a small purr.

After digesting the cake and chatting for a while, Alain coaxed Asseniah down from the beam and the troupe continued on their way to Arelia.

CHAPTER 12

Present Day - Arelia

Melody had decided it was time to tell Alain she was pregnant. The train was parked on the side of the Highway, in view of the Arelian rift guards, waiting until the sun came up in Greensvale City so that Alain could go straight to Queen Prarny and announce their arrival. Gathering up her courage, Melody entered the du Maurier's caravan, so quietly it took them a moment to notice she was there. When they did, Arrahbella took one look at the young girl's nervous face and put her book down.

'I think it's time for some tea,' she said, and left the room.

Alain put down the paragraph he had been rearranging in the air and set aside his pen and notebook. 'Melody.' He patted the chair that Arrahbella had just vacated before noticing a rebel word still hovering in front of him. Frowning, he pointed to the notebook sternly. The word jumped around a little before obeying.

Melody climbed onto the chair, tucking her legs beneath her. Alain waited patiently until she was ready to begin, placing his hands steeple-like under his chin. She fiddled for a while, flapped her wings, looked around the room, then, finally, took a deep breath.

'Alain?'

'Yes, Melody?'

'I have something to tell you.'

'Mmm...' He was beginning to feel nervous as well.

'But, I'm scared that you'll be disappointed in me.'

That surprised him. 'Melody, it would take a lot for you to disappoint me.'

'Don't say that, 'cause then if you are disappointed it'll make it worse.'

He studied her for a moment, tilting his head to one side. 'I promise that I will think about whatever it is you tell me before I react.'

She sighed, shuffled in her seat, beat her wings again, then looked Alain squarely in his kind, wise, blue eyes.

'You know how there was that herb mix-up a couple of weeks back.'

Alain nodded slowly.

'Well... I'm pregnant, Alain.'

Alain continued to watch her, trying to keep a blank face as his mind went a little fuzzy and his heart beat faster.

'Are you sure?' he managed, though his mouth had gone dry.

'Yes, I'm sure.'

He nodded again.

'You should have seen Chester's face when I told him. He was so happy, ecstatic.'

'Are you happy, Melody?'

'Yes. I am. I know you don't think I'm ready and I know you didn't want any children in the circus for a while and that's perfectly understandable. I didn't think I was ready either, but now that it's happening, I believe I am ready and I'm so happy. I'm excited. We're going to keep it, Alain, I couldn't bear to give it away.'

She watched him, waiting for his reaction. Alain's eyes were fixed on the ground as he stroked his beard and his mind whirred with thoughts. He took some deep breaths, trying to slow them down. Yes, he had wanted to keep her child-free for a while longer but maybe that was because he knew it would make her grow up even more, or that she and Chester might want to leave the troupe.

But, he thought, it's quite possible to continue running a circus with a baby in tow. It will work out.

He looked up. 'Melody, you know you don't need my approval. I hope that when you first talked to Arrahbella about the Griffinseed she made it clear that you were free to stop drinking it whenever you liked.'

'I know, but I don't want you to think that I don't respect your reasons for not having children. This *was* an accident.'

'Melody.' He leaned closer. 'The only thing that concerns me is your happiness, so if you're happy about this, then I'm thrilled for you.'

'Really?'

'Really.' He leaned back, his expression turning serious. 'But, there's one condition.'

Melody waited, chewing her bottom lip and

fidgeting anxiously.

Alain's face softened. 'You'd better let Arrahbella and I baby-sit frequently.'

Melody smiled, wiping away some tears before throwing her arms around his neck.

'Thank you, Alain.'

'You realise that Izan will take it under his care,' he told her. 'And Sora and Asseniah will want to play with it constantly, and Mariette will go mushy over it. You and Chester will be lucky if you ever see it.'

She laughed. 'I'm sure we'll see it when it starts crying.'

'Probably.' He released his hold on her and studied her for a moment. 'I guess I should tell Arrahbella to stop the Griffinseed, then.'

'Umm... actually, do you think you could keep this to yourself for a bit? Chester and I want to keep it between ourselves for a bit longer. I'm sorry, Alain, I know you hate keeping things from Arrahbella but just for a little while?'

'She may be able to give you herbs and things that can help.'

'I know, and I'll be sure to tell her if I do need anything but just for now...'

Alain looked reluctant but agreed. 'Okay,' he said. 'Though she may know already.'

Melody smiled. 'Probably. Thank you.'

She left the room quickly, leaving Alain to fiddle with his beard as he pondered her news.

While Alain and Chester went to see Queen Prarny in her dark green castle, the troupe potted around in the field where the train was parked, trying to adjust to the deep blue grass, blue trees, golden water, and multi-coloured buildings (the name Greensvale, as Chester had once explained, had nothing to do with the colour; it came from the woman who had settled the city many centuries ago). A posse of Royal Guards then accompanied Chester as he went to visit his former troupe while two more followed Alain back to the train to protect it from any over-enthusiastic fans.

Around mid-morning, when the nausea of colour-shock had subsided slightly, Melody, Sora, and Asseniah headed into town to peruse the clothing shops. The stone-paved streets were wide but crowded. People stopped in the middle of the path to gossip or grouped around the seductive shop windows to gush over outfits they couldn't afford. The air was warm and had a strange aroma to it, which many people had simply described as being the smell of colour.

'Oh, Sora, look at this one,' Melody said, as she eyed a white lace and pink satin skirt and top ensemble sitting on a mannequin in the front of a large spotless window. Arelian fashion was a strange mix of all the fashions along the Highway, including the Da'Laarwickan javvii-hide wraps, although they had been slightly bedazzled and modified.

'That's pretty, but look at those shoes!' Sora pointed to the shiny black leather shoes with oversized buckles and ridiculously high heels sitting below the outfit. 'You'd never be able to walk in them.'

Asseniah pointed to a long white coat adorned with

unicorns and roses standing in the neighbouring window.

'I'll bet that costs a bit,' Melody told her.

'Look everyone, the Freak Show must be in town,' came a silky voice from behind them.

The three performers turned to see a pretty young girl with purple hair and eyes staring at them coldly. She was surrounded by a group of immaculately dressed girls of about the same age, all smirking at the troupe members. 'And looking at their clothes, I'd say that being a Freak doesn't pay too well.' She put on a fake look of concern.

'I wouldn't pay to see them,' said a girl with a short blue bob, as the others laughed.

Sora, who was actually looking rather elegant today in a long-sleeved green dress, gave her a hard look and turned to walk away.

'Hey, Melody,' the purple-haired girl called after them. 'Keep your Freak hands off of Chester. Find someone your own age from your own planet.'

Melody kept walking. It was moments like these that she was glad her wings were invisible. Sora, however, stopped and turned. She casually walked over to the cackling group and, within seconds, the main girl was sitting in a puddle of golden water, unhurt but dazed. Sora smiled down at her and returned to her friends.

In the afternoon, when the troupe was meant to be returning to set up the tent, Alain and Arrahbella were sitting in chairs on the grass beside the train, sipping cranberry and lemon tea, when Izan came running into view from the direction of the town, looking panicked, his long legs bent in fast strides. Alain stood up as he neared and spied a short, middle-aged man with bright red hair running after Izan, wielding an axe. Alain sighed.

'Alain, help!' Izan called, as he reached his Ringmaster.

'What have you done, Izan?'

'He's the husband of a woman-'

Alain cringed. 'What is the one rule I impose on you?'

'No married women or men, I know, I know, but I swear she told me she was unmarried and Arelians don't wear rings or anything.' Izan turned and, seeing the man was almost upon him, let out a yelp, raced into the open doorway of the dining car and called, 'Sanctuary! Sanctuary!'

Alain gave Arrahbella an exasperated look before facing the angry man who slowed and stopped in front of him.

'Sir, I request permission to board your train and continue my chase.'

'I tell you I didn't know she was married,' Izan shouted. 'She said she wasn't.'

'Are you calling my wife a liar?'

'Well, yes, but for what it's worth, she's a beautiful lady who knows how to have a good time.'

The man turned as red as his hair.

'Izan, enough,' Alain warned.

'Come out and fight me properly, coward. I demand a duel.'

Izan laughed.

'What is your name, sir?' Alain asked, calmly.

'Goodwin of Greensvale City, sir.'

'Well, Goodwin of Greensvale City, do you have any powers?'

Goodwin looked insulted. 'Of course I have powers.'

'And what are they?'

'They're with wood, sir. I'm a carpenter.' He lifted his axe to show Alain the wooden hilt that had been intricately carved with an image of the city.

'Very fine, Goodwin, very fine, but this is Izan Bell.'

Goodwin looked uncertainly at the magician standing in the doorway. Izan was examining his nails as though already bored with the situation.

'If he's one of the most powerful beings along the Highway why isn't he working for a king somewhere? Why's he in a circus?'

Alain decided to ignore this insult. He turned to Izan who smiled.

'Because, Izan is a performer whose first love is to entertain. You may duel with him, sir, but you will lose. That is, in fact, why he was running from you, he did not wish to harm you.'

Goodwin's face fell as he let the axe drop by his side. 'But, I must avenge my wife.'

Alain saw the girls returning with Chester.

'Look,' he said, nodding toward them. 'Here comes Izan's sister and her partner.' Goodwin looked at the girls, his eyes widening as he recognised Chester. 'And, as you can see,' Alain indicated in Arrahbella's direction, 'I am married myself. Izan lives with us, he knows to respect marriage, and he'd never knowingly love a married woman.'

Goodwin opened his mouth to speak, but Alain put his hands on the small man's shoulders.

'No, sir, go home to your wife and find out why she's being unfaithful. I can only imagine what it must be like for a man to discover his wife is loving other men. Go and find out why she's unhappy, Goodwin, and give her what she needs.'

Goodwin was looking at the blue ground with tear-filled eyes (golden tears against fiery red eyes). Chester and the girls had stopped walking to discuss why there was a man with an axe crying in front of Alain. In the kitchen car, Oleg had appeared behind Izan, waiting in readiness in case he was needed.

Goodwin sighed, turned, and dragged his feet and axe back into the town. Alain let out a sigh of relief as Izan whooped and punched the air.

'Alain, my eternal gratitude,' he said, bowing.

'I didn't even have to use any magic,' Alain mused.

'Really? Impressive.'

'Try to be more careful, Izan.'

'What am I supposed to do when they tell me they're not married?'

'Well, I take it you weren't in an inn if the husband managed to find you. Did you go back to her house?'

Izan opened his mouth, then closed it again.

'And it didn't look like a man may have lived there?'

'Alain, this woman was half naked by the time we got through her front door. I wasn't exactly admiring her furniture.'

Arrahbella couldn't help but smile as Alain rubbed his

brow in exasperation.

'Izan, stay out of their houses.'

'Okay, okay.' The magician disappeared inside to scrounge for food. Chester, Melody, Sora, and Asseniah moved inside as well as Alain sunk into his chair again. Arrahbella took one of his hands and massaged it.

That night, after an energetic reception from their first Arelian audience, the troupe went into town to enjoy themselves into the early hours of the morning.

Alain and Arrahbella were the first to arise the following day (with the exception of Oleg, who had been up at dawn to exercise as usual). They had only just walked through to the kitchen and were preparing tea and breakfast when there was a knock on one of the outside doors. Opening it, Alain found one of the morning shift guards standing on the step, looking somewhat more nervous than a guard should.

'Good morning, sir,' he said. 'Forgive me for the interruption but there's an Arelian here to see you.'

Alain frowned. There was something odd about that introduction.

'Okay, what's the problem then?' He thought, perhaps, it might be some Chester-crazed fan.

The guard shuffled uncomfortably. 'It's just that... His name's Ikrael, sir, and he's an outcast. He's not supposed to even be in the city. I tried to turn him away but he insisted and he's not someone I wish to argue with.'

Too curious to feel annoyed at the way the guard was reacting to this supposed outcast, Alain peered out at the blue surrounds but couldn't see anyone.

'Alright, then, show him in.'

The guard didn't seem to like this answer. He leaned in close to Alain. 'I really don't think you want to do that, sir.'

Annoyance finally pushed curiosity out of the way. 'No, it's alright, bring him in.'

The guard sighed before stepping down onto the grass once more. A moment later, Alain had to force his eyes to stop widening in wonder as the visitor stepped up into the train. He was a thin, tall, ghost of a man, with snow white hair, milky skin that accentuated the web of veins beneath it, and white eyes that made you feel as though you were looking at a corpse. Even his lips were such a pale shade of pink that they were barely visible, and when he opened his mouth to talk, the redness of the inside made you wonder if he had just finished a meal of raw, bloody meat.

Now Alain understood the guard's fear; anything so lacking in colour could not possibly be Arelian.

Arrahbella, still standing by the counter, had also frozen at the sight of the newcomer. Her head began to inexplicably throb and she reached up to massage it.

'Alain du Maurier?'

'Yes.'

'My name is Ikrael.' His voice had the same raspiness to it that people have when they're recovering from a cold, only his was permanent. 'Ikrael from the Black Mountains.'

It took a moment for Alain to realise that Ikrael was reaching out to shake his hand, by which time the Wordmaster had hesitated a little too long for it to be considered polite. He could feel every bone in Ikrael's cold, thin hand.

Ikrael's eyes hadn't left Alain's, but now that the introductions were done he turned them to Arrahbella. Alain was studying him too much to notice that his eyes had widened at the sight of her, but when they remained on her, not turning back to meet his own, he came back to his senses and cleared his throat.

'This is my wife, Arrahbella.'

Ikrael nodded to her, an eerie hunger in his eyes as they moved up and down her curvy form.

'Hello,' Arrahbella squeaked.

'Arrahbella, how about some tea?'

She gladly turned back to the sink.

'Would you like some tea, Ikrael?'

'Yes, thank you,' he said, his eyes now on Arrahbella's long hair, cascading down her back.

'Won't you sit down?' Alain gestured to a chair. Ikrael finally turned his eyes back to Alain and sat across from him at the table.

'What can I do for you?'

'I've heard about your circus,' he began, as Arrahbella set the mugs down and sat on Alain's left, rubbing her forehead. 'I hoped I might be able to join.'

Alain wasn't surprised. 'Well, I'm always happy to consider new people, but it depends on a number of things.'

'Like what?'

'Well, if I have a need for your particular powers or abilities, for example. Whether you can work well in a team, whether you're passionate about entertaining people, those kinds of things.' Alain already had a pretty good idea that this man was not right for their troupe; something about him was unsettling, but he tried to keep an open mind because he hated turning outcasts away.

'I have magic,' Ikrael said. 'Lots of magic.' He was very hard to read, no expression at all.

'Do you know how to use it?'

'I've spent all of my life on my own. It's the one thing I've learned to use very well.'

For no obvious reason, Arrahbella shuddered. Alain felt it, but if Ikrael had noticed he didn't show it.

'Well, we already have a magician, and our jester is quite handy with magic too, so I'm not sure that-' he was cut off by Arrahbella squeezing his arm. Ikrael looked down at the table.

'Perhaps we should see what he can do, Alain?' She spoke out loud and Alain wished that she had entered his mind instead.

Ikrael's lifeless eyes shot up and widened again.

'Ikrael,' Arrahbella continued. 'Tell us a bit about yourself.'

Ikrael started a little, recovered, looked at the table, then back at Arrahbella where his eyes stayed while he spoke. 'There's not much to tell. I was born colourless and my mother took me to the palace to try and get me cured but no one could do anything. They all hated the sight of me, so they kept me in a hidden prison cell until I was old enough to look after myself then they took me out to the Black Mountains by the Red Sea and told me not to come back. That's all, really.'

'You poor man.'

This made Ikrael smile, but it was a smile that showed horrible pointed teeth. His eyes seemed to leer even more hungrily at her.

'Alain, why don't we take Ikrael into the practice room and get Izan in there and he can show us a few of his skills?'

Before Alain could respond, however, Chester entered the dining car, still looking very sleepy, one hand to his head. He looked up to greet Alain and Arrahbella, but when his purple eyes fell on Ikrael he jumped and stepped backward in horror. He looked to Alain for explanation but the Ringmaster just stared back with a quizzical expression.

'Morning, Chester,' Alain said, when the jester didn't speak. 'Ikrael, this is our jester and one half of the trapeze act, Chester from the Apricot Meadows.'

Ikrael gave a slow nod of greeting.

Chester's mouth opened and closed a couple of times before he found his voice. 'Alain, may I see you for a moment? Arrahbella, you may want to come too.'

If Ikrael was insulted by this he didn't show it. His eyes had returned to Arrahbella.

'Nonsense, Chester,' Alain said, as he rose from the table. 'We can't leave our guest on his own.' He, in fact, had no desire to leave Arrahbella alone with this man but he couldn't be rude and he sensed some urgency to Chester's request. Even so, he was slightly irked at Chester for making him leave. 'Excuse me, Ikrael, I'll just be a moment.'

Ikrael gave a nod of his head, his eyes not leaving the

Earthling. Alain briefly squeezed Arrahbella's shoulder before following Chester into the girls' room. When Alain had pulled the door across, Chester spoke in an urgent, frightened whisper, trying not to wake the three sleeping girls.

'Alain, do you know who that is in there?'

'Ikrael from the Black Mountains. An outcast who wishes to join our troupe.'

'Exactly. Ikrael has been an outcast since his birth. He's a legend. A monster. The stories about him are horrific. He shouldn't be anywhere near Greensvale City. You can't let him join the circus.'

'You've heard stories about him?'

'Yes, everyone in Arelia has. Bad stories.'

'And he's an outcast?'

'Yes.'

'Chester, what part of the concept "circus" don't you understand? Are we not all outcasts who have had stories made up about us?'

Chester narrowed his eyes. 'No, not all of us are.'

It wasn't the first time Alain had forgotten that Chester was the only "normal" one among them.

'Well, there you go. You've been brought up to believe that he is a monster, but have you actually *seen* him do any of these evil deeds you've heard about?'

Chester looked away. 'People don't make up stories like that, Alain.'

Alain's expression became stony. 'Yes, they do.'

The jester shook his head. 'Nevertheless, you don't want that man anywhere near this troupe. I, for one, don't want him anywhere near Melody. We shouldn't leave Arrahbella in there with him.'

'We have to give him a fair try-'

'Alain, if there's one fault with you it's that you don't believe anyone else. Yes, you're wise, and you have good instincts, and you know what's best for people most of the time, but you need to learn to give people the courtesy of trusting that they may be right sometimes.'

Alain looked away.

A scream and a crash sounded from the dining car. Alain and Chester hurtled back into the kitchen where they found three chairs lying on their sides and Arrahbella backed up against the kitchen bench with her eyes closed. Ikrael's body was pressed against hers as he trapped her there with his arms. His mouth was sucking on her neck. The outside door opened and the guard hurried in, jumping over a fallen chair as he rushed to help Chester and Alain (and it took all three of them giving their most) to pull Ikrael off of Arrahbella. The Arelians then dragged him to the door as Arrahbella slumped to the floor and Alain checked her for injuries.

'Get out of here, you filthy monster,' the guard shouted, as Ikrael ran away towards the Blue Forest. 'Is she alright?' he asked Alain.

'Yes, I'm fine,' Arrahbella panted.

The guard nodded and returned to his position outside. Chester watched as Alain sat Arrahbella in a chair, stroking her hair, hugging her, and talking soothingly.

'We were just talking and he lunged across the table at me,' she said. 'He was so fast, like a snake.'

'Shh. It's alright, he's gone.'

Sora, Asseniah, and Mariette entered the room, having tumbled out of their beds after hearing the scream. They took one look at the seated couple before turning to Chester for explanation.

'Good morning, ladies,' he said, too cheerfully. 'You're just in time to help me make breakfast.'

They took the hint and set about preparing food in silence.

Later, Alain gathered everyone in the kitchen and, after telling them all what had happened, handed the floor over to Chester.

'There have been a lot of stories, over the years,' he said, quietly. 'Ikrael sneaks into the city at night and takes people. Some of them he plays with and then lets them go so that they can tell us what happened to the others. He tortures them, rapes them, eats all the ones he kills.' He stopped and looked away, swallowing hard. 'I've lost two friends to Ikrael.'

'Can't Prarny do anything about it?' Sora asked in a horrified whisper.

'She's tried, and Queen Vaya tried before her. They've sent whole armies, up to one hundred men, but none of them ever come back and no remains have ever been found. I don't think anyone wants to admit that he could have us all if he wanted. No one knows what to do about it so they just let it go, although, there are rumours that prisoners get left in the Black Mountains as a kind of peace offering.'

A collective shiver ran around the group. Alain had his arms around Arrahbella and he closed his eyes at the thought that such a creature had been in his train and touched his wife. He pulled her closer and buried his face in her hair, inhaling the scent of incense. Chester had tried to get her out of the room and he had just waved aside the warning because it would have been *impolite*. He would never forgive himself for that.

'But why would 'e want to join our circus?' Mariette wondered.

'Probably so that he could have access to a larger amount of people and carry out his evil deeds in more places than just Arelia,' Chester answered, his eyes steely.

And, indeed, he was right.

That night, as the troupe filed out of the kitchen car door after dinner, heading toward the tent, Alain remained standing by the table, a worried look on his face.

'I don't think you should be alone, Bella,' he said.

'I'll be fine,' Arrahbella assured him. 'There are guards outside and Ikrael's gone back to the Black Mountains.'

'That doesn't mean that he won't come back.'

She put her hands on her hips. 'Alain, go and entertain the Arelians. That's the job we came here to do, so stop being silly and go and do it.'

Alain remained unconvinced, but, after a moment's hesitation, he stepped forward, kissed her, and left the train. The excitement and business of the show soon had his thoughts distracted and by curtain's close he had almost

350

completely forgotten about Ikrael.

'Wonderful performance, troupe,' he said, as they stood outside the tent. About half of the audience was filing out past them, talking in excited tones and paying compliments, while the rest waited around for their psychic readings. 'Really great. I'm so proud. Mariette, will you go and get Arrahbella please?'

'Oh, I do love Arelia,' Izan beamed, as Mariette headed toward the train.

'The audiences are amazing here,' Sora agreed, breathlessly, as she played with a fire ball, passing it from palm to palm.

'Yes, but we knew Arelians were amazing,' Melody added, rubbing her nose against Chester's once he had stopped doing back flips.

Asseniah kicked at the dirt moodily, hating being on the ground when she was all fired up and energised.

Alain smiled at them all, about to praise them again when…

'Alain! Alain!'

Mariette came running out of the train, a piece of paper in her hand, panic and fear written all over her face. Alain's heart skipped a beat.

'Alain, Arrahbella is not in ze train, but zere was zis.' She handed him the paper. There were only two words written on it, in a hand that looked like a four-year olds: "She's Mine." Alain closed his eyes and swayed. Oleg quickly steadied him. Chester took the paper from Alain's hand and read it.

'Ikrael,' he said.

Melody and Mariette gasped. The troupe looked from Chester to Alain. Alain took a few deep breaths, fighting a wave of nausea. When his head had cleared he raced into the train and searched it from end to end. Arrahbella was nowhere to be found. He raced back outside and called the nearest guard over.

'My wife was taken from our train right under your noses. How?'

'I have no idea, sir. It isn't possible. Are you quite sure? Maybe she has just stepped out for a while.'

Alain showed him the note.

'You'll have to take me to Ikrael's home in the Black Mountains,' Alain told him. The guard was not pleased with this idea, but he had his orders. 'Izan, Oleg, you come as well,' Alain continued. 'Chester, go with Mariette and tell the crowd that there'll be no readings tonight, tell them she's unavailable, make it sound as though she's unwell.' He faltered. 'Then, join the rest of the troupe on the train. Dwarves, stay with the girls. I want you all inside the train as soon as possible.'

Everyone hurried to do his bidding, except for Melody who watched Alain and her brother hurrying off – desperately hoping they would return safely with Arrahbella – until Fenton doubled back and pulled her into the train.

The four men had not gone far when Alain cursed and stopped. 'Sweet Mythos, this is going to take forever.'

'It is a fair way, sir,' the guard agreed.

They were hurrying along the path that led to the

Blue Forest. Houses dotted the laneway, and a little further up they saw a large fenced arena where some feridons were kept. A feridon was Arelia's beast of transportation, consisting of a horse-like body, a wildebeest-style head, and scales and fins down its torso that complemented the gills on its neck.

'They'll be faster,' Izan said.

He led them over to the paddock, jumped the fence, herded four startled feridons out of the gate, then dashed back into the stables to grab saddles and bridles, which he magically threw over the beasts. Alain climbed on awkwardly, not caring that they were doing little more than stealing (he hoped they would be returning them), and they followed the guard down the path.

Racing along at a canter, they were able to reach the Blue Forest quickly, but then their progress was slowed by the overgrown path. Branches that looked like bony fingers snared their cloaks and clothes, shredding their skin, and trying to pull them off of the feridons. Alain and Izan were able to clear some away by magic, but this did little to help their speed.

As Izan fought with a particularly tangled knot of foliage, Alain closed his eyes and looked into his mind, hoping Arrahbella was trying to contact him through their psychic connection, but he found nothing. The knot cleared and they moved on, Alain oblivious to the fact that he was trembling violently.

A good hour later, the trees thinned, and the guard slowed down, raising his hand to signal to the others that they should do the same. Before them rose cracked, jagged peaks and rocky terrain, all of it pitch black, hardly discernible against the night sky. Nestled in amongst the uneven mountain base, two squares of yellow glowed brightly; the windows of Ikrael's cabin – a cabin made of black tree logs, camouflaging it against the mountains. To their left lay the Red Sea, lapping softly at the stony shoreline, giving off an eerie red light as the moon reflected off its bloody surface.

'I won't go any further,' the guard whispered. 'My duty is done.'

Alain knew he couldn't persuade him otherwise so he climbed off of his nervous feridon and handed the reins to the guard. Oleg and Izan did the same, then the three of them crept quietly up to the cabin, tripping on loose rocks, the humans cutting their hands on the sharp stone. When they reached it, Oleg stood back out of sight as Alain and Izan peeked into the window.

The cabin was a single open room, furnished sparsely with a crooked table, a chair, a kitchen area, and a messy makeshift bed, all of which, on closer inspection, turned out to be made from human bones. The wooden floor was splattered with blood stains and other strange colours that could have once been anything. The largest stains were situated around the base of a thick wooden stake, stuck in the floor, reaching nearly as high as the cabin roof. Arrahbella was sitting on the floor, her legs stretched out in front of her, her arms tied behind, wrapped around the stake. A dirty gag was in her mouth, and her rapidly rising and falling chest was covered only by her pretty lace bra; her top lay in shreds on the floor. Her eyes were closed, tears falling slowly. Ikrael was all over her; fondling, kissing, licking, scratching, biting, reaching up her skirt...

Alain looked away and took some deep breaths. When Izan crept over to the door, he made himself follow. They stood around the door, prepared themselves, and nodded to each other.

'Door, open.'

The door swung open violently. Alain ran into the room and was instantly blasted aside by Ikrael. Arrahbella screamed into her gag as she watched Alain hit the floor. Cursing himself for not entering first, Izan threw his power out in front of him as he raced into the room, slamming Ikrael back against the wall and holding him there from a distance, summoning all the magic he could muster, feeling the strength of Ikrael's own power working against him frantically.

'Alain! Alain! Wake up, damn it. I can't hold him,' Izan shouted, scared for the first time in his life at the possibility of being overpowered.

One of Ikrael's arms was working itself free but, just then, Oleg lumbered into the room and pinned each of Ikrael's arms to the black cabin wall. On the floor, Alain came to, shook himself, remembered where he was, pushed his aching body up, and dashed to Arrahbella's side. He managed to get the gag out of her mouth, then fumbled with the rope binding her hands.

'Hurry up, Alain, he's strong.' Izan, and even Oleg, were struggling to hold Ikrael. Sweat dripped down the magician's forehead as he turned a strange shade of grey.

'Rope, untie yourself!'

The rope obeyed and fell to the floor. Arrahbella weakly moved her arms and rubbed her bleeding wrists while Alain undid Izan's cloak from the magician's shoulders and wrapped it around her.

'Do you need me to come back?' he asked Izan, as he lifted Arrahbella into his arms.

'No, I'll be fine. Just get her out of here.'

Alain looked at Ikrael. The monster's eyes were still on Arrahbella, even as he tried to fight against Izan's magic. Alain shuddered and hurried out of the cabin.

'You too, Oleg.'

'But-'

'Go!'

The giant released his grasp on Ikrael and fled to the edge of the forest to help Alain get Arrahbella on to the feridon. Bloodcurdling shrieks filled the air and echoed off the mountains. The lamps went out. Silence filled the eerie landscape. A moment later, Izan stumbled out of the cabin.

'He's either dead or very close to it,' he panted up at them with a smile, before promptly collapsing at Oleg's feet. Oleg hefted him up onto his own feridon while the guard took charge of the other.

They rode as fast as they could with the injured passengers, finding their way in the dark thanks to the skilled beasts and the odd light created by a full moon on blue trees.

When they reached the paddock, they were greeted by the feridons' owners, an elderly couple, who had been out searching for their lost stock.

'Thieves! Scoundrels! Take our stock, will you?' She had a large voice for such a small woman.

The guard jumped down and raised his hands. 'Calm down, lady. I am Herriot of the Royal Guards. Your fine beasts have just aided us in a Royal quest. You should be proud of such fine animals. They have been trained well.'

The woman's furious expression changed to one of pride as her husband lowered his pitchfork.

'Well, that's very kind of you, sir.'

'I'm sorry we had to take them without your permission, but we were in a frightful hurry and as you can see they're all back safe and sound now.'

'Oh, yes, no worries at all.'

Oleg took hold of both Arrahbella, who had fallen asleep out of sheer shock and exhaustion, and Izan, as Alain practically fell off his feridon and handed the reins to the smiling owner. Then, he carried his wife back to the train where Herriot the Guard informed his colleagues of what had happened before taking his leave for the night. By morning, the story would be all over Arelia.

Alain stepped up into the kitchen car, blinking in the sudden brightness. Everyone was around the table. Melody, Chester, and the dwarves jumped up when they saw him, but he only looked at them long enough to make sure they were all accounted for before walking past them. When he reached his caravan, he lay Arrahbella on the bed, took off her boots and skirt, and pulled the covers up to her shoulders, kissing her on the cheek. Then, he pulled up the bedside chair, sat down, and put his head in his hands.

A short while later, there was a knock on the door. Alain mustered up the strength to call them in. Not that he really felt like seeing anyone, he just wanted to be left alone with his wife.

Sora entered, carrying a tray. 'Here,' she said, setting the tray down on the bedside table and picking up the mug of tea. 'Athenaine root. It'll refresh you.'

He didn't feel like it but he took it and sipped. The effect was instant, Sora could see his shoulders relax. She gestured toward the other item on the tray; a sandwich.

'I know you're probably not hungry, but it's there if you want it.'

'Thank you, Sora.' It was barely more than a whisper.

'Melody's sleeping with Izan, Chester's with us, but he said if you want someone sleeping nearby then he'll sleep next door.'

Alain considered this. 'No, it's better that he stay with you girls, but, if two of the dwarves wouldn't mind sleeping next door, that would be good.'

Sora nodded. 'I'll ask them. Goodnight.'

'Goodnight.'

She left. Not long after, there was a knock at the door followed by Dell poking his head in.

'Phan and I are just next door, Alain. Let us know if you need anything.'

'Thank you, Dell.'

He closed the door and the train fell silent. The night passed slowly.

Around mid-morning, when everything was beginning to seem surreal to Alain and his head felt little more than a ball of lead balancing on his neck, Arrahbella opened her eyes. She blinked a couple of times, saw Alain watching her, and smiled.

'Alain,' she said. 'Have you been awake all night?'

He nodded. Arrahbella sat up and the covers fell slightly, revealing the scratches and bite marks that would leave scars of the night before. He wished he had thought to put some balm on them. Her eye make-up was streaked with tears, her hair was tangled, there was dirt on her face and body; Alain didn't think she had ever looked more beautiful.

'You look exhausted. Come to bed.'

He shook his head and felt the room spin. 'Do you need anything? Tea? Water? Food?'

'I need you to come to bed.'

'No, if I go to bed I'll fall asleep.'

'Yes.'

'I don't want to go to sleep. I need to keep watch.'

She reached out and took a hand in hers. 'Alain, you need to get your strength back or you'll be useless anyway.'

'I'm fine. I've gone without sleep many times before.'

'Alain,' her voice was so lyrical, so soothing. 'I need you to hold me.'

Alain sighed, took off his shoes, shirt, and pants, and climbed into his side of the bed. Arrahbella snuggled down next to him as he put his arms around her. He fought to stay awake.

'You scared me,' he whispered.

'You scared me, when you came in and he blasted you

359

aside. I was sure he'd killed you.'

'So was I.' He paused for a moment. 'I'm sorry. I don't know how he got past the guards.'

'Neither do I. One moment I was slicing carrots, the next I was blacking out. When I woke up, I was in his cabin. I tried to call you, but he'd blocked the connection.'

'I shouldn't have left you alone.' His voice was beginning to strain and Arrahbella felt a wetness against her cheek as tears fell.

'Shh, let's not talk about it now.' She moved her head to kiss him and he fell asleep in an instant.

The rest of the week passed slowly and without incident. Everyone was on edge, especially Alain. Once Izan had regained consciousness he assured his Ringmaster that Ikrael had been dead, or at least barely alive, when he had left the cabin, but Alain would not be able to fully relax until they had left Arelia completely.

In the middle of their second week in the colourful world, Chester was invited to a birthday party for one of the Players; the actor who had played Oberon in *A Midsummer Night's Dream*.

'I don't want you sleeping on your own, Melody,' Alain told her over supper. 'You can sleep in our room. Chester can wake you when he returns.'

'Alright.'

'And, Chester, be careful.'

'I will be, Alain. I don't plan on drinking tonight.'

Alain nodded as Chester stood up, kissed Melody on

the top of her head, and left for the Juggling Ant Tavern.

'Well, then,' Melody said to Sora and Asseniah. 'It looks like we can have a girls' only night.'

'Sounds good,' Sora replied.

'And what exactly am I meant to do?' Izan asked.

'You're not going to see anyone?'

Izan shook his head. He had only just started performing in the show and going out again. 'Not tonight. I feel like an old man.'

'You could have a civil conversation with the other grown ups in the train, Izan,' Alain suggested.

The magician snorted. 'Hardly.'

Alain smiled.

'Well, you're welcome to join us if you like, Izan, but we'll be talking about boys, clothes, and hair.'

'Yeah, including those hot guards outside,' Sora added.

'My dear girls, those are three of my favourite topics. If we could talk about me as well then I'm in Heaven.'

Sora and Melody laughed while the others rolled their eyes at each other and Asseniah contemplated her fork with almost obsessive interest.

Later that night, Melody took a pile of cushions from her caravan and arranged them on the du Maurier's floor as Alain attempted to read in bed, his thoughts constantly distracted since Arrahbella's kidnapping.

'Have you picked out any baby names yet?' he asked her, giving up on his novel.

'No. But if you have any suggestions let me know. There are so many good names, I don't know how I'm meant to settle on just one.'

'I'm sure you'll know the right one when you find it.'

Melody sighed. 'I hope so.'

Alain smiled as Arrahbella returned from the kitchen carrying three mugs of tea on a tray. Asseniah had helped her, so she hadn't been alone.

'Are you sure you don't want any Milksap, Alain?' she asked, as she handed a mug to Melody.

Alain shook his head. 'No. I want to be alert.'

'But you've hardly slept since last week.'

'I'm okay,' he assured her, taking the mug from her. Deciding to lighten the mood, he sniffed the liquid suspiciously.

'Alain!'

'What?' He gave her an innocent look and took a sip.

Arrahbella sighed, trying not to smile. She walked around to the other side of the bed and climbed in, taking up her own mug once she was settled.

'I wouldn't drug you against your will,' she grumbled, feigning injustice.

'You would if you thought it were in my best interest.'

'That's not true, I respect your wishes. If you want to walk around like a zombie then you go right ahead.' She put her tea down, folded her arms, and put her nose in the air. Melody watched them with unreserved adoration.

Alain put his tea down, winked at Melody, and turned to Arrahbella, putting his hands on her shoulders.

'Arrahbella,' he said quietly into her ear. 'I know that

if you were to send me into a drug-induced coma it would be done out of the incredible, knee-weakening love you have for me.'

Arrahbella couldn't keep up the act and started giggling. She turned and put her arms around his neck.

'Now I know what to do next Valentine's Day,' she said.

They kissed. Melody's heart tingled and she looked away, feeling slightly intrusive.

After talking for a while they all lay down and Alain dimmed the lamps by command.

Something troubled Arrahbella. She tossed and turned, images trying to reach her but not quite coming through clearly. Alain didn't want to sleep until she had settled, and when she finally did he lay awake for what seemed like hours, one arm around her as he stared up at the ceiling where shadows jumped and danced in the lamplight.

When Melody awoke the next morning, she found she was still on the cushions in Alain and Arrahbella's room, both of whom were fast asleep. Quietly, she got up and went to see if Chester was next door, but there was no sign of him there either. Frowning, she pulled on some clothes and snuck into her brother's room.

'Hi Melody,' Izan drawled sleepily, as she checked his bed and couch.

'Have you seen Chester?'

'As I have only just opened my eyes, no. Although he was in my dreams...'

'Never mind, sorry I woke you.'

She left the room and eventually the train, heading for the Juggling Ant.

As soon as Melody had shut the kitchen door behind her, Arrahbella woke with a start.

'Alain. Alain. Wake up.'

'What is it?'

'It's Chester.'

Alain peered through bleary eyes at the empty pile of cushions.

'Is he hurt?'

'No. But Melody will be if we don't stop her.'

Not fully understanding what she meant, Alain leapt out of bed and the two of them scrambled to get dressed.

They walked through the caravans, finding Izan's caravan empty and the three girls only just waking up. Outside, Oleg was exercising.

'Oleg, can you please keep an eye on things? We have to go into town and I'm not sure where Izan is.'

'He's there.' Oleg pointed to a tall cloaked figure in the distance.

'Izan,' Alain called. The magician stopped and waited for them. 'Where are you going?'

'Melody went off by herself,' Izan explained, wearily, his face pale. 'She said something about looking for Chester. I was going after her, she shouldn't be alone.'

'We're coming with you.'

'I don't think this is Ikrael,' Arrahbella told them. 'I did at first but now I think it's just Chester.'

The men looked at her with confusion, but she had

turned and started walking again.

By this time, Melody had reached the Juggling Ant and was speaking to the barman.

'There was a party here last night,' she said, 'for the Players. Were you on?'

The barman shook his head. 'Nope. But Meela was. Meela.' He waved a barmaid over. Meela finished serving a tray of drinks to a table of middle aged women (who were gossiping away as though their lives depended on it) and approached the bar.

'Yes?' She was a tall woman with short green hair and bright yellow eyes.

'This young lady would like a word.' The barman left them to talk.

'You were on last night? When the Players had a birthday party?'

'Yes.'

'Did you see Chester?'

'I did. I served him a couple of times.'

'Do you know when he left?'

Meela, knowing who Melody was, didn't particularly wish to answer. She hesitated, tapping an empty glass on the bar with a long purple fingernail. 'It was kind of strange actually,' she finally said. 'He was having a good time, only wanted non-alcoholic drinks, then, the next time I saw him, he looked really drunk and there was a girl all over him. A few of the Players tried to pull her off but he ended up leaving with her. He didn't look too well.'

It took Melody a moment to find her voice. 'Do you

know who the girl was?' she croaked.

'Oh, yes. She was from the Honey River House, just down the road. The Honey girls always come in here to pick up their clients.' Meela reached out and patted Melody's shoulder sympathetically. 'Is that all?'

Melody nodded. 'Th…Thank you,' she stuttered. She walked out of the tavern, oblivious to all else, her feet dragging, her head in a fuzz. Once outside, confusion turned to disbelief and anger. She ran down the street, pushing past people. As she passed a store she was stopped by the bold words of a newspaper headline; "Chester the Cheating Jester." It was accompanied by a photo of what looked like Chester leaving the Juggling Ant, leaning heavily on a girl whose features were obscured. Positively fuming, Melody continued running until she reached the Honey River House. There, she paused for a moment, silently praying to Mythos, before throwing the doors open and storming into the parlour.

The interior looked like the inside of a normal hotel, if a little bedazzled: there were lush red curtains hiding doorways off of the parlour; paintings of deliciously curvy nude women, most of them holding or eating fruit; cushioned chairs for the clients to wait in; a beautiful chandelier that did little to help the dim atmosphere (although it probably wasn't meant to); and a chipped tiled floor. A polished wooden bar sat directly in front of the entrance, behind which stood a well dressed, middle aged woman.

'Good morning,' the woman began, as she set down the book of accounts she had been going through. She had a beehive of purple hair and glowing golden eyes that sat behind a pair of purple spectacles.

'No, it is not,' Melody replied. 'My boyfriend is here and I want to know where.'

'Please, ma'am, there's no need to raise your voice, most of my clients are still in bed.'

'I don't care. I want to know which of these rooms Chester is in.'

'I'm sorry, I can't reveal any client information.'

'So he is one of your clients.'

The woman faltered. At that moment, Alain, Arrahbella, and Izan, having already been to the Juggling Ant and spoken to Meela as well, entered in a hurry but Melody didn't notice.

'I didn't say that,' the woman continued. 'I can't tell you whether someone is or is not here.'

'Well, I *know* he's here so you wouldn't be telling me, now, would you? I just want to know which room he's in or I'll bash down every damn door in the building.'

The woman looked frightened.

'Melody,' Alain rumbled quietly.

She turned to face them and crossed her arms. 'What?'

Before Alain could answer, Arrahbella gasped as she was hit by another vision. The vision showed her which room Chester was in and, when it had passed, her eyes shot up to one of the doors on the second floor before she realised too late that she had given his position away. She looked at Melody, hoping the girl hadn't noticed, but Melody was already running up the curved wooden staircase that sat to the left of the bar. This was one of those times when the young girl wished she could use her wings as it would have been much faster, but she didn't think the woman with the beehive hair could keep a secret for very long.

'Which one's he in?' she called, as she walked along the balcony, though she already knew. She stopped at the central door, room 3, and tried the handle.

'Melody, please, don't,' Arrahbella pleaded.

'Izan?' Melody begged, as she twisted the locked handle furiously.

Izan stepped forward, waved his hand, and the door unlocked.

'What?' he asked, seeing the looks the other two gave him. 'I'm on her side.'

Melody threw open the door, her eyes going straight to the large half-canopy bed as a sultry brunette sat up in surprise. The sheet was barely covering her obviously naked body. Her lips and breasts were far too large, as were her aqua-coloured eyes, and her nose was pointy and thin. Next to her, on the far side of the bed, Chester lay sleeping, also barely covered and fully naked.

The sound of the door banging open woke Chester. He felt a throbbing in his head and moaned before rubbing his eyes and slowly sitting up, blinking as he looked around, puzzled by the unfamiliar room. Then, he saw Melody.

'Melody? Where are we?' As he spoke his eyes fell on the girl sitting next to him. 'Oh, hi.' He looked at Melody again, waiting for her to explain who this girl was and why she was in his bed.

Then, his sleepy brain began to start ticking. He

368

noticed the girl was naked, he noticed he was naked, he realised that Melody was not smiling, and he noticed the strange contraptions around the room that could only be found in a...

'Oh, Sweet Arelia,' he breathed and turned to Melody with wide eyes. 'Melody? Melody!'

But Melody turned and left the room, walking back down to the parlour with thumping footsteps as Chester jumped out of bed, found his pants, threw them on, and raced out after her, all the time calling her back.

'Melody. Melody, I swear I have no idea what's going on here. Melody, please, wait.' He hurried out onto the balcony, looking down at the group below him. The brunette followed, not bothering to put a thread of clothing on, and stood beside him.

'Melody, please stop.'

But Melody didn't stop. She pushed past Alain and Izan and walked out into the street. Izan gave Chester a murderous look before going after her.

'Alain, what's going on?'

But Alain waved his hand, shook his head, and walked out as well.

Only Arrahbella stayed, so Chester ran down the steps to her. By now, other girls and clients had appeared in their doorways to watch the action. The beehive haired lady didn't know quite what to do with herself, though this was certainly not the first time something like this had happened, and certainly not the first time with a celebrity.

'Arrahbella,' Chester pleaded, looking desperate and

terrified. 'Arrahbella, please, go into my mind. Tell me I didn't.'

Outside, Alain realised that Arrahbella wasn't following and went back into the foyer where he found both she and Chester with their eyes closed. He stood back and waited, watching the strange contrast of serenity and anxiety emanating from the pair.

After a moment, Arrahbella opened her eyes, a puzzled expression on her pretty face.

'I'm sorry, Chester, it's blank,' she said. 'I've never known anyone's memory to be blank before, even when they're heavily drunk. It's strange.'

'That's got to mean something, doesn't it?' he asked.

'I don't know, Chester. I'm sorry.'

'You could ask me, you know,' the girl said from the balcony. 'I can tell you exactly what he did, in every minute detail. I remember it very well.'

Purple tears trailed down Chester's porcelain skin, his delicious mouth twisted in worry. Alain took a step toward him.

'Chester-'

'You know I'd never be unfaithful to her, Alain,' he whispered.

'Chester, go and get dressed, pay the girl if she needs to be paid, and come back to the train, okay?'

Chester looked defeated. He nodded slowly, turned, and dragged himself back up the stairs. Alain and Arrahbella didn't wait for him, instead they returned to the train where Arrahbella set about getting breakfast for those who hadn't eaten. Melody had shut herself up in her room, but she stormed through to the practice room as the others were eating only a few moments before Chester entered the dining car, looked at them all, and moved through to his room.

Alain couldn't eat. He went to the door of the practice room, inset in its little alcove between the fridge and the cupboard so he was relatively sheltered from view of the others, and listened as Melody cried, screamed, threw things. He slid down the wall and sat on the floor, listening to her sobs grow fainter, his heart aching at the sound of how hurt she was. Eventually, Melody fell silent but he continued to sit there. The others left the dining room slowly, moving through to the girls' room or outside. Arrahbella went over to check on him, but before she could say anything, Melody opened the door and looked at them with a red, tear-streaked face.

'Arrahbella,' she sniffed. 'Can you go and question the girl? See what she says and make her tell the truth.'

'Of course, Melody.'

'Take Izan with you,' Alain said.

As Arrahbella left, Alain looked up at Melody and waited.

'He wouldn't, would he, Alain? He wouldn't do that to me.'

'No, Melody, I don't believe he would.'

'But, there doesn't seem to be any other explanation.'

'No, that's true.'

'But, then, I don't understand.'

Alain patted the floor next to him and she sat down.

'Melody, sometimes people do get so intoxicated that they don't have control over their actions. That girl did

371

look like you. Chester may have been too drunk to tell the difference.'

'She looked nothing like me. Her breasts were bigger than mine.'

Alain smiled sadly. 'He may not have noticed that either.'

'How could you not notice them? Even if you were drunk, they were massive.'

'Even so.'

'But Chester's never been that drunk. He's not a big drinker.'

'Actually, he has, when he was in love with you but still hadn't told you.'

'But there's no reason for him to get drunk like that now. I mean, he's been so happy lately, with the baby and everything.' She paused. 'He tried to ask me to marry him the other day, after what happened to Arrahbella, but I wouldn't let him because everyone was scared and it didn't feel right. I know he wants to marry me though, and he's been the one worried that I'm going to leave him for someone my own age. It doesn't make any sense.'

'Well, if you stopped him from talking about marriage maybe he took it the wrong way?'

'No, he understood. I made sure that he understood.' She put her head in her hands. Alain put his arms around her.

'Wait until Arrahbella comes back,' he said, quietly. 'Hear what she finds out.'

'I don't think he did anything. I just can't believe that he would and maybe that's wrong but I just can't. My eyes say he did, but my heart doesn't agree. It just doesn't seem logical and it doesn't *feel* right. I mean, you know Arrahbella would never be unfaithful, don't you?'

Alain released his hug so that he could look at her. 'Melody, I don't think you can ever truly know. I mean, you do everything you can, and you hope that they're happy, and you hope that they feel loved, and you hope dearly that they'd never seek love from another, but I don't think you can ever truly believe that they wouldn't, and you probably shouldn't, because things happen and humans are easily tempted. It's a sad fact.' He paused and sat back against the wall. 'Having said that, I do trust Arrahbella with all my heart and believe that if she were ever unhappy she would soon let me know. But, I also have the added privilege of knowing that she saw her future with me, so I'm probably not the best person to ask about this.'

'You have an unfair advantage.'

'That's right.'

'Well, yes, you do, but not because of Arrahbella's psychic powers. It's because you and she are a rare pair.'

'I am lucky, aren't I?'

'Yes. Very.'

'Well, you are too. Chester is a good man and I know that he loves you. I do worry sometimes that you'll face some problems with your age difference but I don't believe Chester would be unfaithful to you, Melody Bell... mainly because he knows that Izan and I would murder him if he ever hurt you, or, at least, maim and torture.'

Melody gave him a sad smile and nodded. 'The poor

guy wouldn't have a hope.'

'Nope.'

They were silent for a moment.

'Come on,' Alain finally said. 'This floor has put my rear to sleep. Let's move into the kitchen.'

Melody smiled as she stood up. 'Acrobats don't get sore rears.'

'Be quiet, acrobat, and help me up.'

Chester was sitting on the edge of his bed. He had been crying for a while but now he was just sitting in silence, his face streaked with purple, trying desperately to remember what had happened. When the door opened and Melody entered he looked up then rose from the bed.

'Melody. Melody, I swear I can't-'

'Stop, Chester.'

Chester stopped but his heart gave another pang and he couldn't help the tears from falling again. He sank down slowly to the bed once more. Melody walked over and sat next to him.

'Chester, don't cry.'

'What am I meant to do, Melody? My heart's breaking.'

'Why?'

'Because I've hurt you.'

'Have you?'

He looked at her, confused and frustrated. 'Melody, this isn't fair. I'm terrified that you're going to leave me and that I've done something to hurt you and you're playing with me.'

'I'm sorry, Chester. I didn't mean to come across that way.'

'I wish I could tell you what happened and why but I don't know, I honestly don't. I've been sitting here trying to remember, but it's just blank. I know it looks bad, but I'd never hurt you, Melody, not willingly or knowingly, and I'd never deliberately be unfaithful to you, and I'd never put myself in a situation where I was in danger of doing so. I made sure not to drink too much because I'm trying to stay alert in case Ikrael comes back, so I don't know how I ended up in that bed.'

'Chester.' She put her hand to his chin, feeling his porcelain skin, gently turning his head until his glistening purple eyes looked into hers. 'Ikrael did come back.'

'What?'

'I asked Arrahbella and Izan to go back and talk to the girl. I mean, she knows what happened and nobody even asked her.'

'I did. She told me that I'd slept with her.'

'Well, she lied. Arrahbella delved into her mind and discovered that a mysterious man had approached her last night, told her that she'd find you drugged up, and paid her a load of money, which he'd stolen only moments before, to make it look as though she'd slept with you and to lie about it. Well, actually he told her to sleep with you, but apparently you were so out of it that you fell asleep when you hit the bed, so she had to pretend.'

Chester was shocked.

'From the girl's memory, Arrahbella saw enough

375

of the man to know that it was Ikrael. He was wearing a robe but she saw his hands and part of his face. He did this, Chester. He drugged you. Somehow, he got into the tavern and slipped something into your drink. Obviously, he wasn't as dead as Izan thought he was and now he's trying to play havoc with us. But, it's going to take more than that to break us up. You're stuck with me, Chester.'

Chester processed all that she had told him, hardly able to believe it.

'I'm sorry I doubted you,' she said, quietly.

'Melody, I doubted myself.'

'Chester.' She got up on her knees so she could cradle his head to her chest.

At lunchtime, Alain called every member into the kitchen car so he could discuss what they would do now that Ikrael seemed to be on the move again.

'We cannot abandon our audiences,' he told them. 'We will perform our final three shows and we will perform them as though nothing has happened in the last two weeks. The tent is a solace, remember, a place to escape, not only for ourselves but for the viewer as well. Izan, Chester, Oleg, and I will rotate watch during the night. Everybody, please, be extremely careful. Do not go anywhere alone. Soon, we'll be leaving for Noir Eternale and maybe then we can start to relax.'

'Funny,' Sora mused. 'I never thought Noir Eternale would be a safer place than Arelia.'

Chester looked down at the table, ashamed at

376

the statement.

'I can't believe I didn't know about this monster,' Alain said to no one in particular. 'I know these worlds inside and out.'

'You're not to blame,' Arrahbella assured him.

'I am,' Chester mumbled. 'I should have told you a long time ago, but we've been raised not to talk about him. Most people think he's only a legend.'

'It's not your fault either, Chester,' Alain, Arrahbella, and Melody said in unison. Chester looked at the table top again.

'Come on, then, gang,' Alain said. 'We've got three days left. We'll be okay.'

But not even Alain's chocolate voice could soothe their anxieties this time.

When the final show came to an end, the troupe packed up and left that very night, hardly daring to breath until the last caravan was out of the rift. A collective sigh could be heard throughout the train as it turned around and headed back along the Highway, now pointed in the opposite direction to the one it had been travelling in since leaving Earth, bound for Noir Eternale.

CHAPTER 13

Noir Eternale

Present Day – Noir Eternale

Fenton peered out of the driving cabin window, trying to see the narrow dirt road in the darkness of the forest.

Need to get us some more stardust for these headlights, he decided, and then slammed on the brakes as something scurried across his path.

'Damned ferrets,' he muttered, chewing his straw of talooey harder than necessary.

Gently pressing down on the accelerator once more, he drove the train along at a snail's pace until the trees of the Pleu Forest finally cleared and a wide patch of grass stretched out before him. Further on he could see the lights of Cheyenne, creating a haze over the town. Driving the train off the road, he manoeuvred the long vehicle with expert skill until all nine caravans were sitting parallel to the forest edge.

'All set, Alain,' he announced, once he had walked through to the neighbouring caravan.

The Ringmaster put down his book. He looked very tired, his hair curling away in all directions as though it were trying to escape from his head.

'Thank you, Fenton. We'll set up the tent to let people know we're here and then you're free to roam the city for a while.'

'Righto, I'll get the others.'

Once the tent was up and ready, looking strangely happy in the bleak world, the troupe headed into town, leaving Alain and Arrahbella to look after the train and have some time alone.

As soon as they reached the edge of the cobblestones, they were engulfed by the familiar smells and noises of Cheyenne. The city's main square sprawled out in front of them, activity flourishing everywhere.

Izan inhaled deeply. 'Have I mentioned how much I love this world?'

'Many times,' Melody replied.

The magician smiled at her, looked around eagerly, spotted a brothel, yelped in delight, and hurried inside.

Mariette took Oleg's arm. She was dressed all in black, hoping to go unnoticed in the dark world. 'We are going to 'ave lunch. Does anyone wish to join us?'

'No, thank you. Chester and I are going to La Luna to spend some time alone,' Melody replied.

'We're going to Madam Harmony's,' Fenton told her. 'They've got excellent gamblers there.'

'And we're going to watch the street performers,' Sora said, and Asseniah nodded.

So, as the others dispersed in various directions, the dancer and the giant headed further into the town centre toward their favourite eatery. As they passed the citizens and tourists, Mariette couldn't help looking at every young male vampire she came across, searching for any sign of familiarity in their features. She was sure that Luc would have stayed in Reine and she could never go up and speak to him if she did recognise him, but her heart couldn't help jumping every time she saw a young blood-sucker with fair hair and a grizzled appearance.

Oleg was keeping an eye on the locals as well. He knew this was Jean-Luc's home town and though he had never seen the man, he still watched for anyone that might look at Mariette in the wrong way.

'Do you still want to go to Sucré Musique?' Oleg asked her, as he avoided a vomiting drunk.

'Yes, ze chef zere is one of ze few who does not abuse 'is gift by making 'is food addictive.'

'Provided it's the same chef.'

They arrived at the café in question and Mariette peered through the kitchen window. A tall, thin man with a very well-kept moustache was sweating over pots and pans that bubbled ferociously, singing in a loud voice as he worked.

'Yes, look, it is Pierre. We are okay.'

The dainty tables and chairs were crowded and spilling out onto the street, but they managed to pick their way through the maze to a vacant set on the corner of the footpath. Oleg pulled out a chair for Mariette before squeezing into his own, accidentally knocking the woman next to him and apologising profusely until she blushed with embarrassment. Across the street from their table, a street performer was levitating a few feet off the ground as small, delighted children ran underneath him. A short way along, a vampire was devouring another vampire under the lamp post, blood running down their neck and dripping into the gutter to be washed down the drain, and, next to them, a man was reciting poetry in a voice that made every listener think of diamonds. Around their table, couples, families, friends, and tourists chatted, sipped, and chewed away the night.

A petite young waitress came out of the restaurant with her notebook and pen in hand, her long brown hair swinging in its ponytail as she walked.

'Good evening, madam, monsieur. What will you 'ave tonight?'

Mariette scanned the menu. 'I zink I will 'ave ze pumpkin and sage risotto, zank you.'

'And for you, sir?'

'Steak and chips. Rare, please.' The steak came from an animal known as a vitan; a ghastly creature that roamed the forests, its coat as inky black as the night-encased world it lived in.

'Very good, sir.' The waitress made a note and walked off, swaying her hips tantalisingly.

When she returned with their loaded-up plates she blinked her blue, bloodshot eyes a few times at Oleg who smiled politely before casting his eyes downward to cut the steak, blood oozing out over the plate.

'You should see when she gets off,' Mariette told him, once the waitress had gone back inside.

Oleg shook his head while he chewed. 'I'm not going

to leave you alone.'

'Oleg, when was ze last time zat you were wiz a woman?'

'It's been a while,' he smiled.

'You should ask her. I will be fine. We will go back to ze train and zen you can come back and wait for 'er.'

He looked at his friend with kind but stern eyes. 'I have no desire for anyone at the moment, Mariette, but thank you for thinking of me.'

Mariette smiled and changed the subject, talking about Ikrael and all that had occurred over the last couple of weeks.

They had moved on to dessert – a chocolate cake smothered in chocolate ganache for Oleg, and a strawberry flavoured mound that resembled a cloud in consistency for Mariette – and coffee when Mariette suddenly dropped her spoon, her wide eyes watching a man talking to the diamond-voiced poet. Oleg followed her gaze, looked the man over, then turned back to Mariette who had gone even whiter than usual.

'Mariette?' he prompted.

But the man was turning away from the poet, his eyes falling on Mariette as he did so. She quickly looked away, covering her face with her hand, expecting shouts to erupt at any moment.

But none came.

Oleg cleared his throat and she looked up, jumping a little when she realised the man was now standing beside their table.

'Mariette?' he said, his rough voice barely more than a whisper.

'Jean-Luc?'

'It is you,' Jean-Luc continued. 'I can't believe it's really you.'

Mariette felt giddy as a torrent of emotion flooded out of her heart. Jean-Luc really did look stunned to see her, however, he also looked worried, worn, old, and bedraggled. His once greying beard was now completely grey and his hair had decided to follow suit, barely leaving any trace of its original black.

''ow are you?' she asked.

Jean-Luc looked at Oleg. 'Would you mind giving us a moment?'

'Are you going to do anything to put her in danger?'

'No. I... I just want to talk.'

Oleg looked at Mariette who nodded.

'I'll be just over there,' Oleg told them, pointing to the street corner. Then, he leaned in as close as he could to Jean-Luc. 'You do anything – raise your voice, hurt her – and you'll have me to answer to.'

Jean-Luc, who had, like most of his race, never seen a Da'Laarwickan before, nodded sincerely. Oleg moved away as Jean-Luc took the chair he had been sitting in, his long, black, ragged trench coat trailing over the edge and touching the dirty ground.

'Mariette, after that night, nobody believed me... well, they believed at first, but when we couldn't find you they just couldn't believe that you had no powers, you were such a talented dancer and whore, they began to think I was lying, that I'd murdered you. They chased me out of the town. I've never gone back, but I think about you every day. I felt wretched for the way I reacted. I shouldn't have done that. I loved you, Mariette. I still do.' He smiled. 'It's good to see you again.'

Suddenly, Mariette realised that the wave of emotion she had felt only moments before was not love, but fear that she was still in love with this man. She actually wasn't. Seeing him all broken, unshaven, and still, apparently, in love with her made her feel rather happy.

'What have you been up to? What happened that night?'

She wasn't sure she wanted him to know. 'I fled. Moved to anozer world. I 'ave a family now, people who love me.'

'That's great, Mariette, really great. I'm really happy for you.'

He sounded sincere, but then, she'd thought he loved her all those years ago and he hadn't loved her at all, despite what he said now. She looked up at Oleg who took the hint and walked back to the table.

'Well, Jean-Luc, it 'as been lovely seeing you again but we really must go.' She stood up.

Jean-Luc looked scared. 'No, please don't go, Mariette, I just want to talk.'

'I 'ave nozing to say to you, except goodbye.' She made to leave but he reached out and grabbed her arm. With rapid reflexes, Oleg took hold of his outstretched arm and squeezed until Jean-Luc was forced to let go.

'Please,' he said, tears in his eyes. 'Please, I need to know what happened to our baby.'

Mariette stopped and studied her ex-lover, almost feeling sorry for him. She nodded to Oleg and he reluctantly released Jean-Luc's arm.

'Out 'ere,' she said. They were getting looks from the other diners so she walked out onto the street. Oleg dragged Jean-Luc after her.

She didn't have to tell him about their son. He might go looking for him and perhaps they would reunite. She wasn't sure if she could handle Jean-Luc having a life with the son she would never see. She also knew how she felt, not knowing if Luc was okay, what kind of person he was, if he was happy. But was Jean-Luc really like that? He didn't love her, so why should he want to know what happened to the child he had made with a "monster"? Perhaps he wanted to kill Luc so that no trace of their relationship remained. No, it was better that she didn't tell him anything about her life, or their son, but if she simply refused to tell him anything he might turn on her again.

'Please, Mariette, I need to know.'

Oleg was ready to knock him out if she asked it. She took a deep breath.

''e was never born. Ze stress of 'aving you turn on me caused a miscarriage.'

His shoulders fell. He believed her and she almost believed that he felt guilty and terrible. He certainly looked it. Mariette dared to hope that she had finally had some kind of vengeance on him. He nodded.

'Goodbye, Mariette. I hope you have a wonderful life.' He moped off into the darkness.

Mariette let out a breath of relief. 'Zank you, Oleg.'

'I think you did the right thing.'

She nodded. 'I 'ope so.'

'Come on.' The giant gently took her arm and together they walked back to the train.

Mariette would tell Alain about her meeting with Jean-Luc later, but now she and Oleg gave him and Arrahbella some more time alone, Mariette heading off to the practice room to dance out her emotions while Oleg went to his room to sketch.

'I'm sorry but there are no seats left,' Oleg called in a booming voice over the rabble of the disgruntled crowd.

'You've barely let anyone in,' argued the werewolf standing at the front of the line. 'What kind of tent can't hold more than a handful of people?'

Shouts of agreement came from those standing behind him.

'Our tent seats two hundred people. I'm sorry, but it's first come, first served. Those of you who wish to may receive a ticket for tomorrow night's performance.'

There was a lot of grumbling as some turned and walked away and others fought their way to the ticket booth where Dell began handing out tickets. Oleg waited until the last of them had walked back toward the town then he helped Dell pack up the booth and they went backstage.

'I wish they had money here, Alain,' he told the Ringmaster, who was standing in the wings. 'They'll tear down the tent one day.'

'Thank you, Oleg. I'll try and think of something.'

'I know you think they deserve entertainment too, but is it worth it?'

Alain looked up at him. 'Yes, it is.'

Oleg nodded and headed to a dressing room.

The Noir Eternalans were, like the Arelians, a noisy lot when it came to being an audience, but theirs was more of a drunken, jeering contribution as opposed to a joyous and enthusiastic one.

Mariette's dancing was as fluid and dazzling as ever, then Sora's knives thrilled and awed. Manipulation came next. Then, Izan performed, enjoying being able to respond to the audience's shouts and comments until they were so riled up that they were standing on their seats. Oleg did his bit then and they calmed down, silenced by his amazing strength.

Melody and Chester climbed up into the rafters while Alain introduced their act and Asseniah watched them from the nest of silks she was cocooned in. As usual, Melody was to do a few swings on her own before Chester joined in from the other side. She took the bar from its hook and held it with one hand as she looked down at Alain, his words having as much of an effect on her as they were having on the audience.

Alain bowed and moved away as Fenton pulled the curtains open and the dwarves started playing. Melody took a deep breath, gripped the swing with both hands, and pushed off from the platform, swinging one leg up and over the bar in the same moment.

What happened next happened in the space of a split second but felt like an eternity for all of those watching. The bar gave way, Melody's hands slipped as it tilted, and the left support rope fell like a limp noodle from the rafters. Instinct made her flap her wings but she found them frozen. Fear gripped her. Her eyes met Chester's, and then she fell, hitting the stage with a sickening thud.

Chester felt the air leave him as he stared down at her motionless body. His senses left too, then came flooding back, spurring him down the ladder as fast as he could safely go.

In the wings, Alain had also lost his breath for a moment but was now giving orders. 'Fenton, curtain. Mariette, out front. Sora, get Arrahbella.' Arrahbella was in the train. He had left her there alone, thinking they were safe from Ikrael.

Sora and Mariette hurried off as Chester reached the bottom of the ladder. Fenton closed the curtains and the dwarves struck up a lively tune. Izan, Alain, and Chester hurried to Melody's side as soon as the curtains closed.

'Melody? Melody?' Chester said, fear making his voice shake. She was on her back, her legs twisted awkwardly, arms outstretched, bent at the elbows in odd angles. He went to lift her head but Alain stopped him.

'No, Chester, we can't move her in case her back is broken.'

Chester was horrified at this suggestion, but he kept his hands away. Alain bent down, putting his ear close to her mouth.

'She's breathing.' His voice was shaking.

'Alain, what about the-'

'I know. Wait until Arrahbella gets here, then we'll know more.'

'Why didn't she use her wings?' Chester's eyes were shining as tears welled.

'Probably for the same reason the trapeze was cut,' Alain replied.

Chester stared at him. He hadn't considered that this may not have been an accident. Above them, Asseniah blinked down anxiously. Mariette had turned the audience's silence into applause again as she continued to entertain and the dwarves played distractedly. Chester continued to say Melody's name, hoping to call her back to consciousness.

Alain felt immense relief when Sora returned with Arrahbella. The psychic knelt next to Chester to examine Melody, her face etched with worry.

'We need to know if her back's broken so that we can move her.' Alain said. 'Can you go in and see?'

Arrahbella nodded and closed her eyes, sinking into Melody's mind. A wave of pain hit her with a force and she fought the urge to retreat. She scanned her body, looking for anything broken or ruptured. There was nothing, but... wait, there was something else, something around her stomach area. She came out of Melody's mind in a hurry and looked at Alain with a shocked expression.

'Is it broken?' Alain prompted when she didn't speak.

'No, nothing's broken, but Alain, she's—'

'I know, I know. Okay, Oleg?' The giant stepped forward. 'Take Melody to her bed. Stay with her and Arrahbella. Chester, you go as well.'

Oleg gently lifted Melody and the four of them left through the back of the tent. Alain looked up at the pair of swirling green eyes staring down at him.

'Have you checked your silks?'

She nodded.

'You're okay to go on?'

She nodded again.

'Alright, we'll finish with you. If anything feels wrong you stop immediately, alright?'

Alain and Izan returned to the wings. The Ringmaster paused for a moment, taking a deep breath, a very uncomfortable knot sitting heavily in his stomach, then, he signalled for Mariette and the dwarves to finish, and for Fenton to open the curtains. Izan was so agitated that small swirls of magic were flitting around his fingers like tiny lightning bolts.

'Is she alright?' Mariette whispered, as soon as she was at Alain's side.

'I don't know.' He was shaking but wasn't aware of it.

Mariette put a hand on his shoulder. 'Shall I go and see if Arrahbella needs any 'elp?'

'No. Stay here with me. We'll close the show once Asseniah's done and then we'll all go together.'

'You zink zis was not an accident?' She suddenly feared that Jean-Luc may have been behind it, out for revenge.

'Earlier, I thought I saw Ikrael in the audience, then I thought I was just imagining it, because when I looked again I couldn't see him.'

This didn't make Mariette feel any better. 'Are you sure?'

'No. But this doesn't feel like an accident. We checked the trapeze twice in safety and for some reason Melody didn't use her wings.' He shook his head.

'I didn't get a chance to freeze her,' added Izan. 'I thought she was flying and by the time I realised she wasn't, she'd hit the ground.'

'I know, but make sure your eyes stay on Asseniah.'

'They are.'

As soon as Asseniah had finished, Alain closed the show with an enthusiasm he did not feel and waited until everyone had left, then, he, Asseniah, Sora, Mariette, Izan, and the dwarves went to the train.

They found Oleg in Izan's room, which is where everyone waited while Alain went through to Melody's room. Melody was on her bed, Chester and Arrahbella crouched at her side. She had only just regained consciousness.

'Melody,' Arrahbella said, in her lyrical lilting voice. 'You fell. Do you remember?'

'Yes.'

'I want you to tell me if you're in pain and where, okay?'

'My back, my head, I don't know, everything.' Her hands moved to her stomach, even though Chester was holding one of them. Tears started to roll down her cheeks and she turned her head slightly to look at Arrahbella. 'Arrahbella, I'm pregnant.'

'I know, honey, I know.'

'Is it alright?'

Chester closed his eyes and turned away.

'I don't know, honey, I have to check you first.'

'Can't you go into its mind and see?'

Chester looked at Arrahbella.

'No. I can't go into the mind of an unborn, especially so early on, it's not fully formed yet.'

Melody looked at the ceiling.

'We won't know how the child is for a while,' Arrahbella continued.

'We have to wait to see if I lose it, you mean.'

'Hey, Melody, don't talk like that. Let me get you what you need and see if we can relax you, okay? Worrying and getting worked up isn't going to help, alright?'

Melody nodded, her mouth quivering.

'Okay. Alain, I need one of the girls.'

Alain left the room and Asseniah entered a moment later. The rest of the troupe set about getting their own supper; no one felt like going into town and Alain wouldn't have let them even if they had.

'Alain,' Mariette said quietly, as they stood in the kitchen. 'Do you think Jean-Luc could have done this?'

Alain shook his head, so did Oleg who was standing close by. 'No, I'm sure that this is Ikrael. Somehow he must have discovered that Melody was pregnant and thought it'd be a good way to get back at Chester and myself.' He looked at the ground, swallowing hard. 'I never thought that he'd follow us out of Arelia.'

Mariette didn't know what to say, but just then Arrahbella came through the door with Asseniah.

'She's sleeping,' she told them. 'I've rubbed balm on her muscles. Hopefully that will help ease some of the pain. Chester's still with her.'

'Thank you, Bella.' He looked around at them all. 'Izan, Oleg, we'll have to rotate watch again. I'll take the first shift.'

'No problem, Alain,' Izan said, as he sat down to his supper. 'I'll take the middle.'

Alain nodded at Izan then turned to Arrahbella. He took her hand and led her into the girls' room, shutting the door before sitting next to her on Mariette's bed.

'What are we going to do?' he asked her, quietly. 'I don't know what to do.'

'The only thing we can do is hope that he reveals himself so we can fight him properly, or that he gets bored with us.'

'What if he doesn't? What if he keeps on doing what he's doing? I can only assume that we're not all dead already because he wants to play with us first.'

'You know, I used to read books about magic and villains, but I never thought I'd be the target of one.' Alain smiled sadly. 'But in all of the stories on Earth, all the books and all the movies, good triumphs over evil.'

'This isn't a story, Bella,' he whispered.

She looked down and he looked away. After a moment,

Arrahbella put her fingers to his cheeks and gently turned his head back to face her.

'We'll be okay, Alain. You've fought people like Ikrael before and succeeded.'

'People died in the process.'

'But you stopped him from taking over Landau.'

Alain didn't say anything.

'From what you've told me, he was as powerful and as ruthless as Ikrael and you beat him. You defeated him and you can defeat Ikrael.'

Alain looked at her with sad eyes. 'I didn't have as much to lose back then.'

Arrahbella's eyes spilled over with tears, making the ice blue colour shine like diamonds. She pulled Alain to her and held him tightly.

None of the troupe slept very well that night. The image of Melody hitting the stage was still crisp in their minds. Izan couldn't stop berating himself for not being able to stop her fall. At around one o'clock in the morning, Alain and Arrahbella went to bed and the magician got up to take over.

Chester had crawled into his side of the bed and was drifting in and out of an uneasy sleep. Not long into Izan's watch, he came out of his doze with fear pulsing through his body. It took him a moment to realise why; Melody was moaning.

'Melody?' he said, blinking the sleep away. He moved to sit up and froze. The sheets felt... wet. As his heart thumped loudly he pulled back the covers. There was blood. Lots of blood. His heart plummeted to his stomach as he realised what that meant.

Melody grabbed his arm, staring at him with tear-filled eyes.

'Chester,' she said weakly. 'It hurts.'

'Melody, I have to go and get Arrahbella,' he said, as calmly as he could.

'No, don't leave me, Chester, please,' she pleaded.

'Melody, I have to.'

'No.'

He turned his head toward the adjoining door and shouted desperately, 'Arrahbella! Arrahbella!'

Arrahbella sat up with a start, not from the calls coming from the next room but because she had just had a very graphic and bloody dream.

'Alain, wake up.'

He hadn't been asleep. He was already pulling on his robe. They hurried into the next room where they were stopped in their tracks by the sight of the blood-soaked bed. Alain felt chills shake him but Arrahbella made herself move to Melody's side of the bed.

Chester was in tears, hysteria beginning to set in. 'Oh, Mythos, Mythos, Mythos. Melody.'

Calmly but forcefully Arrahbella said, 'Get out of the bed, Chester.'

Having heard the commotion, Izan burst into the room. 'What in Mythos' name is...' His voice trailed off as he, too, saw the bed. 'Is that Melody's blood?' he asked, horrified.

'Yes, Izan,' Arrahbella told him. She had knelt down and was stroking Melody's hand. Melody was awake but in a daze, unaware of what was going on.

'Arrahbella, do something,' Chester cried in distress.

'Izan, get the girls. Tell them to bring warm water and towels.'

Izan left quickly.

'Alain, get Chester out of here.'

Chester interrupted his distressed pacing to glare at Arrahbella. 'I am not leaving.'

'Chester, I need you to leave.'

Melody had begun to moan again, tossing and turning in fits.

'No, Arrahbella, I'm not going anywhere.' His voice had a threatening tone to it.

Arrahbella stood up quickly. 'Chester, if you don't leave this room now I'll have Alain force you out.'

Chester glared furiously at her. Alain moved to take his arm, but Chester jolted away and stormed out of the room.

'Alain, you go too,' Arrahbella said, kneeling back down. 'This is a female's situation now. Don't let any of the boys in, especially not Chester.'

Alain left the room as Mariette, Asseniah, and Sora entered.

'What's 'appening Arrahbella?'

'She was pregnant,' Arrahbella answered. Melody had passed out again. 'I need warm water and towels and now.'

They hurried to get everything.

396

'It's alright, Melody,' Arrahbella soothed, still stroking her hand. They had taken Melody's leotard off before putting her into the bed so there were no blood-soaked clothes to take off. 'It's okay.'

In Izan's room, Izan, Chester, and Alain were waiting in anxious restlessness. Chester, wearing only his loose white pants, couldn't stand still, walking to and fro by Izan's bed. Izan was sitting on his bed, fully dressed. Alain was on a chair near the door that led to Melody and Chester's room.

'So, did we know that she was pregnant?' Izan asked.

'Three of us did,' Alain replied.

'Arrahbella didn't?'

'No.'

'But you did?'

'Yes.'

'Of course you did.' He wasn't surprised but he was a little hurt.

'They wanted to keep it to themselves for a while.'

'But they told you.'

'They had to tell me Izan, from the circus' point of view.'

Izan snorted. 'How long?'

'Only a few weeks.'

'Since the herb mix-up thingy?'

Alain nodded.

'Do we have to have this conversation?' Chester blurted. 'I mean, it's not like it matters anymore.'

Alain and Izan gave each other a look. Chester continued to pace, wringing his hands, sniffing, his wet face shining purple in the lamplight. Then, he stopped. 'This is ridiculous. There's four people in that room with her and I'm not one of them. Your wife has some nerve kicking me out, Alain.'

Alain's emotions got the better of him. 'Oh, grow up, Chester!'

'Grow up?'

The Wordmaster stood up. 'Did it occur to you that Arrahbella may have asked you to leave because you were making her worse?'

Chester stared at him, unable to answer.

'You're crying, Chester, you're pacing up and down, sobbing. Melody could hear you and it was distressing her. Now, I know you're upset, we all are, and I know you're scared, but I'm seriously starting to reconsider giving you my permission to marry Melody if this is how you're going to react every time a crisis comes up. If you can't be strong when she needs you most, if you can't be calm and collected even when you're dying inside, then I'm not sure if you really are the best man for her.'

Chester looked murderous. 'Well, if you remember, Alain, you said I don't need your permission.'

'You need mine,' Izan said. 'And I'm with Alain. Seriously, Chester, you're my best friend but you're being ridiculous.'

Chester couldn't believe what he was hearing; here he was devastated that he had just lost his child and terrified he was going to lose Melody as well and these two were telling him he was being ridiculous?!

'Oh really?' he fired back. 'Well, I'm sorry if I'm not as cold and heartless as the both of you.'

'Chester, sweet Mythos,' Alain breathed.

The jester's eyes narrowed. He walked across the room until he was close to Alain.

'You know this is your fault,' he said in a low voice. 'You had to invite Ikrael into the train, and your wife had to be so nice to him that he fell in love with her, and now, because he hates you for refusing to let him into your circus, and because he wants your wife, he's trying to hurt you by taking away the next dearest thing to you. So, I may be crumbling under pressure, Alain, but it's your fault she fell, it's your fault my child died, and if Melody dies, I'll be blaming you for that too.'

The words hit hard. Alain looked away.

'Chester, that's not fair,' Izan said. 'Alain's not responsible for Ikrael being a madman. You can't blame him for trying to be nice to the guy, Alain's nice to everyone. And, Ikrael has it in for you as well. You tried to warn Alain when you saw him sitting in our kitchen.'

As Chester opened his mouth to argue, Sora stuck her head through the door. 'Would you three be quiet? Geez.' She disappeared again.

Chester walked back over to the end of the room, sunk down on the floor by the bed, and tried not to cry, without any success. Alain sat down again as well.

A moment later, Asseniah walked into the room, dropped down beside Chester, and wrapped her arms around him. It made him cry even more but she waited until he had quietened. Alain couldn't help smiling sadly as Asseniah surprised him yet again. When she got up, she walked over to Izan, hit him on the arm, then glared reproachfully at Alain, making him shift uncomfortably under her mesmerising green stare. Then, she returned to help Arrahbella. Chester had stopped crying. He was sitting on the floor, leaning against the bed, hands in his lap, legs outstretched, staring at the carpet, looking worn and defeated.

They sat in silence for a while, the only noise being the occasional shaky exhale from Chester. Finally, Mariette poked her head around the connecting door.

'Chester?' He looked up. 'You aren't to look.'

Chester waved a hand indifferently, indicating that he wouldn't. Just for good measure, Izan stood up and spread his cloak, bat-like, in front of Chester so that he couldn't see even if he tried to.

Mariette disappeared for a moment, then, she, Sora, and Asseniah filed out of the room carrying bloody towels, sheets and the quilt, and the basin of hot water. They walked past Alain who watched, then wished he hadn't as he saw that the basin was filled with what the miscarriage had expelled. He rapidly shut his eyes but found the image remained so he opened them again. When the girls had gone, Arrahbella entered the room.

'Chester?'

Izan looked over his shoulder and dropped his arms as Chester got up and walked over to her.

'She's asleep. She has been in and out of consciousness for a while but she's asleep now, which is good. I'd like to stay with her for a bit longer just to keep an eye on things. I can't tell you that she's going to be okay yet.' He nodded and looked at the ground. 'And, I don't think I have to tell you that she's lost the baby.' He nodded again. 'I'm sorry, Chester.'

'May I see her?'

'Yes, but she's only asleep. She'll be able to hear you and I don't want her woken up. If you start crying or say anything that might distress her then you'll have to leave.'

He nodded.

'Okay. You two stay here.'

Melody lay fast asleep but the sheets had been changed and the quilt removed so that only a few fresh sheets and a blanket covered her. As Chester drew closer he could see how pale she looked. He knelt by the bed and took her hand in his. Arrahbella sat in the bedside chair.

'Hey, Melody,' he said, quietly. 'It's Chester. I'm here.' He brushed a ringlet from her cheek and stroked her hair while he spoke. 'You have to hang in there, okay, honey? And when this tour's over, we'll go back to Varatalé and you and I'll go away for a while, okay? Just the two of us. We'll go anywhere you want to go. But you have to hang in there, alright, sweetie? Arrahbella's taking care of you, so you're in the best hands you can be in. And I'll be nearby if you need me.' He pressed his face to hers before kissing her on the cheek. He could feel tears coming again but didn't want to leave her side. Arrahbella gently touched his arm but he jerked it away.

'I have to go now, honey, but I'll be just next door.'

He kissed her again. 'You'll be okay. I love you.' He let go of her hand and walked out of the room. He didn't stop in Izan's room though; he continued on until he reached the practice room, ignoring the bloody mess the girls were trying to clean up in the kitchen. There, he exploded; yelling, punching, crying, swearing, cursing Mythos, Arelia, and Ikrael, and letting the anger overtake him.

When he was exhausted enough to stop, he walked back through to Izan's room. Izan had been in to see his sister and now Alain came out. Arrahbella had told him to check on her every fifteen minutes in case she needed something.

'You should get some sleep, Chester,' Alain said. 'You're exhausted and you can't do any more for her tonight.'

Chester shot him a deathly stare. 'Alain, if it were you in my position, and you didn't know if Arrahbella was going to make it through the night, and you couldn't even be by her side, would you be getting any sleep? Would you even care enough to show the slightest bit of emotion?'

'No, I wouldn't be going to sleep and I'm not even going to answer that second question.'

'Then don't tell me what I need to do. Regardless of how childish you think I'm being, I'm a grown man and I can take care of myself.'

Alain shook his head in disbelief.

'I might go to sleep,' Izan said. 'If Oleg's happy to take watch.'

'I'll go and ask him. I need to see if the girls are okay anyway. Will you sleep here?'

'Yeah, you and Chester can stay here, I don't mind, I

402

can sleep through anything.'

Alain nodded and walked through to check on the girls, who were still cleaning up in the kitchen, and to wake Oleg who needed to be informed about all that had occurred.

The rest of the night passed without event. As Izan slept, Chester and Alain sat in the dim lamplight, exhausted but unable to sleep, Alain checking on Arrahbella every fifteen minutes, leaving once to get her a cup of tea, then checking every twenty minutes. He had Oleg watch the other end of the train mainly, making sure the girls and the dwarves were safe and sound. It seemed Ikrael was content with all he had done for that night, though.

At around seven in the morning, Arrahbella stuck her head into the room, looking very tired.

'Chester, you can come in now,' was all she said before disappearing again. The two men followed her.

'I'm feeling more confident,' she told them. 'I think if there were going to be any more complications she'd have had them by now. It's just a matter of her regaining strength. Alain and I will go to bed. You should try and sleep too.'

'I won't.'

'Well, just be aware that when she does wake up, she's going to be very upset. She may even be depressed, Chester, and she'll probably blame herself and think that you're angry with her.'

'I'm not-'

'I know that, but she may feel that way and you just have to understand that she could feel responsible for this and she may feel that way for a while and we all just have to help her through this, okay?'

Chester looked mutinous. 'Would I do anything else?'

Arrahbella rubbed her forehead. 'Chester, you're doing it now. You're taking it out on us. Now, if Melody wakes up and starts thinking you're angry with her you're going to get upset too, and you're going to be moping around and taking it out on the troupe and you mustn't, Chester, you really mustn't. Just be calm and soothing and patient, okay? Melody will pick up on it if you're not.'

Chester just glared and shook his head. 'You people really have very negative views of me, don't you?'

Alain sighed.

'Chester?' came Melody's weak voice.

He hurried to her side. 'Hey, Melody, I'm here.'

'Chester.' She was awake, but only just. Her eyes flicked from Chester to Arrahbella who was standing behind him. 'Arrahbella? Is the baby okay?'

Chester didn't know what to say. He looked at Arrahbella who nodded to him. It was better that it came from him. He struggled for a moment.

'Melody, you...' He didn't know how to word it. 'You had a miscarriage. The baby's gone.'

Melody closed her eyes. Her lip quivered. After a moment, she opened her eyes again.

'Did you see it?' she asked, and Alain, standing at the foot of her bed, flinched at the memory.

'No,' Chester answered.

'Did you?' she asked Arrahbella.

'Yes.'

'Did it have wings?'

Chester's heart ached even harder.

'It was too early to tell,' she whispered. 'You weren't very far along, Melody, so it was barely formed.'

Melody looked at the ceiling. Tears started to run down her cheeks onto the pillow, wetting her hair. Small sobs escaped her. She faced Chester once more.

'I'm so sorry, Chester.'

'Hey, no,' he soothed, stroking her hair. 'It's okay, Melody.'

'I'm so sorry.'

'Shh. You have nothing to be sorry for.'

Arrahbella stepped forward. 'Melody, you need to sleep. You're still very weak.'

It didn't help. Melody kept crying. Chester continued to stroke her hair, trying to calm her. Arrahbella looked at Alain who nodded and stepped forward.

'With your permission, Chester,' he said.

The jester looked from Alain to Arrahbella to Melody. Melody had covered her face with her free hand. Her shoulders shook, and she choked on tears. Chester gave Alain a nod. Alain sat on the edge of the bed then he gently took Melody's hand and moved it away from her face. She opened her eyes enough to see Alain then she shut them again, knowing what he was about to do.

'Wait,' Chester interrupted. 'Will she be awake enough to let us know if she needs anything?'

'Yes, Chester,' Alain replied. 'I do know what I'm doing.'

Arrahbella gave Alain a warning whack on the arm but, thankfully, Melody hadn't noticed the underlying animosity.

'She'll wake up if anything's wrong,' he assured Chester.

Chester looked at Melody then nodded again. Alain wrote the word "sleep" in the air and pushed it gently toward Melody.

'Sleep, Melody Bell, sleep softly but soundly.'

Melody fell asleep instantly, even showing a slight smile as Alain's command sunk in.

'Alright,' said Arrahbella. 'We'll be next door if you need us.'

Chester nodded. He let go of Melody's hand so he could climb in next to her on the other side of the bed where he took hold of her other hand. Alain stroked Melody's hair then followed his wife through to their room as Oleg entered to check that all was well.

Chester eventually fell asleep, out of sheer exhaustion, as did Alain and Arrahbella, though not before Alain had finally allowed his own emotions to come through, weeping for Melody and the unborn child.

During the night, Arrahbella had a vision. Not having the heart to wake Alain, she passed it along psychically. His nightmare of a lifeless Melody being carried along on a river of blood was replaced by an apricot-coloured meadow where Melody, a few years older than she was now, was on her knees among the flowers, laughing as the most utterly gorgeous four-year-old Alain had ever seen flew in circles around her. The tiny wings of the child were white with purple edges. Her large eyes were purple, and her bouncy, shoulder-length hair was a dark purplish-brown with an underlying coat of gold, which only revealed itself in the sunlight, creating an almost goddess-like glow around her.

'Eralaina, don't go too far,' Melody warned, as the child flew out of Alain's vision, then she laughed and followed, using her own visible wings to catch up to her daughter.

Arrahbella's voice filtered into the picture, as though coming straight from the sky. 'I don't know about anyone else,' she told him. 'But, whatever happens, Melody and Chester will obviously make it through this, and they will have a child.'

She watched as a smile crept across his face, making her smile as well, then she moved closer to him, nuzzled her nose into his cheek, and fell asleep once more.

When Chester woke, sometime around midday, he found Melody awake and looking at him. He was still holding her hand.

'Hi,' he said softly. She didn't answer, didn't even show that she'd heard. 'How are you feeling?' He sat up, but she looked away.

'Empty,' she replied after a moment.

He didn't know how to respond to that. She looked at him again, saw him looking down at the pillow, and misinterpreted his silence.

'I'm sorry, Chester,' she whispered. 'You must be so upset.'

'Of course I'm upset, but you have absolutely nothing to be sorry for.'

'You told me I should stop doing the trapeze. I should have listened to you.'

'I'd never tell you to stop doing the trapeze. We both talked about it and decided it would be okay.'

'I couldn't move my wings.' She was crying again.

'I know, honey. That's because Ikrael had frozen them.'

'I should have rechecked the trapeze.'

'Melody, stop it. This wasn't your fault. Don't you dare think that this was your fault.'

'You were so happy when I told you I was pregnant. I've never seen you that happy.'

'Of course I was happy, Melody, but-'

She rolled over so that her back was to him.

'Just leave me alone, Chester. I just want to be alone.'

Chester had no intention of leaving and was about to protest when Arrahbella, who had walked into the room in time to hear the last sentence, made her presence known by clearing her throat. Chester suppressed his annoyance, dutifully getting out of the bed and dressing while Arrahbella asked Melody if she was in pain or needed anything. Melody said 'no' to both questions but Arrahbella rubbed balm over her muscles once more and went to make her some revitalising tea. Chester left the room and, eventually, the train, going into town with Izan where he had alcohol for breakfast as Izan got some exercise in the brothel across the street. Alain was rather irked that they had left without asking, but he took the time to talk to Melody and read her some poetry until she fell asleep once again.

When Melody's eyes fluttered open some hours later, she saw Chester sitting by her bed, watching her calmly, stroking her hand.

'Hey, honey, how are you feeling?'

'I'm so sorry, Chester.'

'It's okay, Melody.'

'I'd understand if you were angry at me.'

'I'm not angry at you, honey.'

And she fell asleep again. Chester continued to talk about nothing in particular as she drifted in and out of sleep and apologised again. It wasn't until late in the afternoon when she awoke properly and sat up. Arrahbella attended to her, forcing her to eat some toast and sip some tea.

'We're going to continue on with the tour,' Alain told the trio as Melody ate. He was leaning against the wall by the door that led through to Izan's caravan. 'We'll omit the trapeze and manipulation, Melody, until you feel up to it again.' She nodded. 'Chester, I've asked Oleg, Izan, and the dwarves to be on constant look out for any sign of Ikrael. If you see him, you are to kill him.' The girls looked at him in surprise. 'I don't think we have any other choice. It's kill or be killed. He's already killed one of us.'

Melody looked down. Arrahbella's head gave a sharp pang and she rubbed it. It had been bothering her quite a bit lately.

'Excuse me,' she said, standing up and walking past Alain, exiting as Oleg entered. The giant was carrying a small bunch of spiny, velvety flowers, the only kind that grew in Noir Eternale, fuelled by lamplight and light injected by odd glowing bee-like creatures called hobbs.

'Here you are, Melody,' he said shyly, handing her the bouquet.

Melody sniffed back tears as she took the flowers. 'Thank you, Oleg,' she whispered and tried to hug as much of him as she could. Oleg patted her head. He stood back and tried to think of something to say but couldn't, so he turned and left again.

'You should know that Izan has taken it upon himself to find Ikrael,' Alain continued. 'I'd rather he wasn't off on his own but there's no use trying to stop him. He won't listen.'

'Shouldn't you be the one looking for him, Alain? It's you he wants.'

Melody was shocked. 'Chester!'

Alain looked at Chester for a moment, his face unreadable, then he turned and left the room.

'What?' Chester asked her.

'You're angry at Alain.'

'Of course I am, Melody. Ikrael is after Arrahbella and so he's trying to hurt Alain. We're being used as playthings in a game.'

'He's after all of us.'

'Only because we're important to Alain.'

'Chester, Ikrael is after Arrahbella, Alain's *wife*. He's

410

sick with worry about that fact alone but he has to try and protect her, as well as all of us, and still run a business and entertain audiences.'

Chester didn't say anything.

'You can't be angry at Alain, Chester.'

'Of course you would take his side.'

'I'm not taking anyone's side. I'm just asking you to try and consider what he's going through.'

'He treated me like a child.'

Melody opened her mouth to argue but a wave of faintness washed over her and she swayed. She leant against the headboard and took some deep breaths.

'We can't let this come between us,' she said, quietly. 'That's exactly what Ikrael wants. Please don't be angry. I need you to grieve with me. I can't get through this on my own.'

He looked at her but again didn't speak.

She looked down at the sheet, her mind suddenly full of thoughts. 'Izan is the one who will have to fight Ikrael if it comes down to it. I could lose my brother, Chester, and it's Alain and Arrahbella he's after, and if he succeeds I could lose...' She stopped as her throat constricted with a sob. Tears fell from Chester's eyes as he saw how scared she was. 'And if both of them can't fight then you're the next most powerful.' She looked up at him. 'Ikrael took our child, Chester. I don't want to lose you as well.'

Chester's anger flooded away but was replaced by an almost unbearable sadness. He pulled her head to his chest and cradled her as she sobbed.

'It's okay, Melody,' he said into her hair. 'We're going

to get through this. It's going to be okay.' If her wings had been visible, they would have been streaked with purple tears.

The troupe's final destination was Kartan. None of them wished to go, they all just wanted to return home, but they knew that they wouldn't be safe there either. Besides, dealing with Ikrael in a foreign place was better than leading him into their home, or so they thought. Plus, there were paying customers in Kartan; people had already bought tickets. So, with a heavy feeling of dread, the train left the turn off to Noir Eternale and headed for the desert planet.

CHAPTER 14

POSSESSION

Present Day – The Highway

As the train made its way quietly along the desolate Highway, rocking in such a peaceful, lilting way that the events of the last few weeks seemed hardly possible, Chester was sitting beside Melody's side of the bed, reading. His eyes trailed over the words, not taking them in, then wandered away to settle on the sleeping girl. After watching her for some moments, he closed his book and went in search of Alain, finding him in the kitchen.

'Yes, Chester?' Alain prompted, looking up from his own book and the bowl of muesli that he was halfway through. The clock on the wall behind him ticked over to ten o'clock, chiming gently.

The Arelian pulled out a chair two seats down from the Ringmaster and studied the table top for a moment. 'I want to apologise, Alain, for telling you that it was your fault. I didn't mean it and I hope you know that. I was scared and angry but I shouldn't have taken it out on you. It's just not fair that he's after Arrahbella and he's attacking Melody.'

'So, it's okay for Arrahbella to get attacked but

not Melody?'

'No, that's not what I meant.'

Alain put his spoon down. 'Chester, this troupe is like one person. If Ikrael's after one of us then he's after us all.'

'I know, look, I just...' He stopped and ran a hand through his hair. 'I know what Melody means to you, and Arrahbella did a lot for her that night. I shouldn't have said what I said. I didn't really mean it, and I'm sorry. It was immature of me.'

'Well, it did hurt, Chester. I know you may not have meant it in hindsight but you did say it and I was already feeling guilty. I do feel guilty. Arrahbella tells me it's not my fault, and it's probably not, but I'm responsible for this troupe. I should be able to protect you.'

Chester saw the worry on Alain's face and realised that Melody had been right.

'I'm sorry, too, for how I reacted that night,' Alain continued. 'And I'm sorry for what happened to Melody. I know how much you both wanted that child and I know that it could be a few years before Melody is ready to try again.' Chester lowered his eyes. 'But, I need to know that she's being taken care of. I need to know that you can be everything she needs, especially right now so that I can take care of Arrahbella. Izan will go off and do his own thing and Oleg looks after the others. And I'm talking about in the future as well. I trust you, Chester, I do, and I know you love her, but...' He trailed off, looking away. 'The way you reacted the other night, turning on us like that, it scared me.'

Chester hung his head. 'I really am sorry, Alain. I'm

going to do everything I can to help you and Izan protect the troupe and defeat Ikrael.'

Alain nodded. Chester stood, reached out his hand, and shook with him, then, he walked to the door.

'Chester.'

He stopped and turned around.

'I know that Melody and I have a strange relationship and not many people understand it. If you ever had any problems with it, you would tell me wouldn't you?'

Chester was surprised that his anger had been interpreted that way. 'Yes, Alain, I would, or I'd talk to Melody. But, I'm one of the people that do understand your relationship; you're her mentor. I had a mentor once myself. I know what it's like, so don't worry.' He smiled and left the room.

Alain sat there for a while longer, thinking. Eventually, he stood and made some teas, then carried them through to his room. There, he found Arrahbella sitting in her armchair, her eyes closed, one hand rubbing her forehead, an open book hanging limply in the other.

'Arrahbella?' he said, quietly, as he set the teas down on the small circular table between the chairs.

She looked up quickly. 'Oh, I didn't hear you come in.' She smiled but Alain frowned. Never in their entire history had he been able to sneak up on her, she could always sense him approaching.

'Are you alright?'

'Yes, just a mild headache.' She picked up her tea and blew on it.

'How long have you had it?'

She shrugged. 'Oh, on and off for a few days. It's probably a result of going from Arelia to Noir Eternale – all that colour and then darkness.' She was making light of it but at that moment her head throbbed and she couldn't suppress a wince.

'Are they bad?'

'No, not really.' But she winced again.

'Why didn't you tell me, Bella?' He spoke softly, his rumbling tones almost therapeutic on her aching mind.

'It's nothing, Alain. We've had other, more serious things to worry about. They're bound to settle down soon. I'm okay.' He watched her take a sip of her tea. It seemed to relax her a little, though she continued to rub her head intermittently.

He couldn't concentrate after that; he'd read a sentence, look up at her as she rubbed her head or closed her eyes, re-read the same sentence, look up again, think worrying thoughts or think about how they might overcome Ikrael, then watch Arrahbella again. She finally went to bed and he followed not long after, lying there awake for most of the night.

The next day they reached Ferdelong's Inn, the halfway point between Noir Eternale and Varatalé.

'We'll only stay for lunch, everyone,' Alain told them, when they had grouped in the kitchen car. 'I know we usually stay the night but I'm keen to get to Kartan as soon as possible.'

Nobody protested. Silently, they filed out of the train

416

and into the Inn.

Ferdelong was much less friendly than the other Innkeepers. He scowled when he saw the large group enter and grumbled as he rearranged tables so that they could all sit at the same one. Then he walked away without offering them drinks.

'At least it's not too crowded,' Oleg observed, looking around the large eating area. 'We should be served quickly.'

'That's if Ferdelong decides to serve us quickly,' Izan remarked, as he perused a menu. He glanced up when nobody responded and realised that all eyes were on him. 'What?'

'You do know that there are people over there, don't you?' Melody said, slowly, pointing to the eight other people in the room, all of them Varatalians.

Izan shrugged and returned to his menu. 'I know.'

The others looked at each other in surprise. Asseniah checked the magician's pulse, found it quite normal, and shrugged at the others. They returned to their menus.

None of the meals were capturing Alain's attention. He wasn't at all hungry. 'Do you want to share something, Bella?' He turned and found her rubbing her head again, eyes closed. 'Bella?'

Again, she looked up quickly. 'Sorry?'

'Do you want to share something?'

'Oh. No. I'm not hungry.' She put her menu down and sat back in her chair, her eyes fighting to stay open.

'We should have stayed in the train,' he said, quietly.

'Don't be silly. We're the ones who have to pay the bill.' She forced a smile but it quickly transformed into another grimace.

Alain turned back to the table, praying desperately, hoping Mythos would hear him despite them not being in the same universe.

As soon as they had eaten all they could and spent a short time digesting, they returned to the train and continued on their way.

That night, having finally drifted off, Alain found his dream-self standing in a long white marble hall that spread in all directions for as far as his eyes could see. Clouds surrounded the perimeter and hovered above him, bathed in pink and gold light. The name "Arrahbella" was floating around everywhere, written in white smoke. Alain was wearing his white pants and white shirt but was barefoot. In front of him, quite a few feet, Ikrael stood, wearing exactly the same attire, the overall effect making him look like some ethereal being.

'Hello, Alain,' Ikrael said, his voice no less raspy in dream-life. The sound made Alain's spine tingle unpleasantly.

'What do you want?'

Ikrael examined his claw-like fingernails. 'I thought it was fairly clear what I want. I want Arrahbella.'

'Why?'

He looked up. 'That's an odd question. If you don't know then perhaps you shouldn't be married to her.'

'You only met her for a moment-'

'So did you.'

It didn't occur to Alain's dream-self to ponder how

418

Ikrael knew this. 'Ikrael, you aren't well. You can't just take another man's wife. Not by force. It's just not done. In any world. You have to find your own woman, someone who will love you in return.'

Ikrael erupted. 'Arrahbella does love me! She told me she loved me by the way she looked and spoke to me.' His voice echoed around the vast space. 'You don't know it. Why would you? You're too busy looking after your beloved troupe to care for her. I love her more than you ever could, Alain du Maurier.'

Words bubbled in Alain's blood stream, words that he usually had no need for, "hate," "despise," "loathe," "detest," "abhor," as well as words like "fear," "horror," "evil," and "helplessness." They were the kind of words that made the user sick if given too much attention and the sudden onslaught of so many made his sleeping body tremble violently.

'Why don't you ask her yourself who she loves?' he growled through clenched teeth.

'I don't need to. I know it and she knows it. She uses her psychic powers to come and visit me at night, in my dreams, and she tells me that she loves me and we mate and eat.' Alain cringed, his fists clenching tightly, words swimming faster. 'We're going to run away together, Alain. We're going to run away and get married and have children.'

'To marry you she'd have to divorce me first,' Alain pointed out, trying to keep his composure. He wished he could make himself wake up.

'Petty things like that don't matter when love is involved.'

'Ikrael, do you really think that you're going to get away with this? There are fourteen of us and only one of you.'

'Oh, I'll get away with it, Alain du Maurier, because love conquers all, and you're all so focussed on protecting each other, but I have nothing to lose and don't care if anyone gets hurt. And, I'm more powerful than all of you put together.'

Alain stared at him, shaking with anger. He closed his eyes and collected all the power in his being. Words and magic twisted together and moved through him at lightning speed. He opened his eyes and shouted, 'Die!'

But his power remained inside his body and the command was nothing more than an angry word. As Ikrael laughed, Alain felt a terror unlike any he had ever experienced.

The scene began to fade as Ikrael's laugh grew louder, echoing around the Ringmaster's head. The last thing he saw was all of the loose words in the air, Arrahbella's very name, fly into Ikrael's body. Then, there was darkness and Ikrael's voice saying, 'She's mine, Alain. Mine.'

Alain sat up quickly, sweating and gasping, hearing his name being said over and over. He looked around fearfully and saw Arrahbella looking at him, concern filling her ice-blue eyes. She was stroking his arm, saying his name, trying to wake him.

'Alain? Are you alright?' Her voice was weak.

A wave of love and relief washed over him, making him shiver. He wrapped his arms around her, holding her as tightly as he could without obstructing her airway, saying

'I love you. I love you' repeatedly. Then, he pulled away to check that his power had returned, writing "love" in the air and feeling immense relief when it appeared in inky white smoke. He turned back to his wife and kissed her passionately but had to break away as all the emotions that had formed a knot in his stomach over the past few weeks unravelled and travelled at astonishing speed through his body until they overwhelmed him and burst out in an explosion of inky black words, phrases, and jumbled sentences, hurtling through the air and covering the room as they had done in Icecess. Then, he broke down in sobs. Arrahbella held him and shushed him and kissed him and soothed him until he quietened some time later. They lay back down, her arms wrapped around him, his head buried in her chest, wetting her gown with tears. Arrahbella continued to stroke his hair and arm.

Once he was feeling more like himself, Alain untangled his hand from hers, wrote "lock" in the air, and pushed it toward the two connecting doors.

'Is that a good idea?' she asked.

'I don't care,' he whispered. Fear was being pushed aside by the need to protect her, to feel something familiar and safe, accompanied by a consuming dose of desire. Looking into her eyes, he found that she was feeling the same way. Alain rolled over until he was on top of her, leant down, and kissed her. Arrahbella slid her hand across his back, pulling him closer, almost desperately. Overwhelming emotion swept through their bodies, leaving them merciless and melting with lust.

Next door, Chester awoke from his restless and

disturbed sleep to the sound of soft crying. Realising that he was alone in the bed, he sat up quickly and looked around the room. Melody was sitting on a pile of cushions, legs drawn up under her chin, her shoulders and invisible wings shaking as she sobbed.

'Melody?' He climbed out of the bed and went to crouch beside her.

Melody wiped her eyes and smiled. 'I was trying not to wake you.'

'Are you okay?'

'It just hurts still.'

'I know. It's going to hurt for a while.' He cradled her and they stayed that way in silence for a few moments. Tentatively, he kissed her and was pleasantly surprised to find she was rather receptive to it.

When Izan walked through on his watch, he found them entangled and beginning to undress each other. Shaking his head, he walked to the adjoining door and turned the handle. It didn't budge. Puzzled, he waved his hand, making a circle of the door transparent. The scene inside revealed itself and Izan quickly turned away. He shook his head again as the door returned to its natural state.

'Geez, can't leave you people alone for a second,' he muttered, walking back toward his own room. 'As soon as we get on the road you turn into rabbits, and when there's a killer on the loose...' He was interrupted by a cushion that came hurtling in his direction as he closed the door to his bedroom.

Another day's journey brought them to the Varatalé turn off. Every member of the troupe pressed their faces to the train window and watched the rift guards wave as they passed, their hearts sinking as it got further away.

In the evening, the twilight of the Highway seemed dimmer than usual, the landscape more desolate than ever. Arrahbella lay sleeping in bed where she had been all day, knocked out from a combination of tea, pain, and the heated herb-bag she wore across her head.

'Arrahbella,' Alain said quietly, stroking a lock of hair from her cheek.

Her eyes fluttered open.

'How are you feeling, honey?'

She forced a smile. 'Like my head is splitting open.'

'Are there any other herb combinations you can try?'

'I've tried everything I can think of, Alain. Nothing's working.'

Alain wished he knew what to do for her. Part of him felt he should know what the problem was, but his mind was so frazzled that it wasn't working properly.

'Do you want me to get you some tea or heat up the herb-bag?'

'No,' she sat up. 'I'll do it, I need to stretch my legs.'

He helped her out of the bed and watched anxiously as she gingerly left the room.

The Earthling slowly made her way through the caravans, wincing as she walked through the thumping music of Izan's, even though it was only on a very low volume. Melody, Chester, Sora, Mariette, and Asseniah were all in the girls' room doing various things as they listened to some more uplifting music in an attempt to boost their spirits.

From the kitchen, Arrahbella could hear Oleg leading the dwarves through some routine exercises in the practice room. She poured some water into a saucepan and put it on the stove to boil. As she placed the herb-bag in the oven, her head seared with pain and she grabbed the counter tightly, her face contorting in agony. She gasped, a couple of tears falling down her cheeks and onto the tiles. The wave of pain dulled slightly and she opened her eyes, only to be hit by another, even worse than the first, and another. She felt something in her head split open and she screamed.

'Alain!'

Her knees gave way and she fell to the floor, sending a stack of dishes flying off the bench as she went down. Having heard the noise, everyone from the neighbouring caravans rushed in. Mariette hurried to the stove where the pot of water was bubbling over as Sora rushed to Arrahbella's side and Melody dashed back through the caravans to Alain's room.

'Alain, quick! It's Arrahbella. Something's wrong.'

Alain threw his book to one side and they raced back to the kitchen, Izan following closely.

Arrahbella was moaning and crying, one hand to her head, her long hair covering her face. Sora had her hands on Arrahbella's shoulders but she looked up when Alain came in and said, 'I don't know what's wrong with her, she can't talk properly, but I think she said "Ikrael."'

A collective shiver ran around the group.

424

Alain's pale skin turned an even deathlier shade of white. 'Thank you, Sora, move away from her now.'

Sora did and stood back with the others, all watching nervously as Alain moved toward his wife, crouched down next to her, and put a hand on her shoulder.

'Arrahbella? What's wrong, sweetie?'

For a moment, nothing happened. Then, Arrahbella's head jerked up suddenly and she stared at him with wild eyes. 'Ikrael,' she gasped, but a moment later she cackled grotesquely in a voice that was not her own; a horrible, rasping voice. She lashed out at Alain forcing him to jump back.

Alain stared down at his wife feeling absolute horror rush through him as two and two came together.

'Sweet Mythos, he's possessed her,' he breathed.

'What?' they asked.

'Ikrael. He's inside Arrahbella's head.'

'How?'

'Through her psychic powers.'

Melody, Mariette, and Sora gasped. Arrahbella was alternating between looking at them evilly, and clutching her head, moaning and weeping.

Alain crouched down again. 'Bella, look at me.' He tried to keep his voice calm but when she looked at him she saw the fear in his eyes and she weakened. Ikrael took over and she lunged at Alain once again.

'Oleg, restrain her,' he called.

The giant hurried forward, pinning Arrahbella's arms behind her so that she was forced to sit on the ground. She tried to struggle but found she was held tight and growled a deep throaty, threatening growl.

Alain's heart was aching, beating ridiculously fast. He kept forgetting to breathe. He was sweating. Thoughts and words were rushing through his head at the speed of light and yet he felt numb and unable to think at all. He had to do something.

'Ikrael, leave her alone.'

An evil raspy laugh was followed by a scream of pain.

'Ikrael, stop this. You love her, why do you want to hurt her?'

Arrahbella gasped, whimpered, grimaced, her head fell backward then she rolled it forward to look at her husband. She looked like a puppet on strings. 'Stop it, Alain,' she whispered. 'You're making it worse.' Her nails were digging into her palms as she clenched her fists in pain.

'Arrahbella?' Alain was trying desperately not to cry. He felt useless. He was stroking her hair, her face. 'Ikrael, why are you doing this?'

Ikrael laughed at Alain's fear, contorting Arrahbella's face as she tried to resist him. A gasp cut off the laughter and Arrahbella faced her husband once again. When she spoke it was her own voice they heard. 'Stop it. He's hurting me because he knows it's hurting you.' She looked into his eyes as she said it, but her words were too much and he looked away, closing his eyes as a cry escaped his lips.

Melody had been fighting back her own tears, as were most of the troupe members, but seeing Alain turn away, with pain and fear written all over his face, was more than she could handle and she began to sob loudly, turning into Chester's chest who wrapped his arms even more tightly around her.

Arrahbella was screaming again and soon Ikrael was laughing.

'Make it stop!' she screamed. 'Make it stop! It HURTS!'

Alain came back to himself. He sniffed, wiped his face on his sleeve, and put his hands to her head again. She was dripping with sweat. 'It's going to be okay, Bella. Just hold on. Keep fighting him.' He became aware of Melody's sobbing and without looking at them, Arrahbella's words still ringing clearly in his head, he said, 'Chester, get Melody out of here.'

Melody heard this and choked back her crying. 'No, I'll be quiet.'

'Chester, take her.'

'No, Alain, I'm not leaving.'

He whirled around with a fierce look. 'Melody, you will leave this room NOW!'

Her lip quivered and she ran from the room, forced by magic. Chester followed.

Alain turned to the others. 'Sora, Asseniah, you go too. Fenton, tell Dell to pull over and stop the engine, then the two of you join the girls in their room. Cravel, Phan, Grent, you as well.' The dwarves hurried off as Alain turned to Izan with a pleading look. 'Izan?'

The magician shook his head. 'I've been trying, but nothing's working.'

'Keep trying.' Arrahbella was kicking at Alain now. 'Can you put her to sleep? This exertion is going to kill her.' He tried to hold her legs still.

A pause.

'It's no good, Alain, it's like he knows what I'm going to do and he's stopping me before I can.' Izan was, as Alain had been in his dream, terrified at being unable to use his power, knowing that Ikrael was able to play with them so easily... and he wasn't even there in the room with them.

Alain let loose with a string of swear words in various different languages.

'She's slicing her hands to shreds,' Oleg told him, forcing Arrahbella's hands around in front of her so Alain could see them. Her fists were streaked with blood.

With Arrahbella's hands in a better position, Ikrael managed to make her twist around and free herself from Oleg's powerful grasp, sending a wave of power in his direction. Oleg fell back against the wall with a loud thud. Alain attempted to grab hold of Arrahbella but her hands found their way around his throat, choking him, before throwing him aside as well. Izan tried a myriad of things but they were all thwarted before they had barely left his hand. Arrahbella knocked Izan aside and lunged at Mariette, her hands grabbing the dancer by the neck and squeezing tightly. Releasing one hand, Ikrael made Arrahbella slap Mariette hard across the face, then return it to choking her. Mariette was knocked back against the cupboards, unable to breathe. Oleg, Izan, and Alain picked themselves up and hurried toward the pair. Oleg got there first and pried Arrahbella's hands from Mariette's neck. Arrahbella was crying because of everything Ikrael was making her do. Her body trembled violently with exhaustion.

Alain erupted.

He spun Arrahbella around so she could look him in the eyes and power flew out of him with such force that the room shook and the others fell to the ground, covering their ears.

'IKRAEL, YOU WILL LEAVE ARRAHBELLA'S MIND NOW AND YOU WILL NOT RETURN!'

The monster's power was weakening anyway and the strength of Alain's command was too much for him. Arrahbella let out a final scream as the psychic connection was torn apart before she collapsed in a heap at Alain's feet. It took a moment for Alain to come down out of his power fury and then he too collapsed, gathering her into his arms, holding her gently but strongly. Her eyes fluttered open for a moment and looked into his. They were calm, normal.

'It's okay, Bella, you're going to be okay. He's gone now.' He kissed her forehead.

'Thank you,' she whispered, and then she fainted.

Alain cradled her head to his chest and rocked her as tears streamed down his cheeks. Oleg helped Mariette up while Izan stood by, helpless, eventually leaving to tell the others (who had been listening intently on the other side of the connecting door) that Ikrael had gone for now.

After many long minutes had passed, where the only sounds were Alain's shaky sobs, Mariette looked at Oleg and said, 'Oleg, take her to her bed. She needs rest, Alain.'

The giant moved forward, but Alain shook his head. 'No, I'll take her.' So, Oleg opened the door for him as he lifted Arrahbella and carried her out of the room. The others quickly stood back to let him through as he entered the girls' room. Melody and Chester were sitting on Mariette's bed, Melody's eyes still red and teary. Alain didn't look at any of them. He walked on until he got to his room where he laid Arrahbella gently on the bed, bringing the covers up over her. Then, just as he had done in Arelia, he pulled up a chair and watched over her.

He had been alone with Arrahbella for a half an hour when there was a knock on the door.

'Who is it?' he asked quietly.

'Mariette.'

'Come in, Mariette.'

She entered. Alain was still by the bed, worry hanging like a cloud around him.

''ow is she?'

'Still asleep.' She could hear the exhaustion in his voice, tiredness and fear making his rich tones even deeper.

''ere.' Mariette held out the herb-bag. It had been warmed up and the faint aromas of the ingredients wafted toward him. ''er 'ead will be zrobbing.'

Alain stared blankly at the bag for a moment before realising what it was. 'Oh, thank you.' Wobbling a little, he stood and placed it on Arrahbella's forehead.

'And zis is for you.' She handed him a mug of tea. 'Asseniah blended peppermint and Minalla so zat it would be calming and refreshing. We were out of Athenaine Root but it should do ze same zing.'

Alain mechanically took a sip, his mind not registering what he was doing.

'Do you need anyzing else?'

'No, thank you, Mariette.'

She walked to the door.

'Mariette? Are you alright?'

She smiled. 'Yes, zank you. I am a little bruised and sore but I am okay.'

Alain nodded.

Mariette hesitated. 'Would you like me to send Melody in?'

'No. Keep her away for now, please.'

'Okay. We are all going to try to sleep now. Izan is taking watch. Let me know if you need anyzing.'

He nodded and she left.

Alain watched Arrahbella sleeping. Every now and then she would whimper or become restless, moaning and crying out, and he would soothe her and stroke her hair and talk gently to her. He would have sent calming words into her mind but he had no strength left after his powerful command in the kitchen.

A while later (it could have been only five minutes or it could have been an hour, Alain had no concept of time right then) there was another knock on the door.

'Alain? It's Fenton, may I come in?'

'Yes, Fenton.' His voice was barely audible from the other side of the door.

'Apologies for disrupting you, sir, but should we keep on? It's not safe to stay parked on the Highway and we need to be in Kartan on time. Unless you wish to cancel the shows?'

Alain did not look up. 'No. The tour goes on. Please start driving again and thank the dwarves.'

Fenton nodded and went to the girls' caravan to relay Alain's words to the others.

'It'd take a lot of Ikrael to make Alain stop the tour,' Izan said.

'The show must go on. You can't deprive the public of their entertainment,' agreed Chester.

'He probably thinks that stopping the tour would mean that Ikrael has won,' added Sora. 'He wants to show him that he can't affect us.'

Melody hadn't said a word since she had been ordered out of the dining car. Chester had been holding her most of the time and she snuggled into his arms.

Eventually, they all went to bed, only because there was nothing else they could do. Oleg went back to his own cabin with Fenton, Grent, Phan, and Cravel.

'I think we should give them some space,' Melody said to Chester, looking up at him.

'I zink zat is a good idea,' agreed Mariette. 'You can boz sleep in my bed. I will sleep in Sora's bed, if she does not mind.'

'Not at all,' the Ormancian replied.

'Thank you, Mariette,' Chester said, as Melody climbed into one side of the double bed. He took off his shirt and climbed in after her as Asseniah hoisted herself up into

432

her hammock, took her stuffed toy yamui into her arms, and cuddled it tightly. Sora stayed in her day clothes, afraid that they would have more trouble that night, and climbed into her own bed, then Chester turned out all but one lamp by magic.

During the night, Alain sent Izan to wake Melody and bring her to his caravan. Nervously, she entered the room and went to stand in front of Alain as Izan closed the door behind her. The Ringmaster didn't look at her straight away, causing her to fidget with the ties on her top as she nervously waited.

'Melody, did you hear what Ikrael did to Mariette?'

She nodded, swallowing before saying, 'He tried to kill her.'

Alain nodded, his eyes on the floor. Melody had never seen him looking so tired or pale. 'When Arrahbella said that Ikrael was hurting her to hurt me,' he paused, closing his eyes for a moment. Melody had to look away. 'I knew that, if he'd already taken Arrahbella, he'd go for you next. He was inside Arrahbella's mind, which means he knows everything about me. If I hadn't have got you out of the room he'd have tried to kill you like he did Mariette.' He was looking at her now but she couldn't look at him. She felt so silly for being upset. She should have known what he was doing.

'I'm sorry, Alain. And I'm sorry for what happened to Arrahbella.'

'I'm sorry too. I feel terrible.'

Melody leant forward and gave him a tight hug, which he weakly returned.

'Get some sleep,' he told her, when she had released him. She hesitated, looked at Arrahbella, then left the room.

Alain eventually lay down next to Arrahbella, but he didn't sleep. He wanted to be awake in case she needed anything, but his body was tired of holding itself up. The rest of the troupe slept in fits or not at all. In the end both Oleg and Izan stayed up on watch together because neither could get their eyes to close.

The following day, the train arrived at Haaj's Inn. Izan appointed himself temporary leader and took charge of the troupe while Oleg stayed in the train to watch over Alain and Arrahbella. The Highway was bathed in twilight; appearing cold and desolate to the troupe, but hauntingly beautiful to the passing traders.

'Cirque du Phantastique,' Haaj proclaimed loudly, when he saw them enter. Haaj was a Kartanian, with rich olive skin, thick black hair, and a small beard. 'But where are the du Mauriers and the giant?'

'Arrahbella is a little under the weather,' Izan informed him. 'Alain and Oleg are with her. We'll just have some lunch and be on our way.'

'I'm sorry to hear that,' Haaj said. 'I hope it isn't too serious.'

'She'll be okay,' Izan assured him, hoping she would be.

'Good, good. But you won't stay longer? I had beds all ready for you.'

'Sorry, my good man, duty calls.'

Haaj nodded understandingly, whipped the pencil out from behind his ear, and began taking their orders.

'Mariette, do you think Haaj should go to Alain and take him some food? It might cheer Alain to see an old friend and he may feel compelled to eat out of politeness,' Melody suggested, once they had all been seated and served. She pushed her risotto around on its plate, occasionally taking a reluctant mouthful, her tastebuds not registering any flavour, despite it being quite delicious.

'No, I do not zink zat 'aaj should go into ze train,' Mariette replied, and Izan shook his head in agreement. 'But I do zink zat, after we 'ave eaten, and Izan is to relieve Oleg, you should go as well and tell Alain zat you'll watch over Arrahbella while 'e comes in 'ere and 'as somezing to eat.'

'He won't leave her side and I don't want to ask him to.'

'Alright, zen, take some food in and sit wiz 'im for a while. Tell 'im, 'aaj would love to see 'im if 'e wishes to come inside.'

They agreed to this. So, when they had all finished their lunch, Izan and Melody took a tray of vegetable pie and lemonade to Alain. They found the scene much the same as when they had left it; Oleg standing by the wall, Arrahbella sleeping, and a drained looking Alain sitting by the bed, head in his hands, dark circles under his eyes prominent against the whiteness of his overall appearance.

Izan nodded to Oleg and the giant left the train. Alain didn't look up.

'Alain?' Melody said. 'We brought you some of Haaj's

food.' She set the tray down on the bedside table. 'And Haaj would love to see you if you feel like going in.'

'I'm not hungry, Melody,' he replied, still not looking up.

'Why don't you try getting some sleep? Izan and I will stay here as long as you need us to.'

'I do not wish to sleep, Melody, not until Arrahbella wakes up and I know that she's okay.'

There was no talking to him, so Melody stood beside his chair and wrapped her arms around him. Alain seemed surprised by this but only because he was so tired that everything seemed a little surreal to him and after a moment he put his hand up to one of her arms and rested it there. Melody was beating her wings ever so softly so that the tantalising scents of Haaj's pie wafted toward Alain. His stomach growled but he didn't seem to notice. Melody held him for quite a few minutes before kneeling down next to him.

'Alain, please eat something,' she said. She took the bowl of pie and placed it on his lap. Alain stared at it blankly then looked at her for the first time.

'I might be able to stomach some toast,' he finally said.

Melody smiled and removed the bowl back to the tray. 'I'll go and make you some.' She headed toward the bedroom door.

'Izan, go with her please, I'll be alright here for a few minutes.'

When they had gone, Alain knelt by the bed and

stroked Arrahbella's hair. 'Arrahbella,' he said. 'Please wake up. I need you to wake up. I can't function without you. I don't know what I'm doing.' He kissed her cheek and rested his head against hers. 'Please don't leave me,' he whispered.

When Izan and Melody returned carrying a plate stacked with three pieces of thick, buttered toast they found him still in that position. They thought he had finally fallen asleep, but he looked up when Melody quietly said his name, again slightly surprised to see her. He returned to his chair and took the plate of toast from her. Melody watched as he nibbled slowly, the dry toast having no taste to him at all.

He had made his way slowly through half of the third piece when Arrahbella started to stir, not fitfully or restlessly as she had done sporadically throughout the night, but calmly as though simply waking from a good night's rest. Alain practically threw the plate of toast at Melody and knelt by the bed.

'Arrahbella?'

Her eyes fluttered open, focused, took in their surroundings. When they found Alain, she smiled.

'Alain,' she said softly, her voice scratchy.

'Arrahbella. Are you alright? How do you feel?'

'My headache's not so bad.'

He smiled. 'Good.' He kissed her cheek, her nose, and her forehead.

'Is everyone okay?'

He nodded, tears making his eyes glisten. 'We're at Haaj's Inn. Everyone's inside having lunch but Melody and Izan are here.'

The siblings smiled at her. Arrahbella moved to sit up and Alain assisted her.

'Do you want anything? Tea? Food?'

'Not at the moment, thank you.'

Melody took the tray of pie and drink and headed toward the door. 'I'll just take these back to Haaj,' she said, and left.

'Do you zink we should stay 'ere a bit longer,' Mariette asked the group, once Melody had explained that Arrahbella was awake. 'Just to make sure everyzing is alright? Or should we get on ze road?'

'It may be best to ask Alain,' Fenton replied.

'I don't think he's up to decision making at the moment,' Melody said quietly. 'Arrahbella may be more like herself but I don't think Alain is. Not until he's slept, eaten, and made sure that she's okay.' She hesitated. 'I've never seen him so scared before.'

'He'll be alright,' Oleg assured her. He had finished his bowl of stew and was now working his way through the pie that Alain had rejected. 'Once he's got his strength back. He's just drained, that's all.'

'Well then,' said Fenton. 'I vote that we stay here for another hour. That gives us an extra hour before reaching Kartan and, hopefully, an extra hour for Alain and Arrahbella to rest up. Besides, I'm rather liking being in the company of other people right now. It makes me feel somewhat safer.'

They all agreed.

An hour later, they started up the train and resumed their journey. By this time, Arrahbella had been awake for the entire hour but was feeling sleepy again so, after some tea and poppy seed biscuits, she lay back down and went to sleep once more. Thankfully, Alain did the same. Izan, Oleg, and Chester rotated watch over them until they woke late the next day, when the train had turned off of the Highway and was travelling down the side road that led to Kartan.

CHAPTER 15

KARTAN

Present Day - Kartan

Alain opened the kitchen car door and stepped down into the soft, sunset-coloured sand. Harsh heat wrapped around him as he blinked in the strong midday sunlight.

'It reminds me of Earz,' Mariette said, as she stepped down next to him and shielded her eyes with her hand. 'Only zis 'eat is not quite as suffocating.'

'I'd forgotten about Earth,' Alain said. 'It seems like a lifetime ago.'

Mariette nodded in agreement.

'Come on, then,' he continued. 'Three more shows, and then we can go home.'

Together, they set off across the desert to the brilliant golden gates of the Mahzar City.

Once they had shown proof of their identity to the guards, the Noir Eternalans walked through the streets of the elaborate city, passing large white mansions, lush gardens, peacocks, and cars that looked like they were the end result of a horseless carriage coupling with a wingless plane. They arrived at the gates of the palace, proved they were who they said they were once again, and were led through the gardens and cool marble hallways to the throne room.

Sultan Kajab, a short, plump man, sat on a throne of unimaginable expense, next to his short, plump wife, Sultana Ressa. Behind them stood five of their ten daughters (they had fourteen children altogether), their eyes shielded by a veil while their mouths remained visible (Alain always found this custom rather odd as lips were seductive things, especially when they were the only part of the body exposed and were plump and coloured, full in the sweltering heat, dimpled occasionally, or munching on juicy fruit and licking the juices from their chin). Two lines of well-dressed guards decorated the walls, golden spears at their sides.

'Ah, Alain du Maurier,' Kajab said, in a booming voice much too large for such a small person. He ripped the last shred of meat off of the bone that he was holding and tossed it aside, prompting a servant to hurry forward and collect it. 'I'd forgotten you were coming. You wish to entertain us, no doubt?' He used his silk sleeve to wipe the grease from his chin.

Alain bowed. Mariette curtsied.

'Hello, Your Highness. Yes, if you'll still have us then it would be our pleasure to perform for you and your citizens.' The words were mixed with magic and delivered in an acceptably enthusiastic tone.

'Of course, of course. Set your tent up outside of the city in the usual place and I'll let the people know that you're here. How long will you stay?'

'Three days,' Alain answered.

'Fine. Fine.' Kajab took some fruit from the platter a servant offered him and ate it while he spoke. 'I trust the tour has been good to you?'

Alain looked at Mariette and cleared his throat. 'It's been... interesting,' he replied. 'Every tour certainly brings new experiences.'

'Good. Good. Well, you and your troupe are welcome in my city. Please inform one of the guards if you need anything at all.'

Mariette waited until they were outside the palace grounds before she spoke. 'Per'aps we should tell Kajab about Ikrael. 'e may be able to give us extra security.'

Alain shook his head. 'This isn't Kajab's battle.'

When they returned to the train, they found the troupe where they had left them – sitting around the dining room table, talking and looking rather bored.

'Everything alright?' Alain asked. He knew by their faces that they had just been talking about him.

'Yes,' answered a few voices at once.

'Okay, well, Mariette and I will start making lunch. Fill in time until then, I suppose.'

Nobody moved. Their eyes went to Arrahbella who stood up slowly and looked at her husband. She looked tired and pale, a dull ache still plagued her head.

'Alain, they'd like to leave the train.'

'We know you want us to stay together,' Izan added, 'so that we're protected, but it's really only Melody, Arrahbella, Asseniah, and Mariette that need protecting. If we split into small groups we should all be okay. It may even be better

442

for us to split up so we're not all in the one place and we're a harder target.'

Alain gave Arrahbella an anxious look, but she simply returned it with one of her serene smiles. He cast his eyes around the group and realised he had no choice. He couldn't keep them cooped up here for three whole days.

'Alright, we can't set up the tent until it gets cooler anyway. Chester, I assume you'll be with Melody?'

'Of course.'

'Alright. Izan, how's Chester's magic going?'

'He's shaping up to be quite powerful, Alain, though not as powerful as me, of course.' He gave a toothy grin which Alain did not return. 'He knows enough to protect the both of them.'

'Oleg, will you stay with Mariette?'

Oleg nodded.

'Be careful, though, you only have strength on your side.'

'We'll be fine, Alain.'

'We'll stick together, Alain,' Fenton said. 'We'll be right.'

'So, Izan, you'll stay with Sora and Asseniah?'

Sora gave Alain an indignant look. 'Alain, you seem to be overlooking the fact that I'm just as capable of protecting this troupe as Chester, Oleg, Izan, and you are. I can command fire and knives and I can fight well. Asseniah and I will be quite alright on our own.'

Alain sighed. 'You're right, Sora, I'm sorry. From now on, you're in charge of Asseniah and I'll put you on night watch as well.'

Sora was happy with this.

'Izan, where will you be?'

'Well, Alain, as much as I'd love to run into town and find the nearest exotic harem girl to spend the afternoon with, I'll go wherever you want me to go.' He hadn't been as interested in pursuing partners lately, but now that they had some time to roam he found his old desires coming back.

'Thank you, Izan-'

'You can go off on your own,' Arrahbella interrupted. 'Everyone's fine.'

Izan looked at Alain who was looking at Arrahbella, but he sighed again and nodded. 'Arrahbella's right. If we live as though we're expecting an attack then Ikrael has already won. Everyone, go out and enjoy yourselves. We won't let one man rule our lives. Stay alert but have fun too. Come back when the sun starts to get low and we'll set up the tent. Then, we're going to give this city one of our best performances yet.' He seemed to transform during his speech, going from tired and weary to more his usual energetic self. His words lifted their spirits and gave them energy. 'Off you go.'

The troupe left hastily.

Alain turned to Arrahbella. 'What do you want to do?'

'Spend time with you, my love, but let's go into town. We need a change of scenery.'

'Do you think the train will be alright?'

'We've never had a problem in Kartan before.'

'It's not the Kartanians I'm worried about.'

444

'I know. You're good at giving advice, Alain, but not so good at following it yourself.'

He smiled sheepishly.

'Come on. It's us he wants, not the train, and I'm pretty sure his last attack weakened him a lot. He may have been in my mind, but I could also read some of his and each attack takes a lot out of him.' She held her hand out to him and he took it, pulled her to him, and kissed her. Then, after checking that all of the doors were locked securely, they left the train.

The pair headed slowly into the centre of town to the Diamond Rain Hotel, a ridiculously extravagant place that was the cheapest of the Mahzar City hotels. Drowning in luxury was not usually the du Maurier's style, but that was really all one could do in Kartan. They had lunch in the fine cuisine restaurant before heading upstairs to the massage parlour to be pampered and fussed over.

The rest of the troupe ate lunch together in a small air-conditioned eatery that smelt of spices and crushed jewels (a popular ingredient), most of them choosing salads over the traditional curries or rice dishes that the Kartanians lived on. Then, they headed off in various directions.

Chester and Melody strolled along the palm tree-lined streets until they reached one of the many lush gardens that sat randomly around the city. They walked hand in hand through the greenery and exotic flowers of all varieties, incredible displays of the creativity of Haros, the Kartanian God of Creation. In the tree tops, Birds of Paradise warbled melodiously, their stunning tails hanging down like rainbows as they plucked fruit and nectar from the branches. Families picnicked while others napped in the shade. A man-made stream snaked a silver path through the spongy grass. The air smelt of heat, fruit, flowers, honey, and spices.

They found a shady patch of grass under a wide, leafy tree where they sat down, Chester leaning against the trunk, sitting on the lumpy earth where the tree's roots were half buried. Melody sat in his arms with her back against his chest, her head on his shoulder, her wings tucked in neatly. They sat in silence for a while, sleepy from the heat and lunch. After a while, Chester tentatively brought up the subject of marriage once again.

'Melody?'

'Mmm?' Her eyes were closed. Chester's hand was stroking her arm.

'I know you don't think I should ask you to marry me while Ikrael's around because you don't want me asking out of fear, but I'd be asking you now anyway, whether he was around or not, and if you want to marry me then I don't see why we should wait. I mean, isn't now the best time because, and I know I shouldn't say things like this, but what if things do turn out badly? Then at least we were engaged. I'd marry you today if I could.'

Melody opened her eyes and moved so she could face Chester properly. She took his hands in hers, stroking the porcelain smoothness as she spoke.

'I don't want you to ask me yet.'

'Why not?'

'Do you love me, Chester?'

446

He was about to say it was a silly question but then decided to go along with it. 'Yes, I love you.'

'And you know that I love you?'

'Well, yes. At least, I hope so.'

'I do. Isn't it enough just to know that?'

He gave her a dubious look.

'We love each other, we live together, and we spend almost every minute of our days together,' she continued.

'Well, we live together, but we live with seven other people, twelve others when we're on the road.'

'Yes, but we're together. How is marriage going to change that? It won't increase our love for each other. If we're living as a married couple would live already then why does it matter when we get married?'

He didn't answer. He had crossed his arms and was frowning, looking boyish as usual.

'At this point in my life, at this very moment, I want to spend the rest of my life with you. Why can't we just be happy knowing that?'

'Are you saying that you never want to get married? That marriage is pointless?'

'No. It's not pointless. I mean, theoretically it doesn't seem to change anything, but you do have to admit that there's something different between our relationship and Alain and Arrahbella's. There is something to be said for being legally bound together, so that people know you're together and partners for life.'

'Exactly.'

'But, I don't know. At this stage I'm not sure if I do

ever want to get married. I mean, if you want to get married, and if I follow my own theory that it won't change anything then sure, we can get married, but not right now.' She paused and lowered her eyes. 'It's like children. I didn't think I was ready, but when I discovered that I was pregnant, and saw how happy it made you, I felt really content. Now that it's been taken away, though, I'm not sure if I want to try again straight away.' She faltered.

'It's okay, we don't have to talk about children now,' he told her quietly.

'I do want children with you, Chester, and I want to be with you forever, but you forget sometimes that I'm only eighteen.'

He smiled, humourlessly. 'That's because you talk more sense than me.'

She smiled sadly. 'Just wait for me a bit longer, okay? I'm just not ready for those things yet.'

They touched their foreheads together, still playing with each other's hands.

'Okay,' he said.

Melody rubbed her nose against his, then they looked at each other with love-drunk eyes and kissed passionately. An oddly clean, silk covered ball thumped down next to their tree and a small boy appeared to collect it, promptly uttering a disgusted 'eww!' before running off to tell his mother about this horrific public display of affection. His mother told him that aliens were different from him and had their own way of living but the boy decided it was gross just the same.

Not far away, Sora and Asseniah were strolling

through the city's largest shopping mall, which was no less extravagant than the other buildings of Kartan. A polished white marble floor stretched long and wide, a line of baby palm trees dotting the islands down its middle. Shop fronts lined either side, their spotless windows displaying items that shone under the bright lights, tempting passersby. At each end of the mall there was a waterfall which gushed down a small mountain of rocks to the pool below where fat goldfish swam lazily. The entire mall was covered in a spectacular domed roof, made of crystal, tinted to keep out the worst of the heat, magic-powered air conditioning doing the rest.

'There used to be a gorgeous silk store just down there,' Sora said, pointing. 'Do you mind if we have a look?'

Asseniah shook her head, her swirling green eyes looking eerie in the artificial lighting.

They walked on. Before they could reach the silk store, however, they passed a window showcasing a grand piano sitting among an assortment of other musical instruments. Asseniah, who had never seen a grand before, was stopped in her tracks.

'That's impressive,' Sora said, smiling at her friend's reaction. She could see her fingers itching to play it. They were pressed against the glass window, her breath fogging a small circle, her eyes wide. 'Come on.' Sora took her hand, pulling her into the store. She walked right up to the store worker; a tall, thin man with extremely neat hair and a small wispy beard.

'Excuse me,' she said.

'Yes, little girl?'

Sora hated being called a little girl but she let it slide this time.

'Do you allow customers to play your instruments?'

'That depends,' he said, eyeing them with unreserved suspicion.

'On?'

'On whether the customer is a serious musician.'

'My friend is a serious musician.'

Asseniah had found another grand piano, a red one, inside the store, and was examining it closely as though it were a remarkable new discovery.

'She's a child,' the worker replied, with an air of disdain. His nose was quite long and he obviously enjoyed looking down it at people.

But, Asseniah had sat at the piano and was opening the lid.

'Hey, wait,' he cried, hurrying over, waving his hands. But when Asseniah began to play he was silenced into awe. He and Sora stood back as Asseniah played gently and then passionately and then quite madly, rapture on her small face, conversing with the piano in a language unknown to anyone else. A crowd slowly formed outside of the shop, listening and watching through the glass. She played for a good ten or fifteen minutes, eyes closed, lost to the world. When the last note had faded away to wherever played notes go, she opened her eyes, closed the lid, stood, stroked it, bowed to the worker, and left the store.

Deeply puzzled, Sora thanked the store worker and followed. She would have to speak to Alain about this later.

The troupe returned to the train in the late afternoon and stood outside while Alain and Oleg checked there were no nasty surprises awaiting them. Izan had not yet returned and didn't show up until an hour later. As they set about erecting the tent in the sandy desert plain, they began to relax a little, hoping Ikrael may not be able to stand the heat of the planet, thanks to his ghostly complexion.

Alain was helping Fenton adjust the footlights when he noticed Melody flying above him, rigging her trapeze. He stood up and put his hands on his hips.

'Melody Bell, what do you think you're doing?'

'It's okay, Alain. I'm ready.'

'I don't think you are.'

She flew down to him, planting her feet on the stage. Not far away, Chester watched their conversation as he helped Sora with her tightrope.

'Alain, I want to do it. I'm going to have to go back up there eventually and we've only got three performances left. I'll be okay.'

Alain stepped closer to her and lowered his voice. 'What if he's still around? What if he tries again?'

'I need to, Alain, I can't just sit back there and watch. Don't let him take away everything that gives me happiness.'

Alain studied her for a moment then looked up at Chester who nodded. Alain sighed. 'Alright.'

'Thank you,' she smiled, and flew back up to the rafters.

Later that night, Alain and Arrahbella were washing up from

dinner when Sora slipped into the room.

'Alain, Arrahbella, may I speak to you in private for a moment?'

'Of course, Sora Mai.' Alain held out a towel so that Arrahbella could wipe her hands, then he put down his own towel and they followed her into the practice room, closing the door behind them.

'Asseniah and I were in the mall today,' Sora told them. 'We walked past a store that sells music.'

'Sells music?'

'Instruments. There was a piano in the window, but it wasn't like a normal piano, it was, well, I drew a picture of it.' She pulled out a piece of folded paper and handed it to Alain who straightened it. Sora had drawn a perfect pencil replica of the piano, with shading.

'That's a grand piano,' Arrahbella informed them.

'A grand piano?'

'Yes, like a normal piano but,' she smiled, 'grander.'

'You should have seen her with it,' Sora continued. 'She was so enchanted by the one in the window, I've never seen so much emotion on her face before; not even when she's eating honey logs. And then I pulled her inside, but the store worker didn't want her to play because he thought she was just a child. I mean, she is, but he didn't think she was a serious musician, and then, inside, there was another one, but it was red, only a couple of shades darker than her hair, and she sat down and played it, I mean really played it. There was a crowd outside and the worker was stunned. Oh, Alain, it was as though they were made for each other, as though

452

they were lovers, as though they shared the same soul. I'd love to get it for her. I thought maybe, if we all pitched in, we could give it to her for Mythos' Feast Day.'

'They're very expensive, Sora,' Arrahbella said with a frown. 'Well, they're expensive on Earth and I'll bet they're expensive here. Everything is.'

'I know. It was a hundred thousand Ghats, which is about thirty thousand Rohans, but she has to have it, she just has to.'

Ghats were Kartanian currency while Rohans belonged to Varatalé.

Alain frowned as well. 'That is quite pricey, Sora. That's about what we made from our first week in Arelia.'

Sora hung her head. 'I know.'

'It's a lovely thought, Sora. What was the name of the store? Perhaps Arrahbella and I can go there tomorrow and have a look.'

'The Harmony Hut. It's about five stores down from the Northern entrance, on the left-hand side.'

'Alright. We'll see what we can do. If we can't get there tomorrow perhaps we can come back after the tour.'

'Okay.'

'May I keep this?' He indicated the drawing.

'Yes.'

'Thank you, Sora.'

Sora left the practice room, feeling a little disheartened.

That night, after a relatively successful show, most of the troupe were able to fall asleep thanks to the coolness of the night. Arrahbella, however, was tossing and turning, mumbling and crying out as she dreamt.

'Arrahbella. Arrahbella,' Alain called, gently shaking her shoulder.

'No, no, no, no, no,' she cried, and suddenly sat up, wide awake, panting slightly. 'No!'

'What is it, honey?' he asked, stroking her hair.

She looked at him, realised where she was, and took some deep breaths.

'What's wrong? What did you see?'

Arrahbella thought for a moment then shook her head. 'I can't remember,' she whispered. 'I honestly can't remember.'

'It's okay,' he said, though he was more than a little concerned.

They lay back down, but their sleep was interrupted twice more that night by the same mysterious dream.

When morning came, Asseniah was woken by Alain gently shaking her.

'Asseniah,' he whispered. 'Arrahbella and I are going to the shopping mall. We'd like you to come too, please.'

The young girl was tired and would have shaken her head, rolled over, and gone back to sleep if it weren't for the fact that a certain piano was at that particular mall and she wanted to see it again. So, she nodded.

'We'll be in the kitchen,' Alain said, before leaving her to get dressed.

Once Arrahbella had made them breakfast, the three of them set off for the city, quiet with sleepiness, Alain and Arrahbella walking arm in arm as Asseniah walked slightly ahead, kicking at the sand. The Kartanians were up and about already, making use of the morning's mild weather. The mall was as packed as usual.

'Sora told us about a music store,' Alain said to Asseniah, raising his voice slightly to be heard over the ambience. 'Could you show it to us?'

Asseniah nodded once, took Arrahbella's hand and led the pair of them through the crowd to the Harmony Hut. There were a couple of people in the store today as well as two store workers, one of whom was the man from the day before.

'Look, that's her,' he said to his colleague, when he saw Asseniah enter. 'She's the one I was telling you about.'

Asseniah was oblivious to this attention; her eyes had fallen on the red piano and everything else melted around her. Alain and Arrahbella watched with amused curiosity as the young girl trailed her hands across the piano then lifted the lid. Then, surprisingly, she seemed to come back to herself, looking up at Alain as though asking his permission to play.

'Go on,' he encouraged.

She sat down, flicked her hair back in a wave of fiery red, and played as passionately as she had done yesterday, drawing more onlookers, and proud expressions from Alain and Arrahbella.

She seemed to be just getting warmed up when she suddenly opened her eyes, stopped mid-piece, closed the lid, and walked out of the store, just as she had done the day before.

'What is wrong with that girl?' the store worker asked Alain, as Arrahbella hurried out after Asseniah.

'I'm not sure,' Alain replied. 'We are interested in the piano though. We'll come back later.' He left the two men looking very pleased and walked out into the mall where he found the girls sitting on a bench a short way up from the store.

'What happened?' he asked.

Asseniah began to make gestures they were familiar with until they deduced that she knew why they had brought her to the store today, and though she was very grateful she did not want the piano, she knew they couldn't afford it. She had stopped playing because she was getting too attached.

'It's alright, Asseniah,' Alain said, sitting beside her. 'If we can find a way to get it for you, we will.'

She shook her head defiantly, stood and began to walk away, signalling that the conversation was over. Alain raised his eyebrows at Arrahbella before following her. They had some market shopping to do so the three of them headed to the centre of the mall, bought some supplies, and returned to the train.

That afternoon, when the troupe was lazing around the train before dinner and the performance, Asseniah found Sora and gave her a meaningful embrace. She then found the du Mauriers in their room and hugged first Alain then Arrahbella, giving her a kiss on the cheek as well.

'That girl fascinates me,' Alain told Arrahbella, once

456

Asseniah had left the room.

'That's because you don't know her story, and because she has no need for words. She's like your polar opposite.'

'She may not use words but she still has a need for them, everybody does, that's why she listens to musicians like Tori and Sarah.'

'True.'

The evening saw a full house as word had spread of Cirque du Phantastique's excellence, and, just as they had done in Noir Eternale, they found themselves turning people away.

'Sora, I'm putting you on first,' Alain told the Ormancian, who was stretching in a back room. 'You were the talk of the city today. The Kartanians love you.'

Sora pulled her leg out from behind her head and lowered it to the floor, making Alain grimace. 'Tightrope or knives?'

'How about knives to begin with, then manipulation and tightrope in the middle, and fire as the finale? It's the fire they love.'

'Sounds exhausting.'

He smiled. 'You up for it?'

She folded her arms and put her nose in the air. 'Don't insult me, Alain.'

He smiled and winked at her. 'That's the kind of performer I raised.' Letting the red divider fall back into place, he continued on towards the stage.

Once he had opened the show, Alain went to stand beside Izan in the wings, both keeping a close eye on the audience. Oleg was on alert too, on the other side of the stage, ready to step in and catch someone if they fell.

Sora walked onto the stage amid the light applause and stood next to the case of knives. The usual twelve were there; Arrahbella's recent Ormanican purchase was back in her caravan for it had not yet completed its training. One by one, Sora called them out of the case and into her hands. The audience applauded again. They were a rather reserved lot, the Kartanians. Sora told Diana to fly around her, gradually introducing the rest until all twelve were soaring around the stage in intricate patterns. It impressed the crowd enough to make a few of them gasp.

Suddenly, Sora felt her knives do something they had never done before; they pulled against her magic as though wanting to do their own thing. Diana was the strongest, Sora had almost lost control of her. She called them back into her hands, then she cast a nervous glance at Alain.

'What does that mean?' he whispered to Izan.

The magician shrugged.

She let her knives go again. They behaved long enough for her to relax and decide that she must have been imagining it, then, they took on lives of their own. Morgana, Hera, and Athena flew out toward the audience while the other nine dived, soared, and flew around the stage. Sora stepped back in shock, then tried to stop them and shield herself at the same time. Alain realised what was happening as Izan cried out 'Ikrael!' and dashed toward the audience, which was scattering in all directions, screaming as the knives flew at them.

'Oleg, catch those knives!' Alain roared. 'Sora get out of there!'

Sora tried desperately to call them back, believing that she could if she just called them hard enough. But it was too late. Both she and Alain gasped in horror as Morgana, Hera, and Athena struck three audience members who fell like sacks among the rows. Alain's heart plummeted to his stomach, his mind froze, and for a moment he was paralysed by shock. Nearby, Oleg was doing his best to catch the knives that were doing their best to pierce his skin.

'Sora, get off of the stage now!' Alain ordered, coming back to himself.

She gave up and fled to Alain's side as the final Kartanian ran from the tent.

'Knives, stop!' Alain commanded, but it did nothing. There were five still flying around, looking for something to sink into. One of them was Diana. She was teasing Oleg by darting around just out of reach. He grabbed for her, but she shot up in to the rafters. Somebody screamed, but Alain barely heard them; his eyes had followed Diana and the blood rushing in his ears had muffled every sound. As he watched, a tumble of red material fell from above, Asseniah plunging with them, landing on her back centre stage. Diana was sticking out of her chest, buried up to the hilt.

'No,' Alain gasped. He rushed to her side. Sora followed as Oleg grabbed the last knife from the air and held all eight tightly to his chest. Arrahbella, tears in her eyes and a hand to her mouth, rushed out from backstage to kneel by Asseniah's head while Chester and Melody approached more slowly, standing a little way back with Mariette and the dwarves.

'Mariette, Fenton, check the Kartanians,' Alain said quietly. His whole body was numb. He couldn't be sure whether he had actually spoken or not. 'Asseniah.'

She was looking at him, uttering small gasps, blood pooling around the knife hilt, a small trickle trailing from her mouth, down her chin. Alain brushed her hair back, unsure of how to help. Both Sora and Arrahbella were audibly crying now, but Asseniah was calm. She looked at Sora, then Arrahbella, then back at Alain.

'Thank you, Alain du Maurier,' she said, so faintly that Alain thought he must have imagined it. Her voice was so melodious, so musical, it made their hearts soar despite the ghastly situation. Alain was stunned and the tears came free and fast after that, so much so he couldn't hold them back. Asseniah gave a final choking gasp, heaved a sigh, and then her swirling green eyes fell still and dulled.

Alain closed his eyes as sadness overcame him. For a moment he was lost. All that was heard was the sobbing of Sora, Arrahbella, and himself. He couldn't leave her like that though, so he made himself open his eyes, sniffed back the tears, put a hand to her unseeing eyes, and closed the lids. Then, he put his hand around Diana's hilt. Feeling sick, his face contorting in sorrow, he pulled the knife out of Asseniah's small broken body, trying not to feel the flesh pulling against the blade. As more thick blood poured out of the now open wound, he put the knife on the stage beside him and sat back on his heels. Arrahbella pulled Asseniah to her chest and cradled her, rocking her back and forth as she cried. Melody crouched down next to Sora and wrapped her arms around her.

After a moment, Alain became aware of someone standing next to him.

'They're dead, Alain,' Fenton told him in a quiet voice. Alain was so numb that it took him a moment to realise who Fenton was talking about.

'Thank you, Fenton.' He took the knives that the dwarf had pulled out of the dead audience members, placing them on the ground next to Diana who sat perfectly still, looking innocent despite the blood. Then, Alain stood up. 'Oleg, the case for those knives is side stage. Sora, can you help him put them away, please?' Sora was still crying and looked as though she was about to protest but she bit her bottom lip, nodded and, grimacing, collected the four bloodied knives before following Oleg off stage.

At that moment, Izan came running in, breathless and angry. Alain stepped down from the stage and met him in the aisle.

'I lost him. I thought I had him but he vanished.' His eyes fell on Asseniah's body and widened in shock. 'Is she..?'

'Yes, Izan.'

Izan was silent, standing stunned in the middle of the aisle. When he spoke again, his voice was stony and grave. 'I have to go after him, Alain. We're not getting anywhere this way. Perhaps it'd be better if there was someone on the outside. I can try to track him and hopefully know what he's up to before he can attack again. I think I have an idea as to

461

where he goes anyway.'

'Thank you, Izan, but I need you here to protect the others.'

Melody had been listening. She joined them in the aisle, standing at Alain's side.

'Alain, he's taken away Melody and Chester's child, my niece or nephew, and almost killed Melody in the process. He kidnapped Arrahbella and nearly destroyed her, and now he's murdered Asseniah and three Kartanians who have nothing to do with us. I have to do something and I'm not able to do anything by waiting around for him to attack. We've tried that and it isn't working.'

'Izan, you can't go. You can't defeat him all by yourself,' said Melody. 'Please don't go. Alain, don't let him go.'

'I have to, Melody,' Izan told her, quietly but firmly.

Alain had been rubbing his brow, but he dropped his hand as though it weighed more than he could bear to lift and sighed. 'Alright.'

'No, Alain, you can't.'

'Melody, I'm going to go, with or without Alain's permission. I'll be fine. I'll keep an eye on him and if he looks as though he's about to attack then I can come back and warn you. Alain and Chester will look after you.'

Melody hadn't cried when Asseniah died, but now, the loss of her friend and her brother going off to face almost certain death were too much and she let the tears come. Chester came up behind her.

'We'll be asked to leave Kartan, so make yourself scarce,' Alain told Izan then, not knowing what else to do, he clapped

462

him on the shoulder, turned, and returned to the stage.

Izan looked at Melody. 'Don't worry, little sister.' He pulled her into a hug. 'I'll be careful and I won't take him on by myself if I can help it. I know Chester and Alain want a piece of him as well.' He kissed the top of Melody's head and brushed her wings gently. Then, he released her, gave her an encouraging look, looking much older than his twenty-two years, and stepped back. He looked at Chester for a moment, shrugged, and pulled him in to kiss him on the mouth. Leaving Chester wide-eyed, Izan strode to the stage and knelt beside Asseniah. He stroked her face and hair.

'Goodbye, sweet girl,' he said. He stood, looked around at every member in turn, then ran out of the tent.

Izan's cloak had only just disappeared around the entrance of the tent when Kajab entered, flanked by four guards, all of them looking very grim. Kajab sent two of the guards to check the dead Kartanians. They crouched beside the bodies, checked their pulses, and shook their heads at their Sultan.

'Mister du Maurier,' the Sultan said. Alain met him in the aisle. 'Three of my people are dead and the rest have fled for their lives. What is your explanation?'

'I have none, Your Highness.'

Kajab was not pleased with this answer, he had been ready for an argument. 'Oh... well, you and your troupe are banished from Vastoo and word shall be spread to every Kartanian region not to look on you kindly. I advise you to leave Kartan and to never return.'

'We shall, sir. May I thank you for all your kindness

over the years and apologise for the loss of life. As you can see, we have lost one of our own.'

Kajab looked over Alain's shoulder at the lifeless form on the stage and faltered. 'Oh, yes, indeed, well, I'm sorry to see that, but I'm afraid the banishment still stands.'

'Of course.'

Kajab made a move as though he were about to shake Alain's hand but then thought better of it, turned, and left, signalling to his guards to collect the Kartanian bodies on the way. When they were gone, Alain sighed wearily before turning back to the troupe.

'Alright, everyone, we need to take down the tent as quickly as we can. Oleg, please take Asseniah's body to the train, put her in the practice room for now, wrap her in one of her silks. Stay with her, I want to make sure she's left in peace.'

'Wouldn't it be better for me to help take down the tent if we need to do it quickly?'

'I'll stay with her, Alain,' Sora said, suddenly.

Alain thought it over. 'Are you sure?'

'Yes.'

'Alright then.' Sora and Oleg left with Asseniah's body as the rest set about taking down the tent.

When they were done, they all returned to the train, storing the equipment in the store room then avoiding the practice room by walking the outside route to the kitchen car, all except for Alain, who walked through the practice room to check that Asseniah's body had been properly wrapped and to tell Sora to join them in the next room. Fenton started the engine and the train rumbled sadly out of the Kartanian rift, Melody's face pressed against the window, trying to catch any sign of her brother.

The troupe sat in silence for a few minutes; there didn't seem to be any words to say. When Alain finally spoke, his voice cracked with emotion.

'We'll go home, everyone. I have no doubt that Ikrael will follow, but, hopefully, we'll be stronger on our home ground. And, we have Izan on the outside. Arrahbella, I doubt you feel like cooking dinner and I, for one, don't feel like eating any, so if anyone wants anything then get your own and then we shall try to go to bed and get some rest, although I know sleep won't be very forthcoming.'

'I'll take first watch, Alain,' Oleg offered.

'And I'll take the middle,' said Chester.

'Thank you, Chester. Sora, do you want to be on watch?'

Sora was looking at the table top. She had no tears left. 'No, Alain, not tonight. I'm sorry.'

'It's fine.'

'The knives will need cleaning though,' she said, finally looking up at him. 'I'd like to do it. I know how to care for them.'

Alain looked at Arrahbella who was staring blankly at the back of a chair.

'Arrahbella?'

'I don't ever want to see those knives again,' she said through clenched teeth, and left the room.

'Thank you, Sora. If you don't mind then that would

be good of you.' He didn't want to leave Arrahbella on her own for too long. 'Goodnight, everyone. Try to get some sleep.' He left.

'Did we know that she could talk?' Chester asked, when the pair had been gone a moment.

'I knew she could sing,' Oleg said quietly. 'She had the most gorgeous musical voice.'

They spent some time in silence, marvelling over the fact that she had been able to talk all along and wondering why she had chosen not to, feeling sadness envelope them as they realised they would never hear her play the piano again, or see her dance with her aerial silks, or know her story.

In their room, Alain found his wife sitting on the edge of the bed, sobbing. He closed the door and went to sit beside her, holding her until she had quietened.

'They were my knives, Alain,' she finally said, despair making her voice heavy. 'And this is all my fault. Ikrael's after me and everyone's suffering because of it.'

'Hey.' He put a finger under her chin and gently lifted her face until her eyes met his. Tears had made rivers down her cheeks. Her eyeliner and mascara were muddied. 'Bella, you can't blame yourself for this,' he whispered. 'This is Ikrael's doing, Ikrael's madness. Yes, he's apparently after you, but only because he's a deranged lunatic who's been shunned from society for no reason other than the fact that he was different and he's grown monster-like as a result, and you were the first person to show him any ounce of kindness. Don't blame yourself for a madman's actions, Bella.'

'But, why didn't I see it?' she cried, desperately. 'What

466

use is being psychic if I can't see things like this? Why didn't I see it coming?'

His heart would have given a pang if it weren't already aching for Asseniah. Then, he remembered something. 'I think you did see it.'

She pulled away and looked at him with a frown.

'At the beginning of this tour, you had a dream, remember? Your head was throbbing, and there was blood, and a girl screaming.'

'That didn't tell me anything. I mean, it makes sense now, but back then it wasn't much of a warning.'

'And last night, you woke up three times but couldn't remember what you'd dreamt. Maybe Ikrael was intercepting the messages.'

Arrahbella considered this. She rested her head on his chest again and he stroked her hair comfortingly.

'I should have stopped the tour after Noir Eternale.'

'You're being hypocritical, Alain.'

'I know.'

'I told you to come to Kartan. You asked me if I wanted to stop after Ikrael took over my mind and I said to keep going.'

'We thought it was for the best. The show had to go on. It always goes on.' He held her more tightly. 'I was so scared. I knew you were back stage, but one of the knives ripped through the back curtain as though it were nothing more than a web.'

He was answered by soft sobbing and the feel of tears soaking through his shirt.

Hours slowly dragged by and eventually Alain realised that Arrahbella had fallen asleep. Carefully, he lay her on the bed, took off her boots, and pulled the covers up over her just as Oleg came through on his watch.

'Oleg,' he whispered. 'Can you stay here for a moment, please?'

The giant nodded. Alain slid off the bed and walked through to Melody and Chester's room where he found Sora curled up next to Mariette on one of the cushion piles. Sora was asleep but Mariette was awake, stroking Sora's hair. Melody and Chester were in bed – Chester facing Melody, Melody on her stomach – apparently both asleep. Alain walked over to the cushions, crouching beside Sora.

'How is she?' he asked Mariette, quietly.

'She 'as only just drifted off. She blames 'erself. She 'as not said anyzing but you can tell.'

He nodded. 'I know. So does Arrahbella.'

'So do you.'

Alain smiled sadly. He had been stroking Sora's hair, but he stopped now to look at Mariette. 'How are you?'

'She should not 'ave died, Alain. If any of us 'ad to go zen it should 'ave been me.'

He frowned at her.

'I am ze one wizout any magic. I am ze one wizout a significant ozer. I am older, much older. She was too young.'

'Yes, she was, Mariette, but don't you think for a second that it should have been you, because it is not true. It is not true. I need you, you're my oldest friend, and Arrahbella needs you, and Oleg, and Melody, and Sora. We need you,

468

Mariette. We needed Asseniah as well. We need everyone here. Nobody should have died, not at Ikrael's hands.'

She managed a weak smile. He had his hand on her shoulder and he leant forward to kiss her cheek.

'Try to get some sleep,' he whispered.

As Mariette settled down next to Sora, Alain moved over to Melody's side of the bed and looked down at the sleeping pair. Inside, mixed emotions were fighting it out for predominance, they had been all night, while he was holding Arrahbella and now; utter despair and a harsh sadness at the death of Asseniah, guilt for having continued the tour, relief that Arrahbella and Melody were safe, concern for Izan, anger and hate at Ikrael, fear at the fact that he was capable of feeling so much hate, confusion at what to do next, the strange leadership quality in him telling him to stay strong for the others and remain clear-headed, and also a twinge of hopelessness. All of these emotions were stirring all sorts of words in him. He could feel them running through his blood, swirling in his head, demanding to be expressed. With a slight shake of his head, he sat on the edge of the bed and put a hand to Melody's shoulder. She hadn't been asleep and she sat up immediately to blink at him in the lamplight. She waited for him to speak but he didn't say anything. He just looked at her for a moment then pulled her to him and hugged her tightly. Chester opened his eyes, saw them, smiled sleepily, then closed his eyes again. After a while, Alain sat back and examined her. He wrote the word "visible" in the air and pushed it over one shoulder then the other. Her wings appeared.

'I didn't know you could do that,' she whispered.

'Neither did I,' he replied, tracing his finger over the bone of one of them and feeling her shiver. 'Izan will be okay,' he assured her, not believing it himself.

She nodded. 'Is Arrahbella alright?'

'As alright as any of us are.'

He sat for a moment longer, looked at Chester, smiled at Melody, then returned to his room. Oleg exited a moment later. Melody stayed sitting for a while until Chester reached a hand up to stroke a wing, then she lay down and snuggled close to him, feeling sadder than she ever had.

CHAPTER 16

FINALE

Present Day - Varatalé

The tip of the manor's Northern Tower came into view as Fenton navigated the train through the green hills of Neapania. Soon the entire building was standing tall and welcoming in front of him. With a weary smile, he pulled the train around the side of the manor, shut down the engine for the final time that year, and walked through to the du Mauriers' caravan.

'She's home, Alain.'

Alain felt an incredible surge of relief. 'Thank you, Fenton. You, Phan, Cravel, Grent, and Dell may go home now. You have been masterful as always and I'm sorry you had to get caught up in this mess.'

Fenton looked genuinely offended. 'You speak about us as though we were separate from the troupe, Alain, and I hope that is not how you think of us. I believed we were more than that. I'll have you know that we'll be staying right here to fend off Ikrael with you.'

'I'm sorry, Fenton. Of course I didn't mean it to sound as though you weren't part of the troupe. And I appreciate your offer to help us, but you should all be with your families, protecting them. I can't send anyone else away and know that they'll be safe. I'm sure Ikrael won't go after you when we're all still here, I really don't think he will, and if at least some of you can be safe then I'd feel slightly better about this whole situation. Please go, Fenton, and be with your families.'

Fenton spent a moment struggling with his loyalty and honour but then sighed. 'Alright, Alain, we'll go, but be sure to get a message to us if you need any help at all. We'll be back in a jiffy.' He shook Alain's hand. 'Mythos be with you.' Alain gave a single nod in thanks and squeezed Fenton's hand in return. The dwarf nodded to Arrahbella then went to speak to his friends.

Alain held his hand out to his wife. 'Come on then.'

She uncurled herself from the chair, took her husband's hand, and together they walked through to Melody and Chester's room where all but Oleg awaited them. They met the giant at the kitchen car door.

'Oleg, Sora, you stay here and keep watch,' Alain instructed. 'Chester and I will make sure the manor is safe.'

There was nothing obviously suspicious about the manor, so the troupe set about moving general items out of their caravans and into their rooms, glad to be back home.

Eventually, the time came when Oleg had to move Asseniah's body. Lifting her as though she were the most delicate thing in the world, he carried her to the entrance hall where the others were gathering.

'Where should I put her, Alain?'

'I suppose we should bury her.'

'Oh no,' Sora intervened. 'We can't bury her, she'd

hate to be put in the ground.'

'Sora's right,' Arrahbella agreed.

'Well, what am I meant to do? I can't very well bury her in a cloud.'

'When our mother died,' Melody said, quietly. 'She wanted to fly, like our father could, so she jumped from the cliff.'

'But if we threw Asseniah off the cliff, she'd still end up in the sea,' Sora pointed out.

'We could burn her body,' Chester suggested. 'Then Melody could fly up and scatter her ashes on the breeze.'

'I don't think I could burn her,' Alain replied, quietly.

'It's done all the time on Earth,' Arrahbella told him.

'At least then she'd still be in Varatalé,' Sora agreed. 'Or the breeze might fly out of the rift, she'd be on the breeze at least. Oh, yes Alain.'

'She always wanted me to take her flying,' Melody added, with a sad smile. 'But my wings weren't strong enough to hold two people.'

Alain sighed. 'Alright. Let's do it now then.' The body was beginning to deteriorate.

'I'll do the burning,' Sora offered. 'It'll be faster.'

'If you wish.'

The troupe made their way out into the middle of one of the surrounding fields, Oleg carrying Asseniah's body, still wrapped in its silk. Arrahbella had gathered a small bundle of herbs and flowers and she carried this in one hand, holding Alain's hand with the other. Sora carried Asseniah's CD player and two of her favourite albums, while Melody carried a small silver goblet, a souvenir from Alain's travels to Earth.

Oleg lay Asseniah gently on the grass and they stood in a circle around her, holding hands, while Alain, then Arrahbella, Sora, and Oleg said a few words. Then, they all bowed their heads as they listened to a few of the songs that reminded them of their friend.

When the last note had faded away on the breeze, they broke their circle. Chester magically floated the red cocoon until it was standing vertically in the air and Melody placed the silver goblet beneath it. Finally, Sora produced a flame in her palm.

'Goodbye, Asseniah,' she whispered.

The flame leapt onto the silk and began to blaze rapidly. Arrahbella passed everyone a sprig of Rose Blossom to hold under their noses as the smell of burning flesh surrounded them. The cremation didn't take very long. When it was done, Chester controlled the ashes so that they fell neatly into the goblet. When the last mote had settled, Melody walked forward, took up the goblet with one hand, covered its mouth with the other so that no ashes would escape, then flew up into the sky. There were a few clouds about, so she chose a low one nearby, a short distance from the manor's highest spire, the tower that Asseniah had called her bedroom. On the ground, Alain and Chester watched Melody anxiously, hoping desperately that Ikrael wasn't around. Melody faced the way the breeze was blowing and upended the goblet over the cloud. Asseniah's ashes sprinkled out of the silver cup, shining red in the sunlight, and danced on the breeze, bouncing through the cloud and floating away out of sight. Everyone felt a wave of calm wash over them as they watched and they knew Asseniah was pleased with her send off.

Melody returned to the ground and the troupe walked back to the manor where they said goodbye to the dwarves and watched them leave.

The performers spent some time on their own then, attempting to wind down from the tour and its events, which was pretty much impossible with the knowledge that Ikrael was still out there watching them plaguing their minds. Melody left Chester to continue unpacking their clothes and went in search of Arrahbella, hoping the psychic could give her some information as to the state of her brother. She found her in the kitchen, making tea.

'Can you see where he is, Arrahbella? Can you see if he's alright?'

Arrahbella shook her head. Her usually happy eyes looked dull and tired. 'No, Melody, I don't want to give his position away in case Ikrael's still tuned into my mind or waiting for me to do so. I'm sorry.'

Melody nodded sadly and left the kitchen. A moment later, Sora entered carrying the case of knives that Arrahbella never wanted to see again. She put the case on the table and opened it. Arrahbella took one look at it before turning back to the tea and concentrating on making it with unnecessary determination.

'Arrahbella?'

'What is it, Sora?' Her tone was cautionary.

'Your knives, they're sad. They know that you're upset

with them and they know what they did and they feel guilty. They didn't want to hurt those people and Ikrael hurt them by forcing them to do so. See, when I play with them or command them they know that it's so they can dance, or so that I can protect myself, not because I want to hurt anyone. I mean, knives are weapons, they're made to hurt, but they also take on the attitudes of their owners, they pick up on vibes, and because you and I take such good care of them, and because I speak to them so much, they're good too, and they're feeling so guilty.'

Arrahbella hadn't turned around. 'They're knives, Sora. How can they have feelings?'

Sora was offended. 'They're made from metal and wood and stones, so they're living things. A carpenter will tell you that his wood is living and you know very well that Alain's poems get temperamental when he doesn't finish them. You know these knives have feelings, Arrahbella.'

Arrahbella did know. She had often wished that she could talk to her beloved knives the way Sora did. She sighed and turned around.

'Asseniah wouldn't want us to neglect the knives,' Sora continued. 'She'd probably want us to display Diana proudly so that we remembered her, not hide them away to forget about. It wasn't their fault; it was Ikrael's.'

At that same moment, Alain was in his study, trying to write about the final leg of the tour in his journal. He was having trouble concentrating, though. The words in his head were jumbling, jamming, jumping around. He told them to settle but they wouldn't. They seemed to be out of control, like his power had been in his dream. The words that came out of the pen were not the words he wanted.

After deciding that he was probably just tired, he read his last sentence to see if it made any sense. His heart skipped a beat as his eyes skimmed the passage. Cold shivers raced down his spine.

"Arrahbella is mine, Alain, mine. And, now, so is your power."

The words were there in black ink following on from Alain's own description of what had happened in Arelia. His mind still hadn't started working when his hand found itself writing again. He tried to stop it but found he couldn't and the horrible sentence "We didn't need Asseniah anyway" scrawled itself across the page in a style that was certainly not his own; messy and childlike.

There was a knock at the door and Arrahbella entered carrying two mugs of tea.

'Sora brought me the knives,' she told him, unaware of his distress, setting a mug down on the desk by the hand that was still holding the bewitched pen. She continued to talk but Alain was watching the pen again as it wrote the word "hurt" in the air.

'No,' he breathed, but he wasn't in control. The word flew at Arrahbella, turning her sentence into a cry of pain as it hit her, making her drop her tea.

'Alain?' she gasped. Alain was already at her side apologising. He had thrown the pen aside, but Ikrael didn't need a pen anymore; he was manipulating Alain's speech so that the apologies turned into a barrage of curses, threats, and commands to hurt her further.

'I don't love you, Arrahbella.' He made Alain say. 'I hate you. I hate you.' It was said with such animosity that her heart ached. Alain was horrified. He covered his mouth with his hands and ran from the room to avoid hurting her further. He got as far as the entrance hall, hurtling down the grand staircase at astonishing speed, tripping all over the place, but, Melody and Chester were there and the abuse started pouring out again.

'You're an annoying, immature little brat, Melody,' he yelled. 'And you're a slut for liking older men.' Tears were streaming down his face. Melody's hand flew to her mouth in horror. Alain turned to Chester. 'And you should be hanged for sleeping with someone so much younger than you, Chester.'

'Alain?' Melody gasped.

Alain shook his head and closed his eyes, pressing his lips firmly together. But Ikrael was not done. Alain's eyes opened and he looked at Melody with agony written all over his face as his mouth was forced to form the words, 'And, I'm glad that child died, Melody. I didn't want you getting pregnant and you know it. I'm glad you fell, just as I'm glad Asseniah's dead.'

Alain cried out in pain, doubling over and almost collapsing to the ground. His heart held his power and Ikrael's grip on it was more traumatic than anything he ever experienced. Arrahbella had joined them now, coming down the stairs just moments after her husband. Sora too, and Mariette and Oleg heard the shouting, appearing only moments later. Alain tried to keep his mouth closed. He put his hands behind his back so that they couldn't write words in the air.

Then, all of a sudden, he was free. He literally felt Ikrael let go at the same moment he heard a shriek from outside and a yell.

'Alain! Alain!' a voice called through the horrible shrieking. 'I've got him!'

'That's Izan,' Melody shouted.

The troupe rushed to the doors, threw them open, and ran outside.

On the grass in front of the manor, Izan stood with his arms stretched out and black magic pouring from them. At the end of the stream of power, Ikrael was encased in a flame of black, almost fluorescent against the darkness, shrieking in pain.

Alain turned to the others. 'Chester, help Izan. Everyone else inside now.'

Chester kissed Melody and hurtled out of the doors while a flurry of protests arose from the others.

'No,' Alain demanded in a tone of finality. 'All of you in the house now.'

Knowing he'd command them otherwise, they reluctantly retreated. 'Sora, Oleg, you're in charge. Make sure that everyone remains out of harm's way.' Giving them something to do helped them obey more complacently. 'And, if Izan or Chester or I fall then I want you, Sora, to come out and take over.'

She nodded solemnly.

Chester reached Izan as the magician fell to his knees. He had to stop, and in the second that he did ease back his power and Chester rose his arm to take over, Ikrael, damaged as he was, sent a bolt of magic in Chester's direction. The bolt would have killed him had he not fired his own magic at exactly the same moment and it only succeeded in sending him sprawling onto his back, the main impact going to his leg.

'Chester!' Melody cried, but Oleg shut the doors and by the time she had raced to the window in the sitting room Chester was up and fighting again. The rest of the troupe crowded around her to watch, kneeling on the window seat, as Alain joined Izan and Chester, taking up a position between them. Izan was swaying, but he took a moment to gather some more strength and then he got to his feet, shaking furiously, and added his own power to Chester's once more.

'Alain doesn't have any protective magic,' Arrahbella said. 'If Ikrael gets free, he'll be the first one he goes for.' Her knuckles were white, gripping the edge of the window sill.

'I zink Ikrael will go for Izan first,' Mariette said. ''e 'as ze most power and he's getting weaker.'

'Can we please not speculate on who's going to be the first to go?' Melody pleaded. 'We shouldn't be thinking about him getting free. They've got him, they just have to hold him until he weakens.'

She was right. Izan had obviously successfully tracked Ikrael and when he had made his move to take over Alain's power Izan had snared him in a magical cocoon that was causing the monster considerable pain and drainage. If he and Chester could keep it up then Ikrael might eventually weaken enough to be killed. But it wasn't looking good; Izan was sweating and pale and Chester didn't have nearly as much power as Izan.

Alain wrote the word "weaken" in the air and pushed it toward Ikrael, but it weakened Chester's magic instead.

'Alain!'

'Sorry!'

Izan let out a cry of exhaustion and fell to his knees once again, his power flow disappearing. For a moment, Ikrael was only surrounded by the faint purple glow that was Chester's magic, but, while it was still weakening him and burning, it wasn't enough to hold him immobile. Ikrael lifted a snowy white arm feebly and pointed it at Alain.

'No, no, no!' cried Arrahbella. She tried to race from the room but Oleg held her fast.

Ikrael shot a bolt at Alain but Chester pushed him aside and warded off the bolt with his own. A flurry of purple and white magic went back and forth, one bolt hitting Alain on the side of the arm, but Ikrael was so weak that it only made a deep cut and sent him toppling backwards. Chester's injured leg gave way and for one heart stopping moment Ikrael was free. He smiled a bloody smile and raised his arms, gathering power.

Alain lifted his eyes to meet Ikrael's, expecting to see there the raw evilness that he had encountered only once before in his lifetime – in the eyes of his biological father. To his surprise, however, there were no signs of evil, no signs of anything in fact, just emptiness. Even so, Alain knew he was about to die. Thoughts of Arrahbella began to rush through his mind, accompanied by an unbearable feeling of failure.

All of a sudden, Ikrael's body made a violent jolt, stopping him from administering the lethal blow. His eyes broke their contact with Alain's and dropped to his side where he found Diana sticking out of his stomach, just below his ribs, buried up to her hilt.

Those inside the manor looked at Sora.

'As if I was just going to stand here and watch,' she said.

Alain breathed a sigh of relief and pushed himself up off of the ground just as Chester recovered and threw his magic at Ikrael once more. Izan, seeing his opportunity, summoned every ounce of strength he had left and, while Ikrael was busy with Chester, sent a wave of agonising power at the monster, Chester strengthening his own, giving everything he had, knowing that it was now or never. Purple and black magic collided, exploding with a force that shook the ground. A bloodcurdling howl filled the valley, echoing around the hills and sending animals scurrying for shelter. When the magic faded, Ikrael was lying in a quivering heap on the scorched grass.

'He's yours now, Alain,' Izan managed to say, though he was barely audible.

'Thank you, Izan, Chester. Go inside now and please keep Arrahbella away from the window. I don't want her to see me do this.' His eyes didn't leave Ikrael's huddled form.

The boys didn't argue. Chester limped over to Izan's side, helped him up, and supported him to the manor doors.

Arrahbella nearly had a heart attack. 'What the hell are they doing?!' She ran out to the entrance hall so suddenly that Oleg missed catching her. Everyone followed. 'You can't leave him out there alone,' she screamed at the men when they entered. 'Are you crazy?'

'It's his war now,' Chester said, and Izan nodded.

'No. No. Alain! Alain!' Oleg held her back as she scrambled for the door. 'Let me go. Let me go!' Mariette went to her side to put her arms around her and she collapsed in a fit of sobs.

Outside, Alain was watching the quivering white monster with disgusted hatred. He didn't waste any time standing there, though, he got to work on his revenge as soon as the manor doors had closed behind Chester.

First, he wrote the word "hurt" in the air.

'This is for Melody and the baby,' he rumbled in a low voice that came heavy with anger. The word struck Ikrael hard and he moaned, too weak to shriek. Alain followed it up with "agony" and "pain."

'This is for Asseniah,' he said, and threw a barrage of "cuts" and "slices" at the heap, each word cutting the deathly white skin and leaving deep red gashes that bled freely.

Ikrael could have raised his arm to defend himself here. He was near death, weak, and in agony, but if he had wanted to survive there was a tiny window of opportunity to fight back between Alain hurling the last command and then spending a moment gathering as much of his power as he could muster for the next. But Ikrael did not move. He simply waited.

'And this is for Arrahbella,' Alain finished. The word "kill" was written in the air and Alain threw all of his power behind it. Every magical cell in his tall body was fired into action, directing all of his power into his hands and into the command. He then thrust it toward Ikrael, hitting him right between the eyes. The monster let out one final bloodcurdling shriek, his body arching in agony, then the white light of Alain's power faded and both men collapsed in heaps on the ground.

In the manor, everyone had stopped dead still at the finality of the shriek, and Arrahbella, feeling Mariette's grip slacken, ran to the doors, threw them open, and raced outside. Alain was doubled over in weakness but he threw out an arm when she approached and roared "STOP!" He had hardly any magic left but, even so, the weak command hit her like a knife and she whimpered with sobs, reaching out her arms, trying desperately to break free of the order and get to her husband.

'Izan, Oleg, make sure he's dead,' Alain said, as the others came nearer, his arm still outstretched in Arrahbella's direction. Izan was only just hanging onto consciousness but he went with Oleg to Ikrael's mangled body. The rest of the troupe stood in a huddle a few paces back from Arrahbella. Oleg picked up Ikrael's body and twisted the head clean off the neck.

'Eww! Oleg, you should warn people before you do that,' Izan said, weakly. 'He's dead, Alain, unless he knows how to regrow his head and come back from the dead... which wouldn't surprise me.'

Alain dropped his arm and, with it, his command. Arrahbella ran forward as he collapsed again on to the grass, blood flowing from the slash on his arm.

'Alain.' She put her arms around his chest and lifted him so that she was cradling him. His eyes fluttered open to look into hers.

'You're safe now, Bella,' he whispered, and then, he lost consciousness. Arrahbella kissed his face and cradled him to her chest as she cried, blood soaking her top.

Sora stormed up to Ikrael's corpse, pulled Diana out of his stomach, produced a flame, and burnt the white body to a crisp, just to be extra sure. Izan gave her a nod of approval then collapsed and fainted as well. As a breeze blew Ikrael's ashes up into the sky and away, Oleg picked up Izan's limp body then headed over to Alain, pried him from Arrahbella's grasp, and carried both men into the manor, the rest of the troupe following, Melody helping Chester as he limped.

Leaving Arrahbella to sit with Alain, Sora to attend to Izan, and Mariette with Chester, Oleg went to make doubly sure there were no traces of Ikrael left and to send word to the dwarves while Melody jumped onto a neighbour's horse and rode into the village for the doctor.

EPILOGUE

Two Years Later – Varatalé

Alain du Maurier couldn't resist. Carefully, he reached out and pulled back the edge of the red velvet curtain, just enough to allow him a glimpse of the audience. The freshly carved wooden benches were almost completely full; only a few empty spaces remained in the top back rows. All eyes were on Mariette, who was entertaining those already seated, while Grent, Phan, Cravel, and another dwarf named Brock (who had joined the troupe when Fenton had decided to retire and settle down with his family) supplied music.

Alain watched Mariette for a moment, then, once the last seat had been filled and the tent flaps of the brand-new tent drawn, he repositioned the curtain and left to do one final check on his troupe.

'All set, Melody?'

Melody was stretching on the floor of one of the preparation rooms. Her wings were visible; they had been ever since the night that Asseniah had died, and a toddler with purple-and-white wings was sitting on the floor next to her, laughing as her mother bent herself into odd shapes. The trapeze artist looked up at Alain, shivered, and smiled.

'Yes, we're ready. Aren't we Eralaina?'

The one-year-old gurgled in response.

Alain smiled. He lifted his hand and wrote "angel" in the air, then sent it over to dance in front of Eralaina. The child promptly reached out, took hold of it, and put it in her mouth to chew.

'Eralaina!' Melody chided.

Alain chuckled. 'It's alright, Melody. A word like "angel" won't harm her. If I remember correctly, you once ate the word "delicious" and told me it was an experience similar to that of eating Earthling sherbet.'

Melody smiled, shook her head, and shivered again. The partition moved and Chester limped into the room, dressed in his jester's outfit. He wrapped his arms around Melody and she stopped shivering immediately. Eralaina wobbled over and lifted her hands up, demanding to be picked up so she could play with the bells on Chester's hat. The couple had spent some time travelling just as Chester had promised they would. When they had come back, Melody had been pregnant again.

Alain smiled and moved on to the next room, but there was no one sitting at the stardust framed mirror. Instead, the Ringmaster found Izan in the wings, standing next to Sora who was talking quietly to Arrahbella's knives. She had built up quite a relationship with them now and they were in-tuned enough with her to let her know immediately if any other force was calling them.

'Ready?' Alain whispered to them.

'Ready and raring to go,' Izan replied. His hair was all silver now and his face faintly lined. Ironically, he had discovered that people found this older look even more attractive.

Dell was standing near the lighting controls. 'All set, Alain.'

The Ringmaster nodded and walked on to the new circular stage. He rolled his neck gently from side to side, shook himself from the shoulders down, and peered up into the rafters. There was nobody there and he smiled sadly at the memory of those swirling green eyes peering down at him from amongst a pile of red hair and material. He let his head fall back into position and felt the familiar surge of pride for his troupe course through his body, stronger than it had ever been.

Oleg and Arrahbella, having packed up the ticket booth, appeared in the wings and Melody handed Eralaina (who was now chewing her way through the letter 'e') over to the Earthling. Alain gave his wife a wink and she smiled. They would eat supper at an Inn or a Tavern or have it late after each show on this tour. He wouldn't let her be on her own again in a foreign world and the practice started right there in their home town.

The last guest was seated and Dell dimmed the lights. Mariette came off stage and joined Alain behind the curtain. For a brief but extended moment, the thrill of performing for the first time in two years ran through every troupe member in a rush of excited chills.

Alain nodded to Dell. The curtains were parted and

the stage lights turned up until they were too bright to look at. Blinded, Alain stepped out into the centre of the stage as the audience cheered and applauded. With a flourish of his hand and in his rich, seductive tones, Alain du Maurier began the show.

'Ladies and Gentlemen, welcome to Cirque du Phantastique.'

****

ABOUT THE AUTHOR

Claire Marie Clements was born in Adelaide, South Australia and has lived there her entire life. She has always loved writing and acting and is currently studying a Bachelor of Arts, majoring in Creative Writing, at Flinders University. Her other interests include music, cats, art, nature, magic, travelling, and social and animal justice issues. This is her first novel, her previous works include two self-published poetry books: 'Pieces – A Collection of Poems' and 'Writing with Light'.

www.ingramcontent.com/pod-product-compliance
Lightning Source LLC
Chambersburg PA
CBHW030238030726
47493CB00023B/94